Master of Destiny

Angela Drake is a Chartered Psychologist currently practising as a freelance consultant. Angela is married with one grown-up daughter and lives in Harrogate with her husband and various pets.

Master of Destiny

Angela Drake

Pan Books

First published 1999 by Severn House

This edition published 2001 by Pan Books
an imprint of Pan Macmillan Ltd
Pan Macmillan, 20 New Wharf Road, London N1 9RR
Basingstoke and Oxford
Associated companies throughout the world
www.panmacmillan.com

ISBN 330 39886 5

1 3 5 7 9 8 6 4 2

A CIP catalogue record for this book is available from
the British Library.

Printed by Mackays of Chatham plc, Chatham, Kent

One

"Find the Achilles heel," said Rex Chance softly, smiling that chilling, raptor smile of his that gave Tessa the feeling she was inclined to loathe him. "When you go out on your next assignment, let that be your new maxim, Tessa."

"Right," she said, smiling back cheerily, giving every evidence of being kindly disposed towards the man who sat staring steadily at her from across his weighty boss/controller's desk. "I'll engrave the words on my heart."

Tessa's smile concealed a number of conflicting emotions, as smiles so often do. She was aware of harbouring a number of negative feelings towards Rex Chance: mistrust, a prickly dislike and a certain awed respect. Chance had been in post for less than a year and had stamped his authority on the department with a vengeance. She recalled with a slight shudder how within the first few weeks of his appointment he had turned the professional lives of his staff upside down and inside out. He was one of those men able to make swift decisions and act on them instantly. You got the feeling he wouldn't balk at anything, be afraid of anyone. No one on the team felt safe any more.

"Well, I think we've had a most useful discussion," smiled Rex Chance, removing his long legs from the desk and getting to his feet. "How about a coffee?"

Tessa watched him uncoil his lithe frame. A few moments ago she had thought of him as a bird of prey. Now she changed tack and began to run through as much reptilian vocabulary as she could muster. Viper, adder, cobra, mamba, python, boa constrictor, alligator. Oh, don't be so childish, she told herself.

She glanced at her watch. "OK then." Her acceptance was

1

polite but half-hearted. It was already ten thirty and she had a huge pile of stuff on her desk to go through before even thinking of going out to interview celebrities and locate their Achilles heels.

Rex Chance pushed aside a mound of files on the shelves lining one wall of his office and unearthed an ancient-looking chrome flask. As he unscrewed the top a delicious fragrance of freshly ground coffee stole into the room.

"Can't bear the office coffee," he said. "It tastes as though it's been brewed from the dust that flakes off worn brake linings."

Tessa tried to think of a witty retort. A little disc of pain throbbed in each of her temples, the result of her lovely evening out with Oliver during which she had drunk far more wine than was good for her. She had also allowed him to spin it out far too long and late for a working girl who has to rise at seven.

This morning had been a disaster from the moment she had got up. Every single pair of her black tights had made her legs resemble those of a zebra once she had pulled them up as far as her knees. How did ladders get into tights when they were innocently sitting in drawers she had asked herself.

Desperate for something to soothe her raging thirst (she really must find out why drinking wine made you so thirsty, – there was bound to be some convincing biochemical explanation) she had yanked a new carton of freshly-squeezed orange from the fridge and begun to wrestle with its cardboard top. It had resisted opening for an age, then had suddenly capitulated without warning, shooting juice all over her beautifully ironed, cream silk blouse – the one and only.

After all that she had had no time for further perusal of her sparse wardrobe and had been forced to resort to throwing on some crumpled black trousers and a dubious fuchsia-coloured silk shirt which she had chosen in defiance of the golden rule that vibrant redheads should always avoid reds and pinks. This particular pink shouted extremely loudly with her hair, and even more so with the freckles scattered over her porcelain-pale skin like crumbs shaken from a packet of ginger biscuits.

"There," said Rex Chance, placing a mug of coffee in

front of her. "Get that down you. You look as though you need it."

His tone indicated that he was probably sending her up and Tessa glowered as he turned away from her and perched on the edge of the desk, swinging his long legs.

She reminded herself of Chance's dangerously powerful position as far as jobs in the department were concerned – including her own of course. When he had arrived to take on overall control of daytime programming at Dartbridge Television every man and woman in the small army of staff working within the various departments had quaked. They had been right to do so; Chance had hurtled through each department like a hurricane, sweeping all before him and leaving terror in his wake.

As regards her own programme, an afternoon magazine and talk show, romantically named *In the Limelight*, he had interviewed each and every member of the team and had instantly and effortlessly sussed out the shirkers and time-wasters; the ones who turned up late, lunched long and left early. They had all now left permanently. She knew that it would be madness not to be cautious.

But caution was not Tessa's strong point.

"Couldn't you be stirring up a hornet's nest with this Achilles heel business?" she demanded, running over their recent conversation. Well, not so much as a conversation as Chance's treating her to a monologue on the best and only way to revitalise *In the Limelight*, which was currently, as he was fond of reminding the team in no uncertain terms, in danger of falling under his controller's cutting-axe. Revitalise it *his* way, naturally.

"I was talking about finding the vulnerable spot, Tessa, not necessarily exposing it." Chance's unusual amber eyes looked steadily into hers.

Tessa felt that Chance might possibly have the power to see deep inside her head. The two little spots of pain in her temples throbbed with renewed vigour.

"Why should we bother to find it if we're not going to spill some beans?" Tessa challenged. "I thought you said our viewers needed fresh stimulation."

"Indeed I did."

"Well then?" she demanded, instantly reminding herself to soften her tone. Keep cool, Tessa, she muttered silently. You need to hang on to this job.

He paused, smiling at her with a kind of fake fond-indulgence that made her want to hit him over the head with something hard.

"I have the impression that despite your protests you do in fact agree that it's a good idea to ferret out the weak spots of our celebrity guests," he commented pleasantly. "Is that right?"

"Well . . ."

"You did, after all, just say quite decisively that you thought viewers would find that kind of thing stimulating."

"Yes, OK, I did. I do. But, is it ethical to do it?"

"Ah." He looked thoughtful, swinging his legs to and fro in an easy rhythmn. "If done in a certain way, yes, I believe it is. But I also believe the most effective way of stimulating and provoking our audience is to fire their imagination . . ." He paused again, inviting her input, infuriatingly superior and pleased with himself.

"Yes. Go on," said Tessa, feeling her teeth clench.

"A skilful interviewer can inspire an interviewee's confidence, draw out hints and suggestions." He raised his eyebrows, seeking her comment.

"Fair enough. Go on some more," said Tessa coldly, refusing to be drawn along like a dancing monkey on the end of a leash. "I need it spelling out for me."

"Oh, I'm sure you know what I'm getting at. Uncovering little clues to get the audience sitting up and really starting to take notice. Getting them curious."

"Mmm, it all sounds horribly manipulative to me," said Tessa.

"Oh, I don't disagree there. But then the whole edifice of the media world rests on manipulation." He lifted his eyebrows. "Surely you wouldn't argue with that?"

I don't think I like this job any more, thought Tessa. She had a nasty suspicion that Chance was simply winding her up to amuse himself. But you never knew with him. And it was hard to fight back if you were not quite sure whether the enemy was directly attacking you.

"We need," he continued thoughtfully, "to provide our audiences with material that invites them to consider, to speculate. We need to persuade them to form theories, make their own judgements. Become do-it-yourself psychologists if you like."

Tessa made a soft, dismissive snorting sound through her lips.

"In other words we need to make the audiences of Dartbridge TV programmes think for themselves."

"Mmm." Tessa looked down at her hands with their small fingers and short business-like nails.

"Surely we're patronising them," Chance insisted relentlessly, "if we insult their intelligence by continuing to spoonfeed them as though they were half-wits."

Tessa had to admit that she quite liked that particular nugget of his philosophy. "OK. I'll accept that. But don't forget that *Limelight* isn't supposed to be a heavyweight programme. It goes out early afternoon. We interview celebrities and keep things nice and cheery and friendly. Isn't the serious stuff supposed to be reserved for late evening viewing?"

Chance frowned. "Times are moving forward, ideas changing. We have to move on as well, Tess."

She gave a small inward sigh. "So how do we move on in *Limelight*? Just what is it that you want to see happening on the programme that isn't happening now?"

"Ah." Chance leaned his elbows on the table and pressed his fingertips together forming a steeple shape. "You see," he said eventually, leaning forward and treating her to an unnerving stare, "celebrities are still presented on TV as god-like, almost magical, figures. That's strange really because political grandees and members of the royal family, who used to enjoy that kind of unquestioning deification, are now regularly stripped bare on camera."

Tessa lowered her eyes, feeling somewhat unnerved by that last phrase. She noticed that the third button of her fuchsia shirt had come undone, revealing a flash of plunging black bra. She felt her cheeks flush warm as she fiddled with the offending button.

When she looked up, Rex Chance was smiling straight at her. She had to admit that he was quite attractive when he smiled as though he might be a human being instead of a reptile or a bird of prey. His brown eyes seemed genuinely warm, sympathetic even.

Tessa realised that he was one of those people it was hard to categorise. She often thought of him as snake-like and lounge-lizardy on account of his mobile features and his long supple body. She thought of him as hawkish too because of his unnerving, pin-you-down, stare. And the contradictions continued when she reflected that, whether a hawk or a snake, he looked strangely out of place in this chrome and black wood office. His dark brown hair was always wild and ruffled. He invariably wore jeans topped with big hairy sweaters which looked as though they ought to be out in the country, sitting under wax jackets whilst their owner strode across a Brontë-style moor in wind-swept northern counties.

"Are you all right this morning, Tessa?" he asked. "You really do look a bit under the weather."

"Rough, you mean," she said tartly, suspicious of his unexpectedly kindly tone. "Too much wine, men and song last night. It's all my own fault."

He gave a little chuckle, looking genuinely sympathetic.

Tessa was momentarily disarmed, then her eyes narrowed speculatively. She was convinced that Chance's unexpected displays of humanity, his kind and gentle smiles, were simply a calculated method of disarming his staff and his rivals (was there a difference?) in order to ensure that he himself always came out on top.

"You'll have to learn to keep your men in check, Tessa," he said, startling her out of her contemplation of his possible ruthlessness and deviance.

"Yes. Well I'm sure you've learned to do that with your women," she retorted.

Another chuckle. Tessa decided that he was not at all put out by her rudeness, and she instantly regretted her lack of finesse. "Sorry, that was a pretty crass thing to say," she told him.

6

He shrugged. He took her empty mug from her hand and placed it beside his on the desk.

"Look, I've really got a heap of things to do," Tessa said, uncertain as to whether the interview was now completed. Chance seemed to be sitting there watching her as though he had all the time in the world.

"Are you asking for permission to leave the room?" His eyes sparkled with amusement as he aimed this witty dart.

She shot him a polar look and rose to her feet. As she walked towards the door, she heard him say, "What do you know about Royston Gable?"

For a brief moment Tessa was put on the spot. The name was familiar but not instantly placeable. She forced her mind to search through its database and come up with something. "The man behind the current debate on intelligence?"

"Yes!" He gave an approving grin.

"Don't sound so suprised," she protested ungraciously before she could stop herself. "I do keep up with the news."

"I never doubted it."

"What about him?"

"Do you think you could do a good job interviewing him?"

Tessa frowned, considering. "On his personal life? He's hardly a big star like our usual celebs. Who would be interested?"

"I was thinking more of an angle on his research."

Tessa looked at Chance puzzled. "Isn't that kind of thing rather specialist for our show? A bit academic?"

"Possibly. But isn't the issue of human intelligence and the ways in which each of us individuals get their allotted endowment one of the most fascinating topics there is?"

"Yes," she said slowly. "I suppose it is."

"Well then?"

"He's big on the suggestion that intelligence is far more heavily reliant on genetic factors than it's currently fashionable to believe," she recalled, warming to the subject. "Isn't that right?"

"As far as I've understood it, yes."

Tessa sighed. "I'm not up to speed on intelligence theory,

7

or indeed many theories at all," she protested flatly. She was worried. Was Chance deliberately setting her up? Was he giving her an assignment which was basically beyond her capabilities? Throwing her into deep waters so that he could watch her flail and then drown?

"But you could soon get up to speed. I got our researchers to dig out all the relevant newpaper clippings on Gable together with his most recent articles to get you started." He picked up some sheets from his desk and handed them to her. She was annoyed to find herself noticing that his hands were large and slender and beautifully shaped.

"Oh my God!" exclaimed Tessa, glancing down at the photocopied articles from learned journals and seeing the frighteningly long titles. "I'm no academic. I got dreadful A-level marks and no university would touch me with a barge-pole."

He shrugged. "Nevertheless you're clearly a highly intelligent young woman. Surely you're not trying to tell me you need a piece of paper with Bachelor-of-whatever written on it in order to be able to read and *think*. Shakespeare didn't go to university, or Beethoven, or Dr Johnson."

"Is this some sort of test?" Tessa enquired, keeping her voice very calm.

"I'm sorry?"

"This assignment. Is it a hurdle I have to clear in order to escape the fall of the axe?"

Chance stared at her, apparently puzzled.

"The axe on my job," she added, spelling things out to assist him.

"No!" He looked genuinely amazed at such a suggestion, running his fingers through his hair and rumpling it even further. "No."

"You're very good at firing people," she pointed out.

Chance sprang down from the desk. "I wasn't trying to intimidate you, Tessa."

"Good. I'm relieved."

"I just thought that you would be the ideal person to interview Gable. Get him to loosen up a bit. He's as tight as a clam with most interviewers."

8

"Get him to loosen up, hmm? What special qualities do I have to do that?" She glared up at Rex Chance. "Remember, I'm not very experienced. It's less than a couple of months since you promoted me on to the interviewing team."

"I hadn't forgotten," he said evenly. "I've been keeping an eye on your performance since then. And last week I looked through the clips of a couple of your recent interviews."

He paused. She would have felt better if he had made some positive comment on what he had discovered. But he remained silent.

"Being young and female?" Tessa challenged. "Are those my qualifications for looking so promising to loosen this guy up?"

"Yes. In part. And that's not sexist," he said swiftly, "it's simply a fact of life."

"Huh!"

"Tessa, I'm asking you to do this job because I consider that your intelligence, your natural inquisitiveness, your stubbornness in getting to the bottom of issues and your ability to worry a topic like a dog with a bone all equip you rather splendidly for the job."

Tessa's mouth fell open. She made a small incredulous sound in her throat.

"The fact that you are also heavily equipped with female charm is merely an added bonus. And," he went on, his smile now laced with mischief, "you're marvellously small, or should I say *petite*."

Tessa straightened her spine and made herself two inches taller.

"But only in stature," he added wickedly.

"Hmm." The hairs on the back of Tessa's neck prickled.

Chance laughed. "Research has indicated that men feel less threatened by small women, feel more inclined to confide in them."

"Hah!"

"Not all men, I would add."

What was that supposed to mean? Tessa wondered.

"Well, what about it, Tessa? Are you going to do this interview with Gable or not?"

9

"Do I have a choice?"

"Sure. You're free to say no."

"And if I did say no, then what?"

"Then," he leaned forward, "I'd just have to give the job to Lucinda."

Tessa felt her eyes flare like traffic lights. Lucinda was the most irritating woman on the team, if not this side of the equator. Lucinda was impossibly posh and plummy and not at all dim. She was also around six feet tall, had fantastic facial sculpturing and a body with the curves of a 1950s screen goddess. Moreover, by dint of sleeping with those in power, but mainly by being the niece of Dartbridge's Chairman, she had just got herself assigned to an absolute plum of an interview with fast-talking French TV cook Yves Saint Rochelle, a man Tessa would have given her wisdom teeth to grill.

You rat, she thought to herself as she looked up at Rex Chance, knowing full well that the words were written quite clearly on her face.

"Come on Tessa," he cajoled. "This is just the job for you. You're sharp. You're bright. And you've got a very individual style about you. Very persuasive, with just a touch of the abrasive. Men like Gable will be eating out of your dainty little hand."

She gave him a sharp and narrowed look. "OK," she said jauntily.

"I want you to read through that stuff tonight," he said, nodding his head towards the sheaf of papers he had given her.

"You're joking," she groaned.

"Well," he soothed, "if you find yourself tied up socialising again this evening you could always do your reading in the bath, in bed . . ."

"And what am I looking for?" she interjected swiftly.

His eyes held hers.

"No, don't tell me," Tessa said, rising and making swiftly for the door. "I think I already know." Find the weak spot, she thought. You swine, Rex Chance.

Chance gave a low chuckle. "Report back to me tomorrow – mmm?"

"OK. Fine. And the interview with Gable?"

"Oh, I'd suggest a preliminary meeting with him tomorrow or the day after if you can swing it. We need to have him on the show early next week, at the latest. No point in lancing a boil when it's already burst."

Tessa winced with a mixture of squeamishness and panic. "Terrific. Well, I hope I'm not going to disappoint you, Rex," she said, edging around the door.

"I'm absolutely convinced you're not."

She gave a barbed smile. "It's fantastic to be able to inspire such confidence. And quite nice too to be referred to as sharp, bright and persuasive."

"Think nothing of it." Chance looked entertained. The telephone on his desk squalled for attention. He picked it up, lodging it between chin and shoulder. High pitched squawks emerged. Chance ignored them. There were more squawks. A female voice, without a doubt, Tessa noted.

"I just hope I'm sharp enough to spot Gable's Achilles heel," Tessa said to him.

"Oh, I'm supremely confident on that score."

"And I'm supremely confident that you've been sharp enough to spot mine," she murmured.

"Quite definitely," he responded, his hand muffling the demands from the telephone, his eyes glinting with amusement.

Rattlesnake, Tessa concluded, striding off into the corridor.

Two

R ex Chance stood at the window of his fourth floor office
and looked down. In the car park below a tiny young
woman erupted from the building, looked up at the grey clouds
hurling down rain and started to run like mad, weaving her way
with dizzy speed between the cars. She was wearing no coat
or mackintosh over her flimsy pink shirt and would surely be
soaked to the skin by the time she reached her car.

Rex noticed that she clutched a huge wadge of files, some
of them edging their way from the pile and appearing in danger
of ending up on the ground.

She eventually stopped beside a red BMW. Observing the
square lines of the car, Rex guessed it would be around ten
years old. It gleamed and sparkled even on this grey day, and
he could tell how well and lovingly the owner had waxed it
by the way the rain slid from its immaculate bodywork like
the proverbial water off a duck's back.

On reaching the car the young woman began a frantic
juggling pantomime, trying desperately to wrench her car
keys from a huge, floppy leather bag and at the same time
hang on to all her files. Inevitably something had to give, and
a number of the files slid from her grasp, fluttering damply
into a large puddle.

She flung her head up to the skies and stamped her foot.
Rex saw her lips working furiously and guessed there could
be some graphic swearing issuing from them.

He was aware that his own lips had curved into an indul-
gent smile as he viewed the engaging pantomime below.
The realisation pulled him up sharp. Watch it! he warned
himself, amused and irritated at this lapse from professional
detachment.

He wondered if his hunch about her was right; if she truly would be the one to pull off his ambition to lift *In the Limelight* out of the doldrums and put it way up there in the top ratings.

She'd work hard, he knew that. She'd work her guts out in fact. She was keen, hungry to do well. He suspected that she herself might not yet be aware of how very ambitious she in fact was. Some women found it hard to acknowledge even in these enlightened times.

When Tessa Clair came to report back to him on what she had been able to discover about Professor Royston Gable she would be fully conversant with all the facts he had given her, would probably have unearthed some more and would already have formed some kind of theory. If she hadn't he would be both surprised and disappointed.

Rex moved back to his desk and stood staring thoughtfully at the full-page picture of Royston Gable which had appeared in the magazine section of one of last Sunday's quality newspapers. There was surely something to discover behind that utterly bland, utterly charming smile. The more he looked at Gable's wide open, guileless expression the more Rex was convinced.

He was also convinced that the secrets of a man who had devoted his professional life to the issue of the nature of human intelligence were just the sort of revelations to strike huge universal chords. And yet the very canny, very experienced journalist who had interviewed Gable for the Sunday magazine had not managed to come up with anything at all unexpected about him. She had said as much in the article, spelled it out, openly admitting defeat.

So maybe Rex was a fool to think that an impulsive novice like Tessa would succeed where an astute, seasoned doyenne had failed. But he had a strong hunch about Tessa, a conviction that the tiny, sparky redhead would turn up trumps.

He glanced at his watch, noting that he had only five minutes before his next meeting with Lady Collingham, the intrepid Chairwoman and Managing Director of Dartbridge television. Was he fully briefed, sure that he was one step ahead?

Of course he was. He picked up his phone and pressed

the button for an outside line, then began to rapidly punch in further numbers.

Tessa drove her BMW out of the car park, turned into the flow of traffic and almost instantly veered off into another office car park, employing one swift clean manoeuvre to slot into the only available space. She had seen Rex Chance watching her – spying on her most probably – from his office window and she had no intention of giving him anything on which to speculate. If she had stayed under his gaze he might have noticed her digging frantically about in her bag to locate her mobile phone. He might have speculated on who she was calling in the privacy of her car when she had free access to the office phones. He might have wondered if she was using work time to have chats with her boyfriend, thought Tessa grimly, listening to the ringing tone sound out.

"Green Vale Golf Club," said a cut-glass female voice.

"Is Oliver Stone available?" Tessa asked crisply. "Or is he out and about on the links already, teeing off or whatever it is golfers do?"

There was a little cough. "Mr Stone signed in a few moments ago," Cut-Glass said. "And if one wished to be strictly correct it is only golf courses by the sea that are called links."

"I've never wished to be strictly correct," said Tessa jauntily. "But thanks for the information. It's always good for one to live and learn, don't you agree?"

Cut-glass appeared temporarily at a loss for words and could manage no more than another little cough.

"So is Olly available to speak to?" Tessa repeated patiently.

"I'll just see. Who is calling please?"

"Tessa. I'm his current bit of stuff. His little flibbertigibbet. Flavour of the month."

"I see." Cut-Glass was now glacial. "Just one moment."

Many moments passed. Tessa riffled through the files, trying to dig out the information on Royston Gable with one hand whilst locating her lipstick and Giorgio scent with the other.

"Hi there, beautiful!" came Olly's voice.

14

"It's OK for some," Tessa protested. "Playing out with the lads whilst we workers toil and sweat."

"Aah! Poor little thing."

"I am indeed. Listen, I won't be able to make tonight, Olly."

"Oh, come on. What's the problem? Has Daniel Day Lewis just phoned?"

"No, no. No one like that!"

"Ralph Fiennes? Mel Gibson?"

"Not my types."

"Al Pacino?"

"Pacino's old enough to be my father – at the very least."

"I've heard that some little moppets really go for father figures."

Little moppets indeed! She felt a tiny flare of irritation. But you couldn't be cross with Oliver for long. He was like a lovable, floppy-pawed puppy. "It's work that's calling, Olly, not rival masculine charms."

"Work!"

"Yes, work. Have you never heard of it?" Tessa asked sweetly. "It's that nasty thing the majority of the population have to spend most of their time doing."

"Now, now, don't try to frighten me away with sarcasm," countered Oliver. "It'll take more than that to put me off a find like you, you gorgeous creature."

Tessa squeezed her eyelids together, conjuring up a picture of Oliver in her mind's eye as he stood in the lobby at his posh snobby golf club. Tall, blond, elegantly turned out, he would be wearing the lazy good-natured smile that was almost permanently in place on his classically handsome features.

The smile was one of the first things she had noted about him on their first meeting. She had been shop-window gazing one Saturday morning outside one of London's most prestigious car show rooms and Oliver, on watch in his sales office, had spotted her instantly. He had dashed out to talk to her, smiling and joking whilst he gestured to a luxury sports car which would suit her down to the ground. When she interrupted his sales spiel to explain that he might have to delay clinching the deal for a few years whilst she made her fortune, the smile had taken on a hint of flirtation. He had insisted on being compensated for his disappointment by taking her out for dinner that evening. In the car of her choice.

Oliver had a lot to smile about, she reflected, being one of those creatures lucky enough to be born with an extremely large silver spoon in his mouth.

Oliver had very rich parents who appeared to dote on him as their cherished only child. He had a fantastic job as a sales director in his father's BMW franchise, an occupation that seemed to Tessa to involve little more stressful activity than driving rich people around in a variety of highly prestigious vehicles which mainly sold themselves.

Oliver's working hours were amazingly flexible and he had no problems in regularly finding time to nip up to the golf club in order to 'get in a few holes', as he put it.

"You don't really mean it about tonight," he protested with mock pleading. "I was thinking of taking you out to a super new wine bar in the very trendiest, darkest corner of Soho."

"We wined and dined last night!" Tessa protested, wondering how Olly's head could stand the thought of more alcohol. Hers still felt as fragile as the filmy membrane inside an eggshell.

"So what? Pleasure isn't to be rationed, Tess." His voice was suddenly almost chiding.

"Look, I'm sorry, Olly, but I do mean it. I simply can't go out living it up tonight."

"This sounds decidedly serious."

"It is."

"I'll promise to have you home by ten thirty. Tucked up in bed, hopefully with me."

Tessa snorted. "Keep your voice down. Cut-Glass will be listening in."

"Then let's give her something worth listening to."

"I really do have to work," Tessa said flatly. "I have to find an Achilles heel. I'll explain later."

"What? Oh come on Tess! Come out with me instead."

"My boss is dangling a juicy celebrity carrot in front of me. If I can pull this interview off it could give my career a real kick-start." Her vivacity flared and then suddenly fizzled. She gave a small sigh. "And if I make a mess of it, I could be out on my ear."

"No problem, popsy," Oliver laughed. "You could move in with me and be my sex slave."

"No thanks. I value my freedom too much."

"OK then. Fine. I think I'm getting the message loud and clear. I give you permission to stay in tonight and do your homework. But no excuses for tomorrow. It's Mum's birthday and she'll never forgive me if I don't bring you along to help celebrate. She's dying to meet you."

"Oh great!" exclaimed Tessa, highly relieved that Olly had at last given in. Sometimes his persistence, whilst endearing and flattering, was a touch wearing. "A birthday. I *love* birthdays. Of course I'll come."

Rex's sister, Vicky, brushed the flour off her pastry-making hands before picking up the telephone.

"Rex!" she exclaimed. "Where on earth have you been all this time?" She pushed a strand of her long dark hair behind one ear, wondering if she had reached that stage in life when she should have it cut short. No, not yet. A face with bones as clean and strong as hers could look mannish without a softening frame.

"Oh, you know, hiding away. Head deeply buried in the sand of work."

"Tut, tut. Now you haven't forgotten about tonight have you? You are coming?"

"Yes, of course. But I could be a bit late. I've some research to catch up on for tomorrow morning."

"The old, old story," Vicky said, laughing indulgently. She was Rex's older sister by two years, and she could never remember a time when he hadn't been driven by some project or other. When he was a little boy it had been the construction of immensely intricate meccano, which had lasted until he discovered the delights of crossword puzzles, books and Brahms. As an adolescent he had become passionate about the countryside and a fearless fighter for the banning of fox-hunting. At university he had gone through a phase of eloquent political fervour, making himself a shoal of friends

17

and enemies. And then he had gone out into the world of work, which aside from one tragically doomed love affair, had claimed the major part of his life ever since.

"If you were any other man," said Vicky, waving her arms in warning at her son Benny, who had abandoned his pad of paper and felt-tip pens and was now decorating his face with the flour on her pastry board, "I'd conclude that 'research' was a euphemism for a pretty woman."

"Is that a put-down, Vicky? Are you suggesting that I never do any research in that direction? Do you think I live the life of a monk?"

"No. You're more like one of those dedicated priests who manages to have every single female in their flock panting for your favours, whilst you stay safely perched up on your lofty pedestal."

"I didn't know I was that exciting."

"Oh, you do have one or two good human points, Rex, even in the human relationships field."

"Who's coming tonight?" Rex asked patiently, knowing that his sister loved him dearly despite her constant innuendoes and digs.

"Me. My lovely husband Doug – I expect you'll just about manage to remember him. And then there'll be our neighbours, Lexie and Tom . . ."

"And?"

"That's all."

"You sure?

"Yes."

"You're not planning to slot in an extra female at the last minute – just to tempt me."

"No."

"That's so hard to believe, my dear, given your match-making track record."

"To tell the truth, I did have someone lined up. Judy from my yoga group. She's fabulously beautiful, wonderfully caring and just recovering from a divorce." Vicky signalled more frantically to her son who was now using his brightest red pen to draw a wobbly face on the round of pastry she had cut for the lid of her apple tart. "Benny!" she chided, clamping her hand secretively over the phone, her brown eyes twinkling warmly with maternal forbearance.

"The caring Judy! God help me!" Rex groaned.

"He did. Judy's recently got herself fixed up with the yoga instructor."

"Thank you, God!"

"You know, Rex," Vicky said in a low quiet voice, "it really does worry me sometimes to think of your living all on your own, living only for your work."

"Vicky, I have both a full social life and a host of female friends. I don't go back to my lonely flat every night with a take-away dinner and a video."

"Hah!" snorted Vicky. "You may have female friends, but that's as far as it goes, isn't it? There may be dozens of willing volunteers to cook for you and even iron your shirts – God help them. But the minute they start getting serious and falling in love with you they get the short, sharp brush-off, isn't that right?"

There was a pause during which Vicky shook her head slowly and lovingly at her mischievous dark-eyed son, who had completed his artwork on her pastry and now smiled back at her in a way which made her heart beat fast with love. She loved her little boy with a tenderness that was almost painful. It had taken four years of disappointment, clinics, tests and doctors' varying opinions before she had produced Benny. And now her life felt as though a huge warm glow had been placed at its centre.

As he turned his head away she caught a glimpse of herself in the firm line of his nose, and then an echo of Doug in the generous curve of his mouth. He was a compact, chunky child, his features mobile, his eyes full of energy and curiosity. But beneath the glossy brown hair the pale face was still only partly moulded, not yet revealing the secrets of his genetic inheritance, those qualities she and Doug had passed on to make him a unique human being.

"You know why that is," Rex said slowly.

Vicky pulled herself back from fondly maternal thoughts of her son and instantly renewed her attack on her brother, determined not to shirk her mission. "Yes, I do know Rex.

But you can't grieve over Eleanor for ever. It's been six years now." Vicky gave a silent wincing grimace. It was only rarely that she dared to mention Rex's old love by name.

"Don't go on Vicky," he warned. "Don't give me the old routine about how it really is time I fell in love again. That kind of delicate human emotion doesn't come about at the whim of experts in the affairs of the heart. No one can manipulate my feelings for me, however skilled and well-meaning they are. Not even you."

"I stand corrected," smiled Vicky. "I simply can't bear seeing good things go to waste. A good man, that is."

Rex guffawed. "Are you talking about me? The potentially ideal husband, sitting on the shelf and going stale like a piece of ripe Stilton."

Oh Rex, thought Vicky, glancing across at Benny and reflecting on all the joys of parenthood. All those riches. Was it wrong to want them for her brother who was so *worthy* of them. And so very alone.

"I'm your sister, Rex," she said in matter-of-fact tones. "I've known you for ever, man and boy. If anyone can put their finger on your good and bad points, I can."

And she could. "Clever and sharp and witty. Always on the ball, always one step ahead of your rivals. And yet good and kind too." She stopped. But, oh so brittle. Few would guess at the tender heart which beat beneath his daunting exterior.

"Is that it, Vicky?" asked Rex. "I'll have to hang up on you in a minute. There are people banging on my door, demanding to be let in for a high-powered meeting."

"No, that's not quite it, Rex. I need to remind you as well that kids love and adore you."

"Ah. You're saying it's time I was making my application to join the worthy profession of fatherhood?"

"Yes."

"Are you absolutely sure you haven't asked a stray female for tonight?"

"Yes."

"And there'll be no personal crusading in the cause of my romantic future?"

"Promise."

"See you around eight thirty, then. And much love to that wicked son of yours. Try to keep him in some sort of order, Vicky, otherwise he might grow up to rule the world, not just your household."

Three

Tessa was sitting cross-legged on the floor of her rented flat in Highbury, north London. Spread around her were the biographical notes Rex had given her on Royston Gable. Tessa had pushed back the furniture and scattered the papers on the floor like so much confetti. Having tossed them down in a totally random way, she now picked up each item in turn, read through it carefully and then allotted it to a certain pile, according to the nature of the information.

At first the task had seemed a chore. Tess had felt resentful, mutinous even, that Rex Chance had presumed to throw all this research stuff at her, knowing full well she'd have to work flat out all evening in order to get her head around the information so that she could hold her own with Chance the next morning.

Arrogant, controlling rat, she muttered to herself with narrowed eyes.

But as she read on, the various articles and press cuttings started to gain some meaning, to develop a thread of coherence. Her curiosity was roused. The materials Rex had thrown at her stopped looking like an assortment of pieces from a variety of jigsaws and began to fit together to form a meaningful picture of a human life. And it was at this point that she stopped being driven by her anxiety to do well and her constant fear of not coming up to scratch and finding herself redundant, and started to enjoy herself.

She had always been fascinated with true-life stories. Her natural curiosity about the inner psychology of human beings and the way in which it showed itself had been one of the reasons she had gone into journalism in the first place. And the profession had never disappointed her on that score. It had provided an endless procession of human stories, stranger than fiction. How one used those stories was, of course, another matter entirely.

Tessa uncrossed her legs, curled into a comfortable ball and re-read some of the materials for a second time before going on to look at the ones she had not yet seen.

She forgot about the time, forgot that she could have been out and about drinking and laughing with Olly in a dark wine bar; even forgot about Rex Chance.

When her flatmate put her key in the lock at midnight, Tessa was still sitting on the floor, but now the papers around her were no longer in chaos, but stacked in neat piles. And the ideas in Tessa's head were correspondingly beginning to fit themselves into a framework.

Trudie flopped down on the sofa. "I'm giving up men," she proclaimed, as though she had just come on stage as a main player in a Shakespearean tragedy.

Tessa looked up. "Again?"

"Don't joke." Trudie leaned against the back of the sofa and put on an expression of tormented anguish.

"I thought you were out with Andrew tonight. I thought he was the answer to all your prayers."

"So did I."

"What happened?"

"I suggested that we had a few days away together. You know, a weekend in Amsterdam or Paris, nothing heavy."

"Sounds a harmless enough idea."

"He didn't seem to think so. He said I was getting too serious, that he wasn't 'ready' to start talking about going on holiday with me yet. He said we should cool things a bit. Give each other some space."

"Oh dear." Tessa pulled a grim face.

"Why does this always happen to me?" wailed Trudie. "Why do men pick me up and whirl me round, then drop me like a hot brick?" She jumped up and flew across the room to stare in the mirror she had hung there specially for that purpose. "Oh, why am I so unattractive?" she wailed even louder.

"You're gorgeous," said Tessa. About ten times as attractive as pompous, self-opinionated Andrew, she added to herself, but was too tactful to say out loud.

"I'm twenty-four," lamented Trudie. "In six years I'll be thirty."

"That seems logical."

"I'll be on the shelf. I'll be an old maid. I'll be on the sexual scrap heap."

"Have you been sleeping with Andrew?" Tessa interposed.

"Yes."

"Was it good?"

Trudie sniffed. "Not bad."

Tessa chewed on her lip, glancing at the neat piles of paper surrounding her. Part of her mind was still occupied with conjecture about Royston Gable. "Why do you sleep with your men even when you're not enjoying it?" she asked Trudie, genuinely curious.

"Oh God, I don't know. They don't stay with you if you don't sleep with them, do they?"

"Do they stay any longer if you do?" Tessa wondered.

"That's really cruel, Tess." Tears sprang into Trudie's huge china-blue eyes.

"Sorry," said Tessa. "I just have this feeling that if you jump into bed with guys too soon they lose that thrill-of-the-chase feeling and move on to the next likely prey."

"Call you old-fashioned or what!" protested Trudie. "You sound just like my mother. 'Keep them waiting, darling. Preserve a little mystery. Make them respect you.'"

"Mmm," said Tessa, inclined to think Trudie's mother had a point.

"You're lucky, Tessa," Trudie said, tossing her long blonde hair and smoothing her hands over her tiny waist and her rounded hips. "You're not bothered about men."

"What?"

"Well, you know what I mean. Having a man and getting married isn't exactly high on your list of priorities. You're a career-girl type." Trudie sprawled out on the sofa, kicking off her skyscraper-heeled shoes and wriggling her poor tortured toes.

"Hmmm!"

"Look at you now," Trudie pointed out to illustrate her assertion. "It's getting on for the middle of the night and you're still working. You wouldn't be crazy enough to do that if you weren't dead keen."

"I'm motivated by fear," Tessa said. "The wrath of the great Rex Chance, to be precise. Controller-in-chief of Dartbridge daytime TV and undisputed god regarding the rise and fall of his hapless minions. For example, me."

"What's he like, this Rex?" Trudie pulled a strand of hair into her mouth and sucked on it thoughtfully. "He can't possibly be as bad as you've made him out. What does he look like?"

Tessa nibbled on the end of her pencil and considered. "Tall, lean, quite nicely put together, I suppose. Dark brown hair, eyes the colour of old brandy. Also intimidatingly clever and completely ruthless. An alligator in crocodile's clothing."

"He sounds gorgeous."

"All a matter of individual taste, my dear," Tessa murmured.

"How old?"

"Right side of fifty, I should guess."

"No, be serious."

"OK. Mid- to late-thirties is my estimate. Ripe, but not yet rotting."

"Invite him round for dinner," Trudie instructed.

"Not likely," Tessa chuckled. "Does a bunny invite a wolf into its burrow?"

"I'll plan the menu, do all the cooking," said Trudie, a gleam of renewed energy illuminating her eyes. "I'll do avocado mousse. I'll do oysters and tiny asparagus spears. I'll do figs in brandy. A real aphrodisiac dinner."

Tessa sat back on her heels, a smile twitching at the corner of her lips. "I've got the feeling you're getting over that smug creep Andrew even as we speak."

"Is that what you truly thought about him?" exclaimed Trudie, horrified.

"As a matter of fact, yes."

"Why didn't you say?"

"Oh come on!"

Trudie chuckled. "I suppose my heart isn't utterly broken.

Just a little dented." She stretched and yawned, opening her pink lips wide and revealing an equally pink mouth with perfect white teeth. She looked at the piles of paper surrounding Tessa and stirred one of them with her foot. "Anything interesting here?"

"I'm not sure," Tessa said slowly. "I haven't found anything I can quite put my finger on. But I've got this really strong feeling there's a missing link somewhere." She sighed, imagining Rex Chance's scorn should she present him with nothing more than a vague hunch regarding some irregularity or secret from Royston Gable's past. On the other hand there was nothing to be gained by inventing things that were simply fictional. That had been tried by other journalists and presenters and had usually ended up with their having a lot of egg on their faces.

"So what now?" asked Trudie, yawning again, this time more loudly and lengthily.

"Bed. Sleep," said Tessa. "I once read somewhere that solutions to problems can sometimes come in dreams. The mysterious workings of the unconscious."

"Is that right?" Trudie said, suddenly interested. "That's never happened to me."

"No, it's never happened to me either," Tessa admitted. "But there's always a first time."

It was just past eight as Tessa deftly slotted her BMW between the narrow lines marked out in the car park. On this spring morning the sky was a pale inky blue more reminiscent of night than day. A translucent moon, as fragile as a torn paper lantern, hung white and ghost-like high over the office buildings.

"Give in moon," Tessa told it, climbing out of the car, her arms crammed with folders and newspapers. "You've done your bit. Go off to wherever moons go in the daytime and have a lovely long rest. Wish I could join you."

On reaching her office she leaned over her desk, opened her arms wide and allowed all she had been carrying to drop on to the desk-top with a huge thump. Some of the folders spilled over the edge on to the floor and she was in the process of

26

crawling around to retrieve them when Rex Chance appeared in the doorway.

"Good morning," he said.

Tessa glanced briefly up at him. He looked quite unreasonably cheerful and together. He looked like a man who had enjoyed a good night's sleep, who had indulged in the luxury of eating dinner the night before and possibly breakfast before he came into work.

"Is it?" Tessa asked, intensely aware of the emptiness of her stomach and hoping it would not begin to voice embarrassingly noisy complaints.

He smiled. "I hope so."

"I didn't see your car downstairs," Tessa said, frowning slightly as she stuffed escaping papers back into a gaping folder. "I was sure I'd beaten you into work."

"I took the tube." He bent down to pick up the last two folders, handing them over politely to Tessa. "Are you ready for our meeting?"

"What? Now?"

"Yes, now."

Tessa glanced up at him. She waited for the standard lies that bosses were so fond of telling in these circumstances. How would he phrase them she wondered?

Would it be: *"I've a frantic day ahead, Tessa. Can only spare you a half-hour slot before a breakfast meeting with Jodie Foster/ Elton John /Sir Simon Rattle. They're flying in specially to see me."*

Or maybe: *"Something really big has come up. I'm going to be tied up every second of the day after nine."*

"I've already poured the coffee," he said. "It'll be going cold."

Well that made a change, Tessa had to admit, following him down the corridor and finding she had to break into a trot to keep up with his long, loping strides.

He motioned her courteously to a chair beside his desk, and placed the afore-mentioned coffee in front of her. She caught a whiff of sharp masculine aftershave, briefly mingling with the heavenly smell of fresh hot coffee. Her nostrils tingled with pleasure.

27

"Right then!" Chance said briskly. "Royston Gable – so, what have we got so far?"

"You mean what have *I* got?"

"Basically, yes. But I have to admit I've done a little homework of my own."

Tessa couldn't avoid a small grin. "I thought as much." She took a long sip of coffee, almost closing her eyes with bliss at this first warm drink of the day. Taking out the research information Rex Chance had given her on Gable, she laid it on Chance's desk in the three piles she had so carefully assembled the night before.

"I've divided him into three parts," she told Chance, aiming for a light tone to conceal her anxiety.

But she saw that he was now suddenly looking stern and predatory, all his easy social overtures over. This was serious. This was work. Reputations and careers were on the line.

"There's Gable's work," she elaborated, "his family, and his love-life."

"Right." Chance looked expectant. "Well?"

Tessa paused. She had found Royston Gable's details completely fascinating – as she found most people's life stories once the hooks of curiosity fastened themselves around her. And she had formed a strong, intuitive impression that somehow Gable's history was too perfect, too blameless, too good to be true. The picture that his details had painted was somehow just a shade too bland. The elements all dove-tailed together just a shade too conveniently. There must have been something awry in his life, some piece of the jigsaw whose edges were marginally askew.

But her dreams of the night before had not been of any help in disclosing to her what the nature of such a misfit piece might be. There was still nothing watertight she could find in Gable's notes on which she could pin a controversial interview. And she was convinced that the cut and thrust of controversy were what Rex Chance was after. As she had dressed that morning she had concluded that she knew quite a bit about Gable and could do a good job interviewing him, drawing out the most interesting points. But it would be a bread-and-butter kind of interview, following the well tried and tested formula that *In the Limelight* was already well known for. Nothing new or sensational. Tame, in fact.

Tessa glanced up at Chance and licked her dry lips. "When I was at school," she began, in the manner of someone embarking on a story, "we used to do these experiments in the science laboratory. After we'd completed them we had to write them up. They always had to be presented under three headings. Method, Observation, Conclusion."

"I remember," Chance interposed dryly.

"It was very important," continued Tessa, refusing to be denied the right to bring her story to its meaningful close, "to be able to justify your conclusion by something you could point to in the observation section. If you couldn't do that you got a big red line through your write-up and a 'See me' at the end of it."

"OK, Tess, you're entertaining me," Chance said, smiling with elaborate patience. "You've grabbed my interest and my total attention. You're also employing delaying tactics. Now get to the point."

"The point is that whilst I've been through Gable's biographical details in a very methodical manner and even though I've made some pretty snappy and relevant observations, I've discovered absolutely nothing that I could justify putting in my conclusion section." Tessa faced his steady brown gaze, her heart making a dull drumming in her chest.

Chance stared at her for a few moments, his eyes shrewd with conjecture. Then he threw back his head and laughed.

"Is this a roundabout way of telling me you've got one or two hunches and nothing whatsoever to back them up."

"Exactly. A bull's-eye," Tessa told him.

He looked at her, and then looked down at the three piles of notes she had sorted with such care and genuine curiosity.

"I've obviously failed in the task you gave me," she said, giving him a glinty glance, "but I trust I'll get full marks for trying?"

Whilst he had clearly been disappointed with what she had told him earlier, now he seemed faintly amused. "Consider them yours. And I won't get out my red pen." His smile slowly faded as a frown of conjecture creased his forehead.

"Right then, even if you haven't got anything watertight, at least let me hear the bare facts you've come up with so far," he commanded.

"OK." Tessa tapped two of the piles of notes on the desk with her index finger and took in a long breath. "These are the family and love-life notes. I couldn't find anything odd or irregular here. In fact I suppose you could say they seem almost squeaky clean."

"I see," Chance said slowly. "That would seem to me rather unusual in the case of celebrities. Doesn't it seem rather hard to swallow?"

"That's one way of looking at it. But, as I said before, Royston Gable isn't a typical celebrity," Tessa reminded Chance. "He's a serious and respected research psychologist, not an actor or a sportsman or a pop star."

"Point taken. But Gable's well on the road to becoming a celebrity. And he certainly doesn't seem to be backing out of the media storm he's stirred up. Indeed, quite the reverse."

"Yes," Tessa agreed patiently. "Do you want me to go on? With my hunches?"

Rex Chance shot her a swift glance of appraisal. "Are you trying to tell me I was straying off the main track of our discussion?" he enquired, raising an ironic eyebrow, and it struck Tessa for the first time that Rex Chance had certain accomplishments she had not previously suspected. When he felt like it he had a sense of humour, and he could play the role of flirt.

"I think you *were* a little guilty of straying," she said sweetly. "Shall I go on?

"Please do."

"In my opinion, the family and love information are quite convincing, because although they're clean in terms of not appearing to conceal anything, they're in no way designed to make Gable look like an angel."

"Ahh. You're saying that they're clean but not suggestive of careful laundering?"

"Exactly. Now this is how the story goes. He was brought up by his mother and step-father in Manchester, went to the local high school and won an open scholarship to Cambridge."

"A very bright kid obviously," Rex commented.

Tessa nodded. "He studied medicine and qualified as a doctor with flying colours. His first job was as a junior doctor at a hospital in north London where he met his future wife who was a specialist children's nurse. They married very soon after meeting each other."

"Baby on the way? Shotgun wedding?" Rex enquired, with a playful grin. "They still used that term in the unliberated seventies didn't they?"

"I'm too young to remember," Tessa responded archly. She allowed a small deliberate pause to elapse. "And I can't answer the question as to whether Gable's wife was pregnant when they got married. I'd planned to make a few investigatory calls before our meeting, you see, but you caught up with me too soon."

Tessa shot her listener another wry, sparky glance and then suddenly realised with horror that she had fallen into the trap of responding to his mild flirtatiousness with some flirting of her own. She issued a stern warning to herself.

"I'm sorry if I seemed to be hassling," said Chance.

Tessa searched his expression for mockery or guile, but failed to find either of those qualities. She discovered herself thinking that if Rex Chance were not her boss, if he were not a man in a position to manipulate her and influence the rise or fall of her future career, then he might be a man she could quite take to.

"Well, anyway, even if she was pregnant, nothing came of it," she told him. "They never had any children."

"And the marriage lasted how long?"

"Five years. He was twenty-eight when they were divorced."

"When was that?"

"Twenty years ago."

"That makes him forty-eight now," Rex mused. "So what happened to break them up?"

"His wife ran off with another man." Tessa paused, looking thoughtful. "A Harley Street gynaecologist." She leaned across the desk and riffled through one of the piles of newspaper clippings extracting a large photograph. "This was on the front page of the *Sunday Courier* the day after she re-married."

Rex stared at the photograph, a typically glamorous wedding shot of a group emerging from a Mayfair registry office. "She's a very attractive woman."

"Yes. Almost as good-looking as he is. And look – ", added Tessa, leaning across and tapping the picture with a pencil – "Gable's standing there among the guests, looking as happy as though he'd just won the lottery. Except there wasn't one to win then," she added with a laugh.

"Clearly everything was very amicable about his divorce and his wife's new marriage – on the surface at least. So what did Gable do after that? Did he marry again?"

"No. And this is where we move on from the family pile of clippings to the love-life pile." Tessa picked up the wadge of pictures and handed them to Rex who leafed silently through them, giving his full attention to each one.

"Quite a roll-call of escorts. Or possible mistresses," he commented eventually.

"Yes," Tessa agreed. "All of them gorgeous, and some of them pretty famous."

"So he must be a somewhat charismatic guy."

"Oh, he is. Well, as you can see, even in a faded mono-chrome newsprint photograph he comes across as drop-dead gorgeous," Tessa observed.

"Does he?" Rex looked again at the pictures.

"Most definitely," said Tessa, noting that Rex had re-evaulated the pictures with a degree of perplexity on his face. Doubt even. "Maybe another man can't see it. But take my word for it, Royston Gable is a real ladykiller."

When Rex Chance glanced back at Tessa she saw that he now wore a faintly injured look. She felt a little pang for him, recalling what it felt like as a woman to have another man extol the virtues of some unreasonably beautiful and sexy female.

"And yet you don't think that any of these intriguing details about his private life is of particular interest?"

"Not as far as any possible dark secrets are concerned. Well, let's face it, he's been perfectly happy to have his private life quite publicly paraded in the press. Some professionals would balk at that, but not him. Of course the fact that he's not afraid of being seen out and about with a series of lovely escorts doesn't mean he hasn't had secret lovers as well, lovers he'd prefer no one to know about. It's possible that he's very good at keeping some of his affairs quiet. But . . ." she stopped, pinching the end of her nose and making a small grimace.

"Go on."

"We're not after digging up a bit of dirt about the odd married or famous woman he's taken to bed, are we? Surely that's an angle that's been done to death."

"It still makes good copy and good TV," Chance observed. "Especially if the wronged husband's a member of the government or the royal family."

Tessa gave a short dismissive shrug. "Finding something quirky about his work would be far more interesting in Gable's case, don't you think? Given that this latest research he's published on human intelligence is a bit of a hot potato." Her eyes challenged her boss, steely and determined.

He did not flinch. "OK. You're convincing me. I'll buy that. So what have you got?"

Tessa let out a sharp sigh of exasperation. "Nothing"

"Come on. There must be something else you've found."

She shook her head.

"OK." Chance picked up the pile connected with Gable's work. "Let's go through this little lot together with a fine-tooth comb."

"Have you been through it before?" Tessa asked suspiciously. "Before you gave it to me. Are you one step ahead and not admitting?"

Now Chance looked decidedly injured. "No, Tessa, I haven't been through these notes in any detail. I did glance at them. But that's all."

Her expression was still dubious.

"OK, I confess," he smiled. "I did read the first chapter of his new book on genetics and intelligence last night."

"I thought it wasn't out yet."

"It was a review copy. I got it from a critic friend on *The Times*."

"Oh!"

33

"Tessa," he said gently. "There's no need to be so prickly. I'm not laying trip-wires for you to fall over. I'm not trying to do you down. I simply want us to work together on this interview with Gable and milk whatever there is in the story to the greatest effect we can manage. I want to boost *Limelight* in the ratings and convince Lady Collingham that Dartrbridge TV is a force to be reckoned with, and growing more so by the hour."

"Really."

"Don't you trust me?" he asked mildly.

"No, not entirely. You're my boss, you see," she added as though that were ample justification for her scepticism.

"Yes. But I am also human."

"I'm sorry to seem doubting," she said gravely.

He sighed. "Let's stop fencing shall we? Now – give me a quick rundown on Gable's career."

Tessa did not need to look at her notes, she knew Gable's CV by heart. "As I've said, he qualified as a doctor, then did the usual hospital placements as a houseman. But then, instead of taking up a specialism and getting a consultancy, he went back to Cambridge and started studying for a degree in psychology and genetics."

"Just a minute," Rex interposed.

"Yes?"

"That would have cost him an arm and a leg. You're only entitled to one state grant for an initial degree. He'd have had to support himself and also pay tuition fees. He wouldn't have been rich then. He wasn't working. So who paid? His parents?"

"His wife, I imagine. Her father owns one of Scotland's major whisky distilleries. She's loaded."

"Ahh. He picked an heiress did he? Is there no end to his accomplishments? And then?"

"He got a starred First in his finals."

"Wow! After that?"

"He was offered a research fellowship at Cambridge. He was one of the youngest of the decade to get one."

"And he's still there?"

"No. He resigned just a few months ago."

"Really! So what he's going to do next?"

"He's going to spend more time writing. He's been offered visiting professorships all over the place, freelance lecturing, consultation work, and after-dinner speaking. According to an article in one of the big nationals he can command fees of a thousand pounds for a two hour seminar on his latest research!"

Chance smiled. "Better than TV hack-work, mmm?"

"I'll say."

"Well, we seem to have been through all the material. So where are the gaps? Where's the Achilles heel?"

Tessa faced him square on, daring to confront those penetrating brown eyes. "There isn't one."

"Oh come on, Tessa. There must be something juicy to get to grips with. Some gaps somewhere at the very least."

"Everyone's life history has gaps, doesn't it?" said Tessa feeling a wave of renewed frustration for her failure to pinpoint a verifiable gap in Gable's history. "And each human life story is filled with little crevices into which supposition and gossip can filter." She looked away from him. "But I can't work with supposition and gossip," she said slowly.

"What are you trying to say?" His voice was suspiciously quiet.

"I don't think I can give you what you're wanting from this interview. I can do a good straight face-to-face with Gable on his research findings. I can talk to him about his marriage and his mistresses. No problem. But as for Achilles heels . . ." She glanced back at him. "I don't hold out much hope of that at all. Certainly not within the time span we've got."

"So?"

"So, you'd better give all these research clippings to Lucinda, hadn't you?" She held her breath.

"Tessa, are you being deliberately manipulative?" he demanded.

"I'm being honest," she told him shortly. "I'm simply saying that if what you're really wanting from me is the kind of spectacular interview where some past dirty work at the crossroads is suddenly brought to light then I can't do it."

"Can't or won't?" he enquired.

"Oh, I've no moral scruples about digging up dirt if it's the truth and the person concerned has been wicked or cruel or criminal. I'm simply saying that I can't guarantee that kind of sensationalism with Gable. Not on the basis of this material at any rate."

Rex Chance drummed his long fingers on the desk top. "The truth can sometimes provide the most electrifying and extraordinary story you can tell," he observed thoughtfully.

"Yes," Tessa agreed, "but the problem is to find it, and then make it stick. I haven't got anything on Gable. I've no amunition to throw at him."

The drumming continued, echoing in Tessa's ears.

"I'm offering you the opportunity of a lifetime here," Rex Chance said evenly. "If you can make a go of this interview we might be looking at getting you a talk show of your own. Writing your own material, drawing up your own lists of possible guests." He raised his eyebrows.

Tessa's heart gave a huge swoop like a high-flying bird sucked into air turbulence. He was talking about her most secret and cherished ambition.

"Yes," she said. "I realise. But I'm still not prepared to hold out any promises about finding Gable's Achilles heel. And I'm certainly not in the business of manufacturing one specially."

There was a long pause.

"So what now?" asked Chance. His tone was calm and reasonable but she heard the underlying note of challenge.

"I don't know." She stood up and started to edge towards the door. "You're the boss," she told him, opening the door and sliding around it. "The ball's in your court, Rex. You've got to decide whether you want me to go on camera with Gable or to get someone else to do it. It's up to you."

Four

"Fool, fool, fool!" Tessa told herself through clenched teeth, walking swiftly down the corridor back to her own office.

Why had she behaved towards Rex Chance with such transparent obstinacy? Why hadn't she hedged or prevaricated, strung him along a bit? She could have hinted at possible loopholes in Royston Gable's history, made much of her hunch that there was indeed some fascinating story to uncover beneath Gable's impeccable personal details and CV. It was always possible at an interview that the unexpected could turn up.

Why had she had to be so damned honest? Virtually talking herself out of the golden opportunity to be given half an hour on screen face to face with Royston Gable, who, she had to admit, was beginning to look like a more and more fascinating interviewee by the minute.

She hurled her piles of notes and cuttings on to the desk and paced around the office, giving out sporadic sighs of angry frustration.

She was well aware that her preference for frankness and honesty went way back to childhood days. She knew too that it was all bound up with her brother, Alec, whom she had adored and hero-worshipped for years, even when he started breaking her parents' hearts with his lies and his laziness and his incurable extravagance.

Alec had never had any truck with frankness and honesty. He had always preferred to win people over with his charm and persuasiveness, and then cheat them with his deviance and secrecy. He had also always been a great promiser. He would borrow money from his long-suffering parents and swear with a hand on his heart to pay them back. But before he did so

37

he would already have run up further debts and would simply persuade them to lend even more.

He had constantly assured them that he would get a steady job, that he would buckle down and earn a regular salary. But instead he had invested his parents' money in a series of glamorous and risky business ventures in partnership with unreliable friends. He had gone bust more times than Tessa could remember.

His optimism about success never left him, however. Even after a string of disastrous failures he had still cheerily proclaimed that the next venture he hatched up would make a fortune, that it was a sure-fire winner, absolutely couldn't go wrong. And when that happened, then of course his parents would get back all the money he'd borrowed from them and much more besides.

Handsome, sweet-talking, irresistible Alec had promised the moon, thought Tessa, idly ruffling the papers on her desk, and he had delivered nothing.

And yet her parents had never lost their trust in him. When Alec's enterprises failed and his friends evaporated (usually with any money that was to be salvaged from the current venture) and he came slinking back home, her parents would welcome him back, soothe his hurt pride, forgive him without reserve, and dip once more into their savings.

And the promises would start all over again.

Eventually, when he had almost drained the family dry, Alec had fallen foul of the law. The police had turned up at the house one night, demanding to see him, talking ominously of charges for fraud. But Alec had already gone. Vanished into thin air.

Tessa's hands stilled as she recalled that it would now be almost three years since her brother had disappeared. And there had never been a single word from him. Not a postcard, not a phone call. Nothing.

For months her parents had longed for his return. Her mother had put fresh flowers on the oak chest in his room, had shaken the plump quilt on his bed and smoothed the pillows. But gradually they had both faced up to reality and given up hope.

Tessa thought of her parents in their little house on the east coast. She tried hard to be a good daughter to them. She telephoned each weekend, she visited them at Christmas and every bank holiday. But somehow she knew she could never make up for the loss of Alec.

Her parents were not yet sixty, but they seemed old and shrunken, worn down with worry and sadness. They were all used up and done for, the poor loves, she thought with a rush of pity and affection. And all because they had not been able to resist believing in their son's hollow and ultimately cruel promises.

So don't promise what you can't deliver, Tessa murmured to herself, suddenly feeling better about her refusal to allow Rex Chance to persuade her to go one step further than the truth in what she had discovered about Royston Gable.

So even if Chance was already on his way to plummy Lucinda's office to offer her Royston Gable on a plate, at least she, Tessa, still had her integrity and self-respect intact.

She gathered up the information on Gable, stuffed it into a large envelope folder and slotted it into her new slim-line filing cabinet.

As she bent to lock the cabinet, she heard footsteps coming along the corridor. She stiffened, knowing instinctively that the firm swift tread was that of Rex Chance.

He knocked at the door and then walked straight in, making her glad she was not in the middle of some delicate operation such as checking that her new, lace hold-up stockings were not about to lose their grip and slide down her legs. Trudie had laid a bet with her that she would never manage to keep a pair holding up for a whole day. She said Tessa's thighs were far too slender to keep the elastic taut. Disgustingly slender, in fact, had been her exact words. It was such a nuisance being so small thought Tessa, flinching slightly as Rex Chance invaded her office and towered over her. When you were small all your clothes either fell or slithered off you. And men had far too great an advantage over you.

"I've just been on the phone to Gable," Chance said. "You're not off the hook yet."

Tessa was not sure if his expression suggested menace, triumph or both. Whatever it was meant to convey, she had a sense of being cornered, bearded in her lair, so to speak. She gave him what she hoped was a basilisk stare and pressed her lips together sternly. Two hot bright flags of colour blazed in her cheeks. "Don't stop there," she said, trying to sound cool. "I hate to be kept in suspense."

He gave a low dry laugh. "Gable's keen to do the interview, but he doesn't want to talk to you face-to-face until you're both on camera."

"Hey, now wait a minute, I thought I'd made it clear that I wouldn't do the interview!" Tessa interjected.

"You made a few noises in that direction," Chance admitted. "But I wasn't inclined to take them too seriously." He gave her the infuriatingly chummy smile of a man who knows he has the upper hand. "And your final words on the subject – spoken only minutes ago, were that the ball was in my court." He paused, raising an eyebrow quizzically. "I presume that my memory isn't playing tricks, Tessa?"

"No," she sighed. "I suppose not."

"So now I'm telling you that I definitely want you to do this interview and that I trust you won't be foolish enough to throw away the opportunity."

Tessa drew in a long breath and then let it out again. "Tell me some more about what Gable said."

Rex Chance leaned against her desk and swung a long leg to and fro. His face had a faintly detached look about it. It reminded Tessa of the look that came over people's faces on trains or aeroplanes when they were listening to music on headphones, tracking the intricacies of a melody line or a song which no one else was able to hear.

She realised that he was working things out in his head, recalling what had passed between him and Royston Gable and forming a judgement on which he would soon act.

"Gable said that he'd seen a clip of you doing an interview with Anthony Mansfield, the cello virtuoso," Rex said thoughtfully.

"Oh yes!" Tessa gave a sudden smile, recalling that particular interview with amusement and a certain warm affection. Mansfield had been prickly, monosyllabic and downright impossible to begin with. She had feared that the interview would turn out to be a complete disaster. But gradually she had coaxed him from his shell, won him round, got him talking. And when he played one of Bach's cello suites at the close of the programme, his bow drew such magic from the strings that the music seemed to have been produced by the mythical god Orpheus himself.

"Gable was highly impressed. In fact he told me quite categorically that he wouldn't hear of having any other interviewer but you. If I don't give him a firm undertaking that you're going to be the one – then he won't do the interview at all."

"Oh!" she exclaimed, half flattered, half terrified.

"So it looks as though you'll either have to go into a harem or decamp to a far-off planet if you want to get out of it," Chance said drily.

"Yes." She levelled him a challenging look. "Well, as long as you don't expect me to perform miracles, I suppose I'll have to bow to the inevitable."

"Oh come on, Tessa. You know you're dying to do this face-to-face with Gable. Admit it!"

"I'd like to do the interview," she said stubbornly. "I just won't promise to unearth any Achilles heels. Muddy or otherwise."

Chance gave a wry grin. "I'm beginning to wish I'd never mentioned the damn things. They've caused nothing but trouble between us."

There was a tiny beating pause. And then a curious throb of tension in the room. Those words, 'between us', they had a certain intimacy about them which Tessa found strangely disturbing. And she knew without a doubt that Chance had read her emotions and read them correctly. She frowned, puzzled by her feelings.

"It's going to be hard to do an interview if Gable won't meet me beforehand," she said.

"Oh, he'll meet you. But not for a tête-à-tête. At a social gathering – more precisely, at a champagne cocktails party at his house." Rex regarded Tessa steadily. "Tonight."

Her heart gave a jolt. "Tonight!"

"Yes."

Tessa bit her lip. She'd promised Olly that she'd go to his

mother's birthday party tonight. She couldn't let him down. Not again. She felt that she'd done nothing but put him off recently. And though she knew he wasn't the great love of her life and she doubted that they'd ever be a serious item, she was genuinely fond of him.

"What's the problem?" Chance asked.

"A previously arranged date. With my boyfriend," Tessa said flatly.

"Surely he'll understand if you cancel?" His brown eyes were calm and unreadable.

"No, on this particular occasion I think he'll be rather hurt. It's special. His mother's birthday."

"A family occasion! Sounds like a serious relationship." Chance raised his eyebrows.

"None of your business," Tessa mouthed to him with a sweet but cautioning smile.

"Quite right. Apologies. So what are we going to do? Because I rather think we have no choice but to turn up at Gable's party – or risk losing the interview."

For a moment Tessa felt horribly trapped. And then she reminded herself that with every problem there was invariably a solution or a compromise. "I'll go to Gable's party and stay for an hour," she said decisively. "Olly can come and pick me up there in time to get me to his house for the start of the birthday dinner."

Chance stiffened slightly, seemed about to protest, then decided against it. "Fine," he said crisply. He sprang athletically from the desk and stood for a moment looking down at her. He took a small step towards her and she could smell the faint tang of his cologne, the sharp male scent of his body.

"It's a black tie affair," he said.

"I don't have a black tie any more, it went into the dustbin with the rest of the school kit!" Tessa suddenly felt light and frothy and mischievous.

"But you've got a very nice pink silk shirt," Chance countered, unabashed. "That would do splendidly." He turned towards the door. "Oh, and incidentally, bearing Gable's likely preferences in mind, I'd recommend a short skirt and high heels rather than trousers."

42

Before she could flash a glance at him to see if he was merely winding her up, he had turned and slipped silently away.

Tessa stood looking at the closed door through which he had disappeared. Her nerves twitched. Her muscles contracted and tensed.

And then the elasticated lace top of the stocking on her left leg suddenly lost its grip and slithered in one swift movement down to her ankle.

43

Five

Tessa went through the clothes in her wardrobe like a whirlwind rushing towards the USA from far out in the Pacific.

The only thing dangling from the hangers that was clean and well pressed was a rather dull, grey shift dress. Last season when she bought it, just after grey had been proclaimed as the newest new black, she had thought it extremely chic. Now it just looked limp and dowdy – and glumly grey.

Rex Chance's suggestion of her pink shirt put that particular garment right out of the frame. And anyway it had purple biro on it, from the night before when she had so assiduously gone through Royston Gable's biographical details, making rapid notes.

Her memory brought back to her Chance's wicked suggestion about short skirts and black stockings and along with the memory came a sudden thought about a very short, very supple, black suede skirt that she had bought in the July sales at Harvey Nichols last year and had never dared to wear. A very, very short skirt. The sort of skirt that only a girl with slim legs could get away with. Any suggestion of extra fat on hips, thighs or calves gave that skirt a licence to make one look like a packet of pork sausages.

Glancing at her watch she realised that she had not nearly enough time to get herself ready before Rex Chance arrived to pick her up.

It had been a long day. She had had to attend a series of mind-blowingly boring inter-departmental meetings with the news team and the religious programmes team and the documentary team. Rex Chance had decreed that all departments must know what each other were doing, must all pull together

44

and think of Dartbridge TV as an entity, not a series of warring factions.

Huh!

The news team, full of themselves and their brilliant ratings, had rattled on far too long and consequently by the time she arrived back at her flat, she had had less than half an hour in which to take a bath, wash her hair, and put on her clothes and make-up.

When Chance arrived, dead on time as she had guessed would be the case, she had not had time to dry her hair and was forced to leave it wet, knowing that when it eventually dried it would do whatever it wanted. Which, in Tessa's case, meant it would end up a close-fitting helmet of riotous russet curls.

"You look like a medieval page-boy," commented Chance, eyeing the short short skirt, the white shirt with its collar turned up and the delicate gazelle-like legs, bare and smooth with a dredging of honey-coloured freckles.

"Sorry, no high heels available," said Tessa, slamming the outer door behind her and following him down into the road where his silver 1962 Mark II Jaguar was waiting, crouched by the kerb. She gazed at it for a moment, delighting in its sleek, rounded beauty.

Chance, meanwhile, was looking at her pink open-toed sandals and smiling broadly. "Those are perfect."

"What do you mean?" Tessa asked, settling herself on the beautifully yielding soft old leather of the Jaguar's seats. "Perfect fashion-wise, or perfect for making Royston Gable worship at my pretty little feet and turn to veritable putty in my hands?" She paused. "I think there could be some rather nasty mixed metaphors there."

"Not mixed, but maybe odd bedfellows," commented Rex Chance, starting the engine which had a low, throaty growl to it, quite different to the smooth purring sound of a more modern machine. "I simply meant the shoes were great with that get-up. Quirky but charming."

Tessa experienced an odd swooping sensation in her stomach. She glanced furtively at Chance. He didn't seem to be sending her up. He sounded truly appreciative of her efforts to present herself in the best possible light for Royston Gable's party. And as though he were paying her a compliment. A definitely male-like compliment made by a sensitive man to a woman he finds attractive.

She gave a little cough. "I'm nervous," she blurted out with brutal honesty.

"Are you? Of what?" He had drawn up at a junction and now sailed out into the flow of evening traffic with supreme confidence, the Jaguar surging powerfully and emphatically forward in complete accordance with its name.

"This whole thing with Royston Gable, I suppose," she said slowly, suddenly finding a continuation of dancing in ritual stalking circles around Chance tedious and unnecessary. They were not dogs guarding their territory, eyeing each other with their hackles raised. They were on the same side for goodness sake. They were colleagues working together for the good and glory of Dartbridge TV!

"You're nervous about the forthcoming studio interview, I take it, not this little party tonight?" Chance prompted, sounding genuinely concerned.

Tessa looked out of the window. She was not sure of the answer. She couldn't quite put her finger on her anxiety about this business with Royston Gable. She was not a highly experienced interviewer, it was true, but she knew she was a good one. She believed that in time she could even make a name for herself. And so she knew that the drone of anxiety that had been with her ever since Rex Chance mentioned Gable as a studio guest was not simple unease about being on camera with him . . .

"Are you nervous of Gable himself?" Rex asked thoughtfully. "Psychologists with a line in genetics must be a pretty daunting breed. He could be formidable."

The question raised a spark of alarm. "I don't know him yet. So how could I be frightened of him?" But somehow, now the idea had been planted, she realised that Rex's question was not to be casually dismissed.

"No, I suppose not." He changed gear and the car leapt effortlessly through traffic lights changing from orange to red. "So is it me you're worried about?"

Her heart now gave a huge lurch. "You?"

"Yes. Me. Your evil wicked boss, as you keep pointing out. A dreadful ogre to be feared."

She turned and looked at him. His brown hair had fallen over his forehead in a rather rakish and appealing way. She had the notion that maybe he was not too happy to think of her as having noted him down as an evil and wicked boss figure. "There was a time when I was frightened of you," she said evenly. "When you first came to Dartbridge and started firing people."

"They all got other slots elsewhere," he pointed out, defending himself. "And I didn't get rid of anyone who really needed a job."

Tessa considered, mentally flicking through the names of the fired ranks. "No, you didn't."

"Of course not."

"Oh well," she said noncommittally, stroking the Jaguar's gleaming walnut dashboard with tender fingers, "maybe you're not so bad after all, Rex."

Royston Gable lived in a large white Georgian house in the most expensive area of London's Mayfair. Its ranks of elegant windows looked out on to a grassy emerald green square, surrounded by classical black railings. In the gathering dusk of an early April evening light streamed from the windows, throwing golden lozenges of radiance on to the garden.

"A touch more upmarket than my place in Highbury," Tessa commented drily, looking up at the house and speculating idly on how much one would have to lay out to obtain a place like that.

"Highbury's one of my favourite places in London," Rex commented, switching off the engine and unclipping himself from his seat-belt. "Also the home of one of the most exciting football teams in England. Are you an Arsenal supporter then, Tessa? Your flat is just across the road from the ground."

"I'm no connoisseur of football. But I go and stroke the police horses when there's a match and lots of shouting going on."

"Maybe I could come along and stroke them too one evening," Rex said lightly. "Listen to the roars of the crowd."

My goodness, we are getting chummy and chatty, Tessa thought, swinging herself in one graceful movement from the Jaguar as Rex opened the door for her.

Walking up the broad steps to the impressive front door of Royston Gable's house, Tessa felt a sudden sharp twinge of apprehension.

"Are you OK?" Rex asked, glancing down at her, instantly noting the slight falter in her usually brisk pace.

"Yes, fine."

"You've gone rather white."

"Have I?" She gave a short dry laugh. "I think I'm getting the sort of feeling poor old Daniel must have had when he was approaching the lion's den!"

Rex Chance put a hand on her arm. "Tessa," he said in a low voice of concern, "Royston Gable may be an esteemed academic, working in a rather scary field of research, but he's just a man. Just another member of the human race. Just one of a procession of guests for *In the Limelight*."

Tessa looked up at him, suddenly noticing how splendid he looked in his evening jacket and white shirt. "Of course he is," she responded cheerily, in no way prepared to share her vague dark premonition about Gable with Rex Chance. Rex may be looking and behaving in a very friendly manner tonight. But he was still her boss. He still had the power to make or break her career at Dartbridge TV.

An impeccably suited young man showed them into a room leading off the oval-shaped hallway and beckoned a waiter forward to provide them with flutes of champagne.

Tessa looked around her, finding the room nothing short of exquisite. The walls were painted in pale primrose like an early morning sunrise whilst the drawn back curtains were in heavy gold brocade and the carpets a soft banana-cream shade. The sofas and armchairs were covered in palest blue and rose watered silk and a huge concert grand piano gleamed in one corner, its lid propped open as though beckoning guests to come and play it.

There were flowers everywhere, huge displays of lilies and

carnations, and the air was thick with their fragrance, mingling enticingly with the sharp scent of champagne poured over brandy and Angostura bitters.

"Bit like Buckingham Palace, don't you think?" Rex whispered with dry irony in her ear. "A touch grand and old fashioned for my taste."

"Ssh." Tessa warned Rex fiercely, spotting a man in a beautifully cut black suit coming purposefully across the room in their direction. She recognised the slim, graceful figure instantly from the photographs she had studied so carefully. So here he was: Royston Gable. In the flesh.

"Rex! So good to meet you in person!" he exclaimed, holding out his hand and greeting Chance as though they were old friends who were about to be joyously united after too long a gap. He released Rex's hand, turning his body slowly. "And this must be Tessa!"

She felt her hand grasped in strangely soft and delicate fingers. "Hello, Professor Gable," she said formally.

"Royston," he said in a low soothing murmur. "So you're the young woman who's going to grill me on screen next week." Eyes the colour of woodland bluebells gazed down into hers, and long sculpted lips tilted sexily at the corners.

Tessa felt as though she were being assaulted, yet in the most unobtrusive, gentle and fastidious kind of way. "Yes," she agreed pleasantly, not wanting to give anything away. She reminded herself that she was here on business, even though she was in the lap of luxury, drinking champagne and being gently eyed up by an undeniably attractive man.

Recalling that Royston Gable was in his late-forties she was impressed by his masculine beauty and his air of timelessness. He reminded Tessa of the breathtaking sculptures she had admired in the Vatican when visiting Rome the summer before. He was all smooth clean lines, from the top of his gleaming silver hair to his glinting patent shoes. By his side Rex Chance, even in his evening dress, looked craggy and rumpled.

Whereas Rex's hair continually flopped over his eyebrows, Gable's was neatly brushed back emphasising the breadth and smoothness of his forehead and the classical shape of his head. His nose had a decidedly Grecian slant to it and his cheek-bones were as sharply defined as knife blades. The line of his jaw, however, was surprisingly square, indicating a formidable degree of determination.

Tessa looked down into her champagne flute where the bubbles rose and fell with ceaseless energy. She was aware of an overwhelming urge to discover as much about Gable as she possibly could, to make the forthcoming interview a real humdinger.

But how?

She was simultaneously aware of Royston Gable's sharp probing gaze appraising her and of a responding jolt within. She turned to check that Rex Chance was still beside her and, noting his rugged, solid presence, she felt enormously reassured. And, after that, she felt astonished at herself to be harbouring such a feeling.

Just as she was adjusting herself to the idea that Chance could actually take on the role of representative of everything that was familiar and safe, there was a loud shriek of, "Rex! Rex! *Darling!*" from behind her. She turned to see a shapely blonde bear down on Rex, grab him by the arm and drag him away to meet her group of friends.

And she, Tessa, was left staring up into the gimlet blue eyes of Royston Gable.

Six

"I fancy your protector has abandoned you," Royston Gable observed, staring down at Tessa with a faintly amused smile on his face.

"My *protector*! He's my boss!" exclaimed Tessa.

"Does that automatically make him your enemy?" Royston Gable queried.

Tessa was about to make a jokey and flippant response in the affirmative when she pulled herself up short. Something warned her not to treat this apparently harmless conversation with Gable lightly. "Of course not. But," she added, unable to stop herself, "I find it rather amusing that you should think of him as my protector."

"Oh?"

"For one thing I'm rather well known for being able to look after myself," Tessa explained.

"And for another?"

"Oh nothing particularly," she assured him hastily, not wanting to be drawn into making any further comments about Rex. Somehow to do that seemed not only unprofessional, but disloyal.

"He wasn't prepared to let you come to this gathering on your own," Gable said, his intense blue gaze never leaving her face.

Tessa stared back at him, a small frown of conjecture creasing her forehead. "He more or less refused the invitation on your behalf unless I extended one to him also. He seemed to feel a need to accompany you personally."

"Really! How very chivalrous of him," Tessa exclaimed rallying from her astonishment and contriving to look cool and unfazed.

51

"I was beginning to wonder," said Gable, taking her arm and drawing her along with him across the room, "if Rex Chance doubted my motives in inviting you along this evening."

There was another inner jolt. Tessa glanced up into Gable's flawless smiling face and felt a worm of unease uncurl inside her. "He probably couldn't resist the idea of unlimited champagne cocktails!" she jested.

"Mmm." Gable's smile changed from the inscrutable to the enigmatic.

He was leading Tessa towards a door at the far corner of the room. She caught sight of a study beyond, a room lined with dark oak shelves and row upon row of books.

"Oh what a fantastic library!" she exclaimed, standing in the doorway and looking around her.

"Please, do go in. Have a look around." Gable made a sweeping gesture of invitation with his arm, as masculine and graceful as the prince dancing in Swan Lake.

Tessa looked along the shelves. There were volumes of Keats and Shakespeare, of Shelley and Dryden. A complete set of Dickens, Hardy and Austen.

"Some of them are first editions," Gable said, watching her enthusiastic reaction with unconcealed interest.

"I'm impressed. And heartily jealous," Tessa said, taking down a copy of *Persuasion* and leafing through the tissue thin pages.

"Jane Austen's last tale," remarked Gable, his eyes on Tessa's face, "with a heroine who is arguably the author's finest creation. Do you agree, Tessa?"

"Anne Elliot is a very lovable and sympathetic character," Tessa responded swiftly, thanking some lucky star above that she had re-read the novel in the past year.

Gable smiled. Tessa sensed that he had set her a test, and that, mercifully, she had passed it.

He indicated other famous novels and offered some further critical remarks, leaving Tessa both impressed and faintly unnerved.

"You're welcome to come and avail yourself of anything you like here," Gable said pleasantly. "At any time you wish."

"Thank you," Tessa told him noncommittally. "That's very generous."

"Not at all. I hope we can become friends, even though I suspect you're planning to give me a rough ride on the programme."

"You think we might no longer be on friendly terms following that watershed," Tessa suggested with a wry smile.

"Oh, I think we shall." Gable pulled at his shirt cuff, straightening it under his jacket sleeve. Again it was a gesture of perfect grace and symmetry.

"I hope so too," said Tessa evenly. "I like to talk frankly to my guests. But I'm not one of those hosts who aim to do a hatchet job on them."

"I couldn't imagine your doing any such thing," Gable said calmly.

"But I can be very direct," warned Tessa.

Gable smiled.

"I gather you didn't want to do a preliminary face-to-face with me before the actual interview," Tessa said, replacing *Persuasion* and scanning across Gable's collection of poetry.

"Yes." Following her gaze he took down a slim volume and fingered it thoughtfully.

"Why?"

"I like the thrill of spontaneity. The cut and thrust of the unknown," he said.

"Living dangerously?" Tessa suggested.

Again he declined to make a verbal reply. His smile was perfectly friendly, but completely unreadable.

"Some guests like to provide a list of taboo topics," Tessa told him, aiming for a tone as neutral as Royston Gable's smile. "Subjects on no account to be touched on. Total no-go areas."

"How interesting. That doesn't apply to me. I have no taboos," Gable said with great assurance, a remark Tessa was to reflect on grimly in the near future, in circumstances considerably more threatening than the present one.

"Where are your medical and psychology books?" she asked him with curiosity, noting that the shelves were completely filled with books representing English, European and

American literature. There was not a text book or a technical journal to be seen.

Royston Gable's eyes kindled with interest at her observation. "How perceptive of you. Most of my visitors never notice the lack of scientific texts in this library."

"So do you have another library elsewhere?" Tessa wanted to know.

"Yes. I do. It's upstairs. I like to have all my scientific information close to hand when I go to bed. You see, Tessa," he said, watching her reaction closely, "I'm one of those people who don't need much sleep. And so if I wake in the early hours then I simply walk across the landing and spend some time in my science library."

Tessa found herself drawn by the magnetism of his probing blue gaze, and yet at the same time felt vaguely repulsed by some hidden personal quality of Gable's which she could not quite pinpoint.

She had a sudden strong desire to end this unexpected private meeting, which seemed to be turning into precisely the kind of intimate tête-à-tête Rex had told her Gable shunned. She wished Rex would materialise and neutralise the strange atmospheric charge she sensed here, on her own with Gable, in his literary lair.

She turned away from him and walked across to the nearby window which looked out on to the square. The bright emerald of the rail-encircled grass was turning to a dark avocado as the light seeped from the sky. Behind her Gable stood very still and quiet, a silent yet vital presence.

Turning back to him she saw that he was looking through the slim volume of poetry he had selected from the shelves. *"Absalom and Achitophel,"* he mused in his low silky voice. "A very fine piece of John Dryden's. Do you know it, Tessa?"

"Vague memories from schooldays," she said smiling.

He held the volume out to her. She was conscious of his watching her as she flicked the pages. The dense lines of print seemed to shiver slightly as she scanned over them.

"Do please take it home with you to read at your leisure," he said.

"Thank you." As Tessa looked up to acknowledge his kind

offer, she noticed that the computer screen on his desk was glowing. The screen-saver motif was one she had not seen before: a series of slatish coloured coils weaving in and out of each other in constantly repeating patterns.

"Those are a little more enigmatic and interesting than flying windows or expanding and contracting beach balls," Tessa commented, nodding towards the screen and giving Gable a wry smile.

"Indeed. Have you any idea what those interlinked coils are? What they represent?" he asked. His tone was calm and pleasant but there was a challenge behind his question. And Tessa felt a huge determination to provide an intelligent answer.

"You're a medic and a research psychologist," she said thoughtfully. "So my guess is that those blobs are something to do with genetics."

"Well done. You're perfectly right. Can you go further than that?"

Tessa riffled through her memory bank of general knowledge. Genes and chromosomes, she thought. She tried to recall biology and physiology lessons at school. And then she had another idea. She looked back at the screen. "Are those blobs DNA material?"

"Indeed they are." He looked genuinely impressed. "What you see on the screen is no less than the basic stuff we're all made of. Those unpromising looking strands and globules make up the actual material and fabric that differentiates each human being from the next. For me it's the most fascinating material in the world."

Suddenly Royston Gable had lost his detachment. As he stared at the screen his expression became fervent, almost evangelical. He looked to Tessa like a man gazing at the object of his most coveted desire.

She had a sudden understanding that Gable's desire, unlike that of most men, was not directed at a woman. The love of his life was a chemical. An acid responsible for the creation of humanity.

As she stared at the restless screw-shaped coils on the screen it struck her that here was Gable's Achilles heel. Or at least the territory where it might be found. This was what Gable really cared about.

A flare of excitement shot up inside her.

The young man who had shown her and Rex into the house now appeared in the doorway of the library. Quietly and respectfully he approached Royston Gable and spoke into his ear.

Gable nodded. "You must excuse me," he said to Tessa. "I'm needed elsewhere."

"Oh fine!" She felt enormously relieved and eager to tell Rex what she had discovered during this unexpected brief interview.

"Please, do come along with me," Gable said, holding out his arm in one of his graceful gestures. Tessa had the idea that she was being commanded to follow him.

Moving to comply with his silent command she wondered if he were unwilling to leave her on her own in his library – if there was something she could discover that he would rather she did not.

Once again excitement seized her, together with a steely determination not to be a puppet under Gable's control but to do as she wished. She opened her fingers and let her little velvet purse slide to the floor, confident that its fall would make no sound on the thick silver-grey carpet.

As she and Gable passed through into the drawing room, and he became swept up in the throng, she murmured to him about needing to retrieve her purse and swiftly slipped back into the library.

Instantly she found herself feeling rather foolish. She was over dramatising things, behaving like a rather amateurish fictional sleuth.

She picked up her purse and prepared to return to the drawing room to find Rex. But she couldn't help having another look at Gable's fascinating screen-saver.

The coils still swirled, linking and locking, then subsequently unwinding and starting all over again. Hypnotising thought Tessa.

She noticed that Gable's leather-bound volume of Dryden's *Absalom and Achitophel* was lying on the desk beside the computer. She recalled now that she had put it there earlier whilst she bent to examine the screen-saver patterns.

She smiled. So I did leave something to come back for after all. I'm not a complete fraud. Reaching out to grasp the volume her fingers made brief contact with the mouse beside the computer keyboard.

Instantly the saver motif vanished and the screen flashed up a page from the document in most recent use. Gable, or whoever had been working on the computer, must have forgotten to close the file when he left the keyboard.

Somehow peeking into a file on screen was not so guilt-making as clandestinely opening up a letter, and Tessa had little compunction in running her eyes over the shimmering lines of print.

The page on screen had no heading or title. It was simply a list of names, dates of birth and addresses.

Tessa frowned. Were these the names of patients of Gable's? She reminded herself that Gable was currently a researcher and a high profile academic speaker. Surely he would no longer have the time to see patients or clients? So maybe these names formed a list of the subjects taking part in his psychological research.

She looked more closely and was interested to note that the dates of birth logged neatly after each name all fell in the same year – just twenty years prior to the present.

A strange feeling of urgency overwhelmed her, and a sure sense that the information unfolded before her was somehow significant and important.

Rapidly unzipping her purse she fished out the tiny notebook and miniature pen she took with her everywhere and swiftly copied out the first four names and addresses. At this point she was beginning to feel decidedly guilty of snooping, but even so was driven by a strong unidentifiable source of motivation – she could not allow this opportunity to take something from Gable's database to pass by.

She zipped up her bag and picked up the slender book of poetry. As she moved towards the door Royston Gable appeared within the door frame. "Tessa. I've been looking for you," he said. The charming smile seemed to Tessa like a piece of medieval writing: beautiful, complex and utterly illegible.

"I left the Dryden behind," she told him with a rueful smile. She found that her heart was thrashing about inside her ribs like a caged animal. Glancing anxiously back at the computer she saw that screen-saver had cut in. The squirming double helixes of DNA were once again engaged in their mysterious, writhing dance. Her heart steadied a little.

"Ah, the Dryden." He made a low chuckle in his throat. "When you return the poem to me next week I shall question you as to your critical assessment of it."

"I'm the one who's supposed to be asking the questions," Tessa told him, making a valiant effort to keep her voice steady and calm.

He gave her a long, level look. "Yes. Of course. I mustn't forget that."

"No." She found herself watching him in the way a rabbit might watch a fox. He was standing in the doorway, completely blocking her route out. She imagined herself walking up to the door, his smiling down at her and moving slightly away, then teasing her by moving back again before she could escape.

For goodness sake, she told herself impatiently. Get a grip on yourself, Tessa.

"There's a young man just arrived," Royston Gable said. "He says he's come to take you away."

"Oh! That'll be Oliver!" She looked at her watch. "Oh heavens! Is that the time?"

"You have to leave?" Gable enquired.

"Yes. I've another party to go on to. Didn't Rex tell you?"

"No."

"Oh!"

"I can see that my party simply doesn't have what it takes to persuade you to stay!" Gable said softly.

"I'm really sorry," said Tessa, running a hand agitatedly through her curls. "I don't mean to be rude. It's a family party I'm going to, a birthday celebration," she said, wincing at the half truth.

Gable shook his head. "It's quite all right, Tessa. I'm not the slightest bit offended."

He stood aside to let her pass through the door and Tessa shot through the crowded drawing room, her eyes scanning the company for a glimpse of Rex Chance. But he and his blonde abductress were nowhere to be seen.

Seven

Royston Gable shut down his computer then moved to the window, sifting possibilities through his mind as he watched Tessa walk along the square. Under the street lamps her hair flamed sunset gold and her legs were silvery pale. She turned on more than one occasion to look back at the house. He guessed that she would be hoping to catch a glimpse of her boss, Rex Chance, and that his failure to materialise was troubling her. Gable had noted the tingle of electricity between the two of them, but he doubted if either had yet admitted it to themselves, let alone each other. He smiled. Human frailties, hopes and self-delusions were endlessly fascinating for him.

As Tessa folded her tiny frame into a waiting car, he reminded himself of the keen intelligence he had seen in her eyes and the strength of character in her lips. She was not a woman to be easily intimidated.

When he had first seen her playing the part of lively hostess on the *Limelight* show he had found himself suddenly becoming enlivened, his senses heightened. He had felt the hand of fate on his shoulder as he determined to meet her, to come to know her intimately. She was infinitely desirable, and yet he knew she could bring him danger – a woman of such keen perception and determination.

He had a sudden image of himself put at risk, skating on the edge of the precipice with Tessa fleeing ahead of him, the gap between them gradually narrowing.

Withdrawing from the window he found himself filled with a calm, pure elation.

Oliver Stone was double parked beside Rex's Jaguar. Dressed

in blue jeans and a crumpled navy linen jacket he was sprawling at ease, drumming a little rhythm on the steering wheel with his fingertips as he waited for Tessa. At regular intervals he tooted gently on the horn just to let her know where he was to be found.

As Oliver was in the habit of availing himself of whatever interesting vehicles were hanging around at his father's Hampstead showrooms he rarely drove the same car for two days together, and was therefore not always easy to identify from a distance.

But this evening he was driving a classic car to beat all classics. And he was eagerly looking forward to seeing Tessa's face when she saw it. Tessa knew more about cars than any of the girls he'd been out with in the past and he was confident she would be impressed.

"Hi," she said to him, sliding herself into the car and then immediately twisting around to look back at the house from which she had just emerged.

Oliver felt a little piqued. He'd been waiting over a quarter of an hour for her. He'd expected a peck on the cheek at the very least, and some awed comment on his current set of wheels.

"What are you looking for, gorgeous girl?" he asked, starting the engine and revving it into a frenzy of lion-like roaring.

"Not what, who," she replied, craning out of the window to look up and down the road. "My boss, Rex, to be precise."

"Maybe he's already left," Oliver suggested, not especially interested in the comings and goings of Tessa's reputedly ogre-like boss.

"No, that's his car." Tessa gestured towards Rex's shiny Jaguar. "He must still be at the party." She bit on her lip, frowning. The invasive, faintly hypnotic image of Royston Gable which had dominated her mind for the past hour now swiftly faded as she recalled Rex's sudden departure from her at the party and the seductiveness of the extraverted blonde who had dragged him away.

Oliver glanced at the silver car, lifting a faintly mocking, faintly contemptuous eyebrow. "So what if he is? A bloke's entitled to his bit of fun, even if he is the devil incarnate – as you've frequently assured me."

"Yes." said Tessa doubtfully, still looking back at the house.

Oliver felt a tinge of annoyance and exerted some extra pressure on the accelerator. The car now sounded like a whole pride of lions in pursuit of a good supper. "So?" he demanded a little fretfully. "What do you think?"

Tessa swivelled round. "Mmm?" she said vaguely.

"Of the car?" Oliver prompted, fondling the Aston's chubby, provocatively sexy gear lever.

Tessa was still reflecting on Rex and instantly thought of his Jaguar. In the nick of time she checked herself from hurting Oliver's feelings with a clumsy and unthinking response which would let him know that her mind was not exclusively on him. "It's fantastic. I've never been in a DB6."

"Well, you aren't now," said Oliver, gently correcting her. "This is a DB5."

"Oh my goodness," said Tessa, making sure to inject the appropriate amount of awe into her voice. "That really is a rarity."

"Certainly is."

"How did you get your hands on this? No don't tell me – it belongs to one of your fabulously rich customers. It's been in for a service and you're just giving it a test-drive to make sure it's up to the mark!"

She recalled an especially hilarious tale Oliver liked to tell of a cherished 1979 Rolls Royce Silver Shadow that he had borrowed one evening from the service department of the garage and had personally driven back to its owner the next morning. "Goes like a bird," he had told the customer.

"Yes," the man had agreed whimsically. "It was certainly doing more than a hundred when you overtook me in my wife's car on the bypass last night."

Oliver was full of stories like that. He was always joking, always laughing. Always light-hearted and playful.

"Not on loan. It's mine," Oliver said. His face had taken on an untypically serious and almost reverent look.

"Well, congratulations," said Tessa, unable to stop herself wondering where he'd got the money. "Don't tell me you've mortgaged your parents house to get it!"

"My kind, honest heart would never allow me to do a thing like that!"

"Hmmm!"

"My mother bought it for me!" he said, with a little smile of gloating pleasure.

"I thought it was *her* birthday."

"Yes. She's always held the view that it's more blessed to give than receive. Especially when her little boy's on the receiving end."

"Oliver! I think that might be blasphemous."

"Sorry."

"You're just a spoiled brat," Tessa told him lightly, at the same time inwardly realising that she was speaking the truth.

"Yeah. Nice isn't it?"

"How's the golf?" she asked knowing that the answer would keep Oliver going for quite a while, leaving her free to review the oddly disturbing events of the past hour. It was becoming clear to her that she was going to have to make a huge effort to focus her mind on the events in hand once she got to Oliver's mother's birthday party.

Because, just for the moment, the only thing she had the remotest interest in doing was mentally running through her recent encounter with Royston Gable; replaying in her mind exactly what he had said to her, the way he had said it and what might lie behind his words. She was burning to make some sense from her curious, jagged meeting with the magnetic research psychologist, to form some theories and then to plan a structure for the forthcoming TV interview.

And the only person with whom she wanted to share her thoughts on the subject was Rex Chance. Odd that, she thought wryly: she, Tessa, actively wanting to be in Chance's company – even if it was only for the purpose of furthering her career.

"That's enough about golf irons and balls. Not that you were listening anyway," Oliver said, reaching out and sliding his hand up her thigh.

"Sorry," she said, pressing her hand on his, firmly but gently halting its upward progress. "You know I'm not the world's most sporting girl."

"Not as far as team ball sports are concerned, I do agree,"

said Oliver. "But there are other types of even more interesting sports." He paused. When she made no response he said, "And talking of balls, when I take you home tonight, is this going to be my big chance to prove to you that I've really got some?"

"Oliver, that's about the crudest proposition I've heard in my whole life," said Tessa bursting into laughter.

"But Tessa, my sweet, you're positively exquisite!" exclaimed Oliver's mother, shimmying down a vast, lushly carpeted hallway and clasping Tessa in an ecstatic welcoming embrace as though they were bosom chums being re-united after a tragically long gap. Whereas in fact this was the first time they had met.

"Oliver, why didn't you tell me Tessa was so gorgeous?" she went on, holding Tessa at arm's length and eyeing her with apparent wonder.

"I did," said Oliver.

"Happy birthday, Mrs Stone!" Tessa said to the older woman, wondering which birthday this would be. She supposed that as Oliver was nearing thirty, his mother must be fifty at least, unless she had been a child bride. Tessa thought she was exceedingly glamorous for a woman who had clocked up half a century.

Her tall, slender frame was encased in clinging burgundy velvet; an ankle-length gown slit up to the thigh at each side and topped with a waving marabou collar.

"Oh, not Mrs Stone, please!" she said to Tessa. "My name's Sharon." There was a pause during which she treated Tessa to a dazzling and somewhat expectant smile. She seemed to be waiting for some kind of comment.

"Mum is very proud to have a famous namesake," Oliver said helpfully.

Tessa forced her mind to work. "Oh! Sharon Stone," she said, smiling. "Gosh, that *is* a good namesake."

"I know, it's really marvellous fun don't you think? And such a good thing I'm a blonde like she is." Sharon patted her shining blond hair. It was cut in a simple, highly expensive-looking bob, with one of those outrageously fashionable short blunt fringes that top London hairdressers were doing at the moment for women who prided themselves on their style and daring. Tessa privately thought if made them look as though they'd just escaped from *Cell Block H*, but there was no accounting for taste.

Sharon grasped Tessa's arm and steered her through the hallway and into the leisure room at the back of the house. Gaudily dressed guests were milling around the edges of a swimming pool shaped like a violin's belly. They were sipping pink champagne, nibbling caviar canapés and shouting their heads off.

"By the way," Sharon said into Tessa's ear as she handed her a glass of pink fizzy, "I have to tell you, Tessa, that, despite my name, I never go without my panties!" She gave Tessa a sly wink and a nudge.

Tessa gave a little start. She had been temporarily locked away in her own thoughts, which kept slipping inexorably back to the puzzle of Royston Gable like iron filings pulled to a magnet.

Sharon's teasing little whisper brought her smartly back to the here and now. Tessa smiled politely and sipped her wine. She hoped some food would appear soon. As usual she had forgotten to eat anything more substantial than a bird's breakfast since the day before.

"Come and meet my husband," said Sharon, drawing a balding, muscular man from one of the laughing groups. "Vernon, darling," she cooed, "this is Oliver's girlfriend. Isn't she a darling? Just like a little china figurine. Tessa, this is Oliver's dad."

"Welcome to our home," said Vernon, pumping Tessa's hand. "Any friend of Oliver's is a friend of ours. And I mean that sincerely."

She was amazed at how such a small man could be Oliver's father. She looked at the willowy Sharon and remembered reading somewhere that a healthy male always grows taller than his mother. So Sharon had married for money, and Vernon for height genes, she thought mischievously, wondering if she was getting tipsy.

Sharon and Vernon chatted with her some more, then glided away, leaving Tessa feeling like a tiny piece of driftwood floating in large and seething ocean. Oliver seemed to have disappeared, rather in the manner that Rex had earlier.

The guests swirling around the pool had obviously been at the party for some time and were showing signs of becoming steadily wrecked. The bellowing and laughter was deafening and the air was thick with cigarette and cigar smoke. From time to time the occasional fully clothed body toppled into the pool with a resounding splash.

Tessa looked around her. This so-called leisure room seemed as big as an aircraft hangar. A spectators' gallery ran around the upper half of it, accessed by number of intricately designed metal stairways. The whole place was tropically hot. The heating must be on at full blast, thought Tessa, feeling a throb of energy like a ship's engine vibrating somewhere deep in the lower innards of the house.

She knew that if she drank the huge glass of champagne Sharon had given her she would probably soon be joining the steadily growing number of guests ending up in the pool. She considered pouring her champagne into the nearest potted palm, and then thought again, realising that an empty glass would merely invite a refill – either from one of the fleet of waiters weaving sinuously through the throng, or from Sharon who would doubtless be much concerned about a guest whose glass was not topped up.

She had a sensation of dislocation, as though she had been catapulted between two entirely different planets in the short space of half an evening. Reality seemed to be evading her. She felt light-headed and wobbly.

She absolutely must find something to eat.

A strange man reared up in front of her. "Hi! Who are you?" He loomed over her, tall and willowy, seeming to sway like the mast of a seventeenth-century sailing ship.

"Tessa," she yelled at him.

"Ella?"

"*Tessa.*"

"Can't hear a damn thing in this place," the man shouted crossly. He looked down at her accusingly as though the din was all her fault. "Are you in the motor business?" he yelled at her. "Everyone else here seems to be."

"No. TV."

"What?"

"Never mind," she murmured. She saw that the man was perpetually glancing over her shoulder, constantly on the lookout for some other guest who might be more beautiful, more important or more interesting than she. She could tell also that he wasn't prepared to abandon her just yet. She might turn out to be more fascinating than he thought.

Tessa sighed. It was going to be one of those awful parties where you had no choice but to be propelled from one person to another like a spinning autumn leaf in a strong wind.

She realised that the need for food was now critical. She thought longingly of something hugely substantial like a plate of sizzling sausages and creamy mashed potato. With a little mountain of frog-green mushy peas. Preferably delivered intravenously for the swiftest effect.

"Excuse me," she said politely to her roving-eyed companion. "I have to go hunting for some supper."

She found her way to a kitchen the size of a small ballroom. There was not a crumb of food to be seen there. In fact the place was so immaculate it was hard to imagine anything as basic as a sausage or a piece of cheese ever sullying its gleaming white surfaces.

Grabbing the arm of a harrassed-looking passing waiter in the hall, she clutched dramatically at her stomach and moaned, "Starving!"

He looked at her and smiled. "The dining room's that way," he told her, gesturing across the hall.

Tessa had just loaded a plate with a number of items of food, so exotic looking she would be hard-pressed to give them a name, when Sharon appeared in the doorway.

"Ooh! Caught red-handed, thieving the goodies!" Tessa exclaimed, feigning guilt.

Sharon wagged an admonishing finger. "Naughty girl," she said smiling and looking anything but cross.

"Where's Oliver?" Tessa asked. "I haven't seen him since I arrived."

"He's been circulating," Sharon said, sounding pleased. "Talking to all the guests and being a good host for once."

She stretched out a slender leg and ran long maroon nails along her stocking, smoothing out imaginary wrinkles. "Maybe he's beginning to grow up at last. I think you've been a tremendously good influence on him, Tessa."

Tessa's heart gave a small jerk. She realised that this was no light throwaway remark. Oliver's mother really meant what she said. And it seemed to Tessa that Sharon's innocent-seeming comment carried with it some rather serious implications.

"Come along with me," Sharon said conspiratorially, waving a beckoning hand to Tessa. She led the way to a narrow private staircase which ran parallel with the back wall of the house. "No one'll see us," she told Tessa, springing up the steps with light athletic steps. "We'll be able to have a few moments together talking girl-talk."

Oh dear, groaned Tessa inwardly, wondering what was coming and having terrible suspicions. She popped a miniature pizza into her mouth and chewed on it hungrily, reluctantly abandoning her plate on to a carved side-table, beneath a huge display of aurum lilies. It seemed rather rude to be stuffing herself with food whilst Sharon was giving her a tour of the house.

Sharon led the way into a bedroom that looked like something out of a lavish 1950s Hollywood musical – a symphony in apricot and gold. The bed was vast, covered with a golden shot-silk counterpane and surmounted by a padded apricot satin headboard in the shape of a giant shell.

"Wow," exclaimed Tessa dutifully.

Sharon chuckled. "Lovely, isn't it?" she said. "But I think when I redo the room in the autumn I'll go for pinks and burgundies. And I'll have one of those draped canopies over the bedhead – you know, the sort of things sultans have in their tents."

"Mmm," said Tessa, inwardly wincing. Her own tastes were for the classic and simple. Not that she could afford much beyond second-hand tat at present. Of course, if she did well enough and got her own show . . . Instantly pictures of craggy Rex Chance and inscrutable Royston Gable snapped up in her mind like pictures from a pop-up book.

Sharon moved across to the walk-in wardrobes which

spanned an entire wall of the room. On moving aside the heavy glass doors, which glided on silent rollers, Tessa saw that the space beyond was as big as her entire bedroom at the flat.

Sharon started riffling among the hangers, plucking out certain garments and tossing them on to the bed in a heap of rainbow colours.

"You'd be most welcome to try any of these on, Tessa," she laughed. "But you're so tiny they'd swamp you." Sharon focused in on Tessa's short suede skirt and simple white shirt, her eyes slightly narrowed in assessment. "Of course you're young. You don't want to wear old lady's things like me. You want some really snappy designer gear for babes."

Tessa laughed. "That'll be the day!"

"Oh, it will be one day," Sharon said. "At least I hope so."

Tessa licked her lips nervously, aware of the intensity on the older woman's impeccably made-up face.

Sharon picked up a very plain white dress and dangled it from her fingers. "When I was a girl," she said slowly, "I lived in the back streets of Birmingham. My father was killed working on a building site when I was six. My mother was left desperately poor. We used to think baked beans on toast for tea was a real treat."

Tessa looked at Sharon gravely, her eyes warm and full of sympathy. "That must have been hard."

"It was hell. I vowed I'd never be poor again. When I met Oliver's father he was already on the way to owning his own garage. Then he got an agency with Jaguar, then another with SAAB. And now he has retail outlets throughout the country. And we are extremely rich." Sharon hooked the white dress on to its hanger and placed it lovingly back in the wardrobe.

"It's wonderful being rich," she said, her voice low and full of feeling. "I love it. Every minute of it. Never let anyone kid you that money doesn't matter."

Tessa felt the force of the other woman's belief and did not have the heart to counter her assertions.

"You could have the same life, Tessa," Sharon went on. "Oliver may not be the world's hardest worker. But then he really doesn't need to be. His fortune is already made." She slid

the doors together again and the mirrors threw out a reflection
of two women facing each other with serious faces.

"I would so like to see him settled," said Sharon. "And
with someone I can like and trust." Her sharp turquoise eyes
beamed into Tessa's, her meaning potent and crystal clear.
"And I happen to know that he's becoming rather keen on
you. I also know that he's the sort of man who needs a little
female guidance to steer him along the right path, if you take
my meaning."

Tessa nodded, trying to conceal her dismay.

Sharon moved towards the door, her long thighs showing
through the slits of her dress. "Shall we go back to the party?"
she said.

Eight

Mercifully Oliver was full of champagne and well over the drink/drive limit by the time it got to midnight and his mother had blown out the candles on her enormous and intricately-iced birthday cake.

He decided to call a taxi to take Tessa home and was keen on accompanying her himself. But Tessa eventually managed to persuade him there was no need, that she would be going straight to bed and to sleep when she got back to the flat, and that he really should stay at the party and help his parents deal with the despatch of all their weary and mostly drunken guests.

As the black London taxi clacked its way from Holland Park to Highbury, her mind emptied itself of the ostentatious and gilded images of Oliver's house and lifestyle, and was immediately filled up with memories of the early part of the evening: the creased forehead of Rex Chance as he steered the Jaguar through the evening traffic and the cool dispassionate eyes of Royston Gable as he prepared to escort her from his personal library.

Tessa opened her purse and checked that the hastily scribbled list of names she had filched from Gable's computer screen was still there. It was! She gave a sigh of relief. And then she stiffened, for the first time asking herself the obvious question as to whether Gable had guessed at her discovery.

She was pretty sure that he had not been instantly suspicious. But it struck her that after he had had time to think things over, he would surely begin to ask himself what she had been doing during the few minutes she was in his library on her own. He would surely recall that he had left an open file on his computer, concealed only by the screen-saver motif.

Of course the names might mean nothing, be of no interest or significance whatsoever. But Tessa had a strong instinctive sense that they were just the opposite.

The reasoning, thinking part of her brain, stifled and redundant for the latter part of the evening, now sprang into life. It was vital that she found more out about Gable. And soon. The interview day was coming closer. Time was running out, and all of it was precious.

But what was it she needed to find out? And how?

She paid the taxi driver and let herself quietly into the flat, not wanting to disturb Trudie. Trudie, however, was still up, lying on her stomach on the sofa watching a late-night film. On the floor close beside her was a box of brandy-filled chocolates swathed in gold ribbon. Her fingers dipped into the box at regular intervals, one smooth movement conveying a new chocolate between box and mouth.

"Hi, had a good time?" Trudie said, squinting up at Tessa's outfit and grimacing. "Haven't you anything more festive than that? I thought you were going to a birthday party."

"This was all I could find that was clean. You know me, I never have a thing to wear." Tessa stood in the middle of the room, looking with unseeing eyes at the TV screen and thinking about Royston Gable's tantalisingly well-concealed Achilles heel.

"How's that gorgeous blond and fantastically rich boyfriend of yours?" Trudie wanted to know.

"Olly? Oh he's fine. On top form." Tessa fondly recalled Oliver's amiable tipsiness at the end of the party. And then, in a flash of brutal clarity, she suddenly perceived the full extent of his idle, untroubled fecklessness. She recalled the barely concealed message that had lain beneath Sharon Stone's parting words as they swapped 'girl-talk' in her lavish boudoir.

Settle down with him, Tessa. You're a good influence. You'll steady him. You could be a very happy, very rich woman with Oliver. And he's keen. Marry him, Tessa.

No, thought Tessa, her nerves shrieking. She could never marry Oliver. And in any case, she wasn't thinking of marriage at all at the moment. It was essential that she break from Olly before he got more serious. The longer she let things go on, leading him to believe she truly cared for him, the more hurt he would eventually be. And Oliver was a truly sweet and lovable man, even if he was a bit of an airhead. She would hate to hurt him.

"What are you sighing about?" Trudie asked. "You've been out to two super parties tonight with two different guys. You should be crowing over your success. I've just been sat here on my own like a poor little Cinderella whose fairy godmother forgot to turn up."

"Ah, poor Trudie," said Tessa, used to this kind of dramatic self pity from Trudie and confident it meant nothing. "I've just got too much on my mind. Work things, not men," she added hastily.

"When are you inviting Oliver round to dinner? Maybe he's got a gorgeous rich lookalike friend he could bring along for me?"

Tessa turned her head slowly and regarded Trudie in all her lovely, slightly slutsy glory. Her gaze moved over the abundant mane of golden hair, the lazy come-to-bed eyes, the full lips that looked as though they had been stung by a tropical insect and needed kissing better. She thought of Trudie's ceaseless quest to find a warm sexual partner who would not treat her simply as a sex machine.

An idea suddenly slipped into Tessa's mind with the smoothness of warmed oil. A possible solution to the problem of how to free herself from Oliver without causing him pain. The scheme was not a noble one, but one which could turn out quite nicely to the satisfaction of all concerned.

"Oh, but hang on," said Trudie, rolling over on to her back, her heavy breasts moving seductively inside her thin T shirt, "what about that dinner party we were planning so that I could meet your boss?"

"Oh yes, the dinner party." Tessa was dismayed to find herself shot through with a vicious stab of female competitiveness. The idea of Rex's coming along to be cooked an aphrodisiac dinner by Trudie, of Rex's being impressed by Trudie's culinary skills, then later succumbing to her lush full-blown sexiness was decidedly upsetting.

"Get out your little personal organiser thing," Trudie instructed.

"Find a window of opportunity in your busy schedule, then pencil him in."

"What about your schedule?" Tessa asked.

"Completely blank," sighed Trudie. "I'm totally available, any time of the day or night for the whole of the forseeable future!"

Oh God, I could do without this, thought Tessa. "OK," she agreed, sounding cheery and casual. "My filofax is at work. I'll have a squint at my schedule when I get into the office tomorrow and have a word with Rex."

"No, that's too vague and fuzzy. You'll just forget or put it off," said Trudie. "We'll make a date now. Thursday, how about that? No excuses."

Thursday, thought Tessa. Her Big Test day. The day of the interview with Royston Gable, by the end of which Rex Chance would either love or hate her! "Fine," she said absently, "Thursday it is!"

"That's settled then," said Trudie, pleased. "Now, don't worry, I'll do all the shopping and cooking." A dreamy expression came over her face. "I'm getting quite interested in this boss of yours."

Tessa went into the bathroom and stripped off her clothes, leaving them in a little magpie-coloured puddle on the floor. She took a shower, brushed her teeth vigorously, and raked her fingers through her curls. After that she felt too energised to sleep and sat up in bed, staring at the list of names she had stolen from Gable's computer and wondering what they could mean.

She picked up her watch and looked at the time. Two a.m. If she didn't try to get some sleep she'd be no good in the morning. Replacing her watch on the small table beside her bed she noticed that the tiny message-screen on her mobile phone was telling her she had some calls to listen to.

Having pressed the message-play button it was Rex's voice that she heard. The sound of it caused her to experience a stabbing pulse of excitement which amazed her.

His voice was brisk, curt and business-like. "Tessa, where the hell did you get to? I need to speak to you. I'll give you my home number. Call me as soon as you get in."

And then later on there was a further communication, even more terse. "Tessa! Don't you ever listen to your messages? Where are you? Call me!"

She did as she was told. The number rang out for several peals and then a rather blurred voice answered. "Yes?"

"Rex?" she said tentatively.

"Tessa. What the hell time do you call this?"

"Just after two in the morning. You said I had to ring. When the boss commands, the lackeys have to obey." She held her breath, hoping the jokiness was not striking a horribly discordant note.

"I've been trying to get through to you since eight thirty," he said in a very boss-like manner. "Why don't you collect your messages?"

"I can hardly do that when I'm at my boyfriend's mother's birthday party." No, no, I shouldn't have said that, she wailed to herself in panic. Making it sound as though I'm really close to Oliver's family. As though I'm about to join them. She felt like an actor who has just made the mistake of speaking some old lines which have subsequently been scrubbed from the script. But how did she improvise to get back to the current script, the one where Oliver was no longer her boyfriend?

"Oh yes, of course. The boyfriend's mother's birthday party," Rex echoed.

Did he sound irritable? Tessa wondered. Sardonic? Jealous maybe? No, his tone simply sounded dry and patient and amused, a tone she was beginning to find he adopted quite regularly.

"What went on between you and Royston Gable?" Rex enquired. "Did you find any grab handles for next week's interview?"

Fresh panic bubbled up. "He was very polite, very charming. Oh, and very generous about lending out items from his library. I've got a leather-bound volume of a hugely long Dryden poem. I think Gable expects me to have read it by the interview day. Maybe he's going to test me on the text!"

"You'll be the one calling the shots, not him," Rex reminded her.

Tessa was brought up short by that remark. It struck her

that during the brief informal interview she had had with Gable earlier he had managed to call a good many of the shots. Now she thought about it she began to fear that she had committed the cardinal sin of letting a future interviewee take hold of the reins, setting their relationship off on entirely the wrong foot. But she wasn't going to let Rex guess at that. "Yes, sure I'll be calling the shots," she countered with what she hoped was convincing confidence.

He seemed about to make a response and then there was a long silence.

"Rex, are you there?" she said, agitated now.

"Yes. Yes, I'm here."

"Oh good. I thought you'd hung up on me."

"Why would I do that?"

"I don't know. Forget it."

"Tessa," he said with a tolerant questioning inflection in his voice, "are you all right? You sound a bit strange all of a sudden, not your usual sparky self."

"I'm OK, Rex. I'm fine. Just a bit tired."

"Look, I shouldn't have hassled you to call me back tonight. Let's leave this talk about Royston Gable until tomorrow morning. I should guess you'll be wrecked after all your partying and champagne swigging . . ."

"No! I'm as sober as a judge. I'm fine. It's just . . ."

"Yes?"

"Nothing. It's nothing," she repeated firmly.

"Come on, tell me!" He picked up on her hesitation, adding, "Of course, if it's something personal that's bothering you then naturally I don't wish to intrude."

"No, no, it's not that!"

"So what is it?" he wondered, his patience seeming positively elastic.

"I just have this . . . feeling about Gable." She couldn't believe she had said that. How could she have assaulted Rex Chance's sharp, professional ear with an utterance so totally wet and feeble? She, Tessa, up and coming chat show hostess of national repute. Hopefully.

"Is this an example of one of your famous hunches and intuitions?" Rex asked.

"Maybe. Oh, I don't know what it is. I just know he's going be a really tough nut to crack. Getting him to give any of his real opinions away on the show is going to be like getting honey from a block of granite."

"You mean," Rex observed evenly, "you're afraid he's going to show you up to be nothing like the tough sharp-question-shooting girl we all believe you to be?"

"Yes, that's just about it." She gave a silent despairing groan. Each time she thought about it the more likely it seemed that this big-chance interview was going to go down like a big squashy meringue.

"He's going to make mincemeat of you, is he?"

"Hey, Rex, come on . . ."

"Maybe I'll give him to Lucinda after all!"

"NO!" She paused. "You rat," she said softly. "You know very well you said that he'd only talk to me."

"Quite." Rex said cheerfully.

"He's creepy!" said Tessa, suddenly wanting to confide in Rex, whatever he thought of her as a result.

"He has a certain rather curious magnetism, I do agree," said Rex drily. "But basically he's just another bloke, Tessa. I certainly haven't noticed your being fazed by blokes. Quite the reverse."

Before Tessa could answer she fancied she heard a noise on Rex's line, a kind of scuffling noise. Or was it simply interference on the connection? No, she could swear it was scuffling. She sat up as straight as a ramrod, the hairs on the back of her neck standing up. Maybe Rex had someone with him. A woman. A lover. The big pushy blonde who had grabbed him at the party. Hell!

"Tessa, have you dropped off to sleep?" Rex asked.

"No," she said feeling horribly miserable all of a sudden.

"Listen, I simply called earlier to check that you were OK after your one-to-one with Gable. I guessed you must have had a pretty heavy evening all round," Rex said kindly. "You'll be whacked. And I want you as fresh as a daisy to pierce through Gable's platinum-plated armour. So get some sleep and we'll have a full and final planning meeting tomorrow morning. Yes?"

77

"All right," said Tessa.

"Eight o'clock. Breakfast in my office?"

"OK."

"Sweet dreams." The line clicked off.

Tessa flew out of bed, grabbed a notebook and a pencil, and began to scribble down every last detail she could recall from her brief encounter with Royston Gable. When she had finished she tore the sheets from the pad and clipped them together with the list of names from the computer. The four names were already imprinted on her memory:

Adam Baddeley

Hilary Charles

Pascal Dumas

Rupert Frobisher

She lay on her back, staring up into the darkness, her mind fermenting with all kinds of new conjectures. She knew she would never get a minute of sleep, her brain waves seemed not only stirred but well and truly shaken.

Her next conscious waking thought was the registering of sunshine streaming into her room and the birds singing a rousing homage to the new day. When she glanced at her watch she registered pure horror to note that it was already eight fifteen.

Nine

Twenty minutes prior to Tessa's discovery that she had committed the criminal offence of being soundly asleep in bed when she should have been in a business meeting, Rex Chance was already postitioned at the window of his office looking down into the car park.

On his desk there were bowls of fresh fruit, plates of croissants and Danish pastries, and an assortment of preserves in miniature jars. His Thermos was in its usual position on his bookshelves, filled with an enticingly nutty blend of freshly ground coffee which he had prepared before leaving his flat some time earlier.

As he waited for Tessa's cherished red BMW to sweep into the car park he reflected on the events of the evening before. Rex had long ago accepted his shortcomings as a party animal. For a start he quickly became irritated by having to make small talk with strangers and he also found great difficulty in suffering fools gladly. Whenever he was forced into a cocktail party scenario he was reminded that an ability to make small talk with strangers who peddled half-baked ideas was one of the main requirements for surviving the evening without coming to blows with anyone.

Last night at Royston Gable's elegant cocktail party Rex had found most of his fears regarding the brittle party scene quickly confirmed. When the busty, lusty blonde who had once worked as a production assistant on his team many years ago finally realised she was getting nowhere with him and abandoned him for more likely prey, he had had no choice but to circulate and converse with a procession of strangers.

He found himself disgruntled and disappointed. He had been very much looking forward to having Tessa at his side as a companion and ally. He had speculated on her social skills in the general cut and thrust of conversation, being pretty sure she would turn out to be highly entertaining and sparky. It had amused him to anticipate the confirmation of his high rating of her. He had also quite simply looked forward to the pleasure of her company.

But after Tessa had been borne away into Gable's sanctum, showing no instant signs of emerging, he had felt like a man in a blazing building with all his friends vanished and no sign of rescue.

He had then discovered, however, that whilst Royston Gable's guests were as ready as the next to peddle ideas, none of them could be accused of being half-baked. They were, in fact, one of the most clued-up, sharp-witted crowds he had ever come across. Almost alarmingly so; and Rex was used to mixing and fencing with some pretty shrewd operators in a variety of fields and professions.

Most of the guests he had spent time with were researchers in the field of human psychology. He had talked for a while to a donnish looking man who described himself as a scholar of the science of the face. He was writing a book called *In the Eye of the Beholder*.

"You see," the scholar had told Rex earnestly, "the appearance and configuration of each individual face is the astoundingly complicated result of a number of different kinds of genetic influences." He had paused, stroking his long Freudian-style beard and musing.

"You mean things like a big nose or cauliflower ears are handed down to us from our parents?" Rex responded with dry irony.

The scholar looked at him with a faintly puzzled expression and Rex had the feeling this man was no longer in touch with everyday common-or-garden lingo.

"Yes, indeed," the scholar had agreed. "In fact, the extent of our biological inheritance is almost too awesome to consider . . ."

"I suppose an individual's environment and general cultural factors also have an influence on his or her face," Rex had suggested, trying to cut through to the simple facts. "For instance, the stress we encounter in our lives must affect how we look – frown lines and so on." He touched the deep creases in his own forehead with a wry smile. "And current fashion must surely have a part to play too – the way in which we all choose to present ourselves in public. If you look at portraits of Victorian men their faces look quite different from the 1990s bloke."

"Ahh," the scholar responded gravely as though this were a startlingly novel thought. "What an interesting proposition. I must go to the National Gallery once again and look at some of the Victorian portraits."

"You'll find a great many hirsutic differences," Rex said with mocking gravity. "Many differing ways of arranging the hair around the face, the presence or absence of a beard or a moustache. And that's only the men."

His joke had fallen on stony ground. The scholar, having scanned Rex's craggy features with pursed lips, had drifted away into the throng, presumably to make further observations on the varied configurations of the human face.

Rex had then joined a group of research geneticists and tried to discover from them if there was any firm scientific proof underpinning Royston Gable's philosophy about the inheritance of intelligence.

Their answers had been both complex and conflicting. And every utterance they made was so peppered with specialist jargon that they might have been speaking a foreign language. Rex had eventually despaired of discovering anything of interest – at least of the sort that could be communicated to a TV audience.

He had moved on through the intense, erudite groups, listening in to their conversations, hoping to pick up some nuggets of information to pass on to Tessa. Sometimes he would interject an opinion, but mainly he kept silent, attentive and vigilant. He wondered what Tessa had made of Royston Gable on this initial meeting. He was confident she would have been able to hold her own with him; she was a match for most blokes he could think of. And yet there was a small seed of doubt which troubled him.

He had the impression that Royston Gable was in some way stringing them both along, playing a private game with them for his own entertainment. He kept rejecting this theory because it had no factual basis, was basically preposterous and also humiliatingly childish. And yet he kept returning to the idea.

After a time he met up with a forensic psychologist who told him that she specialised in working with the police to track down serial killers. She had worked with police departments in Johannesburg and New York and was now advisor to the Metropolitan police in London. She was all of twenty-nine, around five foot two and definitely awesome. What was it with these small delicate women? he had wondered. Were they about to take over the universe?

Her name was Sarah Blayney. For someone who was the scourge of axe-men and stranglers she was remarkably fragile and feminine looking. Her Scotch-mist grey eyes gazed up at him from a shiny halo of soft brown hair. She projected an image of sweet gentleness, wistful appeal and the kind of vulnerability that would have most men queueing up in order to protect her. If she had not told him the nature of her grisly trade he would have marked her down as a social worker or a nurse, someone in the caring professions. And yet when she talked of her work it was clear that she was not only enthusiastic and competent but remarkably tenacious and determined as well.

As he listened to her Rex found himself snapping into professional mode and assessing Sarah Blayney as a possible guest on *In the Limelight*. "Tell me about catching serial killers," he said crisply. "Are the police getting better or worse at it?"

She smiled. "Even as recently as two years ago the police were pretty hopeless at tracking down spray-gun shooters and rapists," Sarah had told him. "But now things *are* changing."

"So what happened two years ago?" Rex asked.

"They hired me!" she said with smiling conviction. "So now we catch them far more quickly."

They had wandered away from the learned groups of guests into the quietness of the kitchen where he had encouraged her to tell him about her talent for sniffing out psychopaths.

"Is your success based on science and research?" he had asked.

"Mainly, although not exclusively."

82

"Really! Tell me more."

"Well, whilst I don't claim to be a psychic, there's somehow a kind of sixth sense involved."

"That's an interesting viewpoint. What would the scientists say about that?"

"They'd laugh me out of court."

"Except that you get results."

"Exactly."

Rex delved into his pocket and handed her his business card. "Would you consider talking about your work and airing your views on TV?"

"Maybe," she said. "Are you inviting me?"

"Perhaps. I'd like you to think about it." He guessed this woman would be terrific on camera. His mind pictured the interesting scenario of Sarah in the interviewee's chair and Tessa asking the questions.

"Why are you here tonight?" Rex had asked her eventually.

"Royston likes to surround himself with success stories," she observed drily.

"Is that so? Go on."

"He likes to be with people who are bright and able and achieving. You won't find any of life's flotsam and jetsam here."

"I see," said Rex, his interest sharpening. "Are you trying to tell me Gable is an elitist? A man only interested in the chosen few, not humanity in all its variety?"

Sarah gave a brief smile. "Maybe."

"How long have you known him?"

"Around two years or so."

"Did you meet him through your work?"

"Yes. He's been very helpful to me from time to time as a consultant on particular cases."

"How so?"

"Advising on the possible genetic component in criminal behaviour, helping me build up individual profiles of possible killers."

"And is there a genetic component?" Rex asked.

"In criminal behaviour there is some evidence of a connection. But with serial killers genetic links are hard to find. It seems as though these particular killers are not born but made."

"Shaped through family disruption and social upheaval?" Rex suggested.

"Exactly."

"And does Royston Gable go along with that view? I thought he was a keen genetics man – believes in the power of nature rather than nurture?"

Sarah shot him a swift glance. "Why are you so interested?"

"In genetics?"

"No, in Royston Gable?"

"I'm a controller in one of the major TV companies. I've been given a rather brutal directive to up the ratings or clear off."

Sarah nodded. "And?"

"And he's a guest on one of my key programmes. I want to make that programme as entertaining and also as legitimate as I can."

"I see," said Sarah.

"Is he simply a colleague?" Rex asked. "Or more of a friend?"

Sarah's mobile face stilled and closed.

"I'm sorry," Rex said swiftly. "I was overstepping the mark with that last question."

"No, no, asking questions is your profession," she said, her sweet smile back in place. "Let's just say that I met Royston as a colleague and that now I hope we can call ourselves friends." She looked down into her glass and Rex's experience told him that there was a private and perhaps painful story behind those simple words. A story Sarah preferred to keep to herself. Fair enough.

He had steered the conversation on to more general topics and a little while after that Sarah had looked at her watch and told him it was time she went home to her husband and her small son.

"Can I give you a call within the next month or so to discuss a possible appearance on *In the Limelight*?" he had asked, as they shook hands.

"Yes, sure." She gave him a card with a selection of numbers on which she could be contacted.

Rex had slipped the card into his inside pocket, wondering if he would, in fact, give her a call. He always asked for a contact number from people who demonstrated potential for future TV appearances. He did it as a matter of routine, almost automatically. It was a kind of precautionary measure, a way of making sure his stockpile of interesting personalities was always amply filled.

He had parted company on warm and friendly terms with Sarah, fairly confident that she would have no problems in holding the fascinated attention of viewers in a one-to-one TV interchange about her work. On the other hand she could well change her mind about wanting that kind of publicity. Not everyone was desperate to put themselves at the pointing end of a camera, despite the myth that people would kill their grandmothers to get on TV.

"Goodbye," he had said as he watched her walk away.

She had turned and given her misleadingly innocent, girlish smile. "See you!" she had said casually and he had nodded, equally relaxed and uninvolved.

It was a casualness he would remember in the near future, when he suddenly found himself desperate for Sarah's help on a matter far more urgent than a TV talk show.

But now, as he waited impatiently for the red BMW to drive into the car park, his thoughts were focused solely on Tessa and her unaccountable lateness. He looked at his watch. He had been totally convinced that Tessa was deadly serious about her work, would always be highly professional, well prepared and punctual. And here she was making one of the most unforgivable, most asinine mistakes in the book.

A spark of anger against Tessa flared inside him. He hated to think of her spoiling her chances of career success by sloppy behaviour. His expectations of her were enormous. And he was damned if he was going to let her get away with letting herself down. And yes, he had to admit it, damned if he was going to let her get away with disappointing *him*.

On his desk the phone pealed out. He picked it up, expecting to hear Tessa's voice, breathless and apologetic. Instead he heard the clipped and urgent tones of the producer on *In the Limelight*.

They had a hurried conversation. Suggestions were aired, decisions made.

Rex crossed once again to the window. He looked at his watch. "Come on, Tessa," he murmured softly with an indulgence that amazed him. "Don't disappoint me. Show me what you can do when you get the chance."

Ten

Tessa flew out of the flat, her hair still wet from the shower, her face bare of any scrap of make-up. She left her car standing in the road, judging that it would be quicker to take the tube than attempt to fight through the morning traffic at the very peak of its congestion.

Clinging on to the grab handles in a packed train buried deep beneath the heart of London, she tried to think of what she could possibly say to Rex Chance by way of offering some explanation of her lateness to the vital breakfast meeting he had planned.

She'd come to the conclusion that the truth was quite simply not good enough. The truth was too humdrum, too tame, too hackneyed even to consider offering. *Sorry Rex, I slept in.* She shuddered at the very idea of uttering such a limp-sounding phrase.

How could she dress the truth up? Make it more dramatic, give it not only credibility but a touch of panache?

There was a fire at the flat, Rex. I had to wait for the Fire Brigade to come with an extending ladder to get me out. It was touch and go.

My flat mate, Trudie, sliced her finger off when she was cutting the bread for her toast. I had to hunt for the chopped off bit and then take her and it to the hospital.

I was abducted in the night by aliens. No, not aliens, actually it was Royston Gable . . .

She gave a low groan. It was vital to say the right thing to Rex. She wanted to be frank with him, she *needed* to be frank with him, both to preserve her own self esteem and to ensure that he continued to regard her as a professional. But she would simply *have* to lie. Cunningly shaped phrases of half truths and deceit swirled in her mind, growing and swelling by the second.

She knocked on his door, bracing herself for the anger on his face, for an onslaught of his razor-edged scorn. She took a number of deep breaths, deep down from the diaphragm, and schooled herself to speak slowly and clearly, and on no account to babble.

Rex appeared in the doorway, leaning his tall, powerful frame against that of the door. He looked craggy and rumpled and, very curiously, not especially angry. He also looked wonderfully solid and strong and quite incredibly sexy.

Tessa had not been prepared to feel such pure, surging delight as a simple result of seeing Rex again. It was, after all, less than twelve hours since she had last seen him. A sense of unreality and confusion overtook her. She recalled her hastily rehearsed lines.

"You're going to loathe, hate and despise me for being late, Rex. You're going to yell at me, you're going to tell me you'll never forgive me and then throw me out." She found herself speeding up now. Babbling was only a breath away. "You're going to pulverise me to a pulp, then lay me in a dark grave and dance upon it. You're going to—"

He took her hand and pulled her into the room. "Tessa," he said patiently, "stop babbling. Have a croissant. Have some coffee."

She twisted around in her chair as he crossed to the bookshelves and unscrewed his Thermos.

"I slept in, Rex. I forgot to set my alarm, and I was still in bed asleep when I should have been here."

"Mmm. Well, no doubt worse things have occurred in this wicked, cruel world on this fine morning."

"I was sure you'd be furious," she said, accepting a croissant and tearing it apart with hungry fingers. "I was convinced I was in for a terrible bollocking – sorry, reprimand."

"You were," he said, placing her coffee on the desk, close to her plate.

"Oh." She stared up at him. "So am I to be spared?"

"I think so."

"Why?"

"Once you indicated that a bollocking was what you expected, I changed my mind."

"Are you playing cat and mouse with me, Rex?" Tessa said after a pause, giving him a narrow, suspicious look.

He smiled. "Nothing as sinister as that. I hate to act predictably, you see. It lures the staff into bovine apathy."

"Huh!" she muttered, polishing off the croissant and covertly considering the merits of the other tempting delicacies on offer.

"Anyway," he went on, "you've been working pretty hard lately, putting in a lot of extra hours and effort. We're all of us entitled to a little human failing from time to time." He accompanied the conclusion of this noble speech by offering her a Danish pastry which she accepted, all the time keeping her eyes on his face, watching him warily as though he were a wild animal who might suddenly show its claws.

Tessa stayed quiet for a few moments, nibbling at her pastry and wondering why he was being so *very* nice to her. "I've been doing some more thinking about Royston Gable," she told him. "Planning my campaign, so to speak."

"Good!" He levered himself from his perch on the desk and began to pace up and down, suddenly snapping into brisk, boss-like vein. "But to be frank with you, Tessa, I think we should cool things on the Gable interview. You've done your homework on him, you know what you're about. It'll go fine."

Tessa had opened her mouth to receive a juicy chunk of glazed apple pastry. She now closed it again, letting the chunk slide out of her fingers and land back on the plate. "Would you mind saying that again?"

"I think we've allowed ourselves to get far too steamed up about Gable. He's simply one more in the procession of guests on *Limelight*. Let's not get things out of proportion here, hmm?"

"Oh," said Tessa, sensing a dismaying anticlimax to this meeting which she had been keenly anticipating. "It's nice of you to say 'we', Rex. I suppose what you really mean," she went on gloomily, "is that *I'm* the one who's got things falsely blown up, *I'm* the one who needs to cool things."

"Come on, Tessa. We're in the entertainment business. We've both been around. We've seen a few things other people haven't. We don't want to get sucked into the exactly the kind of drama and hysteria Gable is trying to stir up. To tell the truth I think we were *both* guilty of imbuing Gable with a god-like significance," Rex said with a wry grin.

"A cardinal mistake for an interviewer – if you'll pardon the continuation of the religious metaphor," she responded smartly, refusing to remain downcast.

He chuckled. Whilst speaking he had been examining the motives behind his words, finding it hard to disentangle his feelings on the issue of Tessa's interview with Gable; the possible reasons why the whole thing had loomed so large in his thoughts, ballooning out of all proportion, disturbing and troubling him. He was not yet aware of the notion of simple male jealousy and rivalry lurking quietly at the back of his mind, for some unconscious censor was keeping it firmly held there, temporarily muffled and suppressed.

"Anyway your preparations for the Gable interview will have to wait," he told her.

"What?"

"There are more urgent matters to consider."

Tessa gaped at him.

"Lucinda's phoned in sick," he said tersely. "She's gone down with food poisoning, unluckily for her. Can't be separated from her bathroom facilities."

"Oh poor Lucinda!" Tessa's exclamation was underpinned with genuine sympathy. She herself had suffered terrible food poisoning after eating some heated-up chicken at a TV awards ceremony only a few months ago. The discomfort and misery had been indescribable. She wouldn't wish it on her worst enemy. Not even Lucinda.

"She was due to do an interview with the zany French cook, Yves Saint Rochelle, this afternoon."

Tessa's heart began to leap about like a frisky spring lamb. "And?"

"And I want you to do it instead."

"Oh God!"

"I've got all Lucinda's preparatory notes and a draft set

of questions. All you have to do is read them through. Get yourself up to speed—"

"But Saint Rochelle is really big," Tessa protested, torn between delight and terror.

"Yes, he is," Rex agreed calmly.

"A household name."

"Yes."

"He's a plum."

"Yes."

"I've never interviewed anyone as high profile as him."

"No. There's always a first time."

"What about Rob, isn't he free?" Rob was *Limelight*'s top male interviewer. Very slick, very smooth, very popular. And currently making no secret of putting out feelers for one or two highly prestigious presenter jobs coming up on prime-time BBC.

"Tessa," said Rex with calm, almost elaborate patience. "Cooking is well known to be a very sexy activity. And Yves Saint Rochelle isn't just one of the most outrageous, funniest cooks around on TV. He's also one of the sexiest. He needs a woman to strike sparks off and bring out the best in him."

"Or the worst!" Tessa groaned.

Rex did not attempt to deny this. He gathered up one of the bright pink folders which were Lucinda's trademark and placed it in Tessa's hands. "Go away," he told her softly. "Read, mark and learn the contents of this. You'll be needed in make-up at one thirty. On the dot."

Tessa stared up at him dumbfounded.

"Take another croissant. Take a peach. Take the whole plateful of Danish pastries if you want," he added, raising an eyebrow.

"Sugary comfort in my hour of need?" Tessa suggested.

"Sugary comfort or not," said Rex his face becoming dark and serious as he looked at her, "you'll be fine, Tessa. You'll be just great."

"You keep saying that," said Tessa, reaching out and picking up the plate of pastries. "I just hope you're proved right."

*   *   *

Rex put a call through to his sister, Vicky. It took seventeen rings before she answered it.

"I'm very busy," she told him.

"Doing what?"

"Grubbing in the garden with Benny."

"Grubbing?"

"We're looking for worms. Benny's set his heart on making a wormerie, or whatever name you give to a collection of live worms."

"An earthium maybe. Is that the kind of thing little boys like to do?" Rex wondered.

"Indeed it is. Slugs and snails and puppy dog's tails etc." Vicky glanced out of the window, noting the intense calm concentration on Benny's face as he crouched on the earth, inspecting his jam jar and its contents of sliding, waving worms. She smiled, her heart turning over with a surge of warm, fresh love. "So what is it you're after this morning, Rex?"

"I'm after alerting my dear sister to switch on her television this afternoon at around one minute to three."

"Shall I see something to my advantage?"

"You'll see a very bright up-and-coming TV presenter interviewing Mr Supercook Yves Saint Rochelle."

There was a pause. "And what's the name of this bright young presenter?"

"Tessa."

"Ah."

"Yes, Tessa." Rex said musingly. He slotted the phone between his ear and his shoulder and leaned up against the bookshelves. He looked at the chair in which Tessa had sat during the past twenty minutes. The image of her was so strong in his mind, she could almost be sitting there still.

He recalled how, as they had talked, her damp hair had gradually dried from the colour of rained-on autumn leaves to the brilliance of a freshly polished copper urn. Its brightness had attracted the first hesitant rays of the morning sun, drawing them into its russet-gold mesh.

"Rex," said Vicky. "There's something about your long

silence and the way you speak this bright young person's name that makes me both suspicious and rather excited."

"Sorry? What was that?" His voice sounded as though it was coming from miles away.

"Would you like to bring Tessa round for dinner?" Vicky asked, her eyes never leaving Benny who was now moving purposefully down the line of cherry trees bordering the lawn, presumably searching for a stick with which to stir his worms. "Celebrate her success with Mr Supercook? Sometime soon?"

"No."

"Maybe later this week?"

"No." He sighed.

"When did you last see her?" Vicky asked, becoming beady and practical.

"Two minutes ago." Tessa had been looking, thought Rex, so delicious he could have eaten her. And those tiny little boots she had been wearing; the soft black leather hugging her exquisite ankles. And the funny, stripey, lovable socks! Magic! Perfection!

"Two minutes ago," repeated Vicky. "Was she showing any signs of hating you, or of finding you utterly repulsive?"

"I don't think so?"

"Is she married?"

"No."

"So what's the problem my dear?" Vicky rapped hard on the window as Benny approached the jam jar waving a vicious-looking forked stick. "NO!" she mouthed at him as he turned, his dark eyes somehow both innocent and mischievous all at the same time.

"I'm too old for her," mourned Rex. "I'm too world weary and cynical. I'm all scuffed around the edges. And she's so fresh and sharp and shining."

"This sounds highly promising," Vicky said, her eyes still fastened on her son and mindful of the welfare of the wriggling captured worms. "A wonderful example of opposites attracting."

"Mmm," Rex said gloomily. "She's got a boyfriend."

"So? That doesn't mean he has exclusive rights. As long as they're not engaged to be married."

"Yes," Rex agreed.

"They are engaged to be married?" Vicky wondered patiently.

"No, I don't think so."

"I'll make a steak and kidney pudding," Vicky decided. "Very homely, very traditional fare. And an old-fashioned lemon syllabub. Bring Mr Supercook too – he could learn something to his advantage."

"Mmm," said Rex.

"I'll have to go," said Vicky. "The lives of several innocent worms are in danger and I don't want my son developing a taste for murder." She put the phone down and ran out into the garden.

Benny was lying on his stomach, his chin on his hands. He had placed the stick with hugely gentle care inside the jam jar, and was now watching fascinated as the worms began to climb it. Vicky bent and kissed him, heartily ashamed of having doubted him.

She returned to the kitchen, dialled Rex's mobile and left a message on its answering facility. "Thursday evening," she said. "You and Tessa. Seven thirty for eight."

Eleven

Tessa spent the morning running over Lucinda's research notes on Yves Saint Rochelle together with her draft script for the introductory section to the programme. Tessa had been reluctant to alter the script at first, sensitive to the feelings of any script writer, even if it was the awful Lucinda. But in the end she had to acknowledge that she simply couldn't parrot Lucinda's gushing phrases. She got out her favourite purple pen and wrote her own alternative script instead.

As the time drew near for the start of the programme she began to feel nervous and queasy. The Danish pastries sat untouched on their plate; she had forgotten all about them. And now, when she really needed some food, her stomach wanted nothing whatsoever to do with them, or anything else for that matter.

She was worried about her clothes, which were basically the shirt and suede skirt she had been wearing the night before, those items being the only ones to hand which were vaguely respectable. But instead of her pink sandals, whose whereabouts defied discovery, she had put on waspish black and yellow striped socks and her beloved black leather ankle boots, bought in Harrods' most recent sale. This combination had seemed a good idea at the time, but now she wondered if the effect was a touch eccentric.

Well, it was too late to worry now and at least one of the kind girls from the wardrobe section had ironed her shirt for her, making her feel much less crumpled.

In the make-up room she allowed a dusting of powder to be fluffed over her cheeks and nose. But not too much. She wasn't ashamed of her freckles and, in fact, felt naked if they were smothered in Pan-Stik.

She went down to Studio Two where the crew were sorting out lighting and camera angles.

"Hi!" called Mike, the senior cameraman, cheerily. "Big day for you, Tess."

"Yes. I just hope I'll still be alive and in one piece at the end of it."

He laughed. "You'll be a wow."

Tessa looked around the set. When Rex had first arrived at Dartbridge TV he had made no bones about disliking the old *Limelight* set, declaring it to be far too fussy and cosy with its squashy sofas, its floral cushions and little rose-shaded lamps. He had instructed the set design team to make radical changes. Now there were slate-grey leather chairs and one dramatically plain glass table framed in blue tinted steel. Everything was sharp and strong and clean-lined. Tessa supposed that was the image Rex wanted the interviews themselves to project.

She sat in the interviewer's chair and mentally ad libbed through her introduction and general line of questioning.

"Oh, I'm getting a beautiful shot here," Mike said, riding his machine in a little closer.

Tessa checked that her shirt buttons had not come undone or her skirt ridden up to show her knickers; just the kind of titillating slip-ups that Mike loved to focus on.

A voice came through her ear piece. "Only ten minutes to go, Tessa."

She gave a start, having been expecting to hear the voice of Geoff, *Limelight*'s producer. But this was not Geoff's voice. "Is that you, Rex?"

"Yes. The set's looking very good on the monitors up here," he said.

"Are you in the control room?" she asked, turning to speak directly into the impartial eye of the camera.

"Yes."

"Where's Geoff?"

"He's off sick in sympathy with Lucinda. I'm standing in for him."

"Oh great!" she exclaimed gamely, at the same time giving a silent groan.

"It'll be good for me," he added. "Doing some hands-on

production work. So you'd better not take your eye off the ball, so to speak, Tessa. Or you'll have me to contend with."

Tessa's heart swung about in her chest as though it had come loose from its moorings. To do the show was one thing, to have Rex Chance personally in charge of proceedings was quite another.

She clasped a hand over her stomach, heartily glad that she hadn't been tempted to eat a second Danish pastry.

"Saint Rochelle's just arrived. He's on his way up," Rex told her.

Oh, why the hell did I choose to do this nerve-wracking job? Tessa asked herself with an inner wail. Why didn't I get a job as a deep-sea diver or a lion tamer? Something easy and relaxed.

From the corner of her eye she could see the long elastic figure of Yves St Rochelle move to stand at the entry to the set. He caught her eye, giving her a cheeky wave and blowing a kiss.

Time seemed to stand still. And then she heard Rex's voice in her earpiece. "One minute to air. Good luck, Tessa. Good luck everyone! Stand by Studio."

One of the production assistants began a countdown. Ten seconds . . . five, four . . ."

The last movement from Mozart's jolly Horn Concerto started up, sending the adrenalin rolling in.

Tessa felt that her heart would burst, it was thumping so hard. Her mouth was hot and gritty, her throat felt as though it had been laid out to dry in the desert. For a split second she was sure she had forgotten her opening lines. And then, as the Mozart romped to a close, she found herself speaking, her voice perfectly steady, miraculously in control.

She said a few words about the absent Lucinda, apologising on Lucinda's behalf for her absence and wishing her a speedy recovery. She then smiled winningly into the camera and asked her invisible audience of millions for their tolerance in putting up with her, Tessa, instead.

"I welcome my guest today with both excitement and admiration. He is quite simply the tastiest, sauciest, sexiest cook around. And of course," – here her voice began to climb

97

to a crescendo – "as you'll already have guessed, he is Yves Saint Rochelle."

Yves bounded on, right on cue, as springy as a jungle monkey. He wrapped his arms, ape-like, around Tessa and squeezed so hard that she gasped out loud.

"Ravishing, ravishing, ravishing!" he cried, burrowing into the soft skin of her neck with an onslaught of kisses as hard and rapid as grapeshot.

Tessa extricated herself, pink and laughing. "Ravished!" she exclaimed.

"You just wait, my darleeng," Yves said in his thick erotic French accent. He sat in the chair beside Tessa and leaned towards her with the eagerness of a dog eyeing up a steak dinner. He radiated sensuality. He was so very, very French.

"To continue the theme of ravishing, my boss here at the studios tells me that cooking is a very sexy activity," Tessa observed, her face grave.

"Then 'e ees a most percepteeve man," said Yves, leaning even closer and giving a wicked and lascivious leer.

"I think that's probably true," Tessa said calmly. "But I can't even boil an egg, Yves. Does that make me less of a woman?"

Yves reeled back in his chair. His eyes rolled dramatically. "My darleeng, *ay-very* woman can cook. You are all born that way. You 'ave all the cooking equipment beelt een." His eyebrows shot up suggestively.

"Yes? Such as?" Tessa wondered what on earth was coming next.

"You all 'ave beautiful breasts full of milk puddings for leetle babies."

"Not much peeling and marinading involved there though," Tessa responded smartly.

And then they were off, joking and fencing and fooling around like old pals having a gossip over a drink in the local pub. Yves became quite outrageous about his adventurous ways of cooking carrots and courgettes and his daring exploits with various members of the opposite sex. It was hard to tell where one ended and the next began.

"Let's talk seriously about cooking for a moment or two . . ." Tessa suggested, giving him a headmistressly eye.

"No, no, let's not," Yves replied, shooting out a groping hand which began working its way up Tessa's thigh.

"God Almighty!" Rex's voice growled in her ear piece. "Get the bastard back on course, Tessa!"

Tessa sweetly but firmly plucked the presumptuous hand from the top of her thigh and returned it to its rightful place in its owner's lap. "Yves," she said sweetly, "tell me about cooking a sexy supper for two."

"No, no. I want you to ask me *eenteresting* questions, you gorgeous lovely creature. Like 'ow many women I 'ave sleep with. I am a Frenchman, we must talk about lurve."

"That'll come later," Tessa told him with mock severity. "Right now, you must sing for your suppper, Yves. Or rather our suppers. We have to talk recipes, Yves. We have to talk cooking methods."

"Oh, so boring! But darleeng, I lurve you when you're being so streect with me. So what ees eet you want me to tell you?" His eyes roamed over her as though he were assessing a ripe fruit and considering the most tender point at which to pierce it.

This is damned hard work, thought Tessa, feeling as though she were running a marathon, but it's the best work in the world. "I have it on good authority," she told Yves, her eyes opening wide, "that the ultimate aphrodisiac dinner is avocado mousse followed by oysters and tiny asparagus spears, ending up with figs in brandy."

Yves shook his head making a show of appearing momentarily nonplussed. He gazed straight into the camera, his huge brown eyes like flashing headlights. "Theese modern young women. Is there nothing they do not know? Nothing I can teach them?" he asked his invisible audience of millions.

"I'm sure there's plenty you can teach me. About cooking," Tessa laughed. "Come on, Yves!"

He turned his glowing amber beam on her. "Listen to thees darleeng. I tell you all about the truly aphrodisiac supper. I tell you a leetle story. One day I go for my shopping in the supermarket. I see a bee-oo-ti-ful young woman in the queue in front of me. In 'er trolley she 'as one avocado, she 'as some oh-so-tender, peenk biff-stek. She 'as a bottle of Château-Neuf-du-Pape. And a leetle tiny pair of lacy pantees."

Tessa gave a low chuckle.

"I could guess what she would be doing later," said Yves. "You understand, yes?"

"I think we all could have a guess," said Tessa.

"A leetle cooking. A leetle seducing. A leetle screwing. Mmm?"

"Yves! We're on TV."

"Oh yes." He wriggled his shoulders and looked excessively pleased with himself.

"And now I tell you the next beet of my story. A year afterwards I go to the same supermarket and see the same young woman. And now her basket is all full up with beeg, beeg packets of nappies!"

"No fillet steak? No wine?" Tessa put on a faintly wistful expression.

"No. She doesn't need wine. She 'as the joy of being a leetle muzzaire." His eyes revolved like two shiny spinning marbles.

Tessa shook her head at him in mocking reproof.

"And so will you one day, my ripe leetle cherry," Yves informed her.

"Be a little mother?"

"Yes. I 'ope so. Indeed I know so."

Tessa smiled. "I hope so too," she said quietly, surprising herself.

As Saint Rochelle had been speaking, rolling out his outrageous phrases in his absurdly exaggerated French accent a thought had occurred to her. Developing and expanding by the second.

She turned to him with an enchanting smile which managed to blend the innocence of an angel with a wicked glint of the devil. Placing her lips almost against his ear, she whispered so that he alone could hear: *"Je crois que vous gardez un secret. Un grand, grand secret."*

Yves was quite thrown for a moment. The smile faded from his face. For a moment he looked not only baffled, but vulnerable. And in that instant Tessa knew that her hunch was dead on target.

She turned to the camera, making eyes at the invisible audience and daring them to guess what she could possibly have said to silence the irrepressible Saint Rochelle. Turning back to Saint Rochelle she gave a mischievously seductive smile. "I think my suggestion was indecent enough to make even you blush. A dark secret – mmm?"

The pupils in Yves' big brown eyes dilated with alarm and she saw that he was pleading with her. That he was truly frightened of what she might reveal.

"No," he said, trying to recover himself. "I nevaire blush. And everything you say is seemply charming."

"*Charmant,*" whispered Tessa.

"Yes. *Sharmon,*" he echoed, his French accent strangely tinged with English vowels.

"So now will you tell us your dark secret?" she asked, a mischievous glint in her eye.

Yves's eyes flared with anxiety. For a moment Tessa thought he was on the point of dashing off the set and vanishing to a far corner of London.

"The true number of women you've slept with?" she prompted, smiling.

Yves Saint Rochelle stared at her, relief flooding his face. The audience of millions would be unlikely to guess at his fleeting discomfiture, for the moment he had understood that Tessa had rumbled him, he had acted with a true showman's instinct and kept his face determinedly turned from the cameras. Now he was confident she wasn't going to shout out his secret he was once again his flamboyant self. "I 'ave to tell you I am ashamed," he said, his eyes holding hers meaningfully.

"Too many to tell the truth about?" Tessa asked, tilting her head on one side.

"Far, far too many."

"Hundreds?" she asked.

He made a pretence of covering his face. "I am a vairee naughty boy when I am young. But not now, you know. Not any more."

"You were married just a few weeks ago, Yves. Isn't that right?"

"Yes." His hand reached out to Tessa's thigh again, his

Angela Drake

fingers executing a little dance. "And now I am vairee good boy."

And then Tessa was smiling at him and shaking his hand warmly, thanking him for coming on the programme and being such a marvellously entertaining guest.

The Mozart came on, even more bouncy and raunchy than before.

Yves Saint Rochelle was dancing round the set, smiling and singing along with the horn solo.

"Aaaah!" murmured all the girls in the control room, slayed by Saint Rochelle's naughty boy sexiness and the happy-marriage ending to his philandering.

"The bastard," Rex muttered to himself up in the control room. But he was smiling, utterly delighted at the way the interview had gone.

"Tessa," he said into her earpiece, "that was simply terrific. Now bring Saint Rochelle up to the boardroom for champagne. I think he could do with it after the shock you gave him!"

Tessa smiled in silent response. When she got up from her seat the nerves in her legs were quivering with the elation of a job well done. She felt ecstatic, on a huge surging high.

"We're invited to have champagne with the big boss," she told Saint Rochelle, when he at last became still.

"No thanks, duck," he said in a very convincing Cockney accent. "I've had enough excitement for one day."

"Were you born within the sound of Bow Bells?" she asked.

"I was born in Paris, you cheeky young madam," he told her. "My parents were on a weekend trip from Clapham. I arrived a month early and surprised them."

Tessa chuckled.

"I've been to France plenty of times since then. Thought I'd mastered the lingo!" he said reflectively. He bent and kissed her cheek. "Zanks for everything, my leetle darleeng. I come on your programme again any time you ask me." He swaggered away, his huge smile firmly back in place.

When Tessa walked into the boardroom, a great cheer went up.

Her eyes sought Rex's. He strode across and gave her a

102

brief hug. "That was simply fantastic," he said, drawing her along to the table where the entire *Limelight* team were busy popping corks.

Tessa looked up at him. His face seemed to swim before her vision. His long straight nose and his wonderful ruffled hair, his marvellous eyes, so full of knowledge and wisdom and sheer maleness.

Rex could hardly bear to look back. It suddenly came to him that if Tessa continued to gaze up at him like that he could refuse her nothing. His feelings must surely be quite transparent to her. She must be able to read him like a hoarding with letters feet high.

"Now all you have to do," he said, dragging himself back to earth, "is nail Gable and you've got it made."

Twelve

Tessa's programme with Yves Saint Rochelle caused more of a stir than anyone had bargained for.

The next day accounts of the interview along with a variety of photographs of Saint Rochelle and Tessa were all over the daily press. The sizzling chemistry generated in the interchange between the two of them seemed to have made an impact on everyone who had watched it. Of course, Tessa's mysterious whisper and the suggestion of an undisclosed secret had made it all the more powerful.

Tessa was astonished that no one seemed to have guessed the truth. The tabloids had all focused on Saint Rochelle's Don Juan activities, comparing his boast of hundreds of lovers with the Catalogue song in Mozart's opera *Don Giovanni*. She had not heard one small voice raised on the issue of Saint Rochelle's Frenchness – or rather non-Frenchness.

Lady Collingham, Dartbridge's chairman, was delighted at the praise and the phenomenal media attention for *In the Limelight*. She came into the studios in person the morning after the show and summoned both Tessa and Rex to her office.

Even before they arrived in her sanctum Tessa had the feeling they were being given an audience with the Queen. And when they were actually admitted into the great lady's presence, she was not disappointed.

Lady Collingham was in her early sixties and most regal in manner. She wore a royal blue suit with a diamond brooch and pearls, and her immaculately groomed hair looked as though it had been carved from Welsh slate.

"Congratulations to you both," she said, rising from her billiard-table-sized desk and giving them each a hearty hand-shake.

"My niece Lucinda will have to look to her laurels," she observed, swivelling to confront the silver tray on the mahogany table beneath the window and offering a choice of dry or medium sherry. "I hear that yesterday's programme got the highest ratings that *Limelight* has ever achieved. Apparently people were switching on in droves even as the programme was almost ending."

"Heartwarming news," Rex remarked drily giving Tessa a covert wink.

Lady Collingham held up a sherry glass and inspected it against the light from the window, after which she gave it a brisk polish with a snowy lace handkerchief. "It's amazing, isn't it, the sort of bush telegraph that operates even in cosy little England. People must have been phoning each other up and saying, 'Switch on!'" She poured sherries with great precision, not spilling a drop. "I think it's absolutely splendid!"

Tessa sipped her sherry dutifully, even though it was one of her least favourite drinks.

"I gather you're doing a further interview this week," Lady Collingham observed to Tessa.

"Yes. Professor Royston Gable."

"Ah, yes," said Lady Collingham musingly. "I met him briefly a few months ago. A most talented and academic man. Almost frighteningly so."

Tessa's nerves jumped. Why was it the word 'frightening' seemed to crop up readily in respect of Royston Gable? And seemed to be curiously appropriate despite his elegant, mild manner?

She glanced across the desk at Lady Collingham, who was staring into her sherry glass, apparently deep in thought. Tessa didn't think Lady Collingham would use the word 'frightening' lightly. In fact, she didn't think Lady Collingham would normally have much truck with either the word or the emotion.

"Professor Gable's area of research is a very sensitive one," Lady Collingham continued. "People become very worked up on the issue of genetics and the inheritance of certain human characteristics passed down in families." She took a sip of her sherry and placed the glass back on its linen mat with elaborate care. "Are you sure Tessa's up to this interview?" she barked suddenly at Rex.

"Yes," he said quietly.

"Interviewing Gable is an entirely different kettle of fish from Mr Saint Rochelle." Lady Collingham's eyes were as cold and hard as grey steel balls.

"Yes," agreed Rex. "I have every confidence in Tessa. And I think she's already proved her abilities as a superb interviewer."

"Oh, I don't doubt it," said Lady Collingham. "But you must realise that the subject matter of an interview with Gable is bound to touch on tricky areas. Tessa can't spend her time larking around with a man of his calibre as she did with Saint Rochelle."

"Lady Collingham!" Rex protested angrily, "I won't sit here and allow you to speak like that about Tessa, as though she were just a piece of the wallpaper. I . . ."

Tessa reached out and touched Rex's hand, warmed by his support, but at the same time desperate to warn him not to go too far. "Rex! Please let *me* say something."

She faced Lady Collingham. "I've done a good deal of research on Professor Gable's life and his current work," she told the formidable Chairwoman, her tone low and steady, entirely firm, even though Lady Collingham's last remarks had stung. "I think the questions I've drafted are fair and honest ones and that they should draw out some interesting information. And," she went on, refusing to be silenced, "if we don't want to take risks on *In the Limelight* then we shouldn't be inviting someone like Professor Gable on the programme at all!"

Beside her, Rex shifted in his seat. He was looking grim, but Tessa knew without a doubt that his sympathies were all with her, not Lady Collingham.

"No," said Lady Collingham briskly. "I rather tend to agree with you there, Tessa. In fact, Rex and I have already been over that particular issue. He knows my feelings. And to be quite frank I have to say that I don't think Gable is a good choice for a *Limelight* guest. We could be biting off more here than we can chew." Here she looked pointedly at Tessa, who looked steadily back.

"Enterprises that take no risks, that break no new ground are like undug gardens," said Rex coldly. "They gradually turn into a wilderness clogged with randomly growing weeds." It was clear that he was talking, not simply about *Limelight*, but about the whole of the Dartbridge consortium.

Colour stole into Lady Collingham's neck, washing up on to her face. "In my view," she said, making a not very convincing show of ignoring Rex's last remark, "Gable is the kind of person who belongs on the late night 'heavy' shows, being grilled by an experienced interviewer who is used to dealing with guests of his calibre."

"No!" said Rex, his voice tight with dissent and anger. "Not so."

"I'm merely offering my opinion," said Lady Collingham. "You wouldn't respect me, Rex, if I were the kind of woman who minced my words."

Rex gave her a hard stare. And then his face crinkled into a grin. "No, I wouldn't."

Lady Collingham turned to Tessa. "Rex is constantly berating me and the board of directors for our conservatism." The faintest glimmer of humour appeared in her cool grey eyes, and Tessa realised that the chairwoman was rather more complex than she had first thought. "He has left me in no doubt that it's high time Dartbridge became more adventurous and contentious in its daytime programmes."

"Correct." Rex gave a brief nod of response.

"I'm an administrator, not a professional," said Lady Collingham. "And so I have to take the advice of those professionals who know what they are doing. At least I must hope that they know." She looked again at Rex. "Thus, if my Head of Daytime Programmes tells me that Dartbridge must start taking more risks – then so be it."

"Thank you, Lady Collingham," he said gravely. "I think you've made a very fair summary of the position. And I'm entirely confident that my decision to invite Gable on to *Limelight* and to give Tessa the chance to interview him will produce the kind of television that will have our audiences sitting up and taking notice."

Lady Collingham drew in a breath, but Rex ploughed

relentlessly on. "We're already significantly up in the ratings on the strength of just one super afternoon slot programme. Now we have to strike while the iron is hot and make sure we consolidate our position. And, I can guarantee you that an interview with Gable is exactly the right vehicle for attaining that goal."

Tessa, looking from one to the other of these two formidable sparring partners, had a sudden uneasy sense of being used as a pawn in their battle of wills. But there was no time to make a protest – Lady Collingham was already in full flow again.

"You're full of fire, my dear Rex," she told him with smiling indulgence, "and most eloquent in driving home your views. But don't forget that *I* am the one who has to deal with all the lawyers who start screaming if we make a botch up of any highly sensitive or political issues. *I* am the one who has to deal with the board, with our sponsors and with all the advertisers who are the lifeblood of the company. If we upset our sponsors then we all go under."

"Look," said Rex. "I take full responsibility on this issue. If the interview with Gable gets Dartbridge into any kind of trouble then I'll carry the can."

"No, *I* shall have to carry the can," Lady Collingham said sweetly. "Ultimately, as far as Dartbridge is concerned, the buck stops here." She tapped the tooled green leather of her desk top. "You could lose your position, Rex, your salary and your career prospects. But I have to bail Dartbridge out if the going gets rough."

"Lady Collingham," Rex said gently, "aren't you getting things a little out of proportion? We're simply talking of one half-hour programme here."

Tessa held her breath. She had always fancied herself as quite bold, but she would never have dared go this far with Lady Collingham.

The grey ball-bearing eyes gleamed dangerously. And then Lady Collingham threw back her head and gave a ripe, bellowing laugh. "Rex, Rex!" she chided, still chuckling. "I have to admit that it really does me good to be put in my place from time to time. Or so my dear husband is fond of telling me." She chuckled some more. And then, appearing to lose interest in the conversation, she abruptly flapped her hands at them and said commandingly, "Oh, that's quite enough for now. Go away, both of you. I've said all I want to."

She got up from her desk and began to gather up the sherry glasses. It was as though her two staff had already left.

Then, just as Tessa was about to move through the doorway, she said sharply, "Be careful, Tessa. When you're interviewing Gable, just . . . take care!"

Rex strode on ahead, moving so swiftly Tessa had to run to catch him up.

"I need to talk to you, Rex," she said urgently. "Now!"

"OK." His face was grim again, the interview with Lady Collingham had clearly scraped over raw nerves.

In the privacy of Rex's room Tessa let her feelings rip. "What the hell was all that about?"

"Lady Collingham and I don't always see eye to eye."

"I'd have to be as blind as a concrete block not to have noticed that."

"It's quite a normal state of affairs. Chairpersons of boards and their hands-on minions are always coming to blows."

"Rex!" she exclaimed heatedly. "Don't you dare hide behind a wall of whacky words. This is my neck coming under the axe, my head on the chopping block. I'm beginning to feel like Anne Boleyn!"

Rex looked thoughtful. "She persuaded Henry to employ a master swordsman. The head came off with one clean swing. Come to think of it," he added, eyeing Tessa's glowing curls with a sly grin, "she had red hair too, didn't she?"

Tessa snorted. "Oh for God's sake, stop joking. This is serious."

"Yes. Agreed. Go on," Rex invited, leaning against the wall and crossing his arms.

"This is just great, isn't it? You want me to interview Royston Gable and go for the jugular. Oh no, sorry. Go for the Achilles heel . . ."

"You went for it with Saint Rochelle," he interposed softly. "Located it and then made the most rivetingly subtle use of it."

"Stop it, Rex!" she yelled. "Be serious!"

"I'm listening," he said quietly.

"OK. Basically you're wanting me to have a spat with Gable and give the viewers a thrill."

"That's more or less what you did with Saint Rochelle," Rex pointed out. "And see where that got us. Up the road of huge publicity and soaring ratings."

"Gable is quite another ball game to Saint Rochelle, as Lady Collingham pointed out, and as you are very well aware." Tessa protested. Her frustration was like a small fire within her, warming her body and her face. She waved her hand in front of her face like a fan.

"I agree. And you're well up to a spat with Gable, just like you were with Rochelle. It will simply be a contest of a different kind."

"That's exactly the point!" Tessa exploded. "You're wanting a head-on collision, lots of conflict and strife! And Lady C wants peace and caution."

Rex nodded sagely.

Tessa let out a stormy sigh. "So why don't I just go and jump off Tower Bridge right now?"

"No, no. Sinking to the bottom of the Thames is a very dismal and cold way to die."

"Huh!" Tessa paced up and down beside the desk, her boots making brisk taps on the pine flooring.

"Listen, Tessa," Rex said quietly, "and I'm being totally serious now. All interesting interviews are contests. If there's no strife, no conflict, then there's no tension. And the whole thing goes off with all the sizzle and sparkle of a soggy Yorkshire pudding."

Tessa sighed. "Fine. But the problem remains; you want one thing, she wants another. And I'm just a little cat's paw in between. It's no fun trying to serve two bosses when they're pulling you in different directions."

"Tessa," he said, putting his hand gently on her shoulder. "It's my belief that you're an up-and-coming star. If you build on the foundations you laid yesterday, then in time you'll be able to dictate all your own terms. You'll have more power than any mere boss figure. Because audience ratings will give you all the power in the world."

110

Her face was stripped of all colour as she glanced up at him. "Oh, I don't know." Her slender shoulders drooped forlornly and Rex's heart felt as though a huge iron hand was squeezing it.

"Don't tell me you've got cold feet again?" he chided gently. "After your triumph yesterday, I don't believe it."

"Rex, Lady Collingham doesn't think I'm up to this next interview."

"Rubbish!"

"Not so! She spelled it out. I'm OK for fooling around with the likes of Saint Rochelle. But as for confronting Gable! Oh no, I'm just a slip of a girl, I'll never manage to square up to him. You heard her, the message was loud and crystal clear." Tessa began to pace once more.

Rex came to stand close to her, putting out a hand and stilling her agitated patrolling.

"And I'm beginning to wonder if she's right," Tessa concluded miserably.

"She's entitled to her opinion," Rex said reasonably. "But I happen to be convinced that she's wrong."

Tessa shook her head and sighed. "Oh, I don't know. I think it was her comment about the possibility of my making a botch of things that really got to me," she declared suddenly. "That was pretty low of her."

"Definitely below the belt," Rex agreed gravely. "But you have to remember that underneath that queenly suit and the pearls our ladylike Chairwoman is as tough and ferocious as a six-foot-four rugby forward with attitude."

Tessa made a small muffled sound that could possibly have been a chuckle. "She made me feel as though I were just a kid. A flibbertigibbet. A lightweight. And I'm not!" she protested heatedly. "Just because I'm small and twig-like doesn't mean I haven't got a brain and a heart – and plenty of guts."

"You're probably one of the gutsiest people I've ever known," said Rex.

She looked at him sceptically. Was he sending her up?

"Tessa," he said, his voice low and husky, "if *I* can believe in you then why can't you?"

"I'm not thinking straight," she said woefully. "I feel limp and jelly-like, as though all my bones have dissolved into porridge. It's all this excitement and conflict. It takes it out of you even more than running a marathon." Suddenly she rallied, clenching her fist and giving the air a ferocious punch. He grinned. Whacked or not, she still had plenty of fight left in her.

"Oh, Tessa," he murmured, unable to stop himself running a tender hand over her bright hair.

Tessa's head jerked up in astonishment.

"Oh my God!" she breathed, assaulted by a symphony of new and wild emotions as she looked into his eyes.

"What is it?" he asked, his eyebrows raised, his lips twitching.

"I'm late for my next assignment," she said wildly, leaping to the door and disappearing through it as fast as she could.

Thirteen

Oliver had come to a decision. He was taking Tessa out
that evening. Just the two of them, a cosy tête-à-tête, and
he was not going to take no for an answer. He telephoned her at
the office and started laying down the law. When Tessa began
to protest he abruptly rang off and around twenty minutes
later turned up at the studios in person, his arms filled with
a profusion of fragrant, nodding red roses.

"Oliver, what on earth are you doing here at this time of
day?" she exclaimed, glancing up from her desk in alarm as
he burst in.

"Coming to pin you down, my gorgeous one," he said,
throwing the flowers on to the desk, then raising her from
her chair and pulling her into his arms.

"Olly! Please, not here in the office!" Tessa protested.

"Listen," he said, making a poor attempt of looking stern,
"you work every hour of the day and night, you don't reply
to my calls, and I haven't seen your lovely face for two whole
days – in the flesh that is. There are plenty of photos of
you decorating the national press, and my mother must have
replayed her video of you chatting up that cheeky so-and-so
Saint Rochelle about a million times. But not once have I seen
the real live you." He lowered his head, zoomed in on Tessa
and pressed a fierce kiss on her lips.

"Olly!" she protested.

"In other words you seem to be hot public property," he
said. "So when it dawned on me that *I* seem to be the only
one who isn't in on the act I started to get a bit pissed off
about it!" He pulled her hard against him and began to kiss
her in earnest.

Tessa felt a lurch of panic and claustrophobia. She struggled

113

and made some muffled protests. But he held her very firmly and, not wanting to humiliate him with a violent bid for freedom, she had little alternative but to wait until he had finished before she could quietly extricate herself.

"For Heaven's sake!" she told him, part of her amused at his outrageous behaviour, part of her unnnerved and angered by his presumption. "I'm at *work*!"

"So?" He raised his shoulders in a casual, friendly shrug.

"Someone might come in and find us." Her mind flew to Rex and she felt slightly queasy.

"You're a big girl now, Tessa," Olly said amiably. "And I'm a big boy. We can kiss whom we like, where we like, whenever we like."

"I don't share that particular philosophy," she said, her voice cold.

If Oliver detected the ice in her tone he gave no sign of it. "This is what's going to happen tonight," he told her. "We're going to a movie; I've booked for the latest historical blockbuster – you like that sort of thing, don't you? And then we're going on somewhere very, very nice for supper. And after that, well . . ."

Tessa began to hedge. "I still haven't written my script for the interview with Royston Gable tomorrow."

"Haven't written your script!" exclaimed Oliver with mock severity. "I don't believe that for one moment. I've always thought of you as the sort of girl who never fails to have her homework in on time."

Tessa furtively shuffled the papers on her desk, pushing her script for the Gable interview to the bottom of the pile whilst Oliver prowled about, peering at the stills from past *Limelight* programmes which lined the walls.

"I really can't believe that you haven't written your script yet," he said, moving back to the desk and staring down at her, his smoothly handsome face moulded into its habitual lazy smile. "But I've never had you down as a liar. So if what you're saying is true, you'd better watch out, Tess, that ogre of a boss will burn you alive!"

Tessa winced. "OK," she admitted. "I have written it. Most of it. But I haven't polished it up yet." She raked her fingers through her curls, making the light spin and dance through the moving strands. "I've had to do a lot of research for this interview, get myself clued up on all sorts of things I didn't know before."

Oliver smiled. He thought it was super that she was a real pro and truly dedicated to her work, and when she looked as hot and earnest and fierce as she did now he felt quite unbearably protective, and also pretty horny. He had to admit, however, that if he were to be totally honest with himself he thought it a shame for her to be under such pressure and that it would be much nicer for her to be like his mother and live a lovely pampered pet poodle existence – with him to provide the pampering.

"You could sit up with your script all night and it still wouldn't be properly 'polished up'. Listen Tess," he went on, adopting a paternal, nurturing tone, "as you yourself said just now, you've done enough slaving preparing for this interview. The best thing you can do tonight is get out and about and have a good time."

Tessa made another assault on her curls. "Oh, maybe you're right. It's just that—"

"God, I'll be glad when this wretched interview with Gable's over," Oliver exclaimed, throwing himself into a chair. "You don't seem to be able to think about anyone else. It's like the bloke's here in the room, breathing down our necks. Kind of 'three in a bed'." He flicked her a crooked and narrow look. "Except that we haven't got around to two in a bed yet, have we?"

"Stop it, Olly!"

He held his hands up in self defence. "Sorry! Sorry! I just feel the need to keep on plugging away." He was smiling and seemingly unperturbed. "I'll wear you down yet," he said softly.

Tessa said nothing. She was taken aback by Oliver's sudden arrival and painfully reminded of the way she had put him off and neglected him. The truth was that she had been so preoccupied with other issues that she had more or less forgotten to include him in her thoughts, let alone her life.

Reflecting on this awoke a prickly sensation of guilt mixed

with a curious defiance. Tessa had always had a hatred of being captured and pinned down.

And yet she felt she had treated Oliver shabbily, that he deserved better. She was coming to realise that Oliver was a complete stranger to being denied what he wanted, that he had always been used to having his heart's various desires granted more or less as soon as those desires surfaced.

He must be exercising the most strenuous self control with her now. She felt a surge of affection for him as she would for a spoiled, charming selfish boy who was trying really hard to be better.

"Pick you up at seven?" Oliver said, sensing her capitulation.

Tessa smiled. "You win."

As a parting shot, he took her in his arms again and placed his lips over hers.

Tessa stood passive and still within his embrace. She allowed him to do what he liked with her lips. She stroked the back of his neck with her hand. She prayed the kiss would soon end.

But when she heard footsteps coming down the corridor she felt her heart begin to struggle like a small and terrified captured animal. She knew without a doubt that the footsteps belonged to Rex and that his finding her like this was just about the worst thing she could imagine.

But Oliver, giving no sign whatsoever of noticing her struggles, merely pressed her tighter against him.

She heard Rex's polite knock and felt the blast of air rush in from the corridor as, following a discreet pause, the door opened.

Her eyes connected with his startled amber gaze as she struggled for breath under the onslaught of Oliver's full, hot lips. She felt as though she were drowning.

"I'm sorry," Rex murmured stiffly, retreating softly back into the corridor and closing the door behind him.

Oliver released her. Smiling, trailing a finger under her chin as a farewell, he too slipped away

Damn, damn, damn. Tessa closed her eyes, fighting a darkness that swirled within her. It was a darkness of self-deception, a persistence in denying the truth and strength of certain desires that had been softly and insistently filtering into her system for weeks. Insistent desires that would no longer be ignored.

Oliver declared the film to be brilliant. "Jolly entertaining stuff, didn't you think?" he said to Tessa, hugging her to him as they jostled their way out of the crowded cinema.

Tessa had only vaguely followed the storyline of the film, her mind being otherwise occupied.

"That bloke, what's-his-name, who played the lead must be knocking on a bit," Oliver observed. "But he can still pull 'em in. God! I hope I'm as on the ball as he is when I'm old."

"Who is 'em'?" Tessa asked.

Oliver chortled. "The chicks. Women. Babes."

"Oh, them!"

"Don't put on such a saintly face. I bet you wouldn't say no to him if he asked you."

"Asked me what? To shag him?"

Oliver looked pained and pious. "Tess!"

"Sorry," said Tess, sounding, but not feeling, regretful. Oliver's banter was irritating her like a tiny stone lodged painfully in a shoe. The criticism behind her thought made her feel mean and low. Even less like relaxing and enjoying herself than she had before.

"It's a bit rough on a guy," Oliver complained, "to talk about jumping into bed, when he's gasping for it and you're carrying on like a vestal virgin."

Tessa could see the point in that. She was feeling worse by the minute. She felt herself to be a dreadful hypocrite in going out with a man and raising all kinds of hopes in him. A man who was perfectly amiable and lovable and would most probably be a skilled and considerate lover. The simple truth was that she didn't truly want to be with Oliver any more, in bed or out. She wanted Rex Chance. Oh hell.

"Yes," she agreed. "I'm sorry, Oliver."

"Accepted." They walked on. "What does vestal mean when it's at home anyway?" Oliver demanded.

"Chaste. There was a Roman goddess called Vesta who was dedicated to celibacy."

"Vesta eh?" said Oliver musingly. "Not too dissimilar to Tessa, what do you think?" He cracked up laughing at his own joke as he unlocked the Aston Martin and insinuated himself into the driving seat.

"You know, Tessa," he remarked thoughtfully, as they erupted into the flow of London's traffic in a roar of acceleration and a high-pitched yelping of tyres. "That's one of the things I like about you."

"Which thing, what?" Tessa queried vaguely. Her mind was occupied with wondering how much rubber had come off the Aston's front tyres as it exploded into the traffic and, more significantly, what Rex Chance would have thought of her behaviour in the office that afternoon. Recalling his startled and then coolly disapproving eyes she shivered with renewed humiliation. She reminded herself that Rex had a lot on his plate at the moment and was highly unlikely to have bothered to think about her at all.

"Knowing things about Roman goddesses and so on," Oliver explained. "I could never remember any of that boring ancient history stuff they taught us at school. You're a really smart little chick, Tessa."

The restaurant Oliver had chosen was situated in a very fashionable corner of the West End close to St James's Palace. Tessa stood under the restaurant's green and gold entrance canopy and watched Oliver manoeuvre the Aston Martin into a parking space more suited to a Mini. He did this with great skill and panache, orchestrating the operation with some throaty and impressive engine roaring, which had passers-by turning to watch.

You're such a show-off, Olly, she thought with a flash of irritation. Instantly she felt mean and contrite. She reminded herself that Oliver's flamboyant flair for cars and his skill in driving had been a part of his attraction for her when she had first met him. She had always found male competence behind the wheel incredibly sexy. She told herself that she had absolutely no right to criticise him on that score.

As she watched Oliver unfold himself from the car she had a sudden memory of Rex as he wove his Jaguar through the traffic. With Rex there had been no scream of tyres, no flourishes, just a quiet, assured expertise.

You low down creature, she chided herself, *you're accepting the generous hospitality of one guy and thinking of another. Ugh!*

She reached out and took Oliver's arm as he came to stand beside her. As she looked up at him she smiled affectionately and gave him a little squeeze.

As they walked through the entrance of the restaurant the head waiter came to greet them personally.

Tessa was quite used to this happening when she went out with Oliver. Because he had limitless ready cash, ate out regularly at all the most famous, smartest places in London and was an extravagantly generous tipper, he always got star status treatment.

But tonight she sensed something a little different going on. Tonight it was her, Tessa, who was the focus of attention rather than Oliver.

"Hi, Lucien," said Oliver chummily. "I hope you're going to look after us really well tonight."

"Of course, sir," Lucien responded with gentle formality. He turned to Tessa. "Miss Clair," he said gravely, "welcome! And may I say how very much I enjoyed your interview with Monsieur Saint Rochelle."

Turning, he led the way into the restaurant.

"See!" said Oliver, wrapping his arm around her waist and pulling her close. "You're famous. If Lucien is a fan, you've really made it big!"

Lucien seated them at a table in a quiet and intimate corner. Everything was supremely simple and stunningly elegant: a buttermilk coloured cloth, pale green candles, cream and bronze carnations, plain white china.

Tessa recognised it as the kind of elegance and simplicity which cost a small fortune.

Lucien was opening champagne. "The Belle Epoque, sir," he told Oliver. "I remembered that it was very much to your liking last time you visited us. I hope you will accept it with our compliments." Here he paused and smiled at Tessa. "A small celebration before your meal, madam. I felt that was in order."

He poured the champagne into glasses shaped like the heads of aurum lilies then placed suede folders with green tassels in front of each of them and glided away as though on oiled castors.

"He's a bit over the top tonight," Oliver said grinning.

Tessa took a sip of the champagne which was golden, robust and delicious. She glanced at Oliver who was busy with the menu, humming happily as he scanned down the list of luxury foods. She felt an ache of unease. It was not the spasmodic stomach-wrenching anxiety that had been a feature of her life since she had agreed to interview Royston Gable, because now that the interview was so close she felt that she had gone beyond apprehension, that the half-hour facing Gable would just simply have to happen. No, this unease was based on the simple guilt that springs from putting on a false face.

Giving a small sigh, she opened the menu and glanced over it. She noticed that it mentioned three different kinds of caviar and gave helpful descriptions of several methods of serving fresh lobster. She also noticed that it gave no information whatsoever about prices.

"I don't really like caviar," said Oliver. "Funny salty stuff. Overrated. I'm going to have good old leek soup to start with and the venison sausages with lots of lovely mashed potato." He smiled at her in triumph, as though he had just successfully completed some highly intricate task.

"I'll have the poached salmon," said Tessa who by now didn't feel like eating anything at all from this exotic menu and would have preferred to go home and make herself a cheese sandwich.

I'm an imposter, she thought with a twinge of dismay. I shouldn't be here at all in this place. All this extravagance and luxury is wasted on me. And I shouldn't sitting here smiling at Oliver and encouraging him to think I might go to bed with him. Or to think that I'm going to be a part of his future.

A sensation of being trapped came over her. She took some deep breaths, straightened her spine and put a pleasant smile on her face. She may not have any loving feeling towards Oliver, but at least she could be polite. She asked him how the car trade was going.

"Fantastic! Never better!" His eyes sparkled. "Dad thinks we're going to hit an all time high with our turnover figure this year."

"That's good," Tessa said.

"I'll say. The bonus share-out should be phenomenal to match. Certainly can't be bad." He gestured to a passing waiter to refill their glasses. "Of course some of those in the rougher side of the trade went to the wall in the recession, poor sods. Thank God we're not in the cheap end of the market, trying to shift clapped out bangers and staggering from one financial crisis to the next."

"There are always people rich enough to buy Mercedes and BMWs and so on," Tessa observed with a wry smile.

"Fortunately, yes."

He tore up his bread, dropped the chunks into his soup and stirred them around. Whilst spooning up the resulting lumpy mixture he embarked on a light-hearted sermon regarding the ins and outs of the bread-and-butter motor trade as compared with the luxury car market.

Tessa, listening to him with only a part of her attention, glanced at his smooth, seemingly amiable features and began to see the beginnings of lordliness and crude insensitivity that can often go hand in hand with easy and assured wealth.

She sectioned her salmon and forced herself to chew and swallow it, all the time wondering how she was going to tell Oliver that it was all over between them.

Just thinking those last few words gave her a start. She had been seeing Oliver for three months now. He was a part of her everyday life. She supposed she would miss him.

Lucien materialised silently at her elbow, and her body gave a small jerk as he spoke into her ear.

"A telephone call for you, Miss Clair."

She looked up. "Yes?"

"Would you care to take it here?" He offered a cordless phone. "Or privately?"

"Here," she said, taking the phone from his hand.

"We have no secrets from each other," Oliver remarked, smiling at Lucien complacently.

Tessa spoke into the phone. "Hello?"

"This is Royston Gable. I do apologise for intruding into your leisure time."

Tessa's nerves gave a violent squeal. *How did he find me? How the hell did he know I was here?*

As if Gable could read her mind, his rich, beautifully lubricated voice continued. "I telephoned your work, Tessa, and they gave me your home number. And then your very kind flatmate gave me the number of your boyfriend's house. And his most helpful mother gave me the number of the restaurant you've chosen to patronise. I do hope you will forgive the intrusion. I shan't keep you long."

Dear God! He's telling me he has the persistence to find out exactly how and where to find me. Any place, any time.

"So, how can I help you?" she asked succeeding in keeping her voice soft and steady, even though her heart was thrashing around like that of a wild bird trapped in a cage.

"I always like to present my lady hostesses with a corsage," Gable said, gentle and silver-tongued. "I know it's rather old-fashioned of me, but there you are. I can't help being old fashioned." A long pause followed.

"I'm sorry, I'm not quite with with you," Tessa's forehead creased into a small frown.

"It's a question of matching up the corsage with the wearer's chosen ensemble."

"Toning shades, is that what you mean?" She spoke crisply, almost brutally, determined not to match Gable's silky coercion.

"Indeed it is. So what shades will you be wearing?"

"I haven't decided yet."

"Dear, dear. Well then I shall just have to play safe with the creams and golds that will match your Titian complexion perfectly."

"Yes," said Tessa, finding herself completely lost for a longer, wittier response.

"Good. Excellent," Gable said. "I'm really looking forward to our meeting tomorrow."

"So am I," Tessa lied gamely. She found that her throat

had dried. She wished Gable would ring off. Wished it quite fervently. "Good night, then," she said hesitantly.

"Good night, Tessa." There was yet another pause. She wanted to cut off the connection but something stopped her.

"Oh, and by the way," he added politely, "you have something of mine." He drew the words out slightly, sending crawls of unease down her spine. She thought of the four names she had stolen from his computer screen. Adam Baddeley, Hilary Charles, Pascal Dumas, Rupert Frobisher. Names now firmly engraved on her memory. Names she had already begun to follow up, two of them with some success.

"My copy of *Absalom and Achitophel*," Gable said softly. "If you've gained as much as you want from it I'd be most grateful to have it back."

"Oh, yes." A huge wave of relief surged. "Of course. I'll make sure to bring it along."

There was another pause. She fancied she could hear him breathing, but maybe it was simply the drumming of her own blood.

"Good night, Tessa." The connection clicked off. There was just the hum of the dialling tone.

Tessa sat fixed and rigid. She felt as though a hawk had swooped down from a clear sky and pecked a strip of skin from her face.

"Well?" said Oliver, reaching over and taking the phone from her hand, breaking her mood. "Who the hell was that?"

"Royston Gable." She hoped Oliver didn't notice the quaver in her voice.

"Can't wait to see you, eh?"

Tessa reached for her glass and took two large gulps of wine. "Just checking up on a few last minute details."

"He's a cheeky bastard, tracking you down here and calling you up as though he owned you."

"A little over the top," Tessa agreed, trying to sound non-committal.

Oliver had long finished his sausages and mashed potato. He looked around for Lucien, eager to see the pudding menu. By some magic Lucien instantly materialised from a far corner and came skimming towards them.

"Hope I'm not in competition with Gable for your favours," Oliver commented grinning at Tessa, whilst seizing the menu and scanning it eagerly.

"No fear of that," Tessa said, noting that her voice now sounded quite normal.

She was too churned up to eat much more herself and merely waited patiently, sipping at her wine, until Oliver had eaten his fill.

She watched him as he worked his way through an elaborate chocolate mousse drawn up into Alpine peaks and topped with a gilded net of spun sugar. She was able to observe him at leisure, for Oliver's gaze and concentration were always totally focused on the contents of his plate whilst eating.

As her eyes traced the lines of his nose and mouth, she found the reality of Oliver's face dissolving into a mist and merging with an image of her brother Alec. She stared, trying to separate the images of the two men. And it was with a huge shock that she suddenly understood that all the time she had been going out with Oliver she had been secretly comparing and confusing him with Alec, the brother she had lost. She had been longing to find Alec, and Oliver had come along as a consolation prize.

But Oliver wasn't Alec. He was himself. He deserved to be loved for himself. But she, Tessa, would never be able to give him the love he wanted.

The fused image of Oliver and Alec faded. And now she saw Oliver once again in the flesh, spooning up his cream and looking very full and satisfied.

Then, without warning, an image of Rex Chance rose up in her mind. Rex looking grim and hard as he faced Lady Collingham in her office. Rex looking at her through cool, reproving amber eyes as she stood clasped against Oliver in her office.

A wave of heat washed through her body, followed by a cold shivering thrill when she glanced again at Oliver and arrived at the full realisation of what she must do. And how there was no way of doing it without hurting him.

When the meal was finally over Lucien ushered them out

on a wing of charm, expressing the hope that he would see them again very soon.

"You will," Oliver said cheerfully, in splendidly mellow mood now that he was well fed and glowing with champagne. Tonight, however, unlike the evening of his mother's birthday, he had made sure not to hit the champagne too hard. And it was not only his driving performance that he was considering. There was the question of another, more intimate kind of performance to consider. And he really did hope that tonight would be the night.

He drove Tessa back to her flat with commendable care, parked the car and switched off the engine.

There was a long silence and Tessa could hear the blood singing in her ears.

Oliver put his hand on her thigh.

"I've got to go in now," Tessa told him. "I must get some sleep."

Oliver put his arms around her and began to press hot winey kisses into her neck. His hand now moved from her thigh to roam hungrily over her breasts, squeezing her nipples through the fabric of her silk top.

"No, Olly," she murmured. "Not tonight. It really is a big day for me tomorrow."

"Not tonight, not tonight," he grumbled amiably. You're like bloody Josephine. A darling frigid little cow."

"No," she said, struggling a little. "It was Napoleon who was the reluctant one."

Oliver laughed. He put one arm around her and held her firmly, pinning her arm to her side. With his free hand he pushed a lever on the side of the seat and Tess was startled to find herself suddenly laid horizontal.

"Neat, huh?" Oliver murmured nuzzling into her neck. "I had recliners fitted specially." He began to stroke the inside of her thigh.

I have to do it, thought Tessa. I have to tell him that it's no good and that it's all over. That I'm never going to sleep with him. That we'd better split up and then he can find someone else.

Oliver's exploratory hand was firm and soft-skinned and

very experienced. She felt him curl his fingers into the soft hairs at the root of her legs. With one assured movement he swiftly wrenched up her skirt and tugged at her panties.

Tessa snapped her legs shut. "No, Olly, please." *Please don't make me have to give you the most awful violent rejection she prayed.*

Taking her by surprise he suddenly rotated her to lie on her stomach, then gave her three firm spanks. "Do you like this?" he whispered. "I've had some very good reports of my chastising technique." His hands were roaming everywhere, his fingers digging into soft flesh.

Tessa felt herself tremble. Rage danced in her head. She was suddenly empowered. She flung her imprisoned arm free and opened the car's door. With a surge of strength she rolled out from Oliver's grasp, landing in a dishevelled heap on the pavement and raising a gasp of shock from a passing late-night dog walker. She got up, pulling her skirt down, her face fiery with humiliation.

"Sorry sweetheart, sorry. I went too far." Oliver leaned over the passenger seat to speak to her. He seemed quite unperturbed and was still grinning, if a trifle sheepishly. "Listen, I'll let you off for tonight. But once you've got your date with Gable out of the way I'm putting up with no more excuses."

"Olly . . ." she protested, but he had already ignited the engine and was revving it into a fury of growls and roars.

"I'll see you tomorrow evening," he shouted through the din. "Oh, and good luck for tomorrow, poppet. Bye!"

Fourteen

O range lights flashed a warning outside the *Limelight* studio: No Entry.

In the control room Rex was scanning the rows of monitors in front of him with a hawk-like eye. He had decided there was no way he could allow anyone but himself to produce this particular programme. He had told Tessa so as soon as she appeared in her office that morning. He had anticipated a fight. Geoff the regular producer was back at work, raring to go; she could well have challenged Rex as to why he had chosen to make such a high-handed change. But her response had been perectly calm and accepting, almost to the point of passiveness.

In fact the quiet solemnity of her whole demeanour had worried him. He had asked her if she was worried about anything, if she was feeling up to the mark. Her reassurances had all been firm and steady, yet curiously evasive and distant. He had felt a twinge of alarm.

Now, watching the monitor's image of her sitting in her interviewer's chair, he noted the tense set of her delicately-tooled jawline. She was more than nervous. She was scared out of her wits.

In contrast Royston Gable was smiling and relaxed, radiating the authority that comes from knowledge and culture.

Gable had insisted on being in place on the set when the show started. With cool assured firmness he had pointed out that, as he was not a nationally known celebrity, it seemed rather grandiose and egocentric for him to go through the charade of making a big entrance.

Rex had taken his point and not been especially concerned about this slight alteration to the usual format. He had also found himself both impressed and irritated by Gable's quiet presumption of getting his own way.

He stared at Tessa's image on the monitor, chewing on his lip. Gable was leaning towards her, his lips moving as he murmured to her, his smile still in place. Rex strained to hear through his ear piece but Gable had placed his hand over the tiny microphone clipped to his lapel and no sound emerged. Tessa's face registered wary alertness. Rex's facial muscles tightened.

The door opened behind him. Turning he saw Lucinda come softly in. She had only just returned to work that morning and was looking pale and ethereally beautiful after her bout of food poisoning.

"You won't mind if I sit in with you, Rex?" she crooned sweetly. "I'll be as quiet as a mouse. In fact I'm still so weak and wobbly I don't think I could create a stir if I tried."

"Help yourself," said Rex, who harboured a secret aversion to Lucinda, another of God's creatures who never dreamed that the world would not fit in with her wishes.

"Gosh," exclaimed Lucinda, eyeing up the monitors, "is that Royston Gable? Isn't he superbly photogenic? Just look at that bone structure! And those amazing eyes – they're exactly the shade of a Scandinavian winter sky."

"Mmm," murmured Rex, noticing how very pale and strained Tessa looked, and having a horrible feeling there was trouble ahead.

"Tessa seems frightfully nervous," Lucinda chirped sounding far too cheerful. "Of course this is rather a difficult interview for someone of her experience to pull off."

"She'll surprise us all," Rex commented.

"I say! She's wearing some rather gorgeous flowers on her jacket," Lucinda commented, squinting at the monitor. "I wonder who gave her those. I shouldn't think she chose them herself. Has she got an adoring boyfriend?"

"Shut up," growled Rex under his breath.

"One minute to air, Tessa," said the Floor Manager.

"Go for it, Tessa," Rex whispered.

The red light flashed. The programme was on air.

Tessa raised her head slightly in a gesture of openness and

confidence. Turning to face the camera, she gave a brief smile and began to speak.

"Our guest on *In the Limelight* this afternoon is a respected scholar in the field of genetics and human intelligence. But Professor Royston Gable is not the typical academic working in an ivory tower. He has been thrown into the media spotlight by his recent claims to have a discovered a gene for intelligence – an IQ gene. And so now he's something of a national celebrity, and we're more than delighted to welcome him here today."

"Good introduction, Tess," murmured Rex. "Keep it up."

Tessa now turned to Gable, who was sitting perfectly still, nodding slightly in acknowledgement of her remarks.

"So you've found the first gene for intelligence. This is pretty hot, controversial stuff, isn't it, Professor Gable?" she challenged.

Gable smiled. "Some people find any new scientific discovery questionable."

"I don't think the general public get very steamed up one way or the other about discoveries in say, the laws of physics or quantum mechanics," Tessa shot back with a challenging smile.

"They probably don't understand them," Gable pointed out reasonably.

"I for one don't!" Tessa admitted, her smile now rueful.

"I could teach you," Gable interposed smoothly.

One of Tessa's eyebrows gave a slight lift. "Thank you, Professor. Now, come on, admit that scientific discoveries touching on big human issues generate huge feeling."

"I'll take your word for it." Gable was suave and smiling now.

"And your claim to have discovered a gene for human intelligence is a real hot potato!"

Gable gave a quietly superior smile.

Tessa leaned towards him, managing despite her diminutive size to convey a touch of menace. "These findings have aroused huge public interest and debate. You can't deny that."

He paused. "Are you suggesting that I would try to?"

"People are talking about your findings in London pubs and

in the underground. I know that, because I've heard them myself."

"You do your research very thoroughly, Miss Clair."

"Go on, Tessa, keep plugging at him," murmured Rex in the control box, letting out a long held breath. "He's a smooth slippery customer and you're doing fine."

"I thought Tessa's voice was quavering badly at first," put in Lucinda pettishly. "But she does seem to be steadying it a little."

"Claiming to have found an IQ gene is surely highly controversial," Tessa said sternly to Gable, as though he might possibly have been making a false assertion. "People will think it means that all the richness of human abilities and talents are completely determined by our genes."

Gable nodded assent, although his face gave nothing away as to his own private views.

"And is that true?" Tessa demanded. "Are we human beings no more than a product of our genetic inheritance, no more directors of our own fate than animals? What about family influences, the role of school and society in the way each one of us develops?"

Gable smiled. "Those factors play a part, it is true."

"But not a particulary important one in your view?"

Again Gable merely gave a patient and enigmatic smile.

"Christ, he's a tough nut," Rex muttered.

"She's going to lose her grip on him, if she doesn't really drive in hard," Lucinda said smugly.

Tessa leaned forward again. "Come on, Professor Gable. Don't be coy. You've openly expressed the view that what we inherit is far more important than other influences in making us into the individuals we are." She reached out to the table in front of her and plucked a newspaper from it. She began to read, '*My research shows that genetic differences direct the whole of our lives, governing all our experiences and what we learn from them*'. That's a direct quote from a speech you gave to an audience of four hundred professionals in the medical and educational fields two weeks ago."

"I congratulate you, Miss Clair," Gable said. "You really have been most thorough."

"So you're telling us that we human mortals are not moulded by experience, we're simply prisoners of our genes? Is that it?" Tessa demanded.

"I think, on balance, that is what my research suggests," Gable agreed. "You do, of course, put my findings in very dramatic terms, black-and-white terms as all journalists are fond of doing. If you read my articles, Miss Clair, you'll see that I use rather less flamboyant language."

"Yes," agreed Tessa. "But the message is the same!"

"Got him!" Rex exclaimed.

Gable gave Tessa a long, silent, patient stare. From the control box, from the screen it looked harmless enough. From where Tessa was sitting she had the sense of being captured, of being strapped on to skates and sent out on to the ice without any prior experience of skating. She felt herself racing ahead, speeding on, flying, still upright, still safe. But any minute she could swerve, lose her balance, go crashing down. She was holding on to stability and safety by no more than a thread.

Looking now into Gable's cold blue eyes those sensations flooded her mind.

She looked away, telling herself these vague but powerful fears gripping her were simply shadows. She raised her head again.

"What do you say to those people who claim that human intelligence can be fostered and improved by a rich and stimulating environment?" she asked.

Royston Gable shook his head patiently, like a very tolerant teacher dealing with a misguided and truculent child.

"Studies of adopted children carried out as long ago as the 1950s showed that children's IQ scores had no resemblance to their adoptive parents. None at all." His blue eyes fixed on Tessa, and she read a silent message there. Something dark and menacing and possibly deadly.

"The quality of the environment made only the slightest difference," Gable elaborated, "for either improvement or the reverse."

"My goodness!" exclaimed Lucinda, her eyes riveted on Gable's face which filled the monitor. "How extraordinary. I always thought one's background and the kind of school one went to counted for everything."

"The studies of twins is even more powerful," Gable continued with polite insistence. "If you test identical twins who have been raised apart, you find that their IQ scores are invariably almost identical. How do you explain that except through inheritance?"

"Gosh!" said Lucinda. "Just imagine that! I say, I'm jolly glad my parents are intelligent."

Tessa made a rapid mental scan through the information she had amassed in preparation for this interview. "Some people claim that IQ tests are unreliable measuring instruments. They say they are far too crude to capture something as complex as human intelligence."

"Do they really?" Gable said pleasantly, raising his eyebrows.

"God! You walked into that one, Tessa," Rex muttered under his breath.

"I believe we can learn a lot about human beings through intelligence testing," Gable elaborated. "However, the most crucial part of my research relies on comparisons of individual subjects' DNA. Deoxyribonucleic acid, the basic stuff of our material existence. It's very hard to argue with a piece of DNA. Can you argue with DNA, Tessa?"

"No." She nodded, conceding this point. "But you have to admit that your research is truly incendiary stuff. Once out of the bottle this genie – if you'll pardon the pun – could be terrifying. Supposing doctors started to use it in prenatal screening—"

"Are you saying that we should not do research?" Gable interposed. "Is that what you are saying, Tessa?" He stared fixedly at her, pinning her down like a collector staking a butterfly to a page. His eyes demanded an answer, and once again issued some kind of warning. Tessa found the control that was usually solid beneath her begin to slip, like gravel stirred up in a fast current. Her throat constricted. No words could get through.

"Is it right that we should suppress information and patronise the public?" Gable asked. "I say no. We should never be afraid of knowledge. Ignorance is never bliss."

She saw the demonic look in his eye and found herself trembling.

"Christ, Tessa," Rex's voice hissed through her earpiece. "He's starting to call all the shots. Get back on track!"

"Does your research mean that parents would be able to know the IQ of their baby whilst it is still in the womb?" Tessa asked.

"Eventually, we shall be able to give them that information. Yes."

"You'd be happy to go along with that. To play God?" Tessa enquired, her voice fragile and husky.

There was a tiny frozen moment and then Gable slowly shook his head as though the question were not worthy of his consideration.

"Have you any children, Professor?" Tessa asked, swiftly following through.

He turned towards her and now she saw a glittering spark leap in his eyes; a glimpse of something both splendid and dangerous like a rapier glinting beneath the shifting waves of a dark lake.

"No," he said softly.

"But you've had many beautiful lady escorts," Tessa went on, her suggestion obvious. Even as she spoke she felt herself dangerously near some jagged edge.

Gable leant forward to the table and slowly poured himself a glass of water. "Don't go too far, Tessa," he murmured, his face turned from the cameras, his voice inaudible to all but her. "You know why."

Tessa found that the thinking, feeling part of her brain had suddenly closed down. For a moment she was totally numb. Deaf, speechless. The scent from Gable's corsage of lilies invaded her nostrils, swamping her with a powerful deadly sweetness.

"Oh dear," said Lucinda with mock sympathy. "She's dried completely."

"Tessa," Rex said urgently, sensing that something was badly wrong. "Ask him some more about the women. Ask him anything. Then wind things up, fast!"

Tessa cleared her throat.

"Have *you* any children, Miss Clair?" Gable asked, leaning forward and smiling in a caring kind of way.

She shook her head.

"What's the matter with her?" Lucinda asked. "She looks like a little rabbit caught in the headlights."

Rex could only agree, realising that Tessa was beyond any prompting through her earpiece. He had no choice but to look on horrified and helpless as Gable quietly proceeded to take over the proceedings, drawing information from Tessa, prompting and guiding her as though they had changed places and she were the guest, he the host. And Tessa simply went along with him. Passive, inert, helpless.

A disaster. For a talk show it was just about the worst scenario Rex could think of.

There were still five minutes of the programme to go. Rex rested his head in his hands and sat out the time grimly. Then mercifully the floor manager started signalling that time was up. And then Gable was shaking Tessa's hand, thanking her suavely for inviting him on to the show, saying how much he had enjoyed talking with her.

The Mozart horn concerto started up and Rex had never before noticed the depth of melancholy and wistfulness in that apparently cheeky theme.

"Well!" said Lucinda, getting up from her seat and smiling in anticipation of a good day ahead chatting with her colleagues, dissecting the interview and finding out just where Tessa had gone wrong.

Lady Collingham rang down from her office. "I want you and Tessa in here, right now," she barked.

With a sigh Rex slung his jacket over his shoulder. Were they both for the chop, he wondered. Would the Chairwoman choose the axe or the sword?

Royston Gable walked from the studios, reviewing the verbal interchanges of the past half hour. Tessa had dared to take him on and had fought bravely, an opponent worthy of his careful attention. The sharpness of her mind pleased him, as did her tenacious curiosity, and one of her intuitive questions had been disturbingly near the mark. It entertained him to think of how she must be puzzling over the names she had seen on his computer screen, but he doubted that even she would make the mental leap required to discover the truth which linked them together.

Gable had an almost perfect visual memory and an image of Tessa now rose in his mind, to be inspected like viewing a portrait. His mouth curved with pleasure as he saw once again the intelligence and energy in her eyes, the soft curve of her neck, the swell of her firm rounded breasts. He was always most aroused by the women who challenged him psychologically. And it was a long time since he had felt as drawn to a woman as he was to Tessa.

Through his exhilaration an inner voice of reason warned him to take care. Tessa Clair could pose him a real threat. She had come nearer to his secret than anyone else; if she came any nearer she could ruin him. Ah yes! But the very anticipation of the danger she could bring was irresistibly seductive.

Fifteen

"It's time you packed in for the day," Rex said, walking into Tessa's office and looking down at her with a mixture of severity and concern.

It was seven that same evening and Tessa was still at her desk. In front of her was a pile of clippings charting the steady rise to fame of Cherry Ripe, a hopeful new star on the pop scene.

Lady Collingham, after tearing several painful strips off her and Rex, had graciously gone on to suggest that Tessa should treat her disastrous interview with Royston Gable in the same way that steeplechase jockeys deal with a bad fall.

"They get straight back up on the horse so as to squash any risk of losing their nerve," she had said with unassailable authority. "I've had plenty of tumbles out hunting, and that's always been my policy too. In fact, trying again is the only way to pull round from any horrible fiasco, whatever its nature."

So, next week Tessa was to front an interview with sixteen-year-old Cherry. Lady Collingham made no secret of her opinion that a fluffy young girl like Cherry would be far more within Tessa's scope than the brilliant and sophisticated Gable. She had also make it plain that Tessa had better be good this time.

"To lose a grip on one interview is a misfortune, to lose two will look like gross incompetence," she had said in stern Lady Bracknell-style tones.

At the end of the interview Tessa had wondered if it would be necessary to exit from Lady Collingham's august presence walking backwards, as a sign of the greatest deference possible. But Rex had stalked out with never a backward glance, so she had followed his lead.

136

"Come on, Tessa," he said to her now. "Leave all this. Your brain must have shut down long ago. Mine certainly has."

Tessa looked up at him. She saw that his face was lined with fatigue. "Yes," she agreed, pushing the clippings into a single pile and pushing them into a folder.

Rex hesitated. "Come with me to the country!" he said.

"What?"

"My sister Vicky has invited me for dinner. She's an excellent cook, and there'll be plenty for an extra one."

Tessa said nothing; he wondered if she had registered his suggestion.

"You're invited too," he said quietly. "I've told her about you."

After a minute Tessa said numbly, "Oh." She looked up. In her eyes there was the faintest glimmer of irony. "OK. Thanks, Rex."

"Are you sure?" Rex said, sounding amazed that she had capitulated so easily.

"Yes." She gave a faint smile. "Don't tell me you've already changed your mind!"

He laughed. "Come on, get your jacket."

Tessa moved zombie-like to the corner of the room where her jacket lay over a chair. She picked it up and stared at it for a few moments as though she did not quite recognise it. Slowly and deliberately she removed the cream and gold lilies pinned to the lapel and dropped them into the waste bin.

Rex watched her, his eyes dark with curiosity.

"Gable gave them to me," she said. "He always likes to give his hostesses a corsage."

"The hell he does. The smooth-talking rat."

Rex held the door open for her. As she walked towards it she suddenly stopped, went back to the bin and retrieved Gable's flowers, inhaling their fragrance. "There was a moment in the interview," she told Rex slowly, "when I wondered if he'd spiked these lilies with a drug to make me feel wobbly."

"Good heavens!" exclaimed Rex.

"No need to be alarmed," she said regretfully. "They're just plain, simple flowers. He seemed to have no difficulty in rattling me without the aid of chemicals."

Rex looked on helplessly, sensing the pain of her humiliation and feeling there was no way he could heal it.

Tessa smiled. "It's against my principles to be cruel to flowers," she said, dropping the lilies into the jug of water in to which she had crammed Oliver's gift of roses. "And he's not going to win that easily."

Vicky watched the Jaguar come up the drive, sleek, shining and silver.

"It's Uncle Rex," shrieked Benny, who had been allowed a generous extension on his bedtime so as to see his favourite uncle.

"Five minutes!" warned Vicky. "And then it's into bed, young man, no arguments."

"Ooh, look there's a lady in the car too," cried Benny. "Is she my Aunty Rex?"

"Er, no, I don't think so. For one thing she'll have a name of her own."

"What is it?" asked Benny wriggling with huge excitement.

"Tessa."

"Tessa, Tessa, Tessa," sang Benny, flying to the front door and heaving it open. Hurling himself through he launched himself on Rex, swarming up his uncle's long body with the speed and elasticity of a baby monkey.

Having attacked Rex with a volley of hugs and kisses, Benny transferred his attention to Tessa, who was standing looking on, a faintly wistful expression on her face.

"Hi!" she said, smiling broadly as Benny's darting, eager eyes met hers.

Benny leaned out from Rex's arms, yearning towards her. When Tessa lifted him against her, he hooked his legs firmly around her waist whilst his hands began an exploration of her face and hair. "A little toffee spot!" he exclaimed in delight, laying a fingertip on one of her most prominent freckles. "And another, and another!"

"Benny!" called Vicky in warning, progressing down the hall to welcome her guests.

"Thousands and thousands of toffee spots," Tessa told Benny.

"Can you wash them off?" he asked, staring hard then rubbing experimentally.

"No. I tried once or twice but it didn't work. Why do you call them toffee spots?"

"When Mummy makes toffee, she puts the spoon in the pan and takes some toffee out and drops some bits into a cup of cold water so she can see if they're cooked. And they turn into toffee spots." He pressed his finger on a freckle at the tip of Tessa's nose. "I think this one's cooked."

Tessa tilted her head and smiled around Benny at his mother. "Hello, I'm Tessa. Thank you for inviting me."

"I hope you won't take my son's uninvited remarks about freckles amiss."

"They're the kindest and most complimentary remarks I've heard all day," Tessa observed drily, shifting Benny's weight on to one hip.

"Oh dear," said Vicky, turning and leading the way into a large high-ceilinged drawing room with heavy velvet curtains hanging at long windows.

"Not so," Rex countered, putting his hand under Tessa's elbow and following on. "I haven't spoken a single unkind word to you."

"No, you haven't," Tessa agreed. "You've been a model of restraint."

"Indeed I have."

"Acting completely out of character," Tessa added. "That's what worries me."

As Vicky moved through the doorway her lips began to twitch with a smile. They sound almost married, she thought. How intriguing.

Doug, Vicky's husband, who had been engrossed in completing *The Times* crossword, rose to his feet to greet them. "Well, hello there. Welcome, welcome!"

He was an impressive figure, tall and thickset with a long intelligent face surrounded by grizzled, wiry curls. He waved his guests in the direction of the seating arrangements: squashy leather sofas and chairs almost completely buried in medical journals and newspapers.

"Five across," he mused, pausing, frowning, his lips pursed. "A spotted horse, eight letters."

"Skewbald," said Tessa, remembering a brown and cream pony she used to ride as a child. She smiled at Doug, feeling an instant warmth for him. His face was creased and lived in, his lips full and generous. I bet he's really huggable, she thought. And lovable too. And quite a few years older than Vicky, she added, noting the deep grooves around his eyes and his mouth.

"Of course, of course. Excellent!" Doug beamed approvingly at Tessa. "Odd isn't it, how some of the straightforward ones elude you. But then I know absolutely nothing about horses. Drinks everyone?"

"Gin!" said Benny, still wrapped lovingly around Tessa. "Gin, gin, gin! Jiminy tonic."

Tessa grinned. "Is that your favourite drink, Benny?" she wondered, and Benny buried his face in her shoulder, putting on a show of sudden shyness.

"Takes after his mother," Doug said. "I'm a whisky man myself."

Benny squirmed down from Tessa's arms and stood looking up at her. He tugged at her hand. "Come and see my wormerie," he commanded.

"It's not obligatory," Vicky murmured.

"I think it is!" Tessa whispered back, smiling as she allowed herself to be dragged away.

Benny bounded ahead up a broad carved oak staircase carpeted in faded red pile which gleamed in the soft light from wrought-iron wall brackets.

"I like your house," Tessa told him.

"A long, long time ago it used to belong to vicars," said Benny. "Lots of them."

"That must be why it has so many rooms," Tessa said, looking along the rows of doors leading off the wide landing.

"Come on!" Benny said impatiently.

His room was a cosy den, cluttered with a great stew of

toys, models and books. Above his bed there was a family of paper dinosaurs dangling from a piece of furry string, and in the corner of the room a heap of battered, chewed teddies and rabbits snuggled together in an old velvet chair.

Tessa felt she could almost reach out and touch the atmosphere of tenderness, care and security pervading this room. She looked at Benny and knew instinctively that when he grew up he would remember all these riches of affection and unconditional love. And that he would understand their preciousness.

"Look!" demanded Benny, jumping up and down. "Tessa! Look! My worms!"

The wormerie was an old fish tank, set in pride of place on a scuffed pine chest.

Tessa went to stand beside Benny. She put her nose against the glass and watched in fascination as the worms curled slowly around their terrain: a humped landscape of garden earth, twigs and little stones. "I think this must be worm paradise," she said eventually.

"Does that mean heaven?"

"Yes."

Benny smiled, confident that his worms were the luckiest in the world. He pointed out each one by name and gravely wished it, "Good night." He then leapt into his bed, snuggled under the duvet and demanded that Tessa tell him a story. "A very frightening one," he specified, giving a little shiver of anticipated fear.

"Let's see," said Tessa, sitting on the edge of the bed and tipping her head on one side in thought. "How should a good story start?"

"Once upon a time," said Benny impatiently.

"Of course. Right then. Once upon a time there was a worm called Wriggler. His skin was bright green. His skin was so bright that he glowed in the dark."

"Did he have red eyes?"

"Yes. As red as traffic lights."

"Did they glow in the dark too?"

"Yes."

Benny put his thumb in his mouth, satisfied that this was a story worth attending to with care.

"He lived in a worm hole at the bottom of a very beautiful garden and he was a very happy worm. But one day . . ." Tessa paused.

"A demon came to eat him," Benny whispered.

"Yes. A demon with X-ray eyes. He was a very hungry demon because he hadn't had his breakfast or his lunch or his tea the day before." Like me, she thought, feeling her stomach growling with hunger.

"Did he like to eat worms?" Benny asked, his voice a mere breath.

"Oh yes, especially bright green ones with red eyes that glowed in the dark."

Benny huddled even further into his duvet, his eyes wide with the thrill of worse terrors to come.

"But you see, Wriggler was a worm with very special powers," Tessa explained. She talked quietly on, making her story ever more fanciful. She had just got to the point where Wriggler had been transformed into a tall handsome footballer and was about to rescue a captured Pop Princess, Cherry Ripe, when she noticed a dark shadow slide on to the wall beside the door. She knew instantly that it was Rex and her heart gave a little falter.

She touched Benny's cheek. His eyes were closing now, his long black eyelashes making small fluttering beats. "Poor Cherry Ripe," Tessa whispered, "she cried shiny pink tears because she longed to be rescued. And there was only one man who could rescue her, and he had to be so brave . . ."

Softly she let her voice die away, seeing that Benny's eyelids had finally flickered into sleep. She gently patted the mound of his body under the covers and softly rose to her feet.

Leaving the room she looked up at Rex and saw that his eyes were filled with a strange dark intensity as he stared down at her.

"Dinner's ready," he said, breaking the brief spell that bound itself between them.

Tessa caught the scent of meat, well seasoned and slowly, tenderly cooked. She smelled warm pastry and the sharp tang of salad dressing. She found that the bitter humiliation and disappointment of the morning was beginning to ease.

Suddenly she felt the eager anticipation of hunger about to be satisfied.

"I didn't know you had such a way with kids," Rex commented as they went softly down the staircase, side by side.

"How could you know? Our sort of work is pretty well insulated from children, isn't it?"

"I suppose it is. A rather false world altogether."

"An exciting one though. And satisfying too. Most of the time."

"Yes." His pace slowed. He put out a hand and stopped her progress. "Are you all right, Tessa? Are you glad you came tonight?"

"Yes, I'm very glad I came."

"You mustn't let what happened this afternoon . . ."

"I don't want your sympathy, Rex," she interrupted sharply. His kindness and restraint were almost unnerving. She wished he would just get back to being himself. Abrasive, forthright, saying exactly what he thought. "And for goodness sake will you stop handling me with kid gloves. It's scaring the hell out of me!"

"I'm sorry," he said stiffly.

Vicky was moving across the hallway, a perfectly risen steak-and-kidney pudding in her oven-gloved hands. She tilted her head on one side, looking up at her brother and his new 'friend' with a quizzical expression and Tessa had the feeling that Vicky's sharp eyes didn't miss a trick.

"Come on!" Vicky chided. "The fruits of my labours in the kitchen need to be devoured without delay."

They ate at a long table in a dark oak-panelled dining room with huge oil portraits hung all around. Faces with sad, grave eyes stared down at them.

"Former rectors of this parish," Doug explained as he lit the candles in an ancient, slightly tarnished, silver candelabra. "They were all lying stacked up in the attic when we moved in. We took pity on them, dusted them off and let them come downstairs to join in the fun."

"I always think you should treat the house ghosts with consideration," said Vicky, inserting a knife into the suet crust of the pudding from which a curl of fragrant white steam rose up. "You never know what revenge they might take on you if you were to be churlish with them." She handed Tessa a well-filled plate and gestured towards the salad. "Do you have any ghosts in your home, Tessa?"

"In my flat in Highbury? If only!" Tessa responded in wry tones. She suddenly recalled a rather good ghost story that her father used to tell her and Alec when they were children. It was the kind of story she would normally reserve for people she knew very well. But, sitting here with Rex's family, even though she had never met them before she felt entirely at ease. The house seemed to exude an atmosphere of companionship, of trust and tolerance and warmth. She took a mouthful of Doug's excellent Pinot Noir and started on her tale.

When she had finished, Doug refilled her glass and asked her what other talents she possessed besides being an enviably good storyteller.

"Making the most awful mess of golden opportunies," she said quietly, twisting the stem of her glass between her fingers. "Well, one at least. On the *Limelight* programme this afternoon."

"No, not an awful mess—" Rex protested, but Tessa cut him short.

"Yes, it was."

"I'm afraid I didn't hear that particular programme," Doug said, looking concerned.

"See it, darling," Vicky corrected him patiently. "It's a TV show."

"Ah. You must forgive me," Doug told Tessa, "I don't watch much TV."

"He's a bone surgeon," Vicky explained to Tessa. "He lives for his work. The only real world for Doug is the operating theatre."

"Did *you* see the programme?" Tessa asked, turning to Vicky with challenge in her face.

"Yes. I thought it was very interesting. And I thought you were excellent, Tessa. I had to miss the last five or six minutes as there was a crisis in the kitchen, but I was really most impressed with what I saw." Vicky saw the tension in the young woman's eyes, something dark and troubled. "So what was the problem?"

"I dried. I let the guest take over the show and interview me," Tessa said flatly. "It's just about the worst sin in the book."

"Leave it alone, Tessa. You're making too much of it," Rex cut in, looking grim.

"You came across as very well informed," Vicky said thoughtfully. "You'd clearly done a good deal of research in preparation."

"She was excellently informed," said Rex stoutly.

Vicky saw Tessa flash him an angry look. "I was like a concert pianist who plays through nearly all the concerto and then completely fouls up the last few minutes. And you can bet your life it'll be those last few minutes that people will remember."

"Oh for heaven's sake, Tessa. Forget it!" Rex snapped. "Forget the whole thing."

"You'd be struggling to forget it, if you'd been eyeball to eyeball with Royston Gable this afternoon," Tessa flashed back at him, her voice tight.

"Oh for God's sake!" Rex clattered his knife and fork on to his plate. "Most especially forget about him! Tedious, bloody man!"

My goodness! Now they're having open hostilities at the dinner table, thought Vicky, utterly charmed. She hadn't seen Rex reacting like this to a woman for years. He had always kept his feelings well reined in, hidden and private. In fact she had suspected that he hadn't experienced very strong feelings about women at all since Eleanor died. He must be very keen.

"I'll go and get the pudding," Vicky said, rising to her feet.

"I'll help you!" Tessa jumped up and began to stack the used plates.

She said to Vicky in the kitchen, "I'm sorry. Squabbling at the table like that. It was unforgivable."

"Don't be sorry," responded Vicky, lifting a lemon syllabub from the fridge. "You were right to fight back. Rex is used to getting far too much of his own way. Single men in powerful jobs often are, I'm afraid."

145

"I don't normally bicker and moan like that. It's just that it's been a bit of a difficult day for me. I'd hate you to get the idea that I was a dreadful shrew," Tessa concluded, giving a wry grin.

"Not at all," said Vicky, polishing glass dessert dishes with a soft white cloth, then placing them on a tray. "I'm delighted to see that you don't shrink from combat. Because if you're going to spend time with Rex, you'll have to be prepared for some battles!"

Tessa stared at her for a few moments. "I love it here," she told Vicky on a rush of impulse. "It's a real home. You can say what you really feel instead of having to pretend all the time."

"Thank you," Vicky responded, her heart warming towards this unusual young woman.

"And Benny is absolutely gorgeous. He's so alert and curious and full of life." Tessa's face was warm with feeling as she picked up the tray and moved to the door. "You must be very proud to have a child like him."

"Yes," said Vicky, her face softening as she thought of her son, safe and happy and sleeping upstairs. "It took us a long time to get him, and even though he's a terrible mischief, he is very, very precious."

She followed Tessa into the dining room, admiring her slight, slender figure. When she first saw her, Tessa had seemed to Vicky little more than a girl; she was so small and slight, so light in all her movements, her smile constantly breaking out and wrinkling the skin around her tilted nose. Vicky understood now that beneath that fragile, pretty-as-peach exterior there was a strong and steadfast personality. Tessa was a woman of conviction and integrity. And of great tenderness too.

Oh yes, this neat, tiny Tessa would suit Rex down to the ground, Vicky was convinced of it. But Rex could be so damned pig-headed and difficult and touchy. He could unwittingly stamp on the seed of a new love without even recognising that it had been well and truly planted. Vicky gave an internal sigh at the mere thought of it. What could she do to help? she wondered. She pondered on the problem as she spooned syllabub into the glasses.

Don't interfere, Vicky instructed herself as she sat down and picked up her spoon. You have to allow people to be happy in their own way, in their own time. What other way can they find true happiness?

Sixteen

At around eleven, with the meal finally over, the four of them relaxed in the sitting room, sipping their coffee and talking together.

Vicky noticed that whilst Tessa talked to her and Doug as though they had all been friends for years she was avoiding even looking at Rex, let alone communicating with him. And Rex was looking steadily darker and grimmer.

Vicky had unobtrusively observed her brother throughout the evening. She knew him well, and was now utterly convinced that something very important was going on between him and this bright young woman, Tessa. The tension between them was as taut and electric as a stretched wire. Sharp, brittle glances were constantly flying between them. One could almost hear the crackle of the sparks as their eyes made contact. *Aah, the path of true love,* she murmured to herself.

She went into the kitchen to refill the coffee pot. Doug followed her. As he began searching in the cupboards for his vintage port she felt a loving, marital quietness fill the room.

"Aha," said Doug with satisfaction, pulling out one of his most cherished vintage ports, a '79 Ferreira.

"Good heavens!" Vicky exclaimed. "Are you going to give them that? They are indeed honoured."

"Mmm. Well, as you know, dear, I've always had a fondness for Rex. And that young woman he's brought along is absolutely charming."

"Doug!" said Vicky, becoming more amazed by the minute. "You never use the word 'charming'. And only very rarely the word 'absolutely'."

"Indeed, no," Doug agreed, squinting in concentration as he poured the jewel-coloured wine into a Victorian glass decanter

148

that Vicky hoped was not too dusty inside. "I am not normally a man of verbal extravagances."

"Certainly not."

"Do you think she knows about Rex's other women?" Doug asked.

"His *former* women," Vicky corrected. "As far as I'm aware he hasn't had a mistress for months."

"Mistress," mused Doug. "That's a wonderfully evocative word, isn't it?"

"Well it has a certain nobility and romance about it that doesn't come with concubine or co-habitee," Vicky agreed. "Anyway, I don't think other women are a problem as far as Tessa and Rex are concerned."

"It's funny how some men can draw women to them like a cross between Don Juan and the Pied Piper."

"I don't think Rex has ever been a Don Juan."

"Compared with myself," said Doug gravely, lifting his port to the light and eyeing it with an assessor's gimlet gaze, "he has most certainly earned that title. Besides you, Vicky, I have never slept with anyone apart from my first wife and my cousin Dawn who seduced me at a family wedding at the tender age of eighteen and three-quarters."

"Ah, poor darling," said Vicky, sidling up to her husband and squeezing one of his buttocks playfully.

"Well I must say Tessa seems an extremely worthy young woman," said Doug, registering the squeeze and looking pleased. "And I just hope Rex treats her with the regard she deserves."

"Yes," Vicky agreed. "I was just thinking it would be nice if they were to talk to each other once in a while."

"Precisely," Doug agreed. "And I was just thinking that the port might do the trick."

But he was to be disappointed. As he and Vicky returned to the drawing room Rex was already glancing at his watch, his face tight and purposeful. "Good grief, is that the time? Thanks, Doug, but we'll have to give the port a miss. We both have an early start tomorrow morning. We really will have to be leaving now."

"Oh, such a shame! I thought you'd be staying over," said

Doug, smiling regretfully at Tessa. "Next time you must come and spend a weekend with us. Benny would be beside himself with excitement. And Vicky and I would be pleased too!"

As Rex rose to his feet, Tessa rose too, throwing Vicky and Doug a little glance of regretful apology.

A few minutes later Doug and Vicky stood in the doorway, smiling and waving as the Jaguar made its way down the long drive.

"You dreadful matchmaker!" Vicky exclaimed to her husband, squeezing his arm affectionately. "I can't believe what you just said to them!"

"Matchmaker!" he protested. "How so?"

"Suggesting that they'd both be coming again. As though they were already an established twosome. Staying the weekend indeed!"

"Well won't they?"

Vicky paused, a tiny wrinkle of a frown on her forehead. "I hope so." She looked at the dark shadows of the trees lining the drive, hearing the wind moving through the branches, its breath like the swishing of long skirts. "But, I don't know . . ." She gave a little shiver and turned back into the light and warmth of the house.

For a time, very little was said in the Jaguar.

Tessa felt wiped-out from the tension and emotion of the day, beyond tiredness now, her body numb even from the drone of fear that had been humming quietly within ever since Royston Gable fixed his polar eyes on her. *Don't go too far, Tessa.* At the memory a streak of apprehension ran down from the base of her neck, as though a piece of bright cold steel had been dropped inside her collar.

Rex, beside her, was grim-faced, his concentration apparently entirely focused on his driving.

They stopped at traffic lights. They were about five minutes away from Tessa's house. Rex imagined those minutes like droplets of mist, sliding through his fingers, evaporating into nothing. "Why are you so angry with me?" he asked, trying to keep his voice calm and even, hearing it in his own ears; harsh, grating and abrupt.

150

She gave a huge sigh and turned to look out of her window. A man and a woman were locked together in a shop doorway, kissing each other with an intensity of passion that she found strangely moving.

"Tessa?" he demanded. "What have I done to make you so damned fragile and nervy? It's not like you at all."

"So you think you know all about me?" she flashed back at him.

"Of course I don't think that."

"If you don't know what's wrong with me, then you can't know me very well," she said bitterly.

The lights changed. He slid the car into first gear and accelerated away cleanly across the junction. "It's all about this farce with Royston Gable, isn't it? The whole fiasco is still bugging you."

"Precisely!" she shouted back. "A farce, a fiasco. And all my fault."

"Oh for God's sake, Tessa. Stop wallowing in self-pity. You may be at the centre of your own life-drama but you're not at the centre of everyone else's."

Tessa drew in a massive breath. She felt her ribs expand, her heart begin to drum. "If you weren't behind the wheel of a potentially lethal car, Rex, I'd thump you with all my strength for daring to say that. To *me*, who's for ever worrying about what other people are thinking and feeling. Vicky's right. You've got too used to having it all your own way. There are times when you're a downright presumptuous, high-handed, callous bastard!"

He let out a wincing sound through his teeth.

"You're so well on in your career now, you're so exalted and so secure in your abilities that you've forgotten what it's like to be climbing the rungs at the bottom of the ladder." She stared once again out of the window, feeling her eyes blazing like torches into the darkness. "Those rungs at the bottom are very hazardous; they feel as slippery as greased poles. You only have to make one wrong move and you fall off. Right back down to the bottom again."

Rex was silent for a time. They turned into her road. It was full of cars, parked there for the night. He drew up as close as he could to her flat, positioned the wheels precisely against the kerb and switched off the engine.

There was a tense, waiting silence between them.

"Have I really behaved so badly?" he said in a low voice.

"I just hated it that you patronised me by pretending the fiasco with Gable was nothing much to worry about. You wouldn't have done that with anyone else. You certainly wouldn't have done it with anyone who you thought had some decent prospects in front of them. You'd have torn strips off them and asked them what the hell they were playing at. You'd have given them a real roasting and told them to pull their finger out, or else."

He bit on his lip, forced to admit that what she said was true.

Tessa had not yet said all she wanted to. "I was expecting to be told off, to be shouted at. I felt I deserved it. And if that's what you'd done, I'd probably have shouted back and after that I'd have felt a whole heap better."

"Yes," he agreed.

"Instead you handled me as though I were a precious piece of china. You treated me as though I was a little girl who's messed up the song she's practised like mad to sing at the party, and all she needs is a kindly pat on the head to reassure her it was just fine, that it didn't really matter a bit."

"Oh God!" he groaned. "That's dreadful. Is that really how it seemed to you?"

"Yes."

Into the long silence that followed there was an intensifying throb of tension and electricity. Rex fancied he could feel each dark pulsing beat of blood being pumped from his heart.

"I did behave in the way you describe, I admit it," he said slowly. "You're right."

She sighed.

He leaned his shoulder against the door, holding himself as far away from her as possible, not daring to trust himself if they should chance to touch each other. The merest unplanned brush of his arm against hers would topple all his firm resolve not to impose himself on her. Kiss her so that she gasped out loud, caress the whole of her tiny, delicate body, enter her and make her his. *Sweet heaven!*

"I'm very sorry," he murmured.

Tessa made a little movement, turning towards him, leaning a little closer. "Have you any idea," she said with low urgency, "what it's like to humiliate yourself in the eyes of the man you've fallen madly in love with?"

His mind bucked and shied away from the words. It took a moment to understand what she had told him. Further seconds to make himself believe it.

He turned towards her. But still he did not touch her. "Have you any idea what it's like to try to reach out to the woman who's been making your heart beat with pain and longing for weeks? To reach out to her when you know she's hurting like hell, and all you want to do is take the pain away?"

She sat, silent and motionless, looking straight ahead of her, making him feel as though she had completely forgotten about him. His eyes moved slowly over the shape of her head, the curve of her neck. She was so extraordinarily tiny, so very slender that his heart contracted with a desire fuelled by a tenderness and male protectiveness he feared she would despise and reject. He guessed that he could span her waist with his hands. And yet her breasts under the simple white shirt were full and rounded.

"Oh no!" she exclaimed suddenly, her body jerking, her voice husky and shaky.

"What? What is it?" He didn't need to ask. He already knew. She'd guessed what was going on in his head, what was going on in his *body*. She was revolted by him, by his lust and desire. When she had talked about humiliating herself in front of the man she loved, the last man she was referring to was him. Of course she was not talking about him, she was talking about her boyfriend, who would have obviously been eagerly watching the programme, noting her every syllable. How could he, Rex, have been such a stupid fool to make such a simple mistake? He tried to sound calm as he spoke, to control his dismay and desperation.

"That car down the road . . ." she said.

He frowned, bemused. He stared hard at her and then followed her gaze. "The Aston Martin?"

"Yes. It's Oliver's."

"Oliver! Your boyfriend?"

"Yes."

"Impressive," he said, attempting to sound light and casual whilst hot jealousy ripped through him at the thought of this unknown boyfriend, this Oliver who was Tessa's man. Did this Oliver make love to her? Did he slowly undress her and kiss every inch of her fragile, silky body?

"I'd completely forgotten," said Tessa. "It's the night of the dinner-party I'd been planning with Trudie, my flatmate." She put a hand up to her face, recalling that she had not given the occasion a single thought after Trudie's excited speculations. "Oh hell!"

"Who was coming?"

"Oliver . . ."

"Of course. And who else?" he asked stiffly. Not more potential lovers, he thought groaning in agony at the mere idea.

"You!"

"Me!"

"Yes. Trudie's dead keen to meet you."

"Oh, marvellous! So the two of you thought you'd do a little matchmaking did you?" His tone was icy with sarcasm. "You put your heads together and planned the ultimate aphrodisiac dinner. You'd turn off the lights, just leaving the candles flickering. Get me nicely in the mood for a spot of romancing. Me and Trudie. Great heaven! I've only just escaped from Vicky's attempts to matchmake me and a yoga freak."

She put her fingers on his arm. "Rex. Things have changed since Trudie and I planned our cosy little dinner."

He plucked her fingers from his arm and returned them to her. "Yes. And?"

"And now I wouldn't let you within a mile of Trudie unless I'd dumped her in a slimy pond first, chopped off all her hair and wrapped her in a sack."

He tilted his head, suspicious and wary.

"Rex, Rex," she whispered softly.

"Tell me. Just spell it out," he snapped. "Straight down the line."

"I thought I already had."

"No. So just do it now!"

"I've finished with Oliver," she told him gently. "It's all over." She reached out and stroked his cheek. "It's you, Rex. Just you."

He stared blankly ahead. "I can't believe it."

"Why? I'd have thought women fell in love with you in droves?"

He gave a dry laugh. In a way that was true. Women did seem attracted to him. And yes, they probably had fallen in love with him – in their twos and threes if not in droves. He realised now how callously he had sometimes treated this small procession of worshippers. Before Tessa came into his life it had been so long since he had experienced the dizzy sensation of falling in love that he had been rather casual about the whole business. He admitted to himself with shame that he had become used to having the upper hand with women. Become accustomed to having them fall in love with him, throw themselves at him, beg for his favours. And all he had wanted from them was a little warm companionship in his bed.

But with Tessa it had been quite a different scenario. Tessa was very much her own person. And she was young and independent and vibrant. She had her own career, her own money. She had a boyfriend. And she had never seemed to regard him, Rex, as anything but her boss.

"Rex?" she prompted.

He looked at her, at this tiny, spirited sprite who had bewitched him in such a short space of time and he felt himself to be as much at sea as a gauche lad of sixteen on a first date.

Tessa could see the strain in his face; she could see that his eyes were resting on her mouth. She made a barely visible move towards him and then suddenly they were in each other's arms and their lips were pressed together. For a few moments the world of reality spun away into the distance.

As he touched her a deep tenderness swelled inside him. It

155

was a sensation he had been starved of for so long that he had almost forgotten its power and sweetness.

His hands moved over her hair, feeling its incredible softness and its magical resilience. His lips caressed her nose, her cheeks, the tiny delicate lobes of her ears. And then returned hungrily, greedily to her lips.

"Rex," she whispered eventually, "I can't go back into my flat. Not tonight . . ."

"No," he agreed. "You damned well can't. You're coming home with me!" His hand tightened round her arm, letting her know that there was no way they could hold back from finishing what they had started. He stroked the back of her neck.

There was a tiny pause. "Yes," she said, making his heart bound. "Yes, yes, yes."

Seventeen

Rex's heart thundered as he started the engine and pulled the car away from the kerb. He had to concentrate hard, feeling himself almost blinded by the sensations sweeping through him. She had said 'yes' to him. After all the uncertainty of the past weeks, the disappointments and foul-ups of the day before, after all the brittleness of this evening when he had felt as distanced from her as though he were at the other side of the world, she had said 'yes'.

As he accelerated down the road, he looked back at the windows of her flat. "It's well past midnight," he said, his voice feeling tight in his throat. "What's this Oliver bloke doing in your flat on his own with your flatmate?"

"A number of extremely naughty and exciting things, I would imagine," said Tessa.

"The fickle bastard!" growled Rex.

"I think I drove him to desperation," Tessa admitted regretfully. "Poor Olly. He wanted heat and passion. He wanted the works, the full monty, and all I ever gave him was the occasional peck on the cheek."

"Good."

"I was just saving myself up for you," she said, suddenly mischievous.

"Don't you dare tease!"

"I won't tease," she promised.

When they reached Rex's house, he leapt out of the car to hold the door open for her. Linked together they ran up the steps and Rex unlocked his front door.

As she walked through into his house his arms reached out and he pulled her hard against him. He bent his head and his kisses were like fire, heating her, making her glow with longing.

Tessa threw out a hand to steady herself, feeling that her legs were threatening to collapse beneath her. Her fingers connected with something smooth and shiny which slid off the edge of the table and fell to the floor with a beep and a clatter.

"Oh dear," she murmured. "Your phone."

"Leave it!" he commanded. His tone was so sharp, so forceful that she glanced up at him, her eyes wide and questioning.

"You're so strong, Rex," she said, stroking her fingers over his collar bone. "So big and powerful. In body and in spirit. Sometimes I feel overwhelmed."

"I'm sorry, I'm sorry." He looked distressed.

"No, don't be sorry," she murmured. "That's what drew me to you in the first place." After I'd stopped loathing you for it, she said to herself silently, amazed that she could once have felt such antipathy for him, when now . . .

This time when he drew her against him his embrace was gentle and protective. Yet even so, Tessa was acutely conscious of the difference she felt in Rex's embrace in contrast with Oliver. Whereas Oliver was willowy, silky and pliable, Rex was all solidity, strength and firmness.

She rested her face against the muscles of his chest. She could hear his heart beating, fast and urgent. She sensed his need and felt an echoing surge of desire.

As they held each other she became aware of the soft warble of the telephone as it lay on the floor. She had a strange confused feeling that it might be for her, even though she knew that was impossible as no one knew she was here with Rex at his house. And at the same time she felt that even if it had been for her then the person who was calling was trying to reach another Tessa, in another life. She had changed, and nothing mattered now except Rex.

He gave no sign of responding to the phone's demand either. After a few warbles it stopped.

Rex sighed. He rested his hand on her throat, then he put his fingers under her chin and tilted her face up to his. She was confronted with his steady, assessing amber gaze – a man used to be being in charge of things; of people, of situations. And yet just at this moment he was a man who was vulnerable, who was pleading with her not to subject him to the pain of a rejection.

Tessa knew how aroused he was, and her desire for him surged through her, ripping into her veins with breathtaking force. She felt his hands on her skin and her lips opened against his, letting him in, thrilling as his tongue entwined around hers.

As they kissed she took one of his hands and drew it inside her shirt, longing for him to cradle the weight of her breasts. Her nipples were already hard and erect and as his fingers made contact with them she heard herself give a low groan of desire.

He pushed her shirt over her shoulders, some of the buttons gave a little tearing snap. She responded by pulling his shirt open so that she could press her bared breasts against his naked chest. And as their skin touched a shiver raced through her body.

She heard him murmuring her name, over and over. And then with one swift, sure movement, he gathered her into his arms and carried her into the room beyond where he lay her down on a long leather sofa. She drew him down beside her, her breathing rapid and jagged. He unzipped her skirt and slithered it over her hips. Then with a firm two-handed grip he pulled off her panties.

"Now!" she whispered fiercely, parting her legs wide, aching for him to come inside her. He drew his hand between her thighs, making her gasp with pleasure as his fingers caressed her soft waiting flesh. She gave a high singing moan and arched her back in a sudden gesture of ecstasy.

And then he was thrusting up into her, hard and deep. And as he did so he stroked her breasts once more and covered her mouth with his, staring down into her eyes.

At first they were like strangers dancing together for the first time; not quite merging with each other's rhythm, still a little awkward with their new intimacy and overwhelmed with the anxiety to please their partner.

Rex held himself back a little, trying to time his strokes with her responses. He saw the anxiety, deep in her eyes, the curious reticence of a female who, despite her hot arousal, on the very brink of reverberating ecstasy does not take sexual surrender lightly.

"It's all right, darling. You're very safe," he told her. "There's no need to fight me, no need to resist." It was hard for him to be controlled, hard for him not to think only of his own climax which was very near. She was small and tight inside, giving him exquisite pleasure. He closed his eyes, praying that his thrusts did not hurt her. And then, miraculously, he felt the final shreds of her resistance dissolve. She was moving with him, in perfect harmony, she was giving herself to him fully and the sensation was unbearably sweet and precious.

"My love," she breathed, lacing her hands around his neck and pulling him even deeper inside her. He felt a tight spasm of ecstasy spiral between them.

Opening his eyes he saw that waves of pleasure were moving across her face like the play of light over the velvety flank of a hillside. And then his own pleasure exploded in a shower of incandescent sparks. Moments of ecstasy almost unbearably sharp and intense.

They lay together, their hands softly twined, as they allowed themselves to sink back into reality. Tessa looked around her, feeling that the very air in the room was tingling with the sensations they had both experienced.

She was aching with pleasure, her body flushed with Rex's touch. She could still feel the delicious little after-shocks of lovemaking, gleaming tremors of sexual delight as she relived the way he had done certain things to her, using all the devices he knew to bring her to a peak of rapture.

A little while later Tessa raised herself on her elbows and looked down at Rex. She stroked his chest, and bent to kiss his thick rumpled hair.

"You taste lovely," she said. "You taste of fresh air and moorland rain and maleness."

"Very poetic," he murmured. "Tell me some more."

"No. No more flattery, not for a while. Vicky told me I mustn't let you get it all your own way."

"Huh!" He pulled her down to him and kissed her lips hard.

Moments passed.

Suddenly Tessa pulled away from him, a teasing, elf-like grin on her face. "Us being here like this, do you think it's a prime case of bonding together in the face of stress in the workplace?" She chuckled, her irrepressible mischief bubbling over.

"You mean you and me against Lady C?" he suggested with a lazy, contented smile.

"Mmm." Suddenly her eyes clouded, and she turned quickly away from him so he would not see her discomfiture. The memory of her failure and humiliation on the programme the day before still refused to leave her, even now when her happiness with Rex was warming her to her very heart and soul.

"It's pure and simple falling in love," Rex said, putting his fingers under her chin and forcing her to face him. "Finding the person you can see yourself wanting to move through the future with."

Tessa said nothing for a time. Then she sighed with pleasure, whispering, "Now who's the poetic one?"

She got up, found her shirt and shrugged it on. "Can I wash my face, get a drink of water?" she asked Rex.

"Through the hall and down the stairs," he said. "Don't be long, I could get lonely."

Groping in the dim light Tessa made her way into the hall. Her bare toes connected with something cold and smooth. A red light flickered and there was the whirring of an answerphone tape. And after that a mellow unmistakable voice which sent shudders through her body. She put a hand to her mouth to stifle the reflex gasp of shock.

"Tessa. This is Royston Gable. I was simply calling to thank you for the excellent opportunity you gave me earlier on to talk about my work. I so much enjoyed talking to you. I do hope you felt the same."

Tessa stood rigid, pressure building on her as she listened to that smooth, silkily menacing voice.

"Good night, Tessa," Gable's voice went on. "Do take great care, won't you?"

There was the click as the connection went off, the scratchy hum of the tape as it rewound.

Tessa stood staring into the silent shadows of the dark hall, her lips numb, her scalp prickling with electric sensation.

Eighteen

Rex came up behind her, snapping on the light and making her blink. He had pulled on a sweater and trousers, but his feet were bare. "Who was that?"

"*Him*," she whispered, pulling her shirt tight around her, feeling her body and limbs as cold as ice.

Rex ran a hand through his hair. "I'm sorry?"

"Him! Royston Gable."

Rex heard the trace of impatience in her voice, her frustration that he had not instantly realised that she could be speaking of no one else but Gable. Damn the bloody man to hell!

"At this time of night!" he said sharply.

"It was a message on the answerphone. It must have been him calling when the phone rang earlier."

"Christ! What a nerve."

Tessa bent and retrieved the phone from the floor. With great care and deliberation she set it on the table beside the pile of notebooks and directories. She then sank down on a nearby carved oak chair. The coldness of the wood bit into her naked thighs. "How did he know I was here?" Tessa murmured. "How did he know to ring me here, just at the moment we arrived?"

"A calculated guess," Rex suggested hopefully, not really believing it. "After all, he knows that we work in the same organisation. He saw us together last week."

Tessa looked up at him shaking her head. "I don't think so. Royston Gable doesn't make calculated guesses. He decides on the information he wants and then goes methodically about obtaining it."

Rex made a tight, angry sound in his throat. "I'm going to get something to put round you. You're shivering so hard I

163

can hear your teeth chattering." He strode off and Tessa heard him banging doors, opening drawers. There was the sound of crockery and the 'ping' of the microwave.

When he came back he had a dark blue dressing gown draped over one arm and two steaming mugs of coffee grasped in his hands.

"Here!" he said, draping the gown around her shoulders, and placing a mug on the table beside her. "Drink that. Get yourself warmed up." He touched her cheek briefly and then sat down on the oak chair that was twin to hers.

They sat in silence for a few moments. Tessa cradled the hot mug in her hands, gaining comfort as her frozen fingers began to come to life.

"I suppose Gable must have been following you," Rex said. It was a reasonable enough conclusion but one which gave him a jolt of unpleasant shock as he said it out loud.

"Yes," Tessa agreed. She took a sip of her coffee. It felt like fire as it slipped down her throat. "Are you ex-directory, Rex?"

"No."

She sighed. "Thank God for that, at least we don't have to agonise over how he got your telephone number. He simply looked it up."

"Tessa," Rex said sharply, "I've no intention of doing any agonising whatsoever as far as Gable is concerned." His eyes bored into hers, stern and unrelenting. "He's obviously a formidably able man. But from what I've observed since I've got to know more about him, he's also an obsessive, manipulative crank. And he's most certainly not a guy worth losing any sleep over."

Tessa pushed a strand of hair from her cheek. "Do you remember my saying earlier on that if you really knew me, you'd realise what had been bugging me ever since the interview yesterday?"

"Only too well."

"It was unfair of me to say that, because I know you understood perfectly how I felt about caving in at the end of the interview, even though you tried to cover it up."

"Not a mistake I shall repeat," he said.

Master of Destiny

"But no one could have guessed that I wasn't simply talking about being furious with myself for messing things up. Not even you. How could you?"

He put his mug down on the table. "Tessa, what are you trying to say?"

"There was a moment in that interview when I suddenly felt jagged and somehow dislocated, as though I didn't quite know where I was, what I was doing." She lifted her head, confronting Rex's steady, intense stare. "I was horribly scared. In fact for a few seconds I felt physically sick with fear."

Rex frowned, rerunning those moments when he had sat watching the monitor, baffled at what had so suddenly and unexpectedly disturbed her professional poise. He said slowly, "So it was some out-of-the-blue sensation of being in danger that made you lose a grip on the interview?"

"A sensation of being in danger is a good description," she agreed, rubbing her hands over her chilled knees. "But it was not exactly out-of-the blue. I certainly knew where it was coming from. And in a way I'd been anticipating it."

He gave her a baffled look.

"He kept staring at me, fixing me with those cold blue eyes," Tessa said. "And somehow I couldn't make myself look away. I was fascinated and repulsed at the same time. But I couldn't look away."

Rex experienced a moment of blinding rage and jealousy. She was talking about Gable as though she were in thrall to him. Almost as though she were in love with him. And only minutes ago he had thought that he, Rex, had made Tessa his alone. He swiftly relocated his thoughts, understanding that her anxiety, her need and her alarm far outstripped any petty thoughts of sexual rivalry. He sprang up and knelt beside her. He wrapped his arms around her and held her close. "Darling, listen to me." He gave her shoulders a little shake. "Listen, Tessa! Royston Gable is just a man, not some kind of wicked demon."

"Is he?" she whispered.

Rex held her away from him, looking into her adorable, delicate face with its wonderful, kissable ginger-biscuit freckles. "Yes. He is."

"So why is he tracking me? Why is he phoning me up after midnight?"

"It's quite possible he's become attracted to you," Rex said, trying to sound calm and reasonable. He stroked her cheek very tenderly. "I have no difficulty in identifying with that. And we both know that he has a reputation for liking gorgeous, exceptional women." He held her close again, fierce and protective. "Although, God forgive me, if he starts trying to come on to you I'll take him apart with my bare hands."

He began to kiss her again, her neck, her hair, a light touch on her lips. He felt desire stirring in him again, a desperate need to be close to her.

She stroked her hands over him as he caressed her, but there was a strange vagueness about her touch. There was tenderness in it, but no urgency. And when he drew back from her he could tell that her thoughts were still bound up with the fears she had just voiced to him.

Rex was a passionate man. But he was also sensitive, especially to the needs of those he loved. Sighing internally he realised that he would have to forgo the pleasure of further lovemaking until Tessa was once again rational and reassured. A brief hot spark of rage against Royston Gable surged up within him. If Gable had walked in through the door at that moment, Rex swore he would have attacked him and given no mercy.

He took her hands in his, cradling them gently. He schooled his voice to be low and calm. "Tessa!" he said softly, as though calling her from sleep. "What exactly did Gable say to make you so afraid?" He tried to imagine how a man could manage to instil such fear – to intimidate such a confident and hard-headed young woman, and in the middle of a live TV show for goodness sake.

She let out a sigh.

"Do you remember?" he insisted. "Can you tell me his actual words?"

"Oh yes, I remember," she said, looking regretful. "But it all sounds so harmless. I feel really stupid to repeat it out loud. You won't be convinced."

"Trust me."

"All right. This is what he said: 'Don't go too far, Tessa. You know why'. Nothing very sensational, you'll have to agree!"

"It was the way in which he said it which alarmed you," Rex suggested.

"Yes. Exactly."

"Don't go too far. You know why." Rex repeated, musing. "And do you know why?"

"Yes, I think I do – in part, at least." She stopped.

"Well?"

Briefly Tessa explained to him about the list of names which had showed up on Gable's computer whilst she was alone in his library. She went on to describe her immediate hunch that these names were somehow significant. And that the initial presentiment had only grown stronger as the days went by.

"He's a research scientist," Rex cut in, unimpressed. "His work is in the field of human behaviour. There doesn't seem anything sinister to me about his having lists of names and addresses on his computer. They'll simply be records of the subjects he uses in his surveys."

"Yes," Tessa agreed.

"In fact it would be surprising if his computer didn't hold lists of names."

"Yes."

"You're not sounding very convinced!"

"I think he guessed that I'd seen the names . . ."

"So! What if he did guess? It's no big deal." He stared at her, frowning. "Is it?"

"No, I suppose not." She spoke like a child who is being chided for a misdemeanour she did not commit. A child who is simply resigned to putting up with all the disbelief and unpleasantness because arguing seems futile.

Rex let go of her hands and thrust his fingers through his hair. "Tessa will you please just tell me what this is all about!"

"I wish I knew," she responded, her face pale and hunted looking.

His eyes locked with hers. "There's something else, isn't there? Tell me."

"Besides seeing the names, I also managed to copy some of them down."

"A true media hound!" Rex interposed, his stern features suddenly relaxing into a smile.

"Yes. I suppose that's true, I did it almost automatically. I was really curious, you see. I had this feeling I'd be able to find something out about those names. Maybe something I could use on the programme."

"But it didn't work out like that."

"Well, I have found one or two things out. But I couldn't use the information on the programme. And now," she said with a hollow laugh, "I can't stop thinking about that little phrase, 'Curiosity killed the cat'. I wish to God I'd never seen those names."

"Oh, come on!"

"He knows," Tessa said bluntly. "Gable knows that I saw the names. He knows that I made a note of some of them. And he knows that I'm curious."

"How could he? He didn't see you looking at the computer. He didn't see you scribbling anything down."

"No. I'm pretty sure he didn't."

"Well then?"

"He just knew. By some kind of intuition. Maybe my face looked guilty, I don't know." Her teeth bit fiercely into her lip. "Oh, but he knew," she exclaimed with a burst of conviction. She recalled the phone call at the restaurant on that last night with Oliver. Gable's smooth-as-silk voice: *You have something of mine, Tessa.*"

"Your face is certainly very open, very readable," Rex said, his voice low and husky as he stroked his fingers tenderly down her cheek. "So, tell me, what did you find out when you followed up the names?"

"I already knew they were all aged twenty, because the dates of birth were filled in beside their names. Now I know that the addresses and phone numbers are current ones, because every house I phoned confirmed that a person of that name lived there."

Rex shrugged. "So?"

"So at least I know this list is either a new one, or an old one that's been carefully revised and updated."

Another shrug.

"All of the young people are in higher education, none is in a job as yet. Two are at Oxford, one at the Sorbonne and one at some college up north."

Rex shook his head. "That's not exactly riveting news, my sweet one. Remember I'm an old hand in this business. There has to be real blood and guts on the carpet before I start getting interested, let alone excited."

Tessa smiled. It was perhaps the first time she had done so since she had listened to Royston Gable's recorded message on Rex's phone. "No, I suppose you're right."

Rex stood up and began to pace up and down. "Right! Let's try to make some sense out of all this jumble of fact and conjecture. We need to get things into some kind of rational perspective."

"Is that a polite way of telling me I'm being irrational?" Tessa asked sharply.

"Yes. And that's not a criticism, simply an observation." He did some more pacing. "OK. This is how I see it. The bottom line of all this is that you've stumbled on a list of names of Royston Gable's research subjects. Some pure, simple, nuts and bolts information. Nothing more."

"Yes," she agreed cautiously.

"In which case, you've nothing to worry about," Rex insisted, determined to overcome her scepticism, her stubborn refusal to be reassured. "I suppose Gable might regard the stuff on his screen as highly confidential information and he could well be annoyed if he had reason to think you'd had sight of it. But what reason does he have to suspect that? And, even if he does suspect, what evidence has he got?"

"None, I suppose." she agreed wearily.

"He didn't see you making your jottings. He wasn't in the room. He simply wasn't there to see you? Am I right?"

"Yes."

"So whatever he believes or fancies that he knows is merely a figment of his imagination?"

"Yes."

"You're going to tell me next that he has internal TV security. That he was watching you on a monitor."

"No," Tessa countered. "There were no cameras in evidence. I looked."

Rex raised his eyebrows. "Did you indeed? That's good. You were professional, you were careful. You were rational. What can you *possibly* have to be frightened about?"

Tessa made a small low sound in her throat. How could she ever convince Rex of the insidious, invisible power she sensed surrounding Royston Gable? She was talking of feelings and intuitions, of insubstantial dark shadows. Whereas Rex wanted to deal in facts he could see and hear and verify. Maybe a strong, confident man like Rex would never be able to understand the power of vague, formless chimeras.

"All you have in your possession is a list of names and addresses," he said crisply. "You can hardly wreak havoc on the research volunteers with that kind of innocuous information can you? Or on him, for that matter."

"No." She shook her head, tilting it away from him so he could not see her expression.

"You're not planning on doing any further investigations, are you?" Rex demanded, suddenly guessing at her unspoken intentions.

"I don't know."

"Does that mean yes?"

"Probably."

"Oh for God's sake, Tessa! Just forget it. Leave it alone!"

Tessa stared up at him, her eyes flaring with determination. "No, Rex, you leave *me* alone to make my own decisions."

He swung around. "What?"

"This isn't a work issue. You can't dictate to me on this. We're not discussing research for a programme."

"So why on earth bother with it?"

"Because I need to know."

"Christ!"

"I'm not asking for work time to do this. I'll do whatever needs to be done in my own time," she told him quietly.

"I'd hoped your out of work time would be spent with me," he said, his voice tight.

She was silent for a few moments. The force of his need

charged the atmosphere with electric tension. "Oh Rex," she murmured.

"I need you, Tessa," he said in a low voice. "I need you to be with me. There is something that's happened between us that makes me know I can't do without you – and I'm not just talking about the sex, although God knows I don't think I'm going to be able to keep my hands off you. Can't you feel it too?"

She nodded, unable to speak.

"I need you to be with me to build on what we've started together. We need time with each other. To be quiet together, to make love, to talk to each other. And we need to do it now, in the present. Now. I want you to come to me, to live with me, to be my one and only love." He clasped both of her hands tightly in his and forced her to look at him.

Tessa saw that the powerful, decisive Rex was momentarily bewildered and vulnerable, that he was searching her face for a crumb of reassurance that he was loved. Not as a figure of power. Just for himself.

"I will come and live with you," she said, stroking his face with gentle hands.

"Soon! Very soon! Preferably now! My God, you certainly need someone to take care of you, you're so bloody single-minded and impulsive. Say yes, Tessa."

"Yes, yes," she said softly. "I will come as soon as I can arrange things. But . . ."

"Yes!"

"You mustn't clip my wings," she said softly.

He looked horrified. "I'd never do that!"

"Wouldn't you? What were you trying to do just a few moments ago?"

"Keep you safe," he murmured, his face so full of tenderness and concern that she felt she would never be able to tear herself away from him, not even for a moment. All she wanted was to be close to him.

"I have to live my own life," she said, quiet but resolute. "Make my own mistakes."

"Yes," he agreed with a long sigh.

"You're used to being a boss, Rex," she told him. "But

we're not at work now. And although I'm wildly in love with you, I don't intend to dance to every one of your tunes."

"I'm hearing your message loud and clear," he responded, his voice tight.

"Don't look so offended. You know you couldn't truly love a woman who just fell in with everything you suggested," she said. "You're the sort of man who wants more than a cuddly, sexy toy."

"Yes," he said in a low voice. "You're right. A compliant woman isn't my sort of woman at all."

As his eyes looked into hers she had the odd thought that he was weighing her words and her philosophy against something in his past. Some*one* in his past. Some dark secret anguish he would perhaps one day feel able to share with her openly.

He put his hand inside her shirt. "Do you think," he said with a wry smile, "that you could forget about the battle of the sexes for while. Maybe even put Royston Gable to the back of your mind? Just for an hour or so?"

He watched her face as he caressed her. He held her against him and spoke her name, murmured endearments. There were so many other things he wanted to say too, to share with her the secrets of his heart. But for the moment the language of their bodies moving together would have to suffice.

Nineteen

Trudie was in the bathroom when Tessa returned to her flat. It was seven in the morning. A grey mist thickened the air, and the damp London streets looked sleepy and unrefreshed.

Tessa had been quite prepared to find Trudie still in bed, quite probably with Oliver. However there was no sign of the Aston Martin in the road, and when Tessa glanced through the open door of Trudie's bedroom she noticed that the bed was neatly made, its covers plump and smooth, whereas normally it looked as though the entire Arsenal football team had trampled over it.

Tessa went through to the kitchen and peered into the fridge. The remains of last night's dinner confronted her: two avocados going brown at the edges, some cold fried potatoes and an almost completely demolished chocolate mousse which reeked of brandy. Tessa took out a carton of grapefruit juice and poured some into a glass.

She sat at the kitchen table, and thought about the incredible events of the last few hours. It was a very long time since she had made love with a man. She recalled her one previous lover, a drama producer with sad, dark eyes who had separated from his wife and moved in with Tessa for a time. He had made use of her to soothe his pain, and then returned home to try to mend his marriage. This man had been a gentle and courteous lover, his caresses had been warm and arousing, but what had happened between her and Rex during the previous night had been of an entirely different nature.

Rex had possessed her totally. He had overwhelmed her with the power of his need. She could feel the echoes of his touch now, on her lips, on her neck, on her breasts, and the memory brought a flush to her face. Her whole body was

173

filled with a tender, throbbing ache of pleasure. Inside her flesh was still heated from the aftermath of his lovemaking. She was like a fire stubbornly continuing to smoulder on a dull misty morning.

She heard the bathroom door open and slow, stealthy footsteps approaching the kitchen.

"Oh! Tessa!" exclaimed Trudie, her eyes wide and surprised-looking, as though Tessa were some kind of apparition.

Tessa swivelled around and smiled at her flatmate. Trudie looked pink and glowing. Her long hair was freshly shampooed and gleaming. It struck Tessa that if Trudie had enjoyed a night of passion then she had made very sure to wash away all the traces.

"Where did *you* get to last night?" Trudie asked, her voice hesitant rather than challenging.

"Rex invited me to dinner at his sister's house. I completely forgot it was the night of our joint dinner party. I'm really sorry, Trudie."

Trudie stared at her warily. And then, without warning, she burst into tears.

"Oh, love!" Tessa reached out and took one of Trudie's hands. "What is it?"

Trudie gulped and snorted and sniffled. "I've been . . . I'm so . . . Oh, I can't . . ."

Tessa got up, stood beside Trudie and cradled her in her arms. "Come on, it's OK. It's all OK." She stroked Trudie's hair and rubbed her soft fleshy back with comforting hands. Feeling Trudie's large heavy breasts pressing against her own, Tessa had a sudden realisation of the force of Trudie's sexy voluptuousness. She had an earthy roll-me-over-in-the-hay quality about her, like an enchanting Regency trollope. And what's more she was one of the most amiable, least vixenish women Tessa had ever come across. Even Tessa's own mother, who was nearly a saint, was more shrewish than Trudie.

"I've been such a bitch," moaned Trudie. "I've been a real cow."

Tessa patted her some more. "Have you really?"

"And you're so nice, Tessa. You're so good."

"Oh, I have my moments of wickedness!"

174

"No, you don't. You're in control of things. Of yourself. Not like me." Trudie raised her head. Her eyes were red and slippery from crying, her nose pink and quivering. She looked like a depressed rabbit.

"What have you been up to, Trude?" Tessa asked, smiling and feeling worryingly maternal.

More tears and sniffling from Trudie. Looking down at herself Tessa noticed that the front of her shirt was now quite wet.

"I can't tell you," wailed Trudie. "I simply can't."

"Never mind. You can tell me all in good time. Just sit there and relax. I'll make some fresh coffee," Tessa said in practical tones, taking the kettle to the sink and filling it. "Did Oliver come last night?" she asked evenly, not realising until the words were out that they could be construed as both apt and ironically sarcastic.

"Yes. He was furious when you didn't show up."

"Oh dear."

Trudie rubbed the end of her nose with her fingers. She looked up at Tessa with a blend of bewilderment and accusation. "How could you do that to him? Stand him up? He's really nice."

"Yes, I know he is." Tessa spooned coffee into mugs, adding two spoons of sugar for Trudie.

"You must be crazy, letting him slip through your fingers," said Trudie with a touch of peevishness, finally letting Tessa know beyond doubt what had been going on.

"I didn't stand him up," said Tessa honestly. "I'd never have deliberately done anything as cruel as that to hurt him. I simply forgot about our dinner party. I mentioned it to Olly the last time I saw him and after that it went clean out of my mind."

Trudie's face registered a procession of clearly identifiable emotions. Surprise, disbelief, suspended disbelief and then renewed doubt. She was like a new recruit at drama school, practising her range of facial gymnastics.

"I'd had a tough day at work," Tessa went on. "I wasn't thinking straight."

"You couldn't really be that keen on him, if you forgot a

date like that," Trudie ventured, looking at Tessa with eyes full of hope.

Tessa realised that the time for confession was close and that she must be very careful about the reaction she would make to Trudie's revelation. Taking up an indignant stand as the jealous, deceived girlfriend, besides being disgracefully hypocritical, would be likely to catapult Trudie into a state of prolonged hysterical remorse. On the other hand a casual, cheery reception would dent Trudie's already fragile self-confidence on the man front. It would not do at all for Trudie to have the impression she was simply taking on Tessa's cast offs, little better than pinching the already picked-over bones from her flatmate's dinner plate.

"Tess," said Trudie, dropping her voice and her head, "I've something to tell you. It's really dire. You're going to hate me for ever . . ."

"Go on." Tessa put down her mug of coffee and turned her gaze slowly towards Trudie.

"Oliver and I – we got on really well. We had a super evening together. He told me some wonderful stories about the customers he takes out for test drives in those fabulous cars he sells."

Tessa leaned forward. "Yes. And?"

"Well, one thing led to another. We got through quite a lot of wine, you see." Her eyes suddenly gleamed with hope, as though she had seized on a cast iron excuse for what was coming next. "We drank one of the bottles of champagne he brought before we even started dinner. Then we drank the other, and then we went on to the still wine . . ."

Tessa smiled, imagining the scene. She saw Oliver getting more and more carried away with his tales of female customers who tore their clothes off and seduced him over the automatic transmission lever, she saw Trudie getting more and more tipsy, nodding away in encouragement like a mechanical, smiling dolly.

"Yes. What happened then?"

Trudie opened her mouth to speak, then closed it again. She looked at Tessa in wide-eyed appeal.

Tessa realised her friend would never be able to get to the

point. The truth was simply too awful for Trudie to articulate. Tessa put down her mug and drew a thoughtful circle on the table with the tip of her finger. "You said that one thing led to another . . ."

Trudie nodded, her eyes as soft and beseeching as those of a spaniel.

"Are you trying to tell me that you and Oliver . . ." – Tessa allowed a small beating pause to occur – "ended up in bed together?"

"Yes," breathed Trudie. "Oh Tessa, please, please don't hate me!"

Tessa stood up and carried her mug to the sink, walking very slowly as though she were in some kind of daze. She ran water into her mug and washed it with careful fingers. Having placed the mug upside down on the draining board, she leaned against the sink and released a long sigh. "I don't hate you, Trude," she said. "In fact, I'm almost glad about what's happened, even though it's a bit of a shock," she added quickly. "After all Oliver and I have been going out together for quite a while."

"I know, I know. I really thought you two were going to be an item," moaned Trudie. "But just these past few weeks you seem to have been a bit cool with him."

"Yes, I suppose I have." Tessa turned to face Trudie. "In fact I've been a bit of a bitch too, I suppose."

"He seemed really fed up about it. He said you could hardly bear him to lay a finger on you," Trudie continued. Colour swept up into her face as she reflected on this. "Maybe it was a lie. I suppose it could just have been a good line to get me into bed."

"No," Tessa broke in. "I have been pretty much playing the part of the ice maiden with him recently. He wasn't lying to you, Trude."

"I suppose he'll go off me now," Trudie said gloomily. "He'll just put me down as an easy lay."

"No, I don't think that will happen."

"But still," she mused, "he did promise faithfully he'd call me at work this morning. And I really believed him."

"He will call you. He will!" Tessa reassured. She considered telephoning Oliver herself the minute Trudie left the flat and making sure he did call. She walked across the room and put her arms around Trudie once again. "Look, this is all a bit of a mess but it's not a tragedy."

"Isn't it?"

"No. You might have pinched my boyfriend but you haven't stolen my lover, Trudie, because Oliver and I never were lovers. I'm sure you knew that."

"Yes. Even so . . ."

"No, listen, there's more. I've fallen in love with Rex, my boss. I've been in love with him for weeks if I'm going to be totally honest."

"No!"

Tessa smiled. "Yes. I spent the night at his house last night." She allowed time for the full meaning behind the words to sink in.

Trudie suddenly burst into uncontrollable giggles. "Oh, if only I'd have known! I could have really enjoyed myself."

"You mean you've been going through all that agonising for something you didn't enjoy!" Tessa protested.

"Oh, I enjoyed it OK at the time. In fact it was terrific. Oliver's really super in bed. It was just all the guilt afterwards. He wanted to make love again before he left this morning, but I wouldn't let him."

"Because you were worried about my feelings?" Tessa was amazed, and immensely touched. "Oh Trude!"

"Yes," mourned Trudie, sinking back into gloom. "Another reason for him not to call me. I'm a cold, hard-hearted bitch."

"First he's not going to call because you're too hot and randy, and now he's not going to call because you're polar and frigid! Come on, Trude," Tessa smiled.

"Oh," sighed Trudie. "I really like him Tess, I really want this to work. You know me, I just want to settle down and be a fantastically loving and sexy wife and an earth mother with lots of kids."

Sharon Stone will adore you, thought Tessa, feeling one or two weights sliding from her shoulders. "You will, you will. I have this good 'feeling' about it."

"One of your hunches?"

"Yes."

"That's OK then. Your hunches are pretty reliable." Trudie got up from the table, took a tissue from the box on the counter, blew her nose very firmly and settled back into a state of happiness. "Gosh, I'm absolutely famished. What have we got to eat?" She peered into the fridge, yanked out the chocolate mousse and began devour it, scraping around the bowl with her fingers. "Hey," she said after a while, "I saw that interview you did yesterday with that psychologist guy. You were brilliant, Tess, fantastic."

"Did you see all of it?"

"Yes. Oliver had taped it. We watched it together last night. Twice actually."

"You didn't think there was anything strange about the last few minutes?" Tessa wondered.

"No."

"You're sure you were watching it?" Tessa teased.

"Yes. Honest. We watched it before we had dinner. We were being ever so stiff-upper-lip and polite then." Trudie wiped her finger around the bowl once more and licked the results. "Why do you ask? What was strange about it?"

"Oh, I don't know. It didn't go exactly as I'd wanted at the end," Tessa said vaguely. If Trudie and Oliver hadn't noticed anything odd about her performance, she didn't feel inclined to rake over it once again.

"You did go a bit quiet for a few moments," Trudie agreed, frowning with the effort of trying to remember. "But it was all fine after that. He got quite chatty, didn't he?"

Tessa laughed. "You could put it that way."

"Anyway you looked really good on screen. You're one of those people the camera really likes, Tess. But next time you go on get yourself something decent to wear. All that black and white; Oliver said you looked like a nun! You ought to have worn that super pink blouse."

"Yes," Tessa agreed meekly. "But it's in the wash, and generally a bit past it."

"Well, go out and buy another. Buy yourself a new wardrobe. You're getting famous now." Trudie's self-confidence was becoming more buoyant by the minute.

179

"I'll tell you something though," Trudie continued, finally accepting that the chocolate mousse was all gone and placing the bowl in the sink. "That Gable chap's a bit on the scary side."

"You think so?" Tessa became suddenly alert.

"Mmm. Really spooky."

"What makes you say that?"

"It's his eyes," said Trudie thoughtfully.

"What about them?"

"They're creepy. Full of secret thoughts."

"Aren't we all full of secret thoughts?" Tessa asked.

"No!" Trudie sounded genuinely surprised at the suggestion. "Well, I'm not anyway. Of course I would have been if I hadn't come clean about Oliver!" Trudie giggled. "But normally, I'm as pure and transparent as water. You know me, Tess, what you see is what you get!" She began to rummage in the fridge again.

Tessa stroked her fingers over the feathery tendrils of hair at the base of her neck. Just thinking and talking about Gable made prickles run across her skin. And Trudie had sensed something too, even though she had never seen him in the flesh.

Trudie reversed from the fridge clutching the plate of sepia-tinted avocados. "I suppose psychologists are full of other people's thoughts," she mused, with a rare flash of insight. "Do you think they can actually penetrate people's minds?"

"No," said Tessa. "They study human behaviour and attempt to understand people. But they're not all-knowing and all-seeing like gods."

Trudie smothered the avocados in bottled mayonnaise and eyed them with anticipation. "Maybe most of them aren't," she said thoughtfully, "but I wouldn't be at all surprised if he is."

Twenty

Rex was in meetings all morning and through lunchtime. Tessa knew this by careful checking with the administrative staff, who assured her that it would be impossible to get a slot to see him until the middle of the afternoon at the earliest. Even Lucinda was having to wait.

There was a certain satisfaction in the way the various women on the team offered this information, as though Rex were their own private property. And pretty special property at that. Tessa smiled to herself, understanding that whilst Rex was well known and a little feared as a tough boss he was also much admired. And much sighed over by the women on the team, both young and old.

She felt no jealousy, no rivalry. She knew that she and Rex belonged together, that what had happened between them had sealed their future. She wondered what the various adoring females would have thought if they had known she had no need to make appointments to grab a few moments of Rex's attention. She would have him all to herself that evening, and all through the night. And the next night, and the next.

She hugged the thoughts to herself, her own very private, very delicious secret. Not even Trudie, who knew the barebones of last night's events, could guess at how serious she was about this new love affair. As far as Tessa was concerned – passionate, impetuous, idealistic Tessa, it was a bonding which was to be for ever, for better for worse, till death us do part.

She threw open the window of her office and breathed in deep breaths of damp fresh air. Energy and well-being surged within her. Last night Rex had brought her fully alive with the fire and tenderness of his lovemaking. I'm in love, she told herself in delight. I'm madly, deeply in love. Fathoms deep in love. And the man I'm in love with loves me back. She shivered with joy and closed her eyes for a few blissful moments, conjuring up an image of Rex, his tall powerful figure, his shaggy rumpled hair, his wonderful amber eyes, sometimes blazing with the force of his convictions, sometimes dark with passion, sometimes melting with the warmth of his humanity. As she thought of a life ahead with Rex, exhilaration surged within her in rolling waves. And with it came an accompanying sensation of belief in herself. A sense of personal strength and assurance. She felt she could move mountains.

Returning to her desk she saw that there were a number of mountains of the paper variety which required her attention. It was time to get to work. And she was ready for it. She was hungry for it.

First there was the programme with the teenage pop star, Cherry Ripe, to think about. The interview was scheduled for the beginning of next week. Tessa had already read up on a good deal of the star's past history during the previous afternoon and had drafted out a schedule of questions. In addition to her own inquiries the research team had come up trumps with some rather interesting details of Cherry's early life. A keen new member of the team had been doing some very thorough homework and had unearthed a tape of one of Cherry's former primary school teachers giving an interview on a local radio station.

The girl had brought the tape in to Tessa first thing that morning, as soon as she arrived in her office. "I think this could be worth listening to, Tessa," she had said, clearly proud of her achievement.

Tessa had played the tape straight away. It had indeed been worth listening to. The teacher had given a dry, deadpan portrayal of Cherry as a pupil. It had been a witty account, told with subtlety and irony. There had been nothing spelled out, nothing said that the national media would pick up on. But it was not too difficult to read between the lines . . .

Tessa had congratulated the young researcher who had left the office looking decidedly pleased.

Now, as Tessa replaced Cherry Ripe's details in a folder and put them on one side, she reflected that she almost certainly had Cherry's Achilles heel nicely in the bag. Maybe I'll use the information on the programme, maybe not, she thought. But it's good to have the choice.

She checked her watch, which told her lunchtime had come and gone, then looked up the schedule for the rest of the day in her personal organiser, double-checking that there were no urgent appointments which would prevent her pursuing some very private research of her own. She tapped her fingers on the desk top, biting her lip and frowning in concentration. Should she go on with this project? Did she really want to? And was it right to do so? Should she simply take Rex's advice and forget about it?

Leave it alone, Tessa, Rex had warned each time she returned to the topic of Royston Gable and his possible dark secrets. So maybe she should take his advice. Maybe she should simply tear the list up thereby destroying any means of furthering her investigations should she weaken and change her mind at a later date. She knew that if she did, in some way Gable would eventually realise that she was going no further. He would be suspicious for a little while after that, but eventually he'd lose interest in her.

She curled her hand into a fist and brought it down sharply on the desk. "No!" she exclaimed out loud. "No, damn you, Professor Royston Gable. I'm not going to back down."

Unlocking her desk drawer, she took out the notebook on which she had scribbled the names from Gable's computer screen. They were now so familiar they echoed in her head like a tune that wouldn't go away.

She knew without a doubt that there was something important to unravel here. Her intuition told her so, her twitchy female nose for a good human story. Although Tessa had never worked on a big national newspaper, like most TV personnel she was a journalist through and through, and she had always considered that journalism was only a few steps away from detective work. The need to know the truth was paramount in both jobs, whatever the risks.

She flicked through the pages of the notebook. She had made a decision earlier on that she would keep all of her information on this particular investigation confined solely to

her simple, reporter-style notebook. She would feed nothing
into the computer, print nothing out, set up no elaborate files.
Whatever she found out would be confined solely to this one
little notebook and what was in her head.

She looked once more at the brief list of names and the
addresses alongside them. She had contacted each of these
four young people, using the pretext of research connected
with a TV programme on higher educational opportunities as
her reason for wanting to talk to the families. Not exactly
the truth, not exactly a lie. But, from experience, Tessa knew
that few people could resist talking to someone who had a
connection with TV. It was a standing joke amongst media
personnel that the general public would do just about anything
if they thought they stood a chance of appearing on TV. One
of those old chestnut jokes that seemed to contain more than
a few grains of truth.

Apart from encountering no resistance to Tessa's suggestion
that she might visit the young people concerned, there had been
nothing in the various responses that had given her any clues as
to a link between the four names. And so it seemed immaterial
which one she followed up first.

The obvious thing was to choose the name with the most
easily accessible home address. Tessa picked up the phone
and contacted the young man who lived in the East End,
only minutes from Dartbridge's offices in London's restyled
docklands.

He was a student, at home on holiday, studying for examina-
tions in the forthcoming term. He answered the phone himself,
and yes, he was in all afternoon. And yes, he would be very
pleased to talk to her and help in any way he could with her
research. Any time she chose. Right now!

Putting the phone down she felt a pang of guilt, recalling
how she had assured Rex that any researching on the Gable
project would be carried out in her own time. But a firm
appointment for the same day was too good to miss; no media
hound worth their salt stared a gift horse like that in the mouth.
Tessa reassured herself that she had put in countless hours of
unpaid overtime in the past year and that Dartbridge were
hardly losing out if she decided to grab one or two back.

She sat for a while considering the line of questioning she would pursue, making mental notes. Reminded by her growling stomach that it had not been fed for some time, she tossed it a quick snack comprising of a somewhat scuffed chocolate bar she found in one of her desk drawers. She then put on a little make-up, sprayed herself with *Miss Dior* and went down to the car park to collect her car.

Negotiating her way deftly through London's complex mobile tapestry of traffic, she found herself constantly glancing in the rear-view mirror to see if she was being followed. She told herself not to be so twitchy and melodramatic, she tried to ignore the voice whispering insistently in her head: *Should you be really doing this?*

Adam Baddeley was a friendly, courteous young man who answered the door to Tessa with a warm smile of welcome as though she were an old friend.

"Hi! Come in, Miss Clair."

"Call me Tessa, no need to be formal." Tessa walked down a narrow dark hallway, almost tripping over an exercise bike which was propped casually against the wall.

"Sorry. That's Mum's," Adam explained, putting out a hand to steady Tessa. "She bought it when they were all the rage. Used it for about three months and then got fed up."

"I can't think of many more boring ways of spending your time than sitting on a bike pedalling away and getting nowhere," Tessa agreed.

"Exactly. I warned her before she got it," he said with an affectionate smile. "But, you know how it is, parents never listen."

"You have to let them make their own mistakes," Tessa suggested.

"Quite so." His smile was a beautiful wide flash of good spirits – and excellent white teeth. "What would you like me to make for you, Tessa – tea or coffee? The tea's Earl Grey and I've got Columbian freshly ground coffee if you're feeling the need for a more hefty dose of caffeine."

"Earl Grey," Tessa said. "No milk, no sugar."

"Super choice. Won't be a minute." She heard him moving about in the kitchen.

She looked around her. The room was tiny and crammed with furniture. Sitting in the midst of it all Tessa felt she should breathe in to create more space. Everything was clean and neat, but there no attempt to create an atmosphere of elegance. The furnishings were ill assorted in style and their colours were jarring on the eye: the carpet a faded blue with pink flowers, the curtains a jumble of red and orange flares like a bonfire.

Tessa looked at the photographs lined up on the mantelpiece. Several were obviously of Adam when he was younger, some of them taken in the company of a woman who she presumed was his mother. Tessa got up and peered more closely.

"Me and Mum in Brighton when I was ten," Adam said, coming back into the room and noting the line of her gaze.

"She couldn't afford foreign travel, but she took me on holidays all over the place in Britain when I was a kid. I think I'm the only guy in my college who's been to Blackpool and Margate." He gave Tessa her tea and offered a plate of biscuits. "Bath Olivers," he said. "I love traditional English biscuits, don't you?"

"Mmm." Tessa sipped her tea and bit into the biscuit. Her eyes swiftly scanned the room once more and then moved back to Adam. He seemed strangely out of place in this huddled little room, like an exquisite piece of bone china on a jumbled market stall. The perfectly brewed luxury tea didn't fit with the surroundings either. Not to mention the Bath Olivers. She looked at the fan-shaped arrangement of the biscuits on the chipped plate, then looked curiously back at the young man who had so carefully placed them there. She noticed that he was not wearing socks or shoes and that his feet were beautifully shaped, the nails white-tipped and perfectly manicured.

Adam had been staring at the photograph of himself and his mother. He replaced it on the mantelpiece, his movements full of tenderness. "Good old Mum," he said.

Tessa smiled. "There's a lot of affection in your eyes when you talk about your mum," she observed.

"She's a super lady," he said. "She brought me up on her own. My father abandoned us both and pushed off to Australia

186

when I was a baby. I don't remember anything about him." He took a delicate bite of a biscuit as he reflected. "Mum had no money, no family to run to for help. She went out and got herself a job, paid for me to go to nursery school and got on with her life. She's a real fighter."

"And do you take after her?" Tessa asked.

He grinned. "I hope so. My father didn't seem to be a very inspiring role model."

"No, I suppose not." Tessa took another sip of her tea, feeling herself beginning to relax and enjoy herself, talking with this personable young man. She noticed that quite a few moments had gone by and reminded herself that she was on a mission. Rather a delicate one at that. "Well, you're probably wanting to know about my research," she said, clearing her throat with a businesslike cough and taking out her notebook.

Adam shrugged. "I'm quite happy to while away some time chatting to you," he said. "You get starved of company when you're studying for exams. It's a desperately monk-like existence." He smiled again. All the little pinpoints of light in the room seemed to fly to his eyes and dance there.

Wow, he's a serious charmer, thought Tessa, amused. "I work for Dartbridge TV," she told him. "We have a few projects on hand connected with higher education. We're just at the preliminary stage of gathering information at the moment."

"What sort of information?" Adam enquired looking interested.

"Well I suppose the main aim is to identify possible participants for a future documentary series." Tessa experienced faint prickles of guilt as the words of explanation slid smoothly off her tongue. Not quite the truth. Not quite lies. Not quite anything.

"Really!" Adam gave a faintly wicked grin. "How are you rating us as possible contributors?" he asked, leaning forwards towards her. "Is it on our social background or our educational achievement? Or just whether or not we have the plain and simple sexual magnetism to pull in the viewers and up the ratings?"

"You seem to have an excellent knowledge of the TV world," Tessa observed, smiling at him. "Do you know some-one on the inside?"

He shrugged. "No. I've no personal contacts at all. I've met a few media people at Oxford. We get quite a few visiting celebrities at debates and so on. And it's all the rage for undergraduates to want to get into film directing so we have film guys visiting to run seminars occasionally and I've talked to some of them."

"Do you want to get into film directing?" Tessa asked.

Adam gave another smile. This time faintly wistful. "You need money to go into that line of business. Some rich backers."

"How do you get those?"

He raised an expressive eyebrow. "The usual way is to have parents who are loaded." The smile developed into a grin. "I haven't." There was no trace of self-pity, no hint of bitterness.

Tessa made a show of scribbling away in her notebook. "Higher education is very expensive," she observed.

"It's hellishly expensive," he said with feeling. "I couldn't have gone to Oxford at all if I hadn't won an open scholarship." He paused, sipping his tea. "Are you planning to look at the cost of higher education in your documentary? I think you should, Tessa. It's going to be one of the really big issues in the new millenium."

"Yes," said Tessa looking up at him. "Well – I'll bear that in mind."

"What did you graduate in?" he asked, fixing her with his splendid denim-blue eyes.

"I didn't."

"No?"

"After I left school I worked as an assistant for a local radio station. My main responsibilities were answering the telephone and making endless coffees for harrassed disc jockeys."

"And then?"

"I persuaded them to let me do the odd piece of research. And after a couple of years I got a job on the research team at Dartbridge TV. Then . . ." Suddenly she stopped. "You're grilling me Adam," she said cheerily. "It should be the other way round."

He made no attempt to deny this. "You're not simply a researcher now, though, are you?"

There was something in the way he looked at her – so knowing, so assessing – that gave Tessa a tiny jolt.

"I do some fronting now. I'm one of the presenters on a talk show."

"I thought so," he said with satisfaction. "You have a very definite, how can I put it, *air* about you. I couldn't imagine you grinding away as a back-room girl in some dusty little cubby-hole."

"Really!" Now Tessa raised an eyebrow.

"Which talk show?" he asked her.

"*In the Limelight*. It goes out every afternoon. Have you seen it?"

He shook his head. "No. I rarely watch TV. And never in the daytime." His smile was faintly smug, indicating that he had better things to do with his time.

"That's a shame," Tessa said. "If you did you could have seen me fronting the programme yesterday. My guest was the research psychologist Royston Gable." The name seemed to hang in the air, a portent, a trigger. Tessa waited, her pulse quickening a fraction.

"Oh, I know Professor Gable," Adam said. "I've been a guinea pig in one of his major research studies since I was a baby." He looked hard at Tessa, his gaze narrowing slightly. "Didn't you know about that?"

"No," said Tessa airily, making her mind focus on the truthful aspect of her response, hoping her face would not betray the lying aspect.

"So this visit is just one of life's amazing coincidences?" Adam suggested, looking amused.

"I got your name from a computer data bank," Tessa told him, feeling as though she had let a genie out of a bottle and now had no chance of coaxing it back in.

"Ah, one of those so-called random searches?" Adam looked knowing.

Angela Drake

"Mmm." Tessa looked down at her notebook. "So what's the nature of this research project, Adam?"

"It's to chart the development of intelligence from birth to maturity."

"I see. And what did you have to do to contribute to this charting exercise?"

"I had to make myself available for an assessment of intelligence every five years."

"I see. Wasn't that rather daunting?"

"No. It was very interesting. Have you ever taken an intelligence test, Tessa?"

"No."

"Well, let me explain. You have to answer a lot of different kinds of questions: general knowledge, mental arithmetic, vocabulary. And then there are more practical things like jig-saw puzzles and spotting the missing parts in pictures and so on. When I was a kid I really used to look forward to it."

"And did Professor Gable carry out these various tests himself?"

"No. His assistants did the testing." Adam gave a boyish grin. "Some of them were very pretty. It was all terrific fun, in fact."

"A pleasure of a toil?" Tessa suggested with a mischievous smile.

"Oh definitely. And we got paid for it. Well, when I was younger, Mum got the money. But now I get it direct. It's come in very useful."

Tessa wrote rapidly in her notebook. "So you must have been one of the subjects contributing to Professor Gable's latest findings?"

"Yes."

"Do his conclusions worry you? His suggestion that we are more a product of our genes than our environment."

"Not in the slightest," said Adam. "I'm proud to be bright and keen and self-reliant, just like my mother."

"Yes." But what about your father? thought Tessa to herself.

"So do I pass the test?" Adam asked her playfully.

Tessa looked up. "What?"

190

"Shall I be hearing from you again?" His glance was winning and sparkling. "About the documentaries. I'd quite like to be on TV."

"Even though you don't watch it?" Tessa asked with a wry smile, standing up and slotting her notebook into her bag.

"Ah, well, appearing is rather different to viewing, isn't it?" Adam guided her back down the dark hallway. "The former being active and positive, the latter merely passive."

"Yes," agreed Tessa.

Adam shook her hand. "I think this is one of those 'Don't call us, we'll call you, situations," he joked.

"I think you're right."

He laughed, quite unperturbed. There were obviously far too many good things going on in his life for him to be worried about whether or not he was going to appear on the box.

"It's been great talking to you, Tessa," he said. "I've really enjoyed it."

"Me too."

He accompanied her into the street and walked companionably with her to her car.

"Nice car," he commented.

"Yes, I think so," she agreed as she slotted her key into the lock.

"They hold their value very well, these late 80s BMWs," Adam said knowledgeably, bending down and running an exploratory finger over the wheel trims.

"I just liked it," smiled Tessa.

"Yes, but you need to have an eye to market values as well," he told her seriously. "And, of course, if you'd chosen the convertible you'd have made a very nice little investment for yourself."

"Well thanks for the advice, Adam," she returned crisply, glancing at her watch and noting how the time had moved on. "I've never yet found a convertible that didn't let in the draughts. Or leak."

"Oh, you can find ones that are foolproof if you look hard enough." His smile was still friendly, but tinged with a slight air of superiority.

Blokes, thought Tessa with a wry grin. Some of them just can't help knowing best. Even the young ones.

She swung herself into the driver's seat and Adam courteously closed the door for her.

"Goodbye, Tessa," he said. "Take care now."

Tessa watched him walk back to the house. His feet were still bare, and he walked with the cat-like grace of a dancer. She started the engine. She found that her stomach was tight, her palms damp. Why? There had been nothing of particular significance to emerge in the interview. Nothing irregular or unusual, nothing challenging or difficult. She had simply had a harmless chat with a very pleasant, confident, quietly assuming young man.

And yet, and yet . . .

Twenty-One

There was a burst water main on the East India Dock road and the rush hour traffic came to a complete standstill. Tessa punched out the office number on her mobile intending to let the reception team know her whereabouts. But, as seemed to happen in times of need, her phone's batteries were flat. It was an hour before the traffic moved, by which time she decided to abandon returning to the office and made her way through the evening crawl back to her flat.

Trudie was in the kitchen doing her make-up. She always did her make-up beside the window over the kitchen sink, she said it was the only window in the flat with the right sort of light.

"Oh, hi!" she said, eyeing Tessa through her mirror as she applied her mascara.

"Had a good day?" Tessa asked, tossing her bag and keys on the table.

"Fantastic!" Trudie refuelled her brush. "He phoned," she announced dreamily. "This morning. Just like he promised. Isn't that terrific?"

"Great," said Tessa drily. "I take it you're talking about Oliver?"

Trudie's anguished expression was of Shakespearean proportions. "Oh Tess, I'm sorry, that was a really tactless thing to say to you."

"No, it's OK."

"You're sure you don't mind."

"No. Honestly and truly."

"He's taking me out to a super restaurant in the West End." She turned, her face glowing with excitement and well-being. "Do you think I look OK?"

193

Tessa viewed the clingy red dress, her eyes drawn to the dramatic and impressive cleavage. She scrutinised Trudie's beautifully made-up face and her mane of honey blond hair, teased into Bondai-beach rollers.

"You look fabulous," she said. "I mean it. You look simply good enough to eat."

"Not too tarty?"

"No."

"Not too fat? Do you think this dress makes my hips look like an elephant's bottom?"

"No. But it does make your boobs look like melons. Those lovely sweet Galia ones, all round and ripe."

"Oh God!" Trudie began to heave at the neckline of her dress, wrenching it upwards.

"Stop it, Trudie. Blokes love big boobs. I once did a survey on the subject for a radio show."

"Oliver probably likes those neat little apple ones," mourned Trudie.

"Oh for heaven's sake, Trude," said Tessa, beginning to lose patience. "He wouldn't be asking you out if he didn't fancy you."

"No, he wouldn't would he?"

Tessa sat down. Suddenly she felt exhausted. The events of the last twenty-four hours swirled in her head.

"Oh!" Trudie exclaimed, suddenly remembering, "there are some messages on the answerphone for you. I should have told you as soon as you got in."

Tessa's heart felt as though it had swooped down to her stomach. "Who from?"

"Rex."

Her heart rose again, taking wings.

"I think you should call him back right away," Trudie said hesitantly. "He's phoned at least three times. He sounded a bit . . ."

"Yes?"

"Well, on the cross side."

Oh heavens! Tessa punched out Rex's number. He answered after only one ring.

"Tessa! Where the hell have you been?"

"In a traffic jam."

"Don't be flippant," he growled. "I'm talking about where you were this afternoon and why you've taken all this time getting back."

"Rex, don't start getting possessive and organising," she warned.

"Organising!" he exclaimed in outrage. "Dear God, have you any idea how worried I've been?"

She started to frame a reply, but he was still speaking. "You left no contact address when you signed out this afternoon. Your mobile was as dead as a doornail. When I phoned you at home your flatmate had no idea where you were or when you would be back."

"Rex . . . !"

"I was frantic, Tess."

She heard the pain in his voice. "Oh darling, I'm really sorry. Listen to me, I hadn't forgotten we were meeting tonight, it's just that I got delayed and—"

"I'm coming over to get you right now," he cut in, his voice tight. "Don't go out. Don't get in your car or get a taxi. Just stay put."

"Rex!"

"I'm not trying to fence you in, Tess. I'm not coming on all macho and possessive just for the hell of it. I'm simply talking about keeping you safe. Now just do as I say, stay where you are and wait until I arrive."

There was a clatter over the line as he slammed the phone down.

Tessa went back into the kitchen, her face tense with speculation.

"Trouble?" said Trudie sympathetically.

"I don't know." Tessa said slowly.

Trudie looked at her with concern. "You've gone terribly white."

"Have I?" Tessa put a hand up to her cheek. Her eyes were troubled and distracted.

Trudie looked worried. "Have you had a row?"

Tessa looked up, frowning in puzzlement. "Sorry, what did you say?"

"Have you had a row with Rex?" Trudie viewed her friend anxiously. "Oh dear, is it all off? He hasn't dumped you, has he?" She gave a small wince. It was a painful question to have to ask, especially in the circumstances.

Tessa suddenly smiled. "Oh Trudie, you most certainly have a one track mind. Men and their machinations."

"Yes, I suppose I do," Trudie admitted. "It certainly takes all my concentration to hang on to one."

"Well don't worry. I'm sure you and Oliver will be fine. And I can assure you Rex hasn't dumped me, so there's no need for you to go and drown yourself in the Thames wracked with guilt for pinching the only other bloke I'd got."

There was the sound of deep and very impressive horn blast from the road. Trudie raised her head. Tessa could almost see her ears pricking up.

"That'll be Oliver," Trudie breathed, flying to the mirror and tweaking one of her curls.

"Yes. That horn's hard to mistake. I don't think there's another car with a horn that splendid this side of the Atlantic, maybe anywhere else in the world," Tessa said with dry irony.

"I'll be off then," said Trudie, hovering by the door, torn between the need to get to Oliver as fast as possible and the reluctance to leave her flatmate who seemed to be in some kind of difficulty.

"Isn't he coming up for you?" Tessa asked, knowing both the answer and the reason behind it perfectly well.

"No. He said he'd wait in the car . . ."

"Can't face me?" Tessa suggested cheerily.

Trudie nodded. "He told me he felt a terrible rat to have—"

"No need to feel ratlike. Give him my love. And tell him that if he doesn't look after my best mate properly there'll be hell to pay."

Trudie swung back into the room and wrapped her arms round Tessa, landing a smacking kiss on her cheek and almost knocking her senseless with a great blast of *Loulou* fragrance. "You're a fantastic mate. I love you, Tessa."

"Thanks. Same to you. Have a great time."

Trudie teetered away on her high heels. Tessa heard the outer door slam, and then a few moments later the deep full roar of the Aston Martin's engine, which was almost instantly superseded with the velvety growl of Rex's Jaguar.

As Tessa opened the door to let him in, he burst through, taking her in his arms and holding her so fiercely against him she felt her bones would snap.

"Thank God," she heard him murmur. "Thank God you're safe." Tessa pulled away from him. He looked drawn and tense. She could tell that beneath his concern a thread of anger was still reverberating. Her behaviour this afternoon had aroused strong feelings in him. Bitter emotions which were still simmering.

But why? Surely a visit to Adam Baddeley, even if it was connected with Royston Gable, even if it had been in work time, was hardly a serious enough misdemeanour to awaken such powerful displeasure. Looking at him now, recalling his fury on the phone she had a swift realisation of how truly formidable he might be in anger. Anyone who made an enemy of Rex was making a grave mistake.

She took his hand and led him upstairs into the flat.

He leaned against the edge of the table watching her as she delved in the fridge and found cheese and a bottle of Australian Chardonnay.

"I can't explain things to you on an empty stomach," she said, glancing at him from time to time, her heart contracting as her eyes renewed acquaintance with his dark craggy features, his powerful lithe frame. He was very wantable and deeply sexy and she could hardly resist dragging him off to bed there and then. But she could tell that the tension within him needed defusing. That he was in some kind of pain. That just at this moment, he needed her understanding even more than her body.

She poured two glasses of chilled white wine and sat down at the kitchen table, gesturing to him to sit beside her.

"Rex," she said softly. "This tension in your face, here and here," she touched his skin with inquisitive fingers, "what is it all about?"

There was a short, painful silence.

"Tell me," she urged.

"No, you tell me, Tessa. Tell me what the hell you were

197

thinking of this afternoon? Shooting off on your own, telling no one where you were going." Sparks snapped and glittered in his eyes. He was like a gun on a cocked trigger, an explosive freshly lit and quietly smouldering.

"I simply went out to do some research . . ."

"Tessa," he cut in tersely. "You know perfectly well that just from the point of view of professional procedure you should never *ever* go out on a domestic visit without leaving a contact number."

She sighed. "Yes. I admit, I was in the wrong there. I should have left an address or a number." She reflected that it was very common for staff to 'forget' to leave a contact number, the forgetting being quite deliberate in order to cover up a much extended lunch-hour, or a secret lovers' tryst. Or just a little plain, simple skrimshanking. The world of TV was pretty high pressure stuff, you needed a break occasionally, the chance to have a little time to yourself. As the thoughts skimmed through her mind, she never ceased watching Rex's face with careful attention.

"Of course you were in the wrong," he told her, not at all mollified. "Leaving an address or a contact number is one of Dartbridge's most important security regulations."

"Yes," she said quietly.

"You should know that, Tess, you've been with the company for long enough, for goodness sake."

"Yes." Tessa drummed her fingers on the table. She did not like the way things were going.

"My God," he burst out, anger springing up afresh, "you could have got yourself into really serious trouble! Didn't you think about that?"

"Trouble as in bother," she asked with slow pointedness, her eyes glinting dangerously. "Landing myself in bother with you? Is that what you mean?"

"Trouble as in danger," he whipped back. "How could you have acted so impulsively? How could you have been so thoughtless and irresponsible?"

Tessa gave him a narrow, icy look. "Have you said all you want to on this subject, Rex? Because I'm getting a little tired of it."

"No I haven't," he barked.

Tessa sighed. She loved him and adored him and wanted him. But she wasn't going to allow him to hector her as if they were still in the office and he was the undisputed boss, she the lowly minion.

"Then you'll have to go," she told him, her eyes holding his with perfect steadiness. "I'm not sitting here in my own kitchen to listen to you trying to browbeat me."

Rex's eyelids flickered. He could sense the sharp bolt of tension between them and it alarmed him. He knew that in her eyes he was being entirely unreasonable. But then there were certain things Tessa did not know, things that would most surely help her understand. He tried to think of the best way to tell her.

Tessa had got up and walked to the window. The view here on the second floor was limited to lines of grey roofs which stretched away into the distance.

She said unsteadily, "Things will never work out between us, Rex, if you try to restrain and control me like this."

Rex got up and went to stand beside her. He put an arm around her. She felt the warmth of his breath on her ear. The tension of discord left her. She felt soft and weak with desire.

"You're right," he said. "And I'm sorry."

Tessa twisted in his embrace, putting her arms around his neck.

Warm, pulsing moments passed.

"I couldn't bear to lose you, darling," he murmured in time, his voice hoarse with feeling.

"You won't lose me," she reassured him. "Not if we can sort all this out."

"I couldn't bear any harm to come to you," he whispered, clasping her hard against him, his fingers weaving within her hair, massaging the bones of her skull.

Tessa snaked her arms around him. She laid her head against his heart. "Did you lose someone before?"

"Yes."

"Will you tell me about it? Tell me about *her*."

"Yes, I will tell you, my darling," he murmured. He gave

a long deep sigh and then fell silent. Tessa could feel the resistance flowing through his nerves, keeping his body tight, imprisoning his voice within his throat. Slowly she unwound her arms from him.

"Let's sit down together, let's drink some more wine," she said gently.

For a time they simply sat in silence, sipping their wine. Tessa's edgy defensiveness had all evaporated. She felt quite at ease with him now, completely at one. The silence did not disturb her. Now the connection between them was re-established she knew that they had all the time in the world to share each other's secrets.

"What was her name?" she asked him calmly.

"Eleanor." He gave a sharp dry laugh. "Like Eleanor Rigby in the Beatles song. The one who kept her face in a jar by the door."

"And did she? Your Eleanor? Did she keep her face in a jar by the door?" Even as she spoke the other woman's name Tessa felt a humiliating twinge of jealousy for this mysterious creature who had been a part of Rex's past long before she, Tessa, had even known he existed. A woman who had exerted such power over his feelings he could hardly bear to bring himself to speak her name.

"She was six years older than me. And she was already married when I met her," said Rex. "That was the beginning and the end of the problem, I suppose. Her being already married. And my wanting nothing in the world so much as for her to marry me."

"Was there no question of a divorce?" Tessa asked. She spoke very calmly, keeping her voice low and even, conscious that he was as tense and wary as a nervous thoroughbred horse before a vital race.

"No. Her husband held a very exalted position in the British judiciary."

"She didn't want to create a scandal which would harm him?" Tessa suggested.

Pain flickered over Rex's face. "She didn't want to leave him because she loved being the wife of a man in such a powerful position. She loved the status of it, the way other people's reverence for her husband's position reflected back on her. She loved the glamour of the social life." The sorrow and regret in his voice was laced through with bitterness. "Oh – and the money. Do you have any idea what top judges earn, Tessa?"

"Yes." She gave a wry little smile. "Riches beyond the dreams of avarice."

"Quite. And a hell of a lot more than a junior producer at the BBC, which was what my job was at the time." He paused and drained his wine glass. Tessa reached across and refilled it.

"I was young and stroppy and demanding," he continued, glancing at her and giving a faint grin in response to her quizzically raised eyebrow at that last statement.

"Has anything changed?" she murmured. "Apart from your getting older?"

He shrugged. "Maybe not. Anyway, I bombarded her with demands. I shouted and pleaded and argued and badgered and cajoled. 'Marry me, Eleanor, marry me!' But she wouldn't be moved. She was one of those women who are astonishingly passionate and abandoned about sex, but as cold as ice when it came to simple human communication and sensitivity. Of course I didn't see it that way at the time. I thought she was utterly fascinating. For me she was beautiful and complex and perfect. I was completely besotted."

Tessa felt a sharp twinge of misery. She had a strong sense of Eleanor's presence there in the room with them. She could feel her female magnetism and the power of her personality asserting itself in the atmosphere.

"Poor Eleanor," Rex exclaimed softly. "She didn't just keep her face in a jar by the door. She kept everything there – her public and her private face, all of her most secret thoughts and longings. I don't think anyone ever knew anything about her inner world, anything about the intensely private person who hid behind her beautiful elegant mask. I most certainly didn't." He fell silent.

"What happened, Rex?" She stared at his face, alarmed by the distress stetched over it like constraining wires. "Did Eleanor have some kind of accident?" That last word sounded puny and trivial. For Tessa knew without a doubt at this point in the story that Eleanor was dead.

"Yes. You could say so."

Tessa touched the back of his hand. He flinched, moving it away. His face had gone very white. He turned back and gave her a long, slow look. The emotion in it was such that Tessa shivered, and glanced away for a moment. She felt humbled, almost overwhelmed to witness such emotion in another human being.

"Say it, Rex," she whispered. "Don't be afraid to tell me."

"Sometimes when I remember what happened the pain seems to have become all worn away, like a sandcastle flattened by the sea," Rex said wearily. "But there are still times when it can spring back sharp and clear, almost as raw and new as it was then."

"Yes, yes. Go on. Tell me what happened."

"The inevitable," he said grimly. "Her husband found out. Oh, we were immensely careful, obsessionally so because she demanded it. On no account must her revered husband the High Court judge ever know about our tawdry affair." His face twisted with a spasm of pain and revulsion. As he hesitated for a moment, Tessa realised that this had been a deeply flawed love affair, a terrifying cocktail of blinding love and flashing hatred.

"But I think the worthy judge knew all along. In fact I think he had Eleanor followed right from the beginning." Again he stopped. Tessa refrained from meeting his eye, from touching him again.

"He had her killed," Rex went on in a flat, even voice. "He hired a professional killer. Eleanor was shot at point blank range whilst in her car, waiting at some traffic lights. She had this beautiful Mercedes convertible and she loved driving with the top down, even in the coldest weather. She was a sitting target, quite literally. She died almost instantly apparently, slumped over the wheel, with blood pouring down her face. She died alone, surrounded by strangers. What a terrible, anonymous, lonely death."

Tessa found hot tears standing in her eyes. She blinked hard, biting on her lip and trying to control her feelings. This was a moment for Rex to think and remember and feel. Pay homage to the mysterious Eleanor. She, Tessa, must temporarily be secondary.

"That night her husband drank a bottle of whisky in a London bar and then threw himself into the Thames."

Tessa reached out her hand and took his. This time he welcomed the contact of her flesh. She could feel her sympathy passing through her skin into his.

"Rex," she said. "I couldn't even pretend to imagine what you must have suffered. But I'm glad that you told me. It's made me understand things I would never have begun to guess at on my own."

He took her hand, turning it over within his, stroking the palm with his fingers. "This afternoon," he said. "When you were missing . . ." His hand moved up to cover his eyes.

"Oh God! I am so sorry," she whispered. "So very, very sorry to put you through that – raking up all those horrifying memories."

"Yes. There were some pretty low moments, I can tell you. You see, Tessa, I haven't allowed myself to love again since Eleanor was so brutally taken away from me. I know that sounds like a horny old cliché, but it's true. And it wasn't a conscious decision, it wasn't something I planned. I didn't say to myself, 'I shall never allow myself to be hurt like that ever again.' I didn't make an avowal to treasure Eleanor's memory for ever and ever and never betray her by loving another woman as much. It was just the way things turned out."

Tessa nodded. "Go on." Keep talking about it, Rex, she thought. Get the poison out of your system. Don't feel the need to cling on to your grief. Let it go. She suddenly thought of her poor grieving withered parents in their little seaside house. Going through their routine, dreary lives, refusing to let go of the memory of the son who had betrayed them. The past was killing them.

Tessa stroked Rex's arm with slow rhythmic fingers, silently urging him on to cleanse his feelings in order that he could renew himself and love again.

"There was guilt too," Rex said, his voice low and pulsing with feeling. A long, uneven sigh escaped from the depths of his chest. "For a long time I felt so guilty. Quite desperately guilty in fact. Her husband might have engineered her death but I had blood on my hands. I was like Lady Macbeth, feeling I could never wash it off."

"How long ago is it since Eleanor died?" Tessa asked.

"Six years."

"And now, has the guilt gone?"

"Not completely. I can live with it." He drained his glass. He swivelled sharply to face Tessa. "But I can't live with fear. Not fear for the safety of the new woman in my life. I thought I was cold and empty, that I wouldn't fall in love again, that I wouldn't ever *love* again." He reached for her hand, his eyes glowing with tenderness as he stared deep into hers. "But it's happened. Like some kind of miracle. I do love you, Tessa. I meant all of those things I said last night. I don't just want an affair with you. I'm so sick of empty affairs. I want to be close to you and share things with you. I want our hearts to beat together, our spirits to twine themselves around each other. Do you believe me?"

"Yes, I do believe you." She stared hard at him, deeply moved. But one small fragment from his verbal outpourings echoed insistently in her mind. Just five words. Echoing, reverberating. *I can't live with fear.*

She chewed on her lip as a new conjecture began to form itself. "You've had another phone call, haven't you?" she said. "From *him*."

His eyes swerved towards hers, sharpening, glinting. "Yes – *him*!"

Twenty-Two

Tessa gave a little cry. She gazed at Rex, her body tense. "Oh no," she moaned.

"Oh yes. I'm afraid so. When I tell you a little more you'll begin to understand why I went over the top with anxiety on your behalf earlier on."

She nodded. "When did he call? What did he say?"

"He left a message on my personal phone in the office. The machine had the message timed at four-thirty p.m. In that polite, bland voice of his he helpfully offered the information that you had just left the house of a young man called Adam Baddeley who lives in the East End."

"Oh God!" groaned Tessa.

"Exactly. When Gable telephones, you sometimes get the feeling you'll be in need of some divine help before too long."

Tessa winced.

"And *had* you just left the house of the said Mr Baddeley?" Rex enquired. He did not wait for her answer. "Yes, of course you had. Royston Gable isn't a man in the habit of getting his information wrong, is he? He went on to say that you'd been at this house for about an hour." He raised his eyebrows.

Tessa nodded a confirmation. Her stomach was feeling bruised and queasy.

"He offered an opinion, in the gentlest most courteous way of course, that it might be better for you not to plan on making any further uninvited visits of an investigative nature."

Tessa drew in a sharp breath. "And was that all?"

"That was the basic drift. Wasn't that enough?"

"Yes, I suppose so," she said gloomily.

"Of course," Rex continued with a grim smile, "you can

205

imagine the way in which it was all said. That silky urbane cordiality of his, with just the merest throb of menace running underneath. When I had finished listening my skin felt as though worms were crawling all over it. And then when it got to six, and seven and eight o'clock and you still hadn't arrived home . . . Well, you know the rest."

There was a short, reflective silence.

Rex longed to extract a solemn promise from her that she would drop all further attempts to satisfy her curiosity about the names on Gable's computer. He told himself he must hold back. Tessa would, quite rightly he had to admit, resist any requests that smacked of macho commands.

"I know what you're thinking," she said with a little smile of mischief.

"Oh yeah."

"Yes."

"Go on then, amaze me."

"You're wanting to put me in a little gilded cage and keep me nice and safe there, singing sweet little songs to you and letting you stroke my feathers from time to time. You're wanting to be all manly and protective. You're wanting to say something like: 'Tessa, for the very last time you must forget about Royston Gable and his computer names.' Am I right? Or am I right?"

"Hah!"

"Look," she said, deadly serious again. "I'm not wanting to make light of this. I know it's no joke. And after what you told me earlier I wouldn't be so insensitive as to trample over your feelings by dashing off to do some casual sleuthing into Gable's past."

"I hear a 'but' coming along."

"You do indeed. I can't give you any guarantees that I won't ever take any risks again. I can't promise you that I'll never go out and walk alone down a dark street, or that I'll never travel on the underground after midnight, or whatever else you might care to think about that's a touch risky. I couldn't have a life if I started making those kinds of promises. No one could. And you yourself would never agree to that sort of dictate."

"No, but I'm a man," he said with elaborate patience. "Simple as that."

"No, it's far from simple," she protested. "Men are at risk too. Maybe not in the same way as women. But men get mugged, men get beaten up. A man could get shot driving in his car with the soft top down."

He drew in a sharp, painful breath. "Oh, Tessa!"

"I'm sorry," she said, her tone insistent. "But these are things that need to be said. How can we be happy together in the future, how can we truly love each other if we have to keep our hidden convictions secret?"

"OK," he agreed, knowing when it was futile to argue further. "Well, let's be practical. What happens next? Do you want to go on with this . . . investigation?"

She pressed her lips together, she rubbed thoughtfully at her cheek. "I'm not sure."

Rex looked at her and sighed. "Oh yes, you are. You're not only sure, you're one hundred per cent determined. I can see it in your eyes." He shook his head in mock sorrow.

"I was born with an over developed sense of curiosity," Tessa said drily. "It's my Achilles heel."

"Mmm," he agreed.

"I suppose you knew that right from the start." she said ruefully. "From the moment you first noticed my existence and began taking an interest in my work at Dartbridge?"

"Yes, I believe I did. I said to myself here's a little ball of dynamite who's going to get herself into real trouble if I don't step in to protect her." He gave her a provocative grin, silently recalling those early days when he had first come to Dartbridge, those days when he had first seen Tessa, days of wonder when it had dawned on him that it was possible to fall in love again.

"You presumptuous, wretched boss-man!" she chided him, indignant and at the same time laughing.

"Maybe I am. That's one of the things Lady Collingham pays me to do: assess the strengths and weaknesses of the staff. So," he continued smoothly before she could open her mouth to challenge him, "dare I ask what are you planning to do next?"

"I've got three more names to follow up."

"Ah yes. The intriguing 'names'. Oh, and that reminds me,

Angela Drake

did Adam Baddeley let slip anything interesting? I'd almost forgotten about him."

Tessa's face clouded with reflection. "No, he didn't.

"Everything in his life was just hunky dory was it? Royston Gable doesn't haul him up to his clinic once a month to drill his skull and do a brain probe."

"Not that he mentioned." Tessa eyed Rex sternly.

"I'm sorry, I was being flippant. Go on."

"Well, here's what I found out. Adam's an only child. He lives with his mother, of whom he seems extremely fond. His father pushed off and left them both when Adam was quite small. His mother had to put him in a nursery and get herself a job. There's obviously never been a lot of money around in the household. In fact, I would think they're still struggling to make ends meet."

"And yet he's in higher education?"

"Yes. He's at Oxford."

"Good for him. But how does his mother afford to fund him?"

"He got an open scholarship. He must be seriously bright, or phenomenally hard working. Or both. I suppose he'll have his fees paid and there'll be some college funds to tap into to help him as well, I would guess."

"So, bright young lad from the East End makes good against all odds?"

"I suppose you could say that." Tessa gave a small frown. "Somehow he doesn't strike you as the stereotype of a poor lad who's made good."

"Why not?"

"He has an air of quiet authority about him. Almost superiority. He could drop into a stately home for the weekend, pass himself off as the honourable Peregrine Steele-Perkins or whatever, and I bet no one would know the difference."

Rex raised his eyebrows. "That's an amusing little fantasy. But otherwise there's very little to go on, is there?" *Tessa, forget all of this*, he was pleading silently.

"No." She considered, and then leaned forward, a flash of enthusiasm lighting her face. "I was puzzled when nothing came out of the interview with Adam. But that's why I want

208

to see the other three. I just know, somewhere deep in my bones, that when I've seen the four of them, some kind of pattern will emerge."

Rex groaned. He covered his face with his hands.

Tessa was about to speak again, and then suddenly she stopped, unable to go on. All of her conjecturing, all her questions of what and how and why and when seemed supremely unimportant as she looked at Rex, sensing the maleness of him, recalling the desolation he had experienced earlier when he talked of his dead lover. Understanding the great force of his need.

Her heart began to speed up. "Rex," she said gently.

He turned his head, watching her warily. "Yes."

"We've been together all evening and we've done nothing but talk."

"Yes." He stared at her, suddenly seeing the invitation in her eyes, in the parting of her lips.

"Now." she whispered. "I need you so much. I want you so much. Let's not talk any more." She took one of his hands very gently in hers.

He stood up. He made a swift, sharp movement and lifted her to her feet, pulling her into his arms. "Oh Tessa, my only darling!" He began to kiss her hair, her forehead, her nose, her lips.

He cradled her against him. He held her very close, letting the warmth of his body pass to hers. There was something so steadying, so deeply *right* about the feelings that swept through him.

He could sense that Tessa felt this too. He could sense it in the pulse coming from her body. He could see it in her face and in her eyes when he drew back from her slightly. He took her hand and she led him into her bedroom. They lay down on the bed together, very still and very quiet, just holding each other.

The curtains were drawn back and a frail lemon-rind moon was framed in the window sailing in and out of the clouds, silvering their faces.

She stroked his cheeks and his forehead and his temples with gentle, featherlight fingers. "Thank you for telling me about Eleanor," she said with a simple humility that touched him deeply.

He turned her in his arms so they could lie even closer still. His fingers outlined the curves of her mouth, of her browbones, her eyes and her ears. Then very softly he began to stroke her throat and then her breasts, rolling the nipples gently against his thumb.

Tessa gave a small moan and moved against him. He raised himself on his elbows and lay over her, resting his lips on hers. Instantly her lips slackened and parted, her mouth opening under his.

They began to make love very slowly, rejoicing in each other's lingering gestures, the feel and touch of skin and hair, of the little pulsing veins that throbbed at every pulse point.

When Rex entered her body she began to breathe very deeply, giving herself up to him instantly. Tonight there was no resistance within her, no tiny shreds of hesitation and fear to hold her back. Tonight she was not just getting to know him, she was rediscovering him, reliving the joys of their previous lovemaking. The sensation of sweetness that came from that renewal somehow intensified the pleasure she felt a hundred times over.

Rex moved inside her, the ecstasy gradually building within him. He felt as though he had been on a long, lonely journey, that he had travelled a great distance, always on his own, always struggling, always battling. And now he had reached a resting place. Eleanor's features began to recede from that dark part of his mind which stored only pain. As he looked into Tessa's face, silvered in the fragile moonlight, the image of his dead lover was gently laid to rest within that store of memories which bring peace and happiness, not pain.

As he moved over Tessa he felt her muscles begin to tense. Tiny flashing sparks of tingling sensation flew from her body to his. Suddenly she cried out, her ecstasy echoing around the room. Surely it would stir every particle in the atmosphere.

And then after some moments of stillness Tessa's hands were tenderly caressing the back of his neck, every disc of his spine. "Let yourself go, darling," she murmured. "You've made me so happy. I won't break . . ."

Later Rex lay beside her. His body was quietly throbbing with a beautiful, deep satisfaction after his tumultuous climax. As he turned to Tessa a huge wave of tenderness overwhelmed him. He reached over and trailed his finger across the softness of her cheek. He had the feeling that he had experienced a rebirth.

They slept a little and then they woke and talked some more. Rex told her about his and Vicky's lonely life at separate boarding schools whilst his father moved around Europe making his way up the ranks of the British Army. Tessa told him about her lost brother Alec and her poor sad parents.

And then they made love again. And much later on they smiled and willed themselves into stillness and silence when they eventually heard Trudie come in and go to her room.

When they woke in the morning they both felt an intense, overwhelming joy.

"I want to stay here with you for ever," he murmured, kissing her lips once again.

"I can hear another of those 'buts' . . ."

"But work calls."

"The necessity of earning of a humble crust?" she suggested playfully.

"Mmm."

Tessa got out of bed and stretched, her body cat-like and svelte.

"Don't," he groaned. "How can I leave when you look so temptingly lovable?"

"Control yourself," she said sternly. "You have troops awaiting your arrival at headquarters, Mr General. And I have an appointment to do a preliminary face-to-face with Miss Cherry Ripe at eleven, in preparation for the programme next week."

"God!" He buried his face in the pillow.

Tessa took herself off to the shower, then opened the airing cupboard outside the bathroom and hurriedly pulled on some clothes that readily came to hand. Namely a rather crinkled purple silk blouse with long legged birds striding across it, and her silver metallic-look jeans which fitted her slender legs like a second skin.

In the bedroom she was confronted with the vision of Rex's naked buttocks as he attempted to discover the whereabouts of the clothes Tessa had wrenched off him the night previously. This was no easy mission for him and was accompanied by a constant stream of growls and muttered curses.

Tessa clasped her hands firmly behind her back to stop them straying to Rex's gorgeous body.

"Good God!" he exclaimed, looking up at her as he pulled on his shoes. "Are you going to work in that get-up?"

"Yes. It wouldn't do to intimidate poor little Cherry with black-suited, high-heeled power dressing."

"I thought that had all faded into the mists of time. Isn't fashion all soft and supple these days?"

Tessa sighed. "Rex, you should stop listening to the drivel our fashion editors spout forth and go and look at real women out and about in Harrods and at the Ritz." She rolled her eyes mischievously.

"Oh, that sort of real woman!" he said with a dismissive grimace. "No, don't go for the type."

They stood very still, staring at each other for a long deep moment.

"What are you going to do about Royston Gable?" Rex asked quietly.

She turned away, her teeth nibbling at her lip. "I'm not sure . . ."

"I am," Rex said.

She swung back. "Yes?"

"I think you should go on with it."

"No, I don't believe it."

"Yes, that is truly what I think. Mainly because I'm pretty sure you won't be able to stop yourself."

"Yes. You're right. Oh Rex, I'm sorry. I hate to do this to you."

"We'll do it together."

"You mean it?" She was astonished. "Truly."

"There's no alternative. Not for me anyway. And to be quite honest I'm getting rather curious myself."

"Are you? Or do you just want to get your own back on Gable?"

He smiled. "Oh, that would be a wonderful bonus. I can't wait."

Tessa went down with him to his car and watched him get in. She hated to see him leave, hated to be separated from him for even one minute.

He pulled the car away from the kerb and then spoke to her through the open window, looking deep into her face. "You do know how very much I love you, don't you, Tessa? Just promise me you won't ever forget that."

"I promise."

He sighed and made a brave show of smiling. And then he drove away.

Twenty-Three

Cherry Ripe, one of Britain's hottest pop sensations, lived with her mother in a luxury penthouse duplex in Chelsea. It was centrally heated to imitate the climate of a tropical jungle and enjoyed panoramic views over the Ranelagh Gardens and the Thames embankment.

Tessa was met at the door by Cherry's mother, Deidre, a slender, pointed-faced brunette dressed in a shiny gold catsuit. It was hard to imagine her being a mother. She looked far too young to have any children at all let alone a teenage daughter.

"Cherry's just talking to her publicity manager," Deidre told Tessa, her eyes enormous with pride. "The poor pet seems to be busy all the time now she's famous." She gave an excited, breathless laugh.

Tessa smiled sympathetically. Silently she was thinking that she could do without having to deal with a mother and a manager as well as the star in question. She hoped Cherry's manager wasn't going to be one of the obstacle-making kind who persuaded the client to keep everyone waiting just to emphasise their preciousness as a commodity. The kind who then proceeded to muzzle their client whenever a slightly probing question was asked.

"Cherry'll be ready to see you in just a minute," Deidre reassured her. "Why don't I show you round the apartment while you're waiting?"

With a silent sigh, Tessa obediently followed Deidre as she took her on a guided tour of the apartment, triumphantly throwing open one door after another. Tessa was invited to marvel at the marble master bathroom with its twin power showers and jacuzzi, to exclaim in wonder at the bedrooms in toning shades of peony pink and to gape at the tennis-court-sized Poggenpohl kitchen with adjoining laundry room, stacked with an array of gleaming stainless-steel machines.

"Never believe people who tell you money doesn't bring happiness," Deidre said. "I'm as happy as the day's long looking after this place."

Having made sure that Tessa had made a comprehensive inspection of all these exciting features, Deidre at last escorted her to the sitting room where Cherry sat sprawled on a white leather sofa. She was dressed in a turquiose suede mini-dress, was sipping diet Pepsi-Cola from a bottle and scowling ferociously.

The moment Tessa met her glance, Cherry flung her head up in the air, tossing her pale-blond ponytail and flashing the whites of her eyes.

Tessa's instant impression was of a very young, exceedingly pretty girl who had landed herself in a situation which terrified her. She guessed that Cherry was constantly wondering just what she had got herself into.

A woman with mannishly short black hair and red-framed glasses was lurking in the corner of the room, whispering into a mobile phone. On seeing Tessa she too offered a scowl by way of greeting.

Tessa groaned internally. She sat down on the opposite side of the sofa to Cherry and gave the girl a big warm smile. "Hi!"

Cherry stared at her, her huge silvery eyes cold and wary. She tossed her ponytail once more.

Tessa glanced around her, seeking some point of conversational contact. The room was lavishly and expensively furnished, but somehow bare and anonymous as though it were still waiting for someone to move in. The walls were covered in silky embossed paper but there were no pictures hanging on them. The room had few ornaments and no sign of a book, a magazine or a photograph.

As Tessa glanced over the vast steel and glass table beside the sofa she noticed a solitary compact-disc cover.

"Is this your latest?" Tessa enquired, picking it up and looking at the provocative and arresting picture on the front.

It showed Cherry standing inside a human-sized silver bird-cage, wearing two deftly tied scarves and a fiercely sullen expression.

"Yeah." Cherry glared at Tessa, obviously not at all pleased by her arrival, and in no way inclined to make herself pleasant.

Tessa scanned through the list of titles on the back cover, at the same time making a mental note that Cherry was likely to be an exceedingly difficult interviewee if she persisted in continuing in this uncooperative fashion.

"Cherry, pet. Take your feet off the settee, there's a good girl," Deidre said, crossing to the table and setting down a shiny coffee pot that looked as though it might be plated with genuine gold.

Cherry glared at her parent. Her feet remained stubbornly motionless.

"Sweetheart," her mother wheedled, "come along, do what your mum says, there's a good girl."

Cherry swung her legs down to the floor in a swift, savage gesture. She tossed her head once more. It was a mannerism that Tessa was beginning to recognise as a nervous response, rather like a repetitive eyelid twitch.

Tessa embarked on an explanation of the format of the *Limelight* show and the kinds of questions she would be asking Cherry when they were on screen.

"Have you done a lot of live TV, Cherry?" she asked, noting that Cherry's head-tossing had accelerated alarmingly as she was giving her spiel.

"Yeah. Enough."

"She's done mostly recordings," Deidre broke in. "She's made some fabulous recordings, haven't you darlin'?" She turned to Tessa. "Do you know, it's wonderful how they make these new mini discs in the recording studio. It doesn't matter if you make a mistake you see, they just keep on doing the songs over and over again until everything's right."

Tessa was aware that Cherry's agent was suddenly terminating her telephone conversation, had snapped down the aerial, and was now striding purposefully towards the sofa across the intervening acres of white shag-pile carpet.

"Plenty of people get nerves before a live TV show," Tessa told Cherry lightly with a comforting smile. "It's not at all unusual, nothing to worry about."

"Cherry doesn't get nerves," the agent barked. "She's a consummate professional."

Cherry gazed up at the fierce dark-haired woman. Her smooth-skinned forehead wrinkled in puzzlement for a moment. But her eyes were blank.

"Fine," Tessa murmured. She turned back to Cherry. "I like the name you've chosen – Cherry Ripe. Did you get the idea from the song?"

Cherry's eyes shifted about nervously.

"The song *Cherry Ripe*," Tessa explained. "My granny used to sing it to me." She hummed a line or two.

"Oh." Cherry looked even blanker than before.

"Cherry Ripe's a good commercial name," the publicity manager snapped to Tessa. "It has a good ring to it. People remember it."

"So what's your real name, Cherry?" Tessa asked.

"Wish I knew," muttered Cherry, inspecting her long midnight-blue fingernails. "Mum never bothered to find out who my father was."

"Cherry never uses her former name now," the manager cut in. "She's Cherry Ripe, like Madonna is Madonna."

"So her real name is a secret?" Tessa wondered, staring hard at the steely manager.

"No. It just isn't of interest."

"OK. Fair enough." Tessa smiled reassuringly at Cherry. "When we're on air, Cherry, I shall probably ask you to talk a little bit about your voice."

"Oh yeah?" Cherry managed to glare and frown at the same time. "What d'you mean?"

"Your *singing* voice," Tessa explained gently. She was coming to realise that this poor girl was scared out of her wits at the prospect of appearing on *Limelight*. "It has a wonderfully individual quality. It's the sort of voice that people can instantly recognise. They couldn't possibly mistake it for anyone else."

"Yeah." Cherry's defensive attitude appeared in no way softened with this praise. "So?"

217

"So," Tessa went on evenly, realising she would have to spell things out very simply and clearly, "I shall ask you to tell the viewers if you had a good singing voice when you were a child. Tell them about when you first discovered you had a good voice and what sort of training you've had. That sort of thing." She smiled encouragingly at Cherry who did not smile back.

"She's been singing ever since she was tiny," Deidre said confidingly. "She used to copy Madonna, dancing round the kitchen, tossing her little head." She leaned forward to Cherry. "Didn't you used to mimic Madonna, darlin'? Don't you remember?"

"No," said Cherry.

"You do, lovey. Of course you do. There was that competition I entered you for when we were at the seaside. You had to pretend to be a famous person. You were fabulous doing your mime of Madonna. Everyone clapped. Now, that's something you can tell the viewers, darlin', they'd all love to hear about that."

Cherry replaced her feet on the sofa and dug her stiletto heels into the leather.

"We don't want Cherry to be compared with Madonna," the publicity manager snapped. "We're trying to build up a very individual, exclusive image for Cherry."

Cherry's glance swivelled between mother and manager. Tessa thought the expression in the girl's eyes bordered on the murderous.

"Did you have singing lessons, Cherry?" Tessa asked patiently.

"No, I don't like lessons. I like to do my own thing. I just sing the way I want," said Cherry. "And I can't read music neither." She muttered something else which Tessa couldn't quite make out.

"There's no need to say anything about that," her agent broke in swiftly.

"Why not?" Deidre asked. "Those are the kinds of things the public are interested in."

The manager's eyes snapped and glittered behind her red spectacle frames. "We don't want to give the impression that

Cherry is limited in any way. It used to be all the rage for pop
stars to claim they couldn't read a note of music and so on. But
nowadays the public demand far more sophistication. They like
to look up to their idols. They admire accomplishment."

Deidre looked huffy. She reached into the tiny gold bag
strung around her shoulder and took out a slim gold cigarette
case and matching lighter. She flicked the lighter and drew
deeply on the cigarette.

The publicity manager scowled, waving the smoke away
with a grimace of revulsion.

"I need a cig too," said Cherry, stretching out to the
gold case.

"Oh darlin,' you know you mustn't smoke," Deidre said.
"Think of your voice, sweet'eart."

"Jeez!" Cherry muttered under her breath. As she picked up
the case and took out a cigarette her manager walked across and
removed it from her fingers. "Oh no you don't. Your mother's
right. You'll ruin your voice if you persist in smoking."

"Bitch," Cherry mouthed with soft venom. "I'll do what I
bloody like."

"You'll do as you're bloody told," the manager said in icy
tones. "You're barely old enough to buy them legally at the
tobacconists."

Tessa glanced up from her notebook. "May I ask how old
you are, Cherry?" she said very politely. "The various articles
I've read don't seem to agree on a figure."

"She's sixteen," the manager said quickly.

Tessa glanced at Cherry, who offered neither confirmation
or denial. Tessa then looked at Deidre who smiled brightly.
"Yes. That's right. Sweet sixteen."

No, thought Tessa. More like fourteen. And then only just.
Tessa recalled the innuendoes made by Cherry's former teacher
on the tape the girl from the research team had found for her.
Suddenly all the hints, all the half-spoken truths and hidden
nuances formed themselves into a pattern. Tessa saw the likely
sad little story unfolding itself like a serial in a women's
magazine.

Cherry had been a sullen, miserable child at school. School
had been an unhappy place, one where she never achieved

much or made any friends. But she had had one asset. A singing voice in a million. A voice with high notes as sweet and pure as a boy-soprano and low ones as raw and earthy as a night-club belter. And once her mother had realised the potential, there had been no stopping her ambitions for her daughter.

Tessa pieced together how things would have progressed from there. As Cherry had been moved from one school to another – a poorly achieving, disruptive pupil who no one felt sorry to wave goodbye to – her mother had taken the chance to lie about her age. Cherry had become gradually older and older. Eventually her mother had removed her from school altogether so that she could pursue her career.

Cherry hadn't protested. She had hated school. Hated not being able to read, not being able to do anything that gained her teachers' approval.

But depriving a child of her education and sending her out to work under the age of sixteen was breaking the law.

Tessa looked at the fussy, protective, greedy Deidre and knew that her exploitation of her daughter was just the kind of thing the tabloids would love to gloat over. The red-framed publicity manager would not come out of it smelling of roses either.

All in all, Tessa judged it would make a sensation to break the story on the programme. Going for the Achilles heel with a vengeance. But Tessa had already decided that she had no intention of doing any such thing. Teasing Yves Saint Rochelle and pursuing Royston Gable she could justify. They were both fair game.

But poor little Cherry. She was an entirely different proposition. Manipulated by her wheedling, ambitious mother, controlled by her gauleiter manager, being forced to perform like a monkey on a chain; the unhappy girl already had quite enough on her plate. Tessa hadn't the heart to make things worse.

She wondered how she was going to explain it to Rex.

"Have you finished now?" the publicity manager asked rudely. "We have another appointment in a few minutes."

"Yes, yes. I think that's all fine," Tessa said, folding her notebook and standing up.

"I don't want to do it," Cherry burst out suddenly.

"I'm sorry?" Tessa looked down at the angry girl who was now on the verge of tears.

"I don't want to come on your programme."

"Why not, Cherry?" Tessa tried to keep calm. Cancelling the star's slot on the programme at this late stage would be a disaster. Rex would go hairless.

"All those questions you ask. They make me nervous."

"Oh darlin'," exclaimed Deidre in dismay. "You have to go on. There's going to be millions watching."

"This is a very good opportunity, Cherry," the manager warned.

"No," said Cherry stubbornly.

"Oh dear," wailed Deidre.

"It's all her fault," Cherry told her mother, nodding towards Tessa. "I felt all right until she came along, asking all those questions." She flung up her head, tossing her hair. "Go away!" she sobbed. "Get out. GO AWAY!"

"Look, I'm really sorry if I upset you," Tessa told the girl, genuinely distressed.

The publicity manager sprang forward, took Tessa's arm, frog-marched her to the door and pushed her through. "Great!" she exploded. "Simply terrific! Have you any idea how fragile and sensitive that kid is? She's like eggshells. And now you've just about ruined my chances of getting her to do anything useful at all for the next week or so."

"I've done nothing of the sort," protested Tessa, taken completely off guard. "In fact I couldn't have been more tactful."

"You could have been a whole lot less nosy and pushy!"

Tessa stared at her.

"You like upsetting people, don't you?" the woman said, eyeing Tessa with dislike. "I saw that programme you did with Yves Saint Rochelle. You made him look a real fool. Well, OK, he is one, but who are you to rub it in?"

Tessa felt suddenly unnerved, as though the ground was shifting beneath her. This could be really serious, she thought.

"Your programme is supposed to be a piece of light entertainment. A harmless, light-hearted, lightweight chat show," the manager went on. "Who gave you the licence to try to turn it into one of those dreadful prying documentaries? You've gone way beyond your brief today."

"No," said Tessa steadily. "I'm working well within my brief, which is to draw our guests out and show them to the viewers as rounded human beings, not cardboard cut-outs."

The manager gave a derisive snort. "I'm going to get on to Lady Collingham and tell her we're only prepared to go ahead with Cherry's appearance on the programme if Lucinda fronts the show."

Tessa bit her lip. Oh hell!

"And I shan't be too complimentary about your preliminary interviewing techniques," the woman went on. "You're like all the rest of these bright young things on TV. Too damned clever for your own good." She went back into the apartment and slammed the door.

Tessa blew out a long breath. Some days she thought that her job was a breeze: lots of fun and interest and action, with a pay-cheque at the end of it all. And some days she thought that even with double the salary she'd have earned her money twice over. Today was one of the latter.

Outside the drizzle that had been falling earlier had been replaced with dry cool air and a sharp breeze. She walked through the streets, enjoying the bite in the air after the stifling heat in Cherry Ripe's apartment.

Walking down into the hollow, clanging underground car park she had an acute sense of being entirely alone and defenceless. A thrill of fear crawled over her skin as she glanced swiftly around her, trying to probe the shadowy corners of the dimly illuminated space. Was someone tracking her, watching her every move? An image of Royston Gable rose in her mind; it was an image that had been growing steadily stronger since the TV interview. In those moments when she was not fully occupied with people or problems connected with work, he seemed to be there with her. But not now, she told herself firmly. Gable might be dangerous, but he was not the sort of man to hang around in a litter-strewn, sour-smelling car park.

As she stood beside her car, fishing her keys from her bag,

she felt a light tap on her shoulder. Her nerves screeched and a dark chill ran through her body. Turning she found herself looking up into the face of a blond young man with the kind of bone structure that had you instantly catching your breath. He was like a Leonardo da Vinci drawing, a Michelangelo sculpture.

"Hello. Am I right in thinking you're the TV presenter Tessa Clair?" he asked, with a smile that could have had Tessa's pulse accelerating, had she not been madly in love with another man. When she nodded, he smiled some more. "I wondered if you'd spare me a few minutes," he said winningly. "My name's Rupert Frobisher."

Twenty-Four

"How did you know where to find me?" Tessa demanded, her face clouding with troubled speculation.

"I telephoned your studio," he told her, the smile never leaving his chiselled features. "I told the girl on the reception desk a few white lies." His hyacinth-blue eyes sparkled. "I wheedled a little . . ."

"And you got full details."

"Right. Where you were going, the car park you were likely to use. The make of your car, registration number." He lifted his shoulders in an elegant shrug, presumably contemplating his infallible skills in charming information from unsuspecting receptionists.

"I'm not sure that I'm over happy about this," Tessa informed him.

"Oh, come along." He tilted his head on one side. "Please don't be angry. I'm absolutely honorable in my intentions and completely harmless."

Tessa found herself unable to suppress a smile. "What do you want?" she asked with a narrow gaze. And what do I need to find out from him? she wondered. Whilst doubtful and worried about Rupert Frobisher's motives in engineering this meeting, she realised that it represented a golden opportunity. There was no question of allowing the chance of gaining some useful information from one of the Gable 'names' to slip through her fingers.

"Please don't look so suspicious, I'm not a seducing wolf on the prowl." He gazed down at her, and it seemed that every nerve in his beautiful sinuous body was quivering with charming entreaty.

"I should hope not. And you wouldn't get very far if you were!" she told him severely.

He glanced around the grimy, echoing car park. "Look, this isn't the most pleasant place to talk. Too jolly draughty for a start. Let me take you somewhere simply fantastic to have lunch."

She laughed out loud.

"No, I'm not joking. This is serious. Have you ever been to the Bird's Nest?"

She shook her head. He was unbelievable.

"No? Well then, now's the time to put that right. It's a simply super little place. Only opened up last year. My uncle owns it."

Tessa succumbed. What the hell, she thought. She said, "In that case, how can I refuse?"

Rupert led the way to a crouching Italian sports car, parked nearby. Tessa lowered herself into the passenger seat. "I'm almost horizontal," she complained. "Doesn't this seat go any higher? I feel as if a dentist might materialise at any moment and start drilling my teeth."

Rupert pressed a button on the dashboard and the back of her seat rose up silently like the sun.

"Sorry about that," he told her. "I was out with my girlfriend last night. We parked by the river for a snog. Well, you know how it is . . ."

Tessa decided that by snog, he did simply mean snog. You couldn't possibly indulge in more serious sexual activity in this car.

Rupert roared out of the car park and headed off into the West End, cleaving the traffic in the manner of Moses parting the Red Sea. Compared with Rupert, even Oliver would seem like a slouch.

"Now, didn't I tell you this was a super place?" Rupert exclaimed with satisfaction as they sat in heavily embroidered armchairs, sipping Bombay Sapphire (Rupert said there was no point drinking any kind of gin other than Bombay Sapphire) and inspecting a menu that was presented cunningly hidden between the dusty covers of an ancient hardback novel.

"Amazing," agreed Tessa, looking around, her vision assaulted by the huge paintings on the walls: disturbing Picasso-style nudes whose expressions suggested they were undergoing torture.

"I'm going to have the basil boccocchini and a tomato salad," Rupert announced decisively. "It's absolutely delicious, I can highly recommend it. Why don't you have the same?"

"Why not?" said Tessa, realising that standing out against Rupert's charming persuasiveness would require the expenditure of a good deal of effort. She judged that her energies should be directed towards finding out what his motives were in engineering this meeting rather than squabbling over the choice of food.

"I'll order a bottle of Veuve Clicquot. You can always rely on a good champagne to wash down almost any kind of cuisine nicely, don't you think?"

"Definitely." Tessa leaned back and eyed Rupert reflectively. She decided to go for the jugular. "Rupert, have you ever met Professor Royston Gable?" she demanded with brutal directness.

Rupert shook his head in smiling regret. "Never, unfortunately."

"Did you see him on my TV programme last week?"

"Alas no. I've only just got back from a spell of sight-seeing in the Canadian Rockies. Super place. Have you ever been there?"

"No. But to go back to my original question. Am I right in thinking that you've been a subject in one of Professor Gable's major research projects?"

"Yes, indeed." When he smiled at her his eyes seemed to lengthen, and the corners of his mouth turned up most engagingly.

Tessa watched him for a moment in silence.

"What have I done wrong?" he enquired, looking wistful and amused.

"I was wondering why you didn't ask me how I knew that you were a subject for Professor Gable's research."

"Well – it's not like being involved with the secret service, is it? Not classified information." His eyes sparkled winningly.

226

"Come on, Rupert! How do you know that I know?" Tessa felt reckless now. Driven only by the desire for knowledge. Desperate to clear the dark fog of mystery that had swirled in her mind for days.

"Adam Baddeley telephoned me to say that you'd been to visit him. Simple as that."

"Ah, I see." Tessa thought for a moment. "So you and Adam are friends?"

"Indeed we are. We're both at the same college. He's a super chap. A wonderful chum."

Tessa noted the ex-public-schoolboy jargon in Rupert's phraseology. She was also struck by the easy self-assurance in his tone, an assumed authority that comes from privilege and status. She guessed that Rupert's experiences of childhood and schooling must have been very different to those Adam had been exposed to.

Their food arrived: a feast for the eye served on square, matt-black plates. The little yellow balls of mozzarella cheese were lined up with careful precision like chess pieces on a board.

"So, you and Adam had never met before you came across each other at college?" Tessa enquired, spearing a ball of mozzarella.

"No, absolutely not." Rupert leaned back to enable the waiter to fill his glass with champagne. "Pure coincidence. Well, you know what they say – the world's an amazingly small place."

Tessa took a small sip of her champagne. It tasted acid and cold on her tongue. She realised that she was in no mood for relaxing and enjoying herself. "So Adam telephoned you to say that I'd been to see him?"

"Yes."

"Does he often telephone you?"

"Hardly ever. We don't see so much of each other out of college."

"Have you met any other of Professor Gable's research subjects?"

"Not one." He gave her a quizzical smile.

Tessa realised that she was beginning to sound like a detective, quizzing Rupert, coming on far too strong. Easy, she told herself. She captured another ball of mozzarella. "It's a pity you didn't see the interview with Professor Gable," she told Rupert casually. "He was a very interesting guest. He had some fascinating things to say about his research."

"It's simply riveting stuff, isn't it?"

"Mmm." Tessa tilted her head on one side, inviting him to expand a little.

"I mean I've always believed people were a product of their breeding. Geniuses are born, not made, that kind of thing. My father owns a stud, you see, he breeds steeplechasers. You get to know a lot about inherited characteristics in that line of business."

Tessa nodded. "So you'll be pleased to have taken part in a research project that seems to have confirmed your beliefs?"

"Oh, rather."

"Have you any brothers or sisters?" Tessa asked, not quite sure why she wanted to know, simply feeling it was somehow relevant.

"No, I'm the one and only. My parents had a lot of difficulty getting started with me apparently." He smiled, giving Tessa the impression that his parents had thought him well worth waiting for. "They're simply super parents," he added, his face lit with affection. "I've been really lucky on that score. Lots of chaps at school had a rotten time when they were little. Parents piling on the pressure or never being there, or splitting up. But mine were just great."

"And have there been some scores on which you've not been lucky?" Tessa asked lightly, hopeful of finding a chink of darkness amongst all this light.

"Nope. I've had a disgustingly easy life," confessed Rupert, grinning broadly as though his good fortune was something he had won like a sports trophy. "And a jolly happy one too!"

I'm getting nowhere, thought Tessa, frustrated. I'm finding out nothing. Maybe I'm asking the wrong questions. Or maybe there simply isn't anything to discover.

She looked at Rupert, serenely eating his lunch, becoming ever more smooth and assured as he sipped his champagne. There was a silkiness about him, an unshakable self-confidence that was most unusual and yet curiously familiar. He reminded her of someone. She gave a little frown, forcing her brain to work and provide her with answers.

The thought that suddenly sprang into her mind sent her mentally reeling. She turned her gaze once more on Rupert, her eyes running over him as he stared thoughtfully at the angry nudes on the wall. Her heart began to beat with drumming insistence. She got up. "Will you excuse me for just a moment? I have to make a phone call," she said to Rupert with an apologetic smile.

For the first time he displayed discomfiture. "Oh. Oh dear! You will come back, won't you? There's the pudding menu to look at. And . . ." he paused.

"Oh yes," Tessa reassured him, astonished to see that he was lost for words. "I'll be back in just one minute. I promise." She felt his eyes on her as she walked away. It seemed that his reaction to the possibility of her walking out on him had aroused a sudden, very marked anxiety. But why? she asked herself. Why, why, why?

She went into the tiny cloakroom, took out her mobile phone and put a call through to the studios.

"Dartbridge Television Consortium. How can I help you?" came a bored, parrot-like voice.

"Tracy – it's Tessa."

"Oh hi, Tessa! How's things?"

"Marvellous, couldn't be better," Tessa responded with irony.

"Oh dear, that bad! Tracy chuckled. "Who do you want?"

"Rex Chance."

"Ooh, there are a lot of us who feel the same way!"

"Tracy!" warned Tessa. "No wisecracks, please!"

Tracy gave a throaty chuckle. "The whole studio knows the two of you have been lusting after each other for months," she said wickedly. "It just took you and him a bit longer to catch on."

"Is that so? Look, Tracy, I'm in a trendy West One eaterie, I've made a quick escape to the cloakroom and I'm in a rush. Please will you put me through to Rex's office."

"Sorry, I can't do that, Tessa. He's in conference with Lady

Angela Drake

C. Are you having lunch with a fella? Honestly, you presenters get all the fun."

"How long will he be with Lady Collingham?" Tessa asked, rolling her eyes.

"Don't know. As long as it takes. She gave us instructions that they were *absolutely not to be disturbed*. On penalty of fatal throat-cutting," she added, tittering at her own joke.

"Oh," said Tessa, dismayed.

"It all seems to be connected with a call we had a few minutes ago from some big publicity agent," confided Tracy helpfully. "She was a terror, a real shrew, shouting and swearing. She said she had to speak to Lady C immediately. And soon after that, Rex got hauled in for an audience in the holy of holies. He's been there ever since. Wish I was a fly on the wall."

Oh heavens, they'll be talking about me, thought Tessa. Lady Collingham will be tearing strips off Rex for letting his staff run around terrorising poor harmless young pop stars. Oh poor Rex, she thought, imagining him exposed to the onslaught of Lady Collingham's sharp tongue. And poor me, she added bleakly to herself, I'll probably already be jobless. "Don't worry," she said to Tracy, aiming for a firm, cheery tone, "I'll catch up with Rex later."

"Shall I give him a message?" Tracy asked, sounding suspiciously detached.

Tessa conjured up a picture of Tracy, one hand steadying her earpiece as she listened to the phone, the other eagerly poised over her computer keyboard, waiting for the message she could e-mail to Rex's computer and then to all the other screens in the secretarial and reception offices.

"Just tell him I called," Tessa said briskly. "I'll be back in the office within the hour."

She walked slowly back to the table. Glancing across the dining room she saw that Rupert was keeping a careful eye on the entry door. When he saw her, he instantly sprang up, smiling in delight, holding out her chair and then settling her into it, replacing the napkin on her lap with a courtesy bordering on reverence.

"Your pudding's arrived," he told her, looking as pleased as

230

if he'd made it with his own hands. "Hot almond pastry filled with spiced dried fruits. You'll find it absolutely marvellous, best thing on the menu. I know you'll love it."

"Thank you," said Tessa drily. "It was good of you to choose for me. And it's lucky that I'm not allergic to almonds or spiced dried fruits."

Rupert showed no sign of appreciating the irony in her tone. He was obviously used to choosing on other people's behalf and had no qualms about his taste not matching theirs.

"Now! You eat and I'll talk," he told her.

"Oh, right. OK." Silently Tessa decided she would damn well talk too if she felt like it. But then she found that the pudding was extremely good, and so she put on a show of being obedient and quiet whilst she ate it. After all, Rupert was picking up the check.

"So, let's get things straight," said Rupert. "You currently have a job as the presenter of a national network TV chat show?"

"Yes, I'm one of the presenters, anyway."

"And you're making a documentary about young people in higher education?"

"Yes, that's right." Tessa felt the lie slip out with remarkable ease. She told herself that a certain amount of harmless lying was necessary and justifiable in the cause of seeking the truth.

"That's absolutely fascinating," Rupert replied, his eyes shining, his smile radiant. "Splendid, in fact."

"Mmm," said Tessa, keeping her eyes on her pudding. Her heart had speeded up as Rupert quizzed her. The tentative theory that had flashed into her mind minutes earlier now began to have substance. And with it came a fresh spark of fear. What did Rupert really want out of this meeting? Why had he bothered to find out her whereabouts, pursue her, provide her with a luxury lunch? If her theory was phoney, then his behaviour was simply a puzzle. If her theory was valid – then she judged there was cause for extreme caution.

Rupert twirled his champagne glass. "Adam mentioned that there might be a possibility of being invited to take part in the documentary." He spoke with the over-elaborate casualness that indicated that he was very interested indeed in her reply.

"That's always a possibility," Tessa said carefully.

Rupert's blue eyes levelled with hers. "You know," he said thoughtfully, "my father's one of those chaps who have influence more or less everywhere. Except the media, funnily enough."

Tessa polished off the last spoonful of pudding and laid down her spoon. "Yes – and?"

Rupert treated her to the most dazzling smile in his repertoire. "I'll be honest with you, Tess. I've been trying to find a way to break into TV for some time now. It's not easy, is it?"

"No," she agreed. "Not if you're hoping to jump straight to the top of the ladder."

Rupert looked a trifle offended. He soon recovered himself. "Well, I don't mind a spot of apprenticeship, but I'm not exactly the kind of guy who's going to spend my time pushing the mail trolley round the studios and making tea."

"No, I can see that," Tessa smiled. "Rupert," she said, leaning forwards towards him, "are you asking me to use my influence at Dartbridge to get you a job fronting a programme?"

"In a nutshell, yes."

Tessa smiled, entertained that he considered her job to carry with it that kind of power. Added to which, Rupert was not to know that she was in hot water with Dartbridge's redoubtable managing director, that she might now be in the position of not having a job at Dartbridge at all if Lady Collingham had decided to wield her axe.

"I thought if I could take part in the documentary I could demonstrate my potential. And after that . . ." Rupert spread his hands in a graceful gesture indicating limitless possibilities.

"I see," said Tessa, entertained to reflect that throughout this elaborate lunch the only thing on Rupert's mind had been a harmless wish to get himself on TV. She let out a small sigh of amusement and relief.

She sat back smiling, idly watching Rupert's slender hands as he signed the bill. They were exquisitely beautiful hands

— as sensual as those of a dancer, and yet utterly masculine. They were, she reflected, as beautifully formed and delicate as Adam Baddeley's bare feet, padding over the dusty path outside his tiny East End house. Her smiled waned. A tiny shiver raced down her spine.

Renewed conjecture swept through her, stabbing her with further racing speculations.

"Will you at least think about it?" Rupert asked. He was almost pleading.

"Yes," she said with perfect honesty, making sure to keep her voice low and steady, covering all the inner agitation. "I will think about it."

"You promise me now," he insisted. "You won't forget!"

"Oh no, I won't forget."

Rupert's face relaxed. He let out a long breath. "Splendid! Absolutely marvellous. Why don't we have a brandy to celebrate?"

"Because I have work to do back at the studios," Tessa told him. "And if you're very lucky, Rupert, you might one day be in the same position."

Twenty-Five

Royston Gable had first reinvented himself at the age of nineteen when he went up to Cambridge on an open scholarship to study medicine.

He had won his scholarship through gutsy hard work against all the odds in a household that was suspicious of cleverness and academic achievement. He had won it through a demonic determination to get away from his home environment in one of the most deprived and Dickensian inner city areas still to be found in northern England in the 1960s.

Royston had been part of the baby boom following the Second World War. He had been one of the illicitly conceived, illegitimate babies who ended up in a charity home, his cot being one in a row of ten in a cold dormitory at the top of an Edwardian mansion house, his carers being a procession of kindly but detached women dressed in nurse's uniforms.

His parents had adopted him when he was eighteen months old, a sturdy, grave-eyed child, quiet, obedient and watchful. Having been deprived of any one stable adult figure with whom to form a loving bond, the little Royston was already frighteningly self-contained and independent, a lone wolf in the making.

His parents saw his self-containment as an indication of strength of character. His mother was proud that her little boy would play for hours on his own, making up his own games and amusements and never ever making a mess, whereas other children were noisy and wilful, rude and demanding.

Royston's adoptive father, Jim, was a clerk in the treasury department at the Town Hall. His mother, Jenny, was a pretty, much younger woman who looked up to her husband on all matters. Whilst she cleaned and cooked and looked after little

Royston her husband took care of all the family finances and the overall maintenance of their modest household.

When Jim died of cancer just before his fortieth birthday, Jenny was not only grief-stricken but utterly helpless, cut adrift from all she had loved and relied on. Within the year she had married Bill, a burly retired merchant seaman, who flitted in and out of light labouring jobs.

Royston was now eight. At the local school he was something of a star. They moved him up into a class with children a year older because he so far outstripped the classmates of his own age.

His teacher recognised the young boy's intellectual potential. In fact his quickness to learn thrilled her, she was so used to working with children who found it hard to retain routine factual information and even harder to grasp new ideas. But Royston was instantly receptive to all that she offered to him.

After a few weeks she had to admit that he was one step ahead of her in more or less every aspect of the curriculum. When he was word perfect on his multiplication tables up to twelve, he took it on himself to write out and learn the tables up to twenty. After history and geography lessons he would go to the local reference library and find books relevant to the topics she had touched on. He could read anything and everything, even the most complex and irregular words. But most of all he was hungry for scientific knowledge. He wanted to learn about nature, about birds and animals and plants. He wanted to learn the laws of chemistry and physics. He wanted to learn everything about the world around him and how it worked.

Realising that Royston's scientific knowledge easily outstripped her own, she borrowed texbooks from the grammar school which her own son attended. She gave them to Royston to study in his own time at home.

It was at this point that burly Bill intervened. For some time he had been uneasy about the boy Royston's quick brain, his liking for book learning and his apparently superhuman memory. Bill especially disliked the way young Royston looked at him with his cool blue eyes as though seeing right through to the heart of him, branding him a clumsy ignoramus.

Mainly unemployed now, drawing the dole and spending most of it on beer, Bill spent hours sitting in front of the TV, his mind fuddled with alcohol. He had taken to giving Jenny the odd swipe if she nagged him about getting another job, or mismanaged the pitiful housekeeping allowance he gave her. Nothing serious, just a little warning to let her know who was boss.

He had seen Royston's eyes on him as he lashed out, the silent condemning thought behind the lad's cool blue gaze. Well, let him think what he liked, the jumped-up clever little devil.

But it was the books that really got Bill going. When he saw the boy with those books, reading them against all odds even when the telly was on full blast, even when he, Bill, was bad-mouthing Jenny for not clearing up the tea things fast enough, his brains seemed to be set on fire with blood-red thoughts.

One Friday evening, when he came in from the pub, he found Royston enthroned at the table like a little emperor, books spread all over the top. He was reading from a textbook, making neat little notes in an exercise book his teacher had given him.

Bill's head split with rage and envy. Sweeping the books and pencils off the table with one savage swipe, he hauled the boy to his feet and slapped his face hard. "We don't want any of that fancy rubbish in here. Keep that for school. Why aren't you helping your mother in the kitchen?" Bill shook the boy until he heard his teeth knock together. "Well, haven't you got a tongue?"

"She's not in the kitchen. She's having a bath." Bill found it hard to know if the boy was afraid or not. Those blue eyes held no clear message.

The flame of Bill's rage burst into a furnace. "So you dare to answer me back, do you? I'll give you learning, lad." He put the boy over his knee and made him scream with pain. Then he sent him to bed for the weekend with the curtains drawn.

"Oh, it seems a shame," said Jenny when Bill forbade her to take her boy any dinner.

Every Friday night Bill engineered a quarrel. The boy's wits were sharp and he tried everything he could think of to avoid the brutal punishment which he knew in his heart was inevitable.

But Bill had sheer brute strength on his side. His ears sang with satisfaction at the rhythmic crack of his big rough hand on the boy's tender flesh. "You cocky little so-and-so. That'll learn you!"

"Oh, don't," wailed Jenny feebly.

"He's nothing but a little bastard," Bill told her with satisfaction. "His mother would have been some no good slag ready to give her favours to any man that asked. Blood will out, Jenny. And there's bad blood there in that lad. You can tell. He needs it knocking right out of him."

When Royston was thirteen, Bill fell in the canal after an extended visit to the pub. Jenny wept all through his funeral, but Royston watched the coffin glide into the hole in the crematorium wall with his cool, clear blue gaze never once flinching.

Jenny's next husband was a double-glazing salesman. He was never violent, but he never took to Royston. And he was never able to find the funds for him to go on school trips to France and Italy.

On the day he left for Cambridge, Royston kissed his mother's cheek at the station and vowed that he would never return home. And he never did. He had little love left for his mother, and no further need of her. He had money from his college scholarship and a generous bursary from the local council. And when funds ran low in the holiday he took a job as a porter in the local hospital.

He trained himself to speak with the rich, deep vowels of the most privileged, well-connected public-school boys in his college. He never spoke of his home, and in time it became generally accepted that he was a boy of gentle birth, an orphan who had fallen on hard times and was to be commended for learning how to look after himself.

He did spectacularly well in his medical finals, and his

Angela Drake

tutor predicted a glowing future for him as a doctor. But Royston was already looking towards another field of learning. The study of the body had been very interesting, but the study of the mind seemed to him far more fascinating. The very thought of it sent a thrill of anticipated power through his body.

Whilst he was working as a houseman in a London hospital he met Belinda, a lively, red-headed Scottish nurse. With Belinda he found a warmth that had always been lacking in his life. "You're a cool customer," Belinda used to tease him. "I'm going to warm you up."

One night she mentioned to him, rather casually, that her father was the owner of a famous whisky distillery and that when she was twenty-one she would come into a considerable amount of money.

Within six months they were married. Royston introduced himself to Belinda's whiskery whisky-manufacturing father as the only son of a doctor and his opera-singer wife who had both been killed in a car accident. Fortunately Belinda's father was not particularly interested in either medicine or opera, and he never asked for any further details of Royston's tragically cut down parents.

Belinda was impressed when Royston decided to study for further A levels in his spare time and gained a place at Cambridge to study psychology and genetics.

"I shall have to turn it down," Royston had told her gravely. "I can't support myself."

She laughed. "No. But I can!"

Royston's new studies took him over. Body, mind and soul. He had found his true vocation. The search for knowledge about the origins of human beings and the formation of their intelligence and personalities fascinated him. He wanted to discover everything that was known about the way in which the different cards shuffled from the genetic pack could produce different individuals. And then to push the limits further with his own research.

Not only had he found his new vocation, he had found his one true love.

"I never see you," Belinda complained. "And when I do

238

you never talk about anything but psycho-genetics. It's like competing with a beautiful mistress."

At first she made a joke of it. But gradually, as Royston became ever more detached, the marriage began to falter.

Belinda realised that Royston had no real need of a loving relationship with one person. In fact he didn't really know how to give and receive love. She had thought that having a baby would help. But she failed to become pregnant. In the course of investigations for her possible infertility she fell in love with her gynaecologist.

Royston was sympathetic to her desire to have a child. He accompanied her on her visits to the fertility clinic and when she told him about her relationship with the senior doctor and asked him for a divorce he was perfectly calm and understanding. And Belinda, in turn, was very generous in compensating him with a chunk of her fortune.

Royston knew he would never marry again. He was married to his new profession. But he still liked the company of women. And now that he was rich and becoming established in an intriguing and prestigious field of research he could attract any woman he wanted.

He transformed himself into Royston Gable the respected scientist and wealthy escort of beautiful women.

With the eventual triumph of his research into the discovery of a gene for intelligence he found himself catapulted into the public spotlight. Suddenly he was not only rich, not only brilliant academically, he was in demand. The wealthy, the famous and the aristocratic came to him for advice on their choice of partners, mindful of the findings of his research. Newspapers wanted articles, TV presenters wanted interviews.

Now he was Royston Gable the magnetic god-like guru whose research had delivered the keys to the secrets of genetics and intelligence. It was a wonderful life.

Royston Gable sat now in his library, carefully inspecting the details he had just received about the movements of a certain young woman who had taken to meeting young men in whom Gable maintained a long-standing interest.

Gable reflected that he had re-invented himself a number

of times. But the last re-invention had been the one he was most content with. And on no account was he going to forgo it because of the insatiable curiosity of a lively young woman in the media, not even one as fascinating and desirable as Tessa Clair.

A part of him had hoped to be able to leave her in peace to get on with her career and her love affair, but another part had longed to be forced into playing the thrilling and dangerous game that would now be necessary to put a stop to her curiosity.

He drew up a list of calls to be made and reached for the telephone.

Rex tried to get Tessa on her mobile phone. It was switched on to automatic-answering mode which frustrated him beyond belief so that his subsequent message was no more than a curt, barked command for her to get in touch with him immediately – if not sooner. This brutishness he instantly regretted. "Damn!" he exclaimed.

He telephoned Vicky.

"Benny, darling, don't do that," came her voice, warm and husky. Then, "Hello!"

"Thank God there's a female in the world who still answers a phone," Rex growled. "This is your tormented brother calling you."

"What's the problem?" Vicky asked calmly.

"Woman trouble. What's that offspring of yours doing that he shouldn't?"

"Stirring the chocolate cake mixture with his worm-stirring stick."

"Yes, I can see why you might want to put a stop to that."

"Rex, Rex," Vicky sighed affectionately. "Don't prevaricate. As Portia said to Brutus, 'Acquaint me with your cause of grief'."

"I thought Portia was the sharp-talking heiress in *The Merchant of Venice*. Don't recall that she had a bloke around called Brutus."

"Different Portia. There was another, less famous one in *The Life and Death of Julius Caesar*. Portia wife to Brutus. She complained that he was for ever musing and sighing, stamping his feet and so on. Being a real pain, in short."

"Is that what reminded you of me."

"Yes. So tell me what's wrong."

Rex sighed. "Nothing should be wrong. Everything should be right. I've fallen in love, Vicky."

There was a little beating pause. "I think Doug and I already knew. Benny, please come away from the eggs – now! Sorry Rex,"

"You knew?"

"It was writ large all over your face when you brought her here the other night." Vicky paused. "Tessa's perfect for you, Rex. What's the problem? It can't be unrequited love. She was just as transparently smitten as you."

"She keeps going AWOL. It's driving me absolutely crazy."

"AWOL," Vicky mused. "The literal translation of that acronym is *absent without leave*, isn't it?"

"So?"

"So, I'd be rather careful if I were you."

"What do you mean?"

"You're not talking about a soldier deserting his post, or a teenager playing truant from school. You're talking about an independent young woman who has every right to a life of her own, without your wanting to check on her movements every second of the day."

Rex gave a low groan.

"Oh dear, is what you've been doing? Ben, my darling, I'd be much happier if you didn't practise your sculpting skills on the butter."

"No. Well not exactly . . ."

"Oh Rex, I'm not unsympathetic," Vicky told him, her voice warm with affection. "I realise you can't help thinking about danger and disaster where a loved one is concerned. That's understandable. But it's a very long time since Eleanor died. You can't let that memory throw a black cloud over the rest of your life. You can't wrap Tessa in a fluffy blanket of safety and keep her permanently joined to you at the hip."

Rex put his hand up to the back of his neck. He felt a

241

strain there, a tightness. He wondered how much to tell Vicky. He decided to say nothing. Why burden Vicky unnecessarily?

"You're a wise woman," he said to her. "And you have knowledge of two Shakespearean Portias."

"Hah! I do try to keep my brain in trim. Staying at home and looking after a young child can be the equivalent in mind terms to what sitting around all day smoking and eating chocolates does to your body."

"What's Benny doing now?"

"He's sidled out of the kitchen and now he's somewhere out of my sight being exceedingly quiet."

"Trouble?"

"Undoubtedly. I'd better go investigate. Goodbye, Rex. And try not to worry too much."

Rex put down the phone. He swivelled his chair and looked out of the window, his face intense with reflection. Above him clouds swirled around a hesitant sun. A jet screamed past, its nose dipping as it prepared for landing.

He did not hear the door open, did not hear the soft click of the security latch as it dropped into place. Was not aware of the soft footsteps as they approached.

Her hands were on his shoulders, her soft lips against his neck, the warm scent of her invading his nostrils before he realised what was happening. He turned, the joy leaping inside him like a shower of gleaming sparks.

"Hello, Mr Boss," she said, squirming on to his knee and raining kisses all over his face.

"Where the bloody hell have you been?" he growled. But at the same time as he chided her, he was smiling and his voice had lost its cutting edge.

"Lunching with a lithe, sexy young blond." Tessa kissed one side of Rex's mouth. "Male. Very well set up in every way." She kissed the other side of his mouth. "He picked up the tab too."

Rex grabbed her, grasping her face and forcing her lips to contact fully with his.

"Aah," she murmured.

"There's no such thing as a free lunch," he murmured.

"Yes. I knew you'd say that." She arched away from him, smiling tenderly into his face, luxuriating in the renewal of the waves of sensation that seemed to roll up as soon as she was in his presence.

"Who was he?" Rex asked softly.

"I'll explain in a minute. But first I want to know if I've still got a job."

"Hmm. Thanks to me you've been miraculously saved from the chop."

"I've been snatched from the lioness's jaws, no less?" She chuckled. "Tell me what happened."

"It appears that during the course of this morning you were unwise enough to get on the wrong side of some commando-style publicity manager."

"Good description. You would have had to conduct your interview sitting in a barrel with a bucket over your head and a gag around your mouth not to upset her." Tessa suddenly became serious. "Truly, Rex, I didn't step out of line. I was tact personified."

Rex smiled. "Lady C is no fool. She understood that."

Tessa watched his expression. "So, she's not going to fire me. Even more amazing, she's being very understanding. What's the catch?"

Thoughts battled in Rex's face. "Two catches," he countered.

She stroked the creases on his forehead with tender fingers. "Yes?"

"She's concerned that there has been a significant problem around both of your most recent interviews. Problems with Gable, and now difficulties with Cherry Ripe – maybe an outright cancellation of the programme."

"I'm getting myself tarred with the brush of trouble? Is that it?"

"I'm afraid that's exactly it."

"Does it bother you, Rex? As my overall professional boss?"

The tenderness in his responding smile made her heart turn over. "That's the other catch," he said.

She put her head on one side, not quite grasping his meaning.

"I can't go on being your boss, Tessa. Now that we're lovers, things have changed for us. For a start I can't be objective about your performance – your professional performance that is," he added swiftly, as Tessa rolled her eyes at him with heavy suggestion. "People in love can't work properly together as boss and staff member."

"No," she admitted sadly. "You're right. Lady Collingham's right as well, I suppose."

"Don't look so sad," he said. "We'll work something out. It doesn't mean one of us is about to join the ranks of the jobless."

"It wasn't that I was looking sad about. It was thinking of this being the end of our working together. I really liked working with you Rex – once I stopped hissing and spitting every time you hoved into view!"

He drew her against him, so their hearts beat together. "So did I. But what we're going to have together in the future will be even better."

There were some delicious moments of silence, until eventually, with great reluctance they pulled away from each other.

"Now – about this young man you were lunching with?" Rex demanded.

Tessa gave him some brief initial details. The way Rupert had appeared in the car park, his persuading her to have lunch with him. The fact that he was in contact with Adam Baddeley. Rex's eyes darkened with fresh anxiety. "Oh Christ! This Gable business. I really feel uneasy about it, Tess . . ."

"No, you mustn't." Tessa suddenly understood the depth of Rex's distress on her behalf. She saw that he was not trying to control her, he simply wanted to keep her safe. Everyone needed someone who cared enough to want to keep them safe. Looking into his frowning, worried face she made an incisive, completely unplanned decision not to tell him about the astonising insight that had come to her whilst she was with Rupert – about her fantastic theory, which could just be true. And if it were true . . .

A little cloud of gloom sailed over her. She had been longing to share her conjecture with him, to seek his opinion. And the thought of having secrets from him was hateful. But her heart told her that just at this moment it would not be right to confide in him.

"Don't worry about me, darling," she said, rubbing her cheek against his. "I'm going to be really careful, really sensible. I'm going to think things through and look before I leap. In fact I won't do anything else at all regarding Gable without discussing it with you first. That's a solemn promise." She took his hands. "Rex, my darling, I love you so very much. And I know how you worry about me. And I think it's wonderful to have someone caring so much."

He held her hands tightly in his. "Tessa, listen, I have to fly up to Scotland for a meeting with my opposite number in Glasgow. Lady Collingham's specific directive."

"Oh hell, how will I manage to do without you for more than two minutes? When do you leave?"

"In about an hour."

"Oh no!"

"Oh yes! Lady C's lending me her car and her chauffeur to get me to Heathrow. Don't look like that! I'll be back tomorrow afternoon."

"Oh well! I'll just have to sit in my flat tonight and weep with loneliness."

He laughed. "I somehow can't visualise that."

"No. Maybe not. I could catch up on the ironing. Far more practical." She smiled at him ruefully. In her mind was the thought that she could spend a little time working on her theory, considering possibilities, digging up information . . .

God, she thought in distress. I love him so very much, and yet I'm already planning a deception.

An hour later, she stood at the window in her office, watching Rex walk across the car park carrying his black document case. He turned, looked up and gave a brief wave. She waved back, blowing kisses. He disappeared into a huge dark blue Mercedes and was gone. Her arms fell to her sides and suddenly she was desolate.

At six thirty, as she was thinking of packing in for the day and collecting a takeaway pizza on the way home, her phone rang.

"A call for you, Tessa," said Tracy on reception. "It's a Professor Royston Gable."

Tessa's heart lurched. A small animal sound came from her throat.

"Shall I put him off? Tell him you're in a meeting?"

"No," said Tessa, gathering her wits. "Put him through." She waited for the appropriate clicks to sound on the line. "Good evening, Professor Gable," she said smoothly, leaping in to take the initiative before he could so much as take a breath.

"Good evening, Tessa."

"What can I do for you?" she asked, all brisk cheerfulness.

"Dine with me."

She laughed out loud. Lunch with one man. Dinner with another. And neither her only love. This was becoming farcical.

"I'm glad to amuse you," he said. "I've been presumptuous enough to book a table at Claridge's. Eight o'clock."

"No," said Tessa.

"Oh dear. Are you already engaged?"

"As a matter of fact – I'm not."

"So, why refuse?" A pause. "Are you afraid?"

"Yes."

"You impress me greatly with your honesty, Tessa."

"Thank you."

"There's no need to be afraid. I shall meet you in the foyer. I shall say goodbye to you in the foyer. Claridge's is a very civilised place. What harm can I do you there?"

Shivers whipped down Tessa's spine. He was scaring her out of her wits. Curse the man. She wouldn't let him bloody get away with it.

"Tessa, I have something to tell you about your brother, Alec. He's alive and well you know . . ."

Her knuckles glowed bone-white as she clutched the phone. "Alec!" she breathed.

"Yes. Alec, the brother you haven't seen for years. Don't you want to hear how you can get in touch with him?"

She drew in a long, painful breath. "Of course I do."

"Well then, come and dine with me and I'll tell you."

"I don't believe you. How could you know anything about Alec?"

"You can find anything out," he said patiently, "if you know how to go about it and you have the motivation and the contacts."

She was silent.

"You may think all manner of ill of me, Tessa. But I don't think you would believe that I would lie to you on such a serious issue."

"No." A rich mixture of emotions swirled within her. Think, don't feel, she told herself. "All right then. Tell me Alec's date of birth," she commanded. "And the colour of his eyes."

Gable made a small noise of tolerant amusement in his throat. And then he quoted Alec's date of birth and the different colours of his mismatched eyes. Correctly. "Do you want further confirmation?" he asked politely.

"No," she told him, knowing that he had already won. That she had no choice but to accept his invitation. That, in some strange, terrifying way, she had no alternative but to allow events to take their course.

Twenty-Six

Claridge's Hotel was as far away from the atmosphere of the Bird's Nest restaurant, where Tessa had lunched with Rupert Frobisher, as a little motor boat is from an ocean liner.

Sitting opposite Royston Gable, Tessa could imagine that she was dining on board a luxurious cruise liner, the sea beneath her calm and level, beyond any breath of turbulence or emotion.

For that was how she herself was feeling: becalmed and flat and numb. Unreal. This can't be happening, a panicky little voice inside her kept insisting. You can't possibly have been so foolish as to accept an out-of-the-blue invitation from this strange, disturbing man. Defenceless cubs should keep well clear of the lion's den.

Quelling the voice of panic with an upsurge of assertiveness, Tessa took a slow sip of wine and looked steadily across the table into Gable's cool blue eyes.

"What I like about Claridge's," he told her, "is that you can eat the very simplest food here if you wish. Just a little grilled turbot with some steamed potatoes if that is what you prefer. I do dislike those restaurants where they crowd too many things on your plate and every item of food is embellished with a purée or a cassis and so on. I really do object to that."

"Yes, you're a purist," Tessa observed.

His eyes sharpened with admiration. "Thank you, Tessa." He folded the menu and laid it down with a single, precise movement. "Well, I shall have consommé and afterwards some cold lobster but I want you to feel free to order whatever you like."

Tessa gave a faint smile. She recalled Rupert and his

248

transparent efforts to guide her choice that lunchtime. Rupert would learn – in time. Learn how to control by insinuation and cunning, which were far more to be feared than simple bossiness.

She watched Gable as he gave the waiter the order. She had always considered Royston Gable a strangely detached and remote man, despite his habit of making personal observations. She realised now that this distance came from his seeming to inhabit a higher plane than his fellow humans, to be looking over their heads and speaking to them with the benefit of his vision of the whole landscape, whilst they saw only their own tiny personal space.

During the interval before their food arrived, Gable created an atmosphere of pleasant sociability, making a show of drawing Tessa out, enquiring about her preferences in literature, her taste in films, her favourite pieces of music in the classical repertoire. He was like a kindly, exquisitely well-mannered head teacher entertaining a sixth-form pupil to dinner at his house, doing all he could to put her at her ease.

Tessa noted that, once again, Gable was the one asking all the questions, the one calling all the shots. She had expected this. She made no attempt to protest, to assert herself and refuse to allow him to hold all the reins of control. She played the game, *his* game. She responded to all his questions with easy, good-humoured cooperation.

"Did you know that Claridge's was originally a common lodging house?" he asked her, prising the white lobster flesh from its shell with clean, incisive strokes. "A brothel to be more precise."

"Yes," Tessa said. "I once did an article on the great London hotels for a local newspaper. The research was very illuminating."

Gable smiled.

"I didn't think the evidence for Claridge's actually having been a brothel was totally convincing," Tessa added. "Although it certainly seems to have had a dubious reputation. And whatever went on in the original house must have been successful, because it soon expanded to five. And look at

249

it now." She gestured around her. She squared up to Gable's penetrating blue gaze. *I'm no pushover*, she was telling him silently.

Gable regarded her with renewed approval. "Good, good," he said in a congratulatory way as he pushed the bone-clean lobster shell to the side of his plate and arranged his cutlery neatly in the centre. How long would he keep her in suspense? she wondered, as they progressed through their dinner. The theory she had been harbouring in her head for the past few hours now seemed like an undetonated bomb. What disaster would occur if Gable were to see into her thoughts? If he should guess at what she was thinking, then what devastating explosion might result?

"Tell me about Rex Chance," Gable said suddenly, as the two of them considered the pudding menu.

Tessa felt prickles in her armpits. "He's a very astute programme controller," she replied carefully, her heart lunging.

"I'm sure he is. But I was thinking in terms of Rex Chance as a human being, as a man." The cool blue eyes levelled with hers.

Tessa felt chilled. She tried to frame some kind of reply, but somehow the task eluded her. To sum up Rex's personality in a few words for the benefit of Royston Gable seemed like a betrayal.

"Lost for words," Gable said smiling. "He must be very special to you."

"Yes, he is," Tessa agreed. "But that's private, Professor Gable."

"Royston," he corrected her.

She nodded.

He watched her for a few silent, unnerving moments. And when their pudding arrived they ate without attempting any further conversation.

"Let's go into the foyer to have our coffee," he decided at the end of the meal. "There's always an interesting procession of human life to observe there. It makes splendid free entertainment."

He led her to a blue sofa in the corner of the big lobby. They sat down together. Behind them was a mirrored wall, so that wherever Tessa looked she seemed to see some aspect of Gable's beautifully shaped head.

"Let me tell you about your brother," he said in the kindest of tones.

Tessa stared at him, dumb and frozen.

"Let me help you remember him," Gable offered. "He was the favourite wasn't he? The golden boy. The son your parents idolised?"

"They loved us both." she countered staunchly.

"Oh yes, I'm sure that's true. They loved you both. You were fortunate to have what people like to call a normal happy childhood."

"Yes, we did."

"They loved you both," Gable went on smoothly, "but they *idolised* Alec."

Tessa found tears springing in her eyes. They were not tears of self-pity, facing up to being second best for all her childhood years. They were tears of compassion for her poor, bewildered, crushed parents who had lost their darling.

"What you say is probably as close to the truth as one could get." She put her cup back on to the saucer. It made a little crash, because her hands were unsteady. She swung to face Gable. From the corner of her vision she caught a glimpse of herself in the mirror, her face flushed, the tilt of her head fierce with determination. "But can you tell me something about my brother that I don't already know?" she demanded.

"I told you on the telephone that I could help you to get in touch with him."

"You know where he is?"

Gable gave her a long look, his eyes chiding her for needing to ask the question. "Of course."

"How do you know these things about my brother, Professor Gable?"

"A mixture of information and guesswork, Tessa."

"That's not good enough," she told him steadily. "That's far too vague."

"Very well, what exactly do you want me to tell you?"

"I want to know where, or who, this 'information' came from."

He shook his head at her. "You're a sharp, bright young woman, Tessa. You work in the media. You're something of an expert in the ferreting out of information yourself. You know how it's done. Surely?"

"I certainly know how I myself operate. And I probably know quite a lot about the way other journalists and TV researchers go about digging and delving," Tessa flashed back at him. "But you seem to me to employ rather different methods. I'm asking you to tell me about them."

"Very well. You've asked me a simple and reasonable question, Tessa. So I shall give you a simple answer," he said evenly. "The information on your brother's antics before he disappeared from you and your parents' lives was perfectly easy for me to obtain. In my capacity as a research psychologist I have access to a number of databases which many people don't even know exist. Medical and educational data for a start. I also have the power and the influence to gain access to other sources of information which are normally secret and protected. Legal and criminal data, and so on." The blue eyes pierced her. "Do you understand what I'm saying, have I answered your question?"

"Yes, I suppose you have," she said reluctantly.

"You seem doubtful," he said, dropping a brown sugar lump into his coffee.

"Trying to imagine what it must be like to have such immense power at your disposal is quite difficult for me," she told him drily.

"Yes, I suppose it must be," he agreed, his eyes glinting with pleasure at her growing realisation of the full extent of his control over other people.

"Do you really know where Alec is now?" she said, her voice hard and insistent.

"Do you doubt me?" he asked. "Do you think I would lie to you about a thing like that?"

She thought for a moment. "No."

"As I began to tell you on the telephone earlier," he said patiently, "when you're rich and influential it's so very easy to find out more or less anything you want." His eyes flared with a renewed gleam of satisfaction. "And also," he went on with a new, low intensity, "it's possible to 'buy' people, to get them to do whatever you want. Anyone you can think of, Tessa. And they will do anything . . ."

Tessa shivered. "So where is Alec?"

"He's in Paris. He rents two rooms in a charming lopsided building in the seventh arrondissement, quite near to the Eiffel Tower."

Tessa took in a long deep breath. "And what sort of work does he do?"

"Sometimes very little. His last job was as a vegetable chef in a hot little restaurant near the Place de la Concorde. At present he's living with a rich older mistress who takes care of his expenses . . ."

"Oh God!"

"Yes, I'm afraid his lifestyle is not one which would give your parents much happiness if they were to find out about it. Alec is a gigolo. He sells himself to rich, older women."

"Do you have his address?"

"Which one, Tessa? The one in the lopsided apartment house, or that of his mistress's house?"

"I presume you have both?"

"Of course."

Her feelings were a battle-ground. There was a desperate desire to gain all the knowledge she could about Alec, to regain contact with him, to reconcile him with her parents. And then there was the even greater fear of how Gable would use his power in order to stop her going any further in her attempts to uncover his shocking secret – for she knew now that he had perpetrated something terrible, although the exact nature and means were still unknown to her. What might he do to clip her wings? What might he do to her family? To Rex?

She felt a sudden, overwhelming need for Rex's presence. She longed for him to be here with her. She yearned for his incisiveness, his wisdom, his reassurance and protection. With Rex close beside her she would be able to decide what to do. Her mind would clear, her body would stop trembling. She would see the way forward. With Rex she would feel empowered. She would feel loved. She would be safe.

Her mind darted here and there, flying down one blind alley, doubling back and fleeing to the next. Encountering only blank walls and darkness. What next? What should she do? What should she say?

She knew that it would be pointless to try to outwit Royston Gable in a game of deviancy. He was a master of the art.

She recalled the golden rule she had learned as a young journalist. The handy acronym of KISS – keep it simple, stupid. Simplicity was always more effective than complexity.

OK. OK. Think! Think!

"What do you want, Professor Gable?" she asked quietly.

He raised his eyebrows.

"You invited me here to persuade me to do something I wouldn't necessarily have planned to do," she said, doggedly calm and soft. "Or maybe not to do something I had planned to do."

"Yes. Excellent!" Gable seemed inordinately pleased with her grasp of the situation.

"Tell me what!" she demanded, knowing that she was whistling in the wind. He was having far too good a time toying with her.

"I'm offering you a little tasty bait," he said pleasantly. "The prospect of being reunited with your brother. I want you to pursue that bait, to find your brother – and then to be grateful to me. I'm sure you follow my meaning."

She was taken aback by his seeming directness. "Grateful as in not going any further in satisfying my insatiable curiosity?"

"Yes. Precisely that." He sighed. "Oh my dear Tessa. You delight me more than I can tell you. You have such a quick apprehension of situations. And such clear, sharp vision. You must have been a joy to teach when you were a child at school."

"Not that I noticed," she told him. She raised her head and locked her gaze into his. "Let's be really honest with each other, Professor Gable. Let me spell things out. You want me to make you a solemn promise that if I find Alec I shall take no further steps in finding out the link between the names I noted down from your computer?"

The words hung in the air, echoing and reverberating. She

had done the unthinkable. She had dared to voice the nature of their silent, shared secret. A secret understood in essence by both of them, but only partly comprehended by her. The silence that followed was like the tense moment between the blinding flash of lightning and the fearful crash of thunder.

"Solemn promises are cheap, Tessa," he said quietly. "Cheap like easy flowing tears."

"So a promise won't do?"

"I'm afraid not." He raised his head in a gesture of quietly dignified, almost imperial authority. "Not on its own, at any rate."

Tessa's heart ticked in her chest with plump painful throbs. She looked around the plush, warm foyer. People ebbed and flowed, meeting up and parting. Most of them were smiling; anticipating a drink with friends, an exquisite meal, the pleasure of shared companionship. There was nothing to suggest that evil was stalking the atmosphere, its outer face bland and innocent-seeming.

"What then?" she asked.

"I need to plant a further suggestion into your mind," he said politely. "And to know that you have properly understood it."

Oh, the monstrous ego of the man, thought Tessa. "Then go ahead," she said coolly.

He let a tiny moment pass, savouring it. "There are two men you love, Tessa," he said, intoning the words with luxurious, slow emphasis. "One is your brother, who I'm afraid has a rather weak capacity for loving others, because he loves himself more, you see. However, I realise that it would be very pleasant for you to have the chance to reassure your parents that he is alive and well, maybe even to effect some kind of reconciliation. Those small blessings I am happy to offer you." He turned to her, his lips smiling, his eyes assessing.

"Go on." Oh, how she admired and loathed the way he manipulated her with his silences.

"The other man you love is Rex Chance, who I believe has a great capacity for love and who idolises you. It doesn't surprise me that you're madly in love with him, Tessa. What your parents could never offer you, Rex is giving you in abundance." This time he did not look at her. The pause was highly charged.

Tessa's body trembled with the impact of the realisation of what he was driving at. "So," she said, her voice shaking with feeling, "you're threatening Rex."

He allowed a further silence to grow. How a silence can mock, Tessa thought.

"Yes," he said finally. "That is exactly the situation. You see, Tessa, I view your unstoppable desire to ferret out the truth which lies behind external façades extremely laudable. But in this particular case, your desire for knowledge could be very damaging to myself personally. And so I'm offering you the opportunity to trade in your curiosity for the safety of the man you love."

He's got me, she thought. And with the understanding came a momentary sense of relief. If Rex was the price to pay for finding out just what Royston Gable had been up to, then there was no difficulty in making the choice.

Her head bowed in thought, her mind totally filled with Rex, she gave a small jerk of shock as she felt Gable's fingers touch her arm. The physical contact with him made her freeze. She turned her head and looked up at him, her heart hammering. But his eyes were quite neutral and calm. He tilted his head, drawing her attention to the figure of a man standing at a respectful distance a few yards in front of her, waiting for a chance to speak.

"Miss Clair?" the man queried courteously.

"Yes."

"I'm sorry to disturb you, madam. There is a telephone call for you."

Tessa glanced at Gable. He smiled, opening his hands in a gesture of acceptance of whatever she chose to do.

She was shown to a private cubicle. Her heart beat fast as she anticipated Rex's voice. "Hello."

"Tessa Clair?" It was a woman's voice. Unknown.

"Yes."

"My name is Charles. Rosemary Charles."

Tessa's mind gave a startled little buck. The name was somehow familiar. But from where?

"I'm the mother of Hilary Charles."

"Oh!" Now her mind began a frantic scramble through endless possibilities. "Oh yes!"

"You know who I am?"

"Yes. At least . . ."

"Listen, I haven't much time, I'll get straight to the point. I saw your programme with Professor Gable last week. I've been meaning to call you since, but . . . well, let's say the shock got to me. I just couldn't believe my eyes. I needed time to think."

She stopped speaking and Tessa could hear her jagged breathing. "Mrs Charles? Are you still there?"

"Yes. Yes, I'm here. I wanted to warn you, Tessa. You could be in danger."

"I think I'm beginning to realise that."

"And I'm not sure that I'm too happy about my own situation either. Anyway, I'm not letting that dreadful man intimidate me."

"So what did you want to tell me?"

"Basically that I think Gable is Hilary's father. The facial resemblance is so startling. And – everything else fits."

"Everything else?" Tessa gripped the receiver, every nerve of her body straining.

"It's a complicated story. I'll try to explain as briefly as I can. You see Hilary's not my husband's child. My husband had a car crash not long after we were married. As a result of his injuries he became sterile. We decided to opt for artificial insemination. I was recommended to a brilliant gynaecologist at a fertility clinic in north London. I got pregnant straight away and we had Hilary. She was like a gift straight from heaven." Rosemary Charles stopped and cleared her throat noisily.

"Where does Professor Gable come in?" Tessa prompted gently.

"I met him once at the fertility clinic. He was there with his wife. He wasn't a Professor then, just plain Dr Gable. And he looked rather different twenty years ago; his hair was light brown and he had a beard. I'd more or less forgotten about him until I saw the TV programme. But seeing Gable as he is now, and then looking at Hilary . . .

Well, the likeness is uncanny. They just must be father and daughter."

Cries of astonishment seemed to reverberate through Tessa's body as theories and conjectures began to form themselves into a clear, sharp image of the terrible truth. "Are you saying that Dr Gable somehow infiltrated his own sperm into the clinic's sperm bank?"

"Yes. That's exactly what I'm saying. Isn't it crystal-clear? I somehow had the feeling you'd guessed. I taped your programme and when I played it back, it seemed to me that you had realised there was something odd in his past. And that he knew you had."

"Yes," breathed Tessa. "But not this! Oh God!"

"Look, I'll have to go in a moment. Hilary and her father are just arriving home. Her putative father, I should say. I've left my work number on your answerphone. You can call me there for a longer conversation tomorrow. We can maybe plan what we should do next."

"Why did you call me here this evening?" Tessa asked sharply.

"I telephoned your flat. When I heard the cryptic message you'd left on the answerphone, saying whom you were with and where, I knew I had to warn you. Listen Tessa, I got on to Gable after the programme and asked a few awkward questions, and his response was not that of a sane man. Don't try and tackle him on your own. Steer clear of him until you're absolutely sure you've got all eventualities well covered." She paused and Tessa heard the sound of a door banging, and laughing voices, one male, one female. "I'm sorry but I have to put the phone down now," Rosemary Charles said crisply. "Call me tomorrow."

She was gone.

Tessa stood in the phone cubicle, frozen into stillness. Her mind was so full she felt that it might overflow. Names rang in her ears, names and incredible relationships. Hilary, Adam, Rupert. Presumably Pascal also. Half-brothers and -sister, and all Royston Gable's 'children'. So who else was involved? How many more 'children' were there?

The information tumbled in her mind like a seething sea of

black water. She began to feel dizzy and unsteady. But she had
to keep calm. And very, very steady. She had to hold on to
this information. She had both to hold on to it and also to hide
it from Royston Gable who was waiting for her only yards
away. And then some time later she had to act on it.

Easily said. Not easily done.

Oh Rex, she sang out in a low moan. Why aren't you
here?

Twenty-Seven

R ex's flight left Heathrow on schedule and arrived in Glasgow five minutes early.

The administrative staff at Tartan TV had booked him into a five star hotel. There was a car waiting to take him there. The driver would wait whilst he freshened up and changed and then would take him on to the studios where he was scheduled to join an evening managerial meeting. Afterwards there was dinner and presumably a good deal of whisky drinking at an exclusive city-centre club.

Throwing his document case, which doubled up as overnight bag, on to the bed he immediately placed a call to Tessa's flat in Highbury.

"Hi there," said a treacly, seductive voice.

"Can I speak to Tessa?" He was aware of his voice sounding as friendly as the grating of a sharpened saw.

"No, I'm sorry. She's not back from the studios yet. Can I take a message?"

"Who is that please?"

"Her flatmate."

"Ah yes, of course. Trudie."

"Yes, that's the one. Can I help at all?"

"No. I don't believe you can. But perhaps you'd get her to call me when she gets in?"

"Yes, sure thing. What's your number?"

He looked down at the phone and reeled off the line of digits printed on the white label. "You can leave a message at the desk if I'm not available."

"Yes, of course. Who shall I say wanted her?" the treacle voice enquired.

"Rex. Rex Chance."

"Oh yes, *Rex*. Tessa's boss. Hi there! I've heard so much about you, I feel I already know you."

Rex sighed. "I can imagine."

"I'll tell her you called. That's absolutely no problem. She's probably out doing research for one of her programmes," Trudie said comfortingly. "She works all the time, Rex! She should get a medal. Maybe you can fix that for her!"

"Thank you so much, Trudie. Goodbye."

"Bye now! And don't worry, Rex. She'll be just fine!"

As Rex put the phone down, fear for Tessa clenched around his heart. There would be a three hour wait before he could try to get in contact again. And suddenly, hundreds of miles away from Tessa, those hours seemed like a lifetime.

Tessa walked back into the foyer. She moved with slow, deliberate steps like someone suddenly discovering they were walking on a surface drenched with oil.

Gable was sitting on the blue sofa in exactly the same position as when she left him.

On seeing her, he rose, turning himself towards her. She saw the movement as though in slow motion. She anticipated the moment when he would fix his eyes on her face.

She breathed in deeply. She steeled every nerve in her body, forcing herself to meet his gaze.

It was a horrible mistake. She knew instantly that her thoughts were like disobedient messengers, beaming out from her mind and radiating from her eyes; their communication as sharp and clear as though spelled out in capital letters on her forehead.

She saw too, with a sense of doom, that there was no question of his ignoring or misinterpreting the message in her eyes. He knew that she had finally uncovered his secret and that she had the means to ruin him.

All of that was conveyed to Royston Gable in no more than a fraction of a second. And immediately he was in control of himself.

"You seem concerned, Tessa," he said with low sympathy. "And you're looking very pale. No bad news, I trust? Nothing serious?"

She shook her head. She made an effort to smile, to affect an attitude of cheery detachment. The results were dismal, making her think that she would have been a disaster if she had chosen the acting profession. "I've had a long, difficult day," she said. "I'm very tired. If you'll excuse me I'd like to go home now." She heard the tremor in her voice and cursed herself.

"Yes, of course. I'll get the man on the door to call a taxi for you."

"Thanks." She could hardly get her brain to work, so insistent was the pounding of her heart. She supposed in some fatalistic way that he would let her go home, and that after that he would work some dreadful retribution on her. But tomorrow was another day, she told herself. And Rex would be home by then. Hope surged up within.

Yet each time she glanced up at Gable she was struck afresh with panic, unnerved by his bland, innocent-seeming smiles.

As they waited in the foyer, watching the taxi draw up, he grasped her arm and squeezed the soft flesh with his fingers until she drew in a breath with the pain of it. "I do hope you enjoyed our evening," he commented pleasantly. "I certainly did."

"Yes," she murmured, not being able to bring herself to say thank you.

"Don't forget what I said!" he commanded softly. "Think of Rex. Think of how you would feel if he were in distress. Think of his safety, and his happiness. Think of all that, Tessa. Promise me!"

"Yes, yes. I will." Inside she found herself tearing apart with silent screams. Please God, let me get away from this man! When she thought of what he might do to her, what he might do to Rex she was filled with incomprehension and outrage. She tried to push all the horror from her mind and simply focus on her longing to get home and have time to think, away from Gable's disturbing surveillance.

The doorman was holding the door of the taxi open for her. She got in and sank with relief on to the cool leather. "Highbury Hill," she told the driver. "Just near the Arsenal ground."

He switched on the meter. "I'm a Tottenham supporter.

myself, love," he said, revving the engine and drawing away from the kerb.

There was something in his voice, some hint of hostility that jarred. She glanced at the man's reflection in the driving mirror. A big, chunky man. A dark, sullen expression. No, not just sullen, menacing.

Her heart pounded frantically in her chest. Seconds passed, they felt like years. She had a sense of having plunged into a terrible black dream. She recalled Royston Gable's silky voice, his assertion that if you were rich enough you could buy anything, buy *anyone*.

Of course. All this had been set up. The driver had been bought. Tears pricked her eyes at the contemplation of her own foolishness.

Fighting to steady her breathing, she made herself concentrate on what really mattered. As the taxi waited at a red light, she flung open the door, stumbled out and set off at a panic-stricken sprint. But the press of people coming out of theatres and restaurants made it impossible to get very far. The driver was soon bearing down on her, grabbing at her arm, his voice tight with anger.

"Ay! Where do you think you're going? You haven't paid me."

She squirmed around to look at him. "What?"

"I want four quid from you."

Tessa saw that the driver was neither malicious nor menacing. He was simply a heavy-jowled man who had been on a long shift, was tired and irritable and none too pleased to be cheated of his fare.

She opened her purse. Her hands shook so much she found it hard to grasp the coins she needed.

"Are you all right, love?" the man asked.

"Yes. Sorry, I'm really sorry. Here's five pounds. I don't want any change."

He stared at her for a few more moments, then turned and walked away. She made her way down the steps into the underground.

Everywhere around her normality was in evidence. People stood on the escalators, calmly gliding up and down. A violinist fiddled away at the entrance to the platforms. Brightly lit trains rumbled in and out of the station.

She looked around her. The sensation of being pursued still gripped her. Don't be so *stupid*, she told herself.

It was three in the morning before Rex returned to his hotel. He had called Tessa's flat twice during the evening, but each time Trudie had answered. The third time a young man had picked up the phone. He had the sound of a man who was slightly drunk and more than slightly annoyed to be dragged away from whatever it was he had been doing.

"Piss off, will you?" he had growled, before Rex had even had a chance to speak. The next time he phoned he got the answerphone message.

Tessa had changed her message from the brief, cheery one he was used to. This message was longer, spoken in a low, tense voice.

"This is Tessa Clair. I have an appointment to dine at Claridge's with Professor Royston Gable at eight o'clock. Please direct your calls there."

Rex packed his case, took a taxi to the airport and booked himself on to the early morning flight to Heathrow.

Vicky was surprised to receive a phone call from her brother at six a.m. that morning.

"Rex, isn't it a little early in the morning for socialising?" She squinted at the radio clock on the bedside table. Beside her Doug stirred and gave a sigh.

"I need your help, Vicky!"

She struggled into a sitting position, frowning, hearing the tension in Rex's voice. "You've only to ask."

"I'm in Glasgow, stuck at the airport. There's some problem with the plane's landing gear. We're not going to get a time for take-off until it's all sorted out." He paused. "Hell!"

"OK, OK," Vicky said, knowing that something was badly wrong when Rex lost his faintly sardonic tone. "What is it you want me to do?"

"I'd like you to go round to Tessa's place and check out if she's there."

Vicky did not hesitate. "Yes, fine. Wait a minute while I get a pencil to jot down the address." She reached for the pad she kept by the bed. Doug made some little grunts, his eyelids flickered.

Vicky scribbled swiftly as Rex dictated the information.

"So what's the problem?" Vicky said, reaching out and stroking Doug's sleep-crumpled cheek as he began to take in what was happening.

"I'm probably making a complete fool of myself – but I'm very uneasy about Tessa. She wasn't home last night. She was out with this guy Royston Gable. The one she interviewed last week."

"Rex, isn't this reaction a bit over the top?" Vicky asked cautiously.

"I'm not worried about her fidelity, Vicky. I'm worried about her safety."

"I see," she said helplessly, not seeing at all.

"Maybe I'm simply being a stupid, over-anxious fool," he said with a sigh.

"If you're worried, there must be a reason," Vicky said practically. "But that doesn't mean there isn't some perfectly simple explanation for Tessa's not being at home. She could have been called away to see her parents for example."

"No!" Rex cut in silencing her. He gave Vicky a brief account of Tessa's interest in Royston Gable. And of the cryptic message on her answerphone.

"I'll get round there straight away and find out whatever I can," Vicky said decisively, snapping on to full alert. "What then? Do I go to the police if she's not there?"

There was a silence. "What would they do at this stage apart from making a note that she's temporarily missing?" he asked. Another pause. Then he said decisively, "No, don't go to the police."

"All right. I won't do anything without talking to you first. Look Rex, I'm sure it'll all be OK."

"Yes. But please don't tell me to try not to worry."

"Don't insult me! Now get off the line," she said affectionately. "I'm going to get dressed."

265

Doug raised his eyebrows as she slammed the receiver down. "What was all that about?"

Calling out from the adjoining bathroom whilst she quickly washed, Vicky gave her husband a brief outline of Rex's concerns. "Poor Rex!" she exclaimed, returning to the bedroom and raking her fingers through her dampened hair. "For this to happen to him, after that dreadful business with Eleanor. He's as psychologically tough as they come, but on the issue of the woman he loves, he's utterly defenceless."

"So where do you come in?" Doug rolled over and put his hands behind his head, watching her with husbandly pleasure as she fastened her bra and pulled on panties, jeans and a sweater.

"I told Rex I'd drive over to Tessa's flat, see what's what."

"Ah. A mission! Do I see the gleaming light of adventure in your eye?" Doug enquired fondly.

"No," she responded. "But much as I love my life as an adoring wife and mother it is rather stimulating to contemplate a dash through London's streets as an alternative to persuading a three-year-old to put on his clothes and battle with him about eating a sensible breakfast of cornflakes rather than four packets of barbecue-flavour crisps."

"Point taken," Doug agreed. "Now don't worry. I'll be here guarding the little offspring of our loins until you return to the bosom of your loving family."

Vicky bent to kiss him.

"Mmm," he murmured. "Pity you can't get back into bed for a while."

Vicky pulled away from him. "I love you," she said, gathering up her bag, checking that her keys were inside. She stopped at the door. "Oh, by the way, the barbecue-flavour crisps are in the cupboard over the sink."

The early morning sunshine, after the previous days of pearly, grey cloud, was so bright it made everything look as vivid as a film.

There was only a trickle of traffic at the moment. Vicky observed the odd surging bus and the shiny little stream of cars, knowing that very soon the stream would swell to a river, then a torrent and eventually a standstill.

She watched a turbaned woman in an African costume of vibrant pink and maroon chattering and laughing as she walked along, one child in her arms, another at her side. They were all beautiful, their skin glowing like polished ebony in the sun.

On a corner, a fruit seller stacked his barrow making it glow with colour. On went oranges, lemons, mangoes, red pawpaws, purple figs, piling up in bright, bulging rows.

A grey cat streaked across the zebra crossing, head down, its ears back, yowling loudly, living dangerously.

"Ouch!" exclaimed Vicky stamping on the brake. "Just missed you, puss. Another of your nine lives gone."

A plump, pasty-faced jogger puffed along, face creased with concentration and effort. Stepping on to the crossing, he slowed to a walk, turned to Vicky and smiled a thank-you.

She smiled back, suddenly filled with a strong pulsing sense of being part of life, part of a timeless, eternal dance.

Early starters straggled across the junction at the end of Tessa's street, making for the underground. As Vicky signalled to turn, she reminded herself that she wasn't just on a happy little outing, sightseeing through the fascinating streets of early-morning north London.

She gave a sigh. "Please God this is all something and nothing," she murmured, her eyes scanning the numbers as she drove slowly along.

There was a showy blue sports car outside Tessa's house. Vicky had little interest or knowledge regarding cars, but she could tell that this one was exotic and very expensive. Idly, she wondered if the car had any siginificance in the story that was about to unfold.

Having rung the bell for flat two which bore Tessa's and one other name, Vicky checked her watch and saw that the time had moved on to seven a.m. Not exactly the crack of dawn for a young woman who had a job to go to. She looked up at the curtained windows above. Everything looked very quiet, very sleepy.

She rang again.

After a time the door opened, revealing a statuesque young

woman clad in a man's white evening shirt. Tousled ripples of thick blond hair cascaded over her shoulders. She blinked at Vicky, her eyelids seeming heavy and still full of sleep. Although maybe it was the weight of yesterday's mascara on her lashes that was weighing them down, Vicky thought irreverently. She smiled at the young woman. "Hello."

"Hi," the woman said automatically back, looking as though there was nothing in the world she wanted to do except get back to bed. She shivered. Her nipples showed like small firm grapes through the fabric of the shirt.

"I'm Rex Chance's sister, Vicky. I was wondering if I could have a word with Tessa."

"Oh my God!" exclaimed the blonde woman. "Is there some bad news? Has anything happened to him? Oh heavens!"

"No, no. Sorry, that was dreadfully clumsy of me. Rex is fine. I was just wondering if I could have a quick word with Tessa?" Vicky was surprised to find herself suddenly sick with fear as the young woman's eyes registered suspicion and then anxiety.

"Are you Tessa's flatmate?" Vicky asked her.

"Yes, I'm Trudie." The young woman stared helplessly at Vicky, her eyes round with conjecture.

"Can I come in please?" Vicky said, finding it necessary to more or less push her way past Trudie who was standing like a permanent fixture in the doorway. She felt herself brushing against breasts which felt quite startlingly round and firm.

Trudie closed the door. "I don't think Tessa's home yet," she said.

"Could you check please?" Vicky asked.

"What's happened?"

"Nothing, most likely. It's just that Rex was expecting her to be home last night. He called quite late on but he just got the answerphone."

"Yes," Trudie agreed. She coloured slightly. "Well, I can certainly tell you she wasn't back before two a.m. I went along to the bathroom then. Her door was open, I could see in."

"Well, could you go look again!" Vicky was becoming impatient. Trudie's ripe, slutsy sexiness was now beginning to seem rather bovine.

268

"Yes! Shan't be a sec."

She went up the stairs. A man's voice came down to meet her. "Trude – are you OK?"

"Fine, fine."

There was a pattering of footsteps and low murmurings. After a time Trudie reappeared. "No, she's not there." She put a hand through her hair, combing through the long strands with agitated fingers. "Oh heavens!"

"Have you any idea where she might have gone? Where she might be?"

"No." Colour flared in Trudie's face as though she had been slapped.

"Trudie, just tell me what you know!" Vicky commanded, catching the scent of a trail to follow.

"She left a note on the table, saying she'd gone to meet that guy Professor Gable at Claridge's." Trudie sighed. "I didn't see it until just now. Well, Oliver, my boyfriend, found it."

Vicky frowned. "Yes, we already know about the meeting with Professor Gable. She'd left a message to that effect on the answerphone too. I don't suppose you'll have heard it."

"No," said Trudie.

Vicky saw the young woman's severe discomfiture and felt a wave of sympathy for her.

"I should have read the note sooner," wailed Trudie. "Oh Jesus, poor Tessa."

"What could you have done?" Vicky asked practically.

"Nothing, I suppose." She put a finger in her mouth and started tearing the nail. "If I'd seen the note I could have told Rex when he rang last night. He could have done something maybe, before anything . . . happened." For the first time she looked Vicky straight in the eye. "I don't trust that guy Gable," she said impulsively. "He's a creep."

"Well, maybe," said Vicky briskly, sensing a stab of real alarm on Tessa's behalf. "But I don't think you should waste time feeling guilty. What matters is what we do now."

"Yes," agreed Trudie.

"Have you any idea at all where Tessa might have gone after her dinner with Professor Gable?" Vicky asked, clutching at straws.

Trudie shook her head. "No. She doesn't usually stay out late. And she always let's me know where she is." She pushed her hair back from her face. "Oh, I hope to God she's OK. Poor Tessa!"

"Don't keep saying that," Vicky warned. "In these kinds of situations there's nearly always a simple reason for the person's absence. She'll be fine. She probably stayed with a colleague from work and is already in her office at the studios." The rallying, sensible words sounded horribly false in her ears.

Trudie's woeful, anxious expression indicated that she was not convinced either.

An air of tension and doom hung around the whole house.

Upstairs the phone rang.

Vicky opened the front door, eager to get away. Crisp, cold air rushed in.

The man's voice called out urgently from upstairs. "Come quickly. It's Tess."

Twenty-Eight

Tessa kept her eyes fixed on the slender vertical gap between the wooden shutters covering the windows. For hours there had been a thick black line showing, an indicator of the darkest part of the night. But imperceptibly the line had turned to pale turquoise and gradually to a translucent rose. Now there was a gleaming thread of golden radiance piercing the gap. She scewed her eyes up against the dazzle.

Checking her watch, as she did almost every minute, she saw that the time had crawled on to six thirty. In the quietness of the room her breathing seemed unnaturally loud and harsh, her heartbeat like the low thump of a kettle drum.

From time to time fear pressed down on her chest like a great, suffocating weight. Sometimes her thoughts were in confusion, tiny terrified animals scurrying in all directions, finding only blocked entries. Sometimes she could think rationally. She would say to herself very calmly: I've been kidnapped by Royston Gable. He's done this amazing thing because I've posed a terrible threat to his reputation. I've no idea what he wants from me . . .

And then for a moment the fear would sweep over her and hot tears would spring into her eyes. *I must keep calm!*

She had already made an exhaustive examination of the room in which she was held captive. She had come to the conclusion that it was depressingly secure. Captive! she kept repeating to herself, the incredibleness of it startling her afresh each time she heard the word in her mind.

She guessed the room to be a medium-sized bedroom on the first floor of a small house. The stairs she had stumbled up the night before had been steep, with creaking wooden boards, so maybe the house was old. Whatever the nature of the house,

271

the room Gable had chosen to keep her in seemed foolproof against escape. There was a heavy, snugly fitting wooden door, double-bolted from the outside. The walls were plain and painted white or some very pale pastel. There was no furniture except for a bed in one corner. The one long, low-set window was entirely covered with a heavy, continental-style wooden shutter with one central opening: the only chink of light in the general darkness. The small adjoining wash-room and lavatory had no window, and nowhere could she find any ornaments or items of furniture or decoration that might have some use as an instrument of escape.

Escape; that word of fantasy and fiction echoed in her head until it lost its impact.

Her body was aching and stiff. She stretched, rotating her arms briskly and windmill-like to get the blood coursing through her veins. She bent from the hip, touching her toes, rising up, bending again. She kicked her legs high in the air like a dancer, first the right leg for ten times, then the left. She went into the bathroom and showered. She went back to the bedroom.

There was a gentle knock on the door. "Tessa?" came Gable's voice.

"Yes," she said wearily, with the bleak despair of one who feels utter powerlessness.

She heard the bolts being drawn back. Gable slipped softly through the door. "Are you well, Tessa?" he enquired.

"No. I don't like being shut up like a disobedient dog." She raised her head, her eyes challenging him, outrage welling up.

"Oh, I am so very sorry about that." He smiled at her with what appeared to be genuine tenderness. This morning he was dressed casually in beautifully cut jeans and a soft blue cashmere sweater which enhanced the brilliant bluebell hue of his eyes. He looked every inch the perfect English gentleman, dressed for a day of relaxation in the country.

Tessa recalled that in the little drama that had occurred the previous evening, Gable had never once raised his voice, had behaved throughout with gentle and impeccable politeness.

Following her panic-stricken flight from the taxi Tessa had battled with her continuing sense of unease as her train roared through the underground tunnels. She told herself that Gable had merely been sabre-rattling during their dinner together, setting out to unnerve her, driving her to a state where she would believe anything of him, even crediting him with having read her thoughts after the conversation with Mrs Charles. Clearly ridiculous.

She had walked swiftly down the road to her flat, constantly looking behind her, staring into the shadows between parked cars and garden bushes. As she stood at the door of her house, raising her key to the lock, the warnings of some sixth sense made her swing around, her body taut with alarm. But it was too late, arms were already restraining her, a soft, sweet-smelling cloth pressing against her nose and mouth.

There had been a period of partially lost consciousness during which she had felt herself floating, dream-like, whilst glowing, fluorescent figures glided through her mind. When she had begun to focus on reality once more, she had found herself in the back of a very luxurious limousine. The scent of new leather had prickled in her nostrils, the barely perceptible silk purr of an engine had whispered in her ear. Her head had ached. Her vision was furred over, as though she was looking through a veil.

Royston Gable had been sitting beside her, his hand holding hers, his fingers on the pulse at her wrist.

"There," he had said soothingly. "Nothing to worry about. Just a temporary loss of full cognition."

She had made a small moan.

He had stroked her hair.

When the car drew to a halt, he had put his arm around her to help her out. He had half-carried her up stairs which squealed on each step. He had laid her on the bed. She had felt overwhelmingly tired . . .

She looked up at him now. So elegant, so impeccable. So mildly mannered and yet so dangerous.

"Did you sleep well?" he asked her now. "What time did you wake?"

"At two forty a.m."

He smiled. "I like your precision, Tessa. That's something I truly admire in you."

"What happens now?" she asked.

"We shall have breakfast together. And while we dine I shall tell you all you need to know about the day ahead."

"I see."

"Come along then! The table is set downstairs. Everything is ready."

A chill whipped through her. She was determined not to show him her fear. "Aren't you going to manacle my hands?" she asked in ironic tones. "Put a ball and chain on my feet? You should be careful; I might make a run for it."

He smiled at her whimsical attempt at a joke. "No you won't. Just keep thinking of Rex. Of keeping him safe. He's been held up in Glasgow by the way. I believe his flight might just about be ready to take off."

Tessa followed him down the creaky stairs. "Where are we?" she asked.

"In the country," he told her. He gestured to a small oak-beamed dining room where a continental-style breakfast of cold meats and croissants was set out.

Tessa sat at the table and looked out of the window. There was a small rose garden, and beyond nothing except vast fields stretching as far as the eye could see. She could be anywhere in the UK.

She served herself with ham and a hard-boiled egg. Anxiety had killed her appetite, but she knew she must eat, must keep up her strength. She cracked the shell of the egg and scooped out the yoke inside.

"I'm glad you're feeling hungry," he said, pouring coffee from a silver flask. He sat down. He said to her: "While you're eating I shall tell you whatever you want to know."

Tessa stared at him. He was truly incredible.

"Maybe it's better for me not to know too much," she said with caution.

"It won't make any difference to what I have planned for you," he responded gently. "You know quite enough already to destroy my current, very pleasant life." He paused, his blue eyes glimmering.

Tessa raked her fingers through her hair. "Yes," she admitted with despair.

274

"Let me run through your discoveries to date," he said with kindly consideration. "You know that I have illegally – and some would say, shockingly – fathered a number of illicit children by means of infiltrating my sperm into a sealed sperm bank." He raised his eyebrows.

"Yes." Tessa looked at the food on her plate and felt sick.

"I did that, you see, in order to gain some of the most fascinating research findings on genetics and intelligence that have ever been obtained." He took a croissant and tore it apart, taking out the warm doughy innards and toying with them, before placing them in his mouth.

"You see," he continued, "the conventional studies of genes and intelligence are fraught with a number of factors that can't be controlled. There are so many variables to be considered – the diversity in intelligence between any two parents for example. Now if you pair the same father with a considerable number of mothers you hold one vital variable constant. Every child of mine has a genetic inheritance from a father known to be of exceptionally high ability. How fascinating it has been to look at the different ways the children turned out depending on the differing ability of their mothers."

The full horror of what Gable had done filled Tessa with revulsion. "You played God," she said.

He nodded agreement. "I think you suggested that to me before, when we were talking together on your TV programme. And you were quite right, Tessa, I did indeed, for a while, play God. It was the most intensely exciting period of my whole life."

Tessa toyed with her knife, her forehead creased in thought. "How did you know the intelligence of the mothers?" she asked, laying the knife on her plate.

"Ah, Tessa. That curiosity of yours; active even in the most dire of circumstances." He gave a low chuckle. "It was easy. All of the women at the clinic and all of the sperm donors had been required to undergo a set of psychological tests, evaluating their intelligence and personality, in order that each sperm donor and recipient could be roughly matched. My only problem was a logistical one. Getting access to that information and infiltrating the sperm bank." He popped a wedge of croissant into his mouth and swallowed. "It didn't take very long to find ways and means."

"I see. My God!" Tessa breathed.

"Of course my current research findings have drawn on other, more conventional studies besides that particular one. But that one was certainly very helpful." He smiled. "And it gave me such pleasure too – watching all those babies grow up. At a discreet distance, of course."

"How many were involved?" Tessa asked. "How many 'children' do you have?"

"Probably as many as a potent sultan in a harem." he said with a smile of ironic satisfaction. "Fathering many children is by no means unusual, Tessa."

"The way you did it was! So you're not going to give me a figure," she insisted.

He reached out and patted her hand. "No, my sweet tenacious investigator, I'm not. I truly don't have an exact one to give you."

"You said you would tell me whatever I asked."

"I'm sorry to disappoint you."

"Will you disappoint me about Alec too? Was that all a hoax?"

"No. You may telephone him whenever you wish, Tessa. You may telephone anyone, in fact! Your personal phone is still in your purse. I never considered removing it."

Tessa considered his words for a moment or two. Somehow this offer was not reassuring. Renewed fear suddenly hit her like a swung plank.

"You're thinking that I'm simply teasing you. Toying with you and enjoying accelerating your fear."

She was silent.

"You're thinking that the only foolproof way for me to stop you sharing your knowledge with others is to kill you," he suggested softly. "And sooner rather than later."

Tessa's blood froze in her veins.

"But I'm not going to kill you, Tessa. I've no wish to kill you. Quite the reverse. I like you far too much for that. In fact I would go so far as to say that I love you."

"Stop it!" she moaned. "Stop all this. Now!"

276

"Why don't you telephone your housemate?" he said calmly. "Leave a message to say you're safe? Tell her as much as you want. Wait for an hour or so and telephone Rex. Or maybe his sister . . ."

"Dear God. What do you know about Vicky?"

"That she has a husband she loves. That she has a dear little boy, whom she and her husband adore. Whom your lover, Rex, adores also. I've made it my business to find out as much about you as I possibly can, Tessa. I've had a very happy and productive few days. I've almost recaptured those ecstatic moments in the fertility clinic. Being God."

At that point Tessa knew that Royston Gable was insane, or whatever the current politically correct psychiatric phraseology for his state of mind was.

Rushing into her mind came two lines from a poem:

> *Great wits are sure to madness near allied,*
> *And thin partitions do their bounds divide.*

She remembered having been struck by them when she read through Gable's leather-bound volume of Dryden's poem *Absalom and Achitophel*. Her attention had been drawn to those two particular lines because of the pencilled exclamation marks beside them in the margin. Had he in some twisted, unconscious way been trying to warn her?

"Don't look so tormented, Tessa," Gable soothed. "I'm not going to hurt you. I know when to admit defeat."

"How soon did you guess I'd noted down names from your computer?" she asked. "Did you watch me?"

"I knew your intentions as soon as you made your predictable excuse about a dropped purse in order to return to the library."

Tessa felt a chill run through her. "Why didn't you stop me?"

"I felt it was fate that had made me careless about leaving the data unprotected. A fortuitous mistake that would bring us together. I realised, of course, that you might attempt to formulate theories as to the links between them. I did not anticipate you would delve and dig through to the truth. Such a tenacious young woman you are!" he said, smiling at her with satisfaction as though she were a clever daughter who had pulled off top marks in an examination.

"Tell me, Tessa," he said with interest, "what prompted you to scribble down those names you found on my computer? Was it merely journalistic nosiness?"

She sighed. "Intuition," she said wearily. "A hunch that they were important. I have a reputation for that kind of thing." She made a deprecating grimace.

"You should never disregard instincts and intuitions," he told her. He leaned forward, an evangelical glint in his eye. "They spring from what psychologists call the 'intelligent unconscious'. Well-tuned minds like yours and mine are truly miraculous creations."

Tessa recoiled inwardly from the crazed grandiosity of his words. "I don't think my intuition has done me much good," she said.

He gave her an affectionate smile. "I have to confess that the knowledge of what you might manage to discover alarmed me at first, Tessa. Naturally I wanted to hold tight to what I'd fought and worked for. But, you know, when you started to get close to piercing the shell of my secret I began to feel a strange sense of release. Carrying a secret as important as mine can be something of a burden. And you have lifted that from me. Unfortunately at the same time you have robbed me of my position at the pinnacle of the research ladder."

He made a significant pause and Tessa trembled inwardly.

"Well, I have had my time of glory. Now I am willing to resign myself to a life of obscurity. I shall go abroad, assume a new identity. My new life will be a little dull after all this. But . . ." he shrugged.

Tessa felt a low whimper in her throat. She kept it suppressed.

"Don't worry, my little Tessa," he reassured her. "You'll be out of here within twenty-four hours. Back with your beloved Rex."

"What do I have to do?"

"Very little."

"Spell it out."

He leaned back in his chair and raised his head. His eyes

shone with anticipatory pleasure. "You must simply permit me to spend a night making love to you. I've wanted you ever since I saw you, Tessa. A night with you, where I shall guide you into the most exquisite pleasure you have ever experienced, will be something I can treasure in my memory for always."

"No," Tessa breathed, her limbs going cold.

"Oh yes, I think so."

"You can't make me do that by threatening to hurt Rex," she said wildly. "That was just an idle threat. He's strong, he's sharp, he's always one step ahead. He can look after himself. And if you went as far as to kill him then everyone would know."

"Oh my dear Tessa, I don't want to kill him. I don't want to kill at all. Think about it rationally and you will understand that I take pleasure in giving life, not taking it away."

A spark of incredible, last ditch hope leapt up. Tessa wondered if she saw light at the end of this nightmarish tunnel. If Royston Gable was not going to kill, either her or Rex, then what real hold did he have over her?

She began to reason with him. She became eloquent in her attempts to make him see the absurdity of what he suggested. To make him see that he would do nothing except hurt her by forcing her to sleep with him.

He simply shook his head, his smile never faltering.

"You can't make me," she whispered.

"Oh yes, I can do whatever I like with you." He leaned forward. He spoke into her ear.

Tessa made a small, keening sound. If she believed what he had just told her, then it was true. He could do whatever he liked.

Twenty-Nine

R ex came off the plane at Heathrow and immediately
telephoned Vicky.

"She's on her way back from Highbury," Doug told him.
"The traffic will be horrendous."

"So what's the news about Tessa?"

Not good, thought Doug. He started to frame words. *My
God!* This was difficult.

"Just say it!" Rex told him tersely. "I'm expecting the
very worst."

"Tessa has been – abducted. I suppose that's the appropriate
word. Yes."

"Oh Christ!" The sound was of an animal in pain.

"She's not harmed." He hoped that was some consolation.

"What do you know, Doug?"

"Vicky phoned me to say there'd been a call from Tessa
to the flat."

"When was that?"

"Around an hour ago."

"And?"

Doug recalled Vicky's terse message. She had sounded
disoriented, unnerved. Apparently Tessa's voice had been as
flat and lifeless and lacking in hope as that of a blindfolded
prisoner awaiting execution. Those had not been Vicky's exact
words. He tried to remember. Everything seemed suddenly out
of kilter. He felt an ache of anxiety very unusual for him. What
had been the word? Ah yes, resigned, that was it. Tessa was
resigned.

Doug began to attempt to explain this to Rex. By his side
Benny was curiously still and quiet, listening in, catching
the mood.

"Right," said Rex decisively as Doug finished. "So basically what we know is that Gable has got Tessa. He's holding her in a cottage, somewhere in the countryside. Searching for a needle in a haystack job, wouldn't you say?"

Doug had to agree.

"There's no time to lose then!" Rex put the phone down, leaving Doug listening to the bleak whine of the dialling tone.

"Come on then, young man," Doug said to Benny. "Time to get ready for nursery school."

There was some argument about whether Benny could take his worm collection to nursery school. Doug reasoned, Benny insisted. A compromise was struck. Benny agreed to take only his worm stick with a promise that at the weekend Doug would help him start a snail collection.

Doug eventually managed to persuade Benny to put on matching shoes rather than the odd ones he favoured and they walked together to the gate, waiting for their neighbour, Jenny, to arrive in her Jeep which could accommodate several lively children in safety and comfort.

As the Jeep turned the corner in the road, Benny began to wave wildly, jumping excitedly from one foot to the other. Doug lifted him into the back of the vehicle.

"Hi Doug!" called Jenny. "Super morning, isn't it?"

Doug nodded agreement. Looking through the window of the Jeep he felt a deep satisfaction to note how Benny, an indulged only child, moved forward to greet the other children, fully at ease amongst the throng. He and Vicky had never envisaged being parents to an only child, they had always imagined they would have several children – a big tribe of a family filling the house and the garden. But no child at all had been forthcoming. He was reminded of how he and Vicky had longed for a baby for so many years. They had more or less given up and then, without warning, amazingly, Benny was on the way. He had been born premature and tiny, it had been touch and go for a few days whether he would survive and then there had been a few further agonising weeks before he had begun to thrive properly.

Doug stood watching the Jeep move away. He saw that

Benny had already forgotten about him, but he waved anyway until the Jeep disappeared from view.

Through all the anxiety on Vicky and Rex's behalf about Tessa, he felt a smouldering glow of well-being at the thought of his miraculous, wonderful son.

Rex did not need to spend wasteful time thinking and planning. In some strange way he had been anticipating this terrible moment. Somewhere in his unconscious, thoughts, schemes and tactics had already been hatching.

He knew instinctively that he had only himself to rely on in planning the overall strategy of finding Tessa. He knew too that there was not much time. There never was in cases like this. Especially when you were dealing with a deranged, devious and very clever mind.

The name of Sarah Blayney had sprung instantly into his thoughts as soon as his worst fears for Tessa's safety had been confirmed. He knew without a doubt that Sarah Blayney, the tiny, dynamic tracker-down of serial killers with whom he had talked at Royston Gable's party was the one person who could help him.

He called her without delay and she agreed to meet him at her house in Swiss Cottage as soon as he could get there.

"Oh dear," she said, opening her front door and gesturing him to come in, "I've had the feeling for a long time that Royston Gable was a disaster waiting to happen. But you can't lock people up for what you suspect they might be capable of, can you?"

Dressed in black leggings and a cream sweatshirt, padding in little black ballerina shoes, Sarah looked about eighteen this morning and as unlikely to provide information on a criminally disposed madman as the most innocent, fresh-faced child.

She led him into her kitchen, cleared a mound of books and building bricks from the nearest available chair, poured him coffee and asked him to tell her as much as he knew.

"Pathetically little," Rex said grimly. "She had dinner with Gable at Claridge's last night. I've already been on to the staff at the hotel. She left in a taxi. Gable left separately, also in a taxi. They wouldn't comment further. I had the impression there had been nothing unusual about his or Tessa's behaviour."

"No, it would all have been very civilised. Gable doesn't like crudeness or brutality. He would consider that very tasteless, very vulgar." Sarah stirred her coffee with slow reflective strokes. "So, presumably you're wanting me to help you find out where he's taken her."

"Yes. I suppose you could also help me to understand what he might be planning to do with her," he said quietly, his expression bleak.

"Let's leave that topic for the moment and try to work out his motivation in taking her. There must be some reason, some logic, some plan behind it. Impulsiveness doesn't figure heavily in Gable's personality."

Rex gave Sarah a quick outline of Tessa's suspicions about the names she had stumbled across on Gable's computer and as much as he knew about her subsequent investigations.

Sarah frowned. "I don't quite understand. Surely it's perfectly reasonable to expect a research scientist in the field of human development to have lists of names on his computer."

"She had a kind of hunch," Rex said, frowning. "She thought there was something unexplained, something odd about that list and the way the names might be linked together. And subsequently Gable seemed to confirm that through vague implications and veiled threats."

"Ah, now that is very much his personal style." Sarah considered for a while. "It seems, then, as though Tessa's hunch had some validity, some real substance."

"She'd tracked down the current whereabouts of all the four names she'd managed to record. And she's seen two of them in person."

"I see." Sarah's eyes narrowed in speculation. "And does Royston Gable know? Does he know that she's actually met any of the named people?"

"Yes, he does."

"Ah."

"Sarah, does it really matter about the names and what's behind them? Tessa is out there somewhere in dreadful trouble. In real danger."

283

"It could matter," Sarah said steadily. "It could help us to understand what he's planning to do next."

"Isn't the most vital thing to locate where she is? Shouldn't we put all our energies into that in the first instance?"

Sarah paused for a moment. And then she nodded agreement.

"So? Where do we start?" He ran his fingers through his hair, trying to focus his thoughts. And then he glanced into Sarah's sharp, assessing blue eyes and saw her intelligence shining through. "You've done some prior thinking on this, haven't you?" he challenged. *A disaster waiting to happen*, she had said.

"You're quite right, I have. I started drawing up a profile of Royston around eighteen months ago—"

"Why?" Rex cut in sharply.

"He's an interesting subject for someone in my profession."

"But your work is with criminals."

"Yes. I'm also interested in those with a psychological potential for criminal acts. I had a sense that Royston's obsessive personality could lead to trouble. And I've kept the profile up to date which could be useful to us."

Rex allowed hope to spring up. "So what do you think we should do next?"

"The person most likely to help is Royston's ex-wife, Belinda. She's possibly the only person he's ever felt real love for."

"Right! Where is she? Can we contact her?"

"She lives in St John's Wood. Just down the road from here. She's at home this morning. She'll see us. I rang her before you arrived."

Rex stared at her. Little Sarah with her schoolgirl scrubbed face and her ballerina pumps. "You're amazing!" he exclaimed, smiling for the first time that day.

Belinda, who had once been Mrs Royston Gable, showed Rex and Sarah into a sun-drenched sitting room furnished in pale apricot and turquoise. As sophisticated in appearance as Sarah was simple, Belinda radiated the vitality and well-being of a woman in her mid-forties who is very much enjoying her life.

Rex stared at her, curious to see the woman who had presumably long ago been in love with Royston Gable, and he with her. She was small, vibrant and red-headed. She wore an emerald suit and a very determined expression. It was possible to imagine that in her youth she might have had certain similarities to Tessa in both looks and personality.

Rex's mind worked feverishly, forming connections, constructing theories. Could it be that Gable's obsession with Tessa was in some way linked with triggered memories of his lost wife. And if so, was that good or bad news? He couldn't begin to answer his own questions.

"So Royston has finally flipped his lid," Belinda said drily. "Poor, driven, damaged Royston."

"Poor Tessa!" Rex commented.

"Yes," Belinda agreed. "Poor Tessa."

"Do you think you can help us?" Rex asked her. "We think this could be very serious. Tessa could be in real danger."

"I'll do all I can," Belinda said. "Believe me, I really will. I've known for a while that Royston was skating near the edge."

"What do you mean?" Rex asked sharply. "How do you know that? Are you in touch with him?"

"Oh yes. We had a very civilised divorce, and we've always remained on friendly terms," Belinda responded evenly. "In fact we had lunch together only a couple of weeks ago. I thought he was in a strangely agitated state. On a high. You know, like someone on heroin."

"*Is* he on drugs?" Sarah asked.

"Good gracious, no." Belinda seemed genuinely startled by such a suggestion. "He's never had any leanings towards addiction. He's never smoked, he's never drunk alcohol to excess. He won't even take an aspirin if he has a headache. Not that he would ever admit to having a headache. Royston is a man who likes to think that he is in complete control of his life. Body, mind and soul."

"And of other people's lives," Sarah put in quietly.

"Oh yes," Belinda agreed. "That has always been a particular fantasy of his."

A control freak, thought Rex, his heart plunging. And Tessa is entirely at his mercy.

"So his drug is the control of other people?" Sarah suggested.

"Yes." Belinda pondered for a moment, her lips pursed, her eyes half closed. "Yes, I think it would be true to say that manipulating other people is Royston's main drug. The way he gets his very best highs."

Rex leaned forward to Belinda and gave her a brief, tense account of Tessa's discovery of the list of names on her ex-husband's computer.

As he spoke he could see Belinda's interest sharpening. There was a glint of recognition in her eyes, a recollection of something long buried in the past.

"I assume these names had dates of birth beside them?" she said.

"They did. And those dates of birth were all in the same year." Rex stared at her, daring to go on; hoping for some kind of enlightenment that would help him get Tessa back.

"Ah. And were those dates twenty years prior to now?" Belinda wondered.

"Yes."

Rex heard Sarah draw in a sharp breath, saw that she was frowning in renewed speculation.

"That's the year after I left Royston. It's also the year after we had spent a very great deal of time and money at a fertility clinic after it became clear that I had a problem in conceiving naturally. I was artificially inseminated with Royston's sperm and miraculously I got pregnant immediately." She gave a whimsical smile. "We were over the moon. And then I lost the baby at four weeks. We tried three more times. Each time I got pregnant and each time I miscarried at four weeks, just like clockwork. It was a desperate time for both of us. And towards the end of it, the thread of hope that had held us together finally broke when I realised I had fallen in love with the gynaecologist who was in charge of my case." She sighed, slowly turning the beautiful emerald ring on her wedding finger. "Oh poor, sad, distraught Royston. I think my failure to carry his babies, and my rejection of him for another man, was the trigger to loosen all the restraints that had bound him. He had a terrible childhood, you see. He had been thwarted at every turn. And then I betrayed him."

Rex felt his mind hum with this new information.

Sarah said quietly, "If you had carried one of your babies to full term, would it have been born in the same year as those young people whose names Tessa noted down?"

"Yes."

Sarah fixed Royston Gable's ex-wife with a long, penetrating look. "Belinda," she said, and Rex heard the quiet, irresistible command in her voice, "what did Royston do in that clinic besides provide sperm which could be introduced directly into your uterus? Besides playing the role of caring supporting husband?"

Belinda smiled. She took a cigarette from a bronze box on the table and lit it, drawing in deeply. "He created a number of other babies, I suspect."

Rex, who had been slumped in gloomy conjecture, jerked upright. Suddenly all his cloudy surmising produced a dazzlingly clear conclusion. "Sweet Jesus! He took test tubes from the sperm bank and put his own sperm there instead!"

"You knew about this?" Sarah asked Belinda.

"I guessed. Well, OK I knew. Not at the time. Later on. As I said, we still kept in touch after I remarried. He developed a passion for studying child development. He became fascinated with the idea of the inheritance of genius."

Rex frowned and bit on his lip.

Belinda drew on her cigarette. "He became fascinated too with his own intellectual prowess. He joined MENSA. He teamed up with psychologists working on new tests of ability. He became completely obsessed."

"So his personality seemed to change around that time?" Sarah suggested.

"I suppose, looking back, you could say that. At the time our divorce came through he called round to see me. He was very polite and caring in his manner. He said he didn't blame me for choosing someone else. He admitted that his life had become completely taken up with his research. And then he made a kind of indirect confession of what he had done. For a while I refused to fully understand what he told me. And then I persuaded myself not to believe it. And finally I said to myself, What the hell can I do about it? Those parents who got Royston's sperm instead of that of some other unknown guy were probably just as happy with their kids as they would otherwise have been. Leave it be, I told myself. Why stir up trouble and unhappiness?"

Sarah let out a long sigh. "Yes, I can understand that view."

"I felt it was so devastating for Royston when I fell in love with my current husband. I was so sorry for him. I suppose he hated my pity." Belinda crushed her cigarette in a huge brass ashtray. She recrossed her slender legs. "So how does all this help you find Tessa?"

"I'm not sure," said Rex slowly. "But it certainly shows us what sort of man we're dealing with. A potentially very dangerous one."

"Where would Royston go?" Sarah asked Belinda. "Where would he take some very precious cargo? A much sought-after prize? Because my guess is that's how he's thinking of Tessa."

"I don't know," Belinda said bleakly. "Truly, if I had the remotest idea, I'd tell you."

"Where were you living at the time of your visits to the fertility clinic?" Rex asked.

"In a flat in Mayfair."

"Would he take her there?" Sarah wondered.

"I shouldn't think so. They're very rarely standing empty. I can give you the address anyway."

"You see," Sarah explained, "I think Royston would choose a location that had some kind of significance in your marriage. A former house. The house of a friend maybe, or a relation. A place where you had a particularly happy time."

Belinda sighed. "Nothing obvious springs to mind. Maybe if I had a little time to think about it—"

"Christ! We have absolutely no time to waste!" Rex exclaimed.

"That's true," Sarah agreed. "But you can't force hidden memories to surface through a simple effort of will. In fact the more you struggle and the more anxious you get, the less likely you are to recall."

Belinda sighed. "I just wish I could come up with something to help you."

Sarah smiled at her. "If we go away and let you have a little peace, you probably will. The brain works in a very curious way. Even now, a part of your mind will be unconsciously searching for relevant information, much as a computer searches through its data bank. Just when you're not expecting it, when you've let your mind relax, some memory will surface."

"Let's hope so," Rex said grimly.

Sarah stood up. "We'll leave you now, Belinda. If you remember anything at all will you let us know? Anything at all."

"Yes, of course I will. I'm really so sorry . . ."

Driving away from Belinda's house Rex pushed the car fiercely through the gears, crushing his foot down hard on the accelerator. "What now?"

"We've got to keep thinking things through logically," said Sarah.

"Easier said than done." His voice was grim. Automatically he flicked the switch on his carphone, putting it into call-receiving mode.

Almost instantly it rang. Both he and Sarah gave a reflex jerk.

Rex tilted his head towards the mouthpiece. "Yes! Hello!"

"Rex? It's Tessa." The voice was very small, very weary sounding.

"Oh my precious darling!" His voice died away, his throat was thick with feeling.

"I'm not . . . hurt," she said. "I'm not . . ."

"Darling, just take your time. Is he listening in?"

"No. He's gone out. It makes no difference. He doesn't stop me from talking to who I like."

"Where are you? Have you any idea at all?"

"No. There are just fields outside. Cornfields, I think."

"Are you in England?"

"Yes. And the countryside around is very flat."

"How long did it take to get there in the car?"

"I'm not sure. I was out for a while. Sleeping."

"What time did you set off?"

"About ten."

"And what time was it when you woke up?"

"Two thirty."

Rex gave a low groan. She could be anywhere.

"Oh Rex. I'm so sorry," she said mournfully. "I'm so very sorry."

"*You're* sorry! What have you to be sorry for?"

"I've brought so much trouble for you."

"Darling, you've done nothing. You're innocent." He was going to add, 'A victim'. He refrained. It was not true anyway. She was a fighter.

"It'll all be over tomorrow morning," she said.

A chill ran through his body. "What will?"

"All of this. Everything . . . It will all come right again."

He felt reality begin to fragment. "What's he going to do?"

"He's not going to hurt me. He's not going to hurt anyone. It's not like you think. He hasn't got a gun or a knife." She gave an eerie, echoing laugh. "It's not like that at all. And *don't* call the police."

"Darling, just tell me. Share it with me. All this misery I can hear. Share it. Don't bottle it up."

"I can't. I just can't say the words." She sounded utterly weary. Defeated. Stoically accepting the fate Gable had decreed for her.

"Rex, I do love you," she said. "I thought I loved you before all this. But now I love you so very much I want to cry when I think about it."

Rex clenched his free fist. He heard a singing sound on the line. Damn. The batteries on her phone were going. "Tessa," he said calmly, "we shall find you. Do you hear what I'm saying? Keep fighting darling. I know you can. I believe in you." The singing subsided, there was just a rushing noise.

"Tessa," he called out, his voice low and firm, "*we shall find you. And soon.*"

He flicked the phone off and reset it. He turned to Sarah. "What did you make of that?"

"I need some time to think," Sarah commented.

"It's not good," he said slowly. "He's planning to kill her, isn't he? That's what she meant about it all being over tomorrow morning."

Sarah shook her head. "She said he wasn't going to hurt her. He didn't have a gun or a knife."

"He's hurt her already, the bastard. If I get my hands on him I'll rip him apart."

"Rex. He's not going to kill her," Sarah said sternly.

"How do we know that?"

"He's a serial reproducer," she said. "Not a serial killer."

He was silent. Then he gave a grim smile. "A neat way of putting it. Are you absolutely certain he won't kill her?"

"I'm very confident," she said.

His mind clicked through other possibilities and suddenly his heart gave one doom-laden thump. "Oh sweet Jesus. He's going to rape her."

"No," said Sarah. "But he may well try to seduce her."

"She'd never . . ." Horror choked him.

"No, she would never betray you with Gable," Sarah said quietly. "But he is an expert at manipulating people – women, especially – into situations where they find themselves coerced into doing things they'd never dreamed of before."

Rex took in a long breath. "You!" he said. "He did that to you."

She nodded. "Whilst we were working together he became attracted to me. He started to dig into my past. He looked up my medical records and found out that I'd had an illegitimate child when I was in my early twenties. That I'd gone abroad to have the child and then given it up for adoption. He never actually presented me with a blackmail threat, but he knew it could be very damaging to me if anyone found out." She stopped. "You see the father of the child was my sister's husband."

"How did Gable seduce you?" Rex asked softly.

"In the gentlest, subtlest way. He became my friend as well as my colleague, he lulled me into feeling safe with him. He took me to dinner one night, and then he delivered his bombshell and I knew I had no choice."

Rex frowned. "And yet you remained friends with him?"

"In a strange way, yes I did. He only demanded the one 'payment'. He's not a hateful, thoughtlessly vicious man, he has a great deal of charm even for someone as experienced and suspicious as me. And it's only recently that he's revealed the deep-rooted nature of the obsessive aspect of his personality. Besides which, I had reasons of professional interest to keep in touch with him."

"I see." Rex did not look reassured.

"If it's any comfort at all, Rex, I can assure you that whatever he does to her, he won't use violence. He won't injure her."

"Maybe not physically," Rex cut in, closing his eyes against the hateful idea of Gable and Tessa locked together. "But psychologically he could wreak havoc."

Sarah did not disagree.

"OK!" Rex said crisply. "Remind me where we're going please!"

"Mayfair."

"Right."

But the address Belinda had given them was occupied by a very elegant retired Cabinet Minister preparing for a sherry party.

"Nothing there," Sarah said as they got back in the car.

"And not a cornfield in sight," Rex added. "Where now?"

"Let's park somewhere and go through what we know to date. And let's phone Belinda and see if cornfields stimulate any useful memories."

But having done this they found themselves little further on.

When the phone rang again, Rex snatched it up as though it were about to escape. "Tessa!"

"It's Doug."

"Doug! What is it?"

"Benny," he said, his voice shot through with dull misery. "He's been taken."

Thirty

From the moment that Royston Gable had told Tessa of his arrangements to abduct Benny, she had known that he had her completely in his power.

There was no way in which she would do anything to risk Benny's safety. When she saw the little boy arrive in a car with a seemingly harmless and kindly looking couple, all her faint flickers of hope had been snuffed out. The knowledge of Gable's total control over her had brought about a sensation of demoralisation which took a temporary stranglehold on her normally buoyant spirit. A terrible numbness seized her.

During the next few hours there were fleeting instants when she could persuade herself that permitting Gable to play whatever sexual games he liked with her was a small price to pay for a child's safety.

And other times when she felt that Rex's love for her must surely be poisoned for ever when he found out what she had allowed herself to be subjected to. She had hated not being able to share her feelings with him during their brief conversation. It had seemed to her that anything she might say to enlighten him would simply make things worse. And then her phone had died on her and he was gone.

She fixed on the next time she would see him. All the menace and the horror would be over. They would start their life together.

But she would be a tainted woman. Gable would have stolen her integrity. She would be soiled.

Having paced the small upstairs room for long enough, she now sat on the bed. Gable had opened the shutters so that she could see out over the fields. He had explained that the windows were triple-glazed. The possibility of breaking them

294

without some heavy implement was impossible. She didn't think she would have tried anyway. The drop below was several feet on to a stone-flagged terrace. She was beyond hope now. Almost beyond fear.

At six thirty Gable brought her fresh clothes to wear, mindful of the forthcoming evening and the night they were to spend together. He placed a pile of glossy bags on the bed, a little smile of satisfaction on his face.

"I think you'll find they fit you perfectly," he said. "You will look beautiful in them."

Tessa glanced at the bags. "Thank you," she said.

"You will be surprised how much you are going to enjoy yourself," he said. "We shall have a little supper and wine. And then we shall go to bed together. You think you are going to be in torment. But it won't be like that."

Oh dear God, he is truly mad.

"Is Benny safe?" she demanded.

"Yes. Perfectly safe. The couple who are taking care of him are very good with young children."

"Who are these people who are willing to kidnap a child?" Tessa broke in. "How did you find someone wicked enough to do a thing like that?"

"They are not wicked," Gable said evenly. "They are good, honest people."

"How much are you paying them?" Tessa asked quietly.

"I pay them a very fair wage. They act as my cook and housekeeper. They've been with me for some years now," Gable smiled at her disbelief. "I first met them when I was directing a national-scale intelligence survey. They were in their final year at a special school. Young people with learning difficulties, with the reasoning ability of a child, but with qualities of loyalty and integrity that have made them invaluable to me." He raised his eyebrows, inviting her to draw her own conclusions.

"You feed them any line you want. You brainwash them!" Tessa exclaimed in horror.

"No, Tessa, I simply offer them the benefit of my knowledge and experience. And I've been very generous to them, giving them money to help their families and so on. And when I have an especially important task for them, they seem to find a great deal of enjoyment in being trusted with the responsibility. They made a very good job of interesting Benny with a little aquarium of worms and reassuring him with the story that they were friends of his parents come to collect him from school. Right now they're keeping him happily entertained with a wildlife jigsaw. He's a very able child, isn't he? Quite exceptional."

Tessa felt sickened at Gable's obsession with an élite of superbrains. "Yes," she agreed shortly.

"Of course, as I told you earlier, a child of his age, even when treated well, can be quite badly psychologically damaged if deprived of his parents for any length of time. At present Benny is happy, but soon he will become anxious about his parents' absence."

Tessa winced, imagining the long term harm that could be done to Benny if this separation from Vicky and Doug were dragged out.

"There's no need to be concerned. Benny will be back with his parents tomorrow," Gable said softly.

"As long as I'm a good compliant girl."

Gable nodded.

"I telephoned Alec," Tessa told him.

"Ah. And what came of that?"

"He and his mistress are holidaying somewhere in the south of France. They're touring the coast. St Tropez through to Monte Carlo. They could be anywhere. I left a message with the housekeeper, asked her to give him my number."

Gable said nothing. He was watching her carefully, analysing her feelings.

"So you didn't lie to me, did you?" she said. "You really did know about Alec's whereabouts."

"Oh yes."

Tessa sighed. In some ways it would have been better if he had lied. She wanted to hate him totally. She wanted him to be completely black, with no chinks of light showing through his devil's mantle. But it wasn't as simple as that. *He* wasn't as simple as that.

"Did you really want to talk to Alec?" Gable asked.

"I don't know. I was almost relieved when he wasn't there."

"That's only natural. For a reunion to work it really has to come from him, doesn't it? Maybe he will call."

"I doubt it. At least I can tell my parents he's alive."

"Then I've done some good for you, Tessa?"

She nodded in silent agreement.

"Now," he said softly, "let's talk of something much more interesting. Let's talk about you and Rex Chance. You're desperately in love with him aren't you, Tessa? Completely enchanted."

Tessa stared at him, her heart speeding up.

"I feel such envy for Rex," Gable said with low intensity. "That he should have captured the adoration of a beautiful, bright young creature like you. He is a very lucky man."

"I'm lucky to have him," Tessa said.

"Do you think he loves you enough to forgive you when he finds out you've enjoyed making love with another man?" Gable enquired gently. He reached out and fingered a strand of her hair. "Because you will, and I shall be sure to let him know."

Tessa forced herself not to shrink away from him. As it dawned on her that Royston Gable was as interested in hurting Rex as he was in possessing her, she found herself suddenly regaining her spirit, her fight. Battling on her own behalf had seemed like a lost cause. But fighting for Rex was something else entirely.

Rex dropped Sarah off at her house and drove straight to Doug and Vicky's.

They were both behaving with incredible bravery, although their faces were ghostly white with strain, etched with lines of terrible pain.

Rex hugged Vicky to him. "Oh God, Vicky, I'm so sorry!"

"What can we do?" she demanded. "This sitting around simply waiting is unbearable."

"What happened?" Rex asked Doug, who was pacing the room, unable to sit still.

"It's not entirely clear," he said, still pacing. "The headteacher

297

says Benny was in school all morning and that he had his lunch with the other children. But he didn't turn up for afternoon registration."

"Don't they supervise children in school playgrounds, for God's sake?" Rex demanded.

"That's exactly what I wanted to know," Doug said. "Apparently one of the lunchtime supervisors had only started that day and there had been some problems sorting out playground squabbles."

"Was that the head's excuse?" Rex demanded. "Hardly reassuring."

"The poor woman sounded quite distraught," Doug said, standing still and rubbing his hand over his wiry hair. "There'll be an official enquiry. She's already talking about putting locks on all the playground entrances."

"I want to call the police," said Vicky. "Someone must have seen Benny being taken. Someone must know something. I have to call them, Rex. I know what Tessa said, but . . ."

"Yes. You're right," Rex agreed, recalling Tessa's plea, but knowing he could not stop Vicky and Rex taking this step. It was surely the only real chance they had of doing something to bring their son back to them.

Just before seven, as the three of them sat tense and silent in the kitchen, Sarah telephoned.

"I know about the child," she said. "Gable telephoned me. He's not going to hurt him." She paused. "Are you hearing me, Rex? He is not going to hurt the child."

"Do you really believe his promises?"

"Yes."

"What exactly did he say?"

"I have the child. He's safe. He will be returned unharmed. That was it, no time specified, I'm afraid. Now, before you blow up again, Rex, listen. Belinda's remembered a country cottage on the outskirts of Cambridge. Gable had toyed with the idea of buying it as a weekend retreat for them both when he was a mature student. In the end he'd decided it was too small. Belinda never saw it, but she remembered that he'd talked enthusiastically about the huge cornfields surrounding it."

"Where is it?" Rex looked at his watch. "Hell, it'll take an age to get out of London this time of evening."

"There's no precise address. She just knows it's somewhere on the south side of Cambridge."

"That's useless!"

"No. It should be possible to find it by keeping calm and using our heads. Try to keep the heart out of it, Rex!"

"OK. Point taken. I'll get a grip on myself," Rex said grimly. "I'll come right over and collect you," he said.

She made a small sound in her throat. "Rex, I'm doing a rather special dinner party tonight for my husband's work colleagues. I'm behind on my schedule as it is. I'll be here for you on the end of the phone, but I can't leave the house."

Rex grimaced with frustration. "I'm sorry, I shouldn't have presumed," he said.

"That's quite all right. Now, I've already looked at the map and I've identified three villages which seem likely." She reeled off the names.

"I'll drive around, ask the local people questions . . ."

"Yes." She paused. "I'll be here for you, Rex. And, remember, he's not going to kill her, or the child."

"No, but he has other ways of doing damage. Don't bother replying to that. I'm on my way."

"And I'm calling the police." Vicky told him quietly when she heard the news. "Now."

Tessa could hear nothing. The house seemed completely silent. There had been comings and goings in the past hour. Gable had driven away again and then returned within the hour. A second car had driven away – presumably Royston's faithful acolytes with Benny. She had never heard the little boy speak, never heard him cry.

She showered in the little washroom, washed her hair and finger-dried it into soft curls. Then she put on the buttercream satin and lace lingerie that Gable had bought for her. It was almost too beautiful to hide under clothes, she thought. She slipped into the emerald green dress he had chosen. An ankle-length, slinky, clinging dress in some soft, silky-knit fabric. The small mirror above the wash-basin suggested that

Gable's choice in gowns was both tasteful and well tuned-in to her own personal style.

Gable came for her around eight. He stared at her for a long moment, his blue eyes glinting with pleasure.

Holding her arm under the elbow he escorted her downstairs to the dining room where a cold buffet was set out.

"You're surely not a man of culinary talents as well as all your other accomplishments are you?" Tessa asked.

"No, no. I bought all this at a delicatessen in Cambridge. Are you hungry, Tessa?"

Be steady, Tessa told herself. Keep a middle course. Not too dull and defeated. Not too brash and assertive. Just nicely controlled.

"Not really. I'll have some prawns and one of these little mushroom tartlets." She reached for a plate.

"And, naturally, you'll have some champagne." He was already easing the cork from a bottle.

He poured the wine and sat down. His eyes fastenened on her. She could hear his breathing in the silence. "Won't you come and sit on my knee, Tessa?" he commanded softly.

Slowly she walked towards him. Lowered herself on to his lap. Stared into his eyes.

Rex drove out of a London in a blazing, furious hurry. The traffic on the M25 orbital was thick, but it was moving. He went out into the fast lane and let the thirty-five-year-old Jaguar show him what it could do. It was not inconsiderable.

He felt strangely lightweight and free now. His vision seemed unnaturally clear and he knew that his mood was extremely dangerous and that he must keep a check on himself.

Ten miles south of Cambridge he turned off the M11 motorway and instantly found himself in flat endless countryside. He drove to Frogcroft, the first village on Sarah's list, made straight for the local pub, ordered himself a beer and started chatting with the customers.

The wine sang in Tessa's head. She frowned, recalling that she had been careful to keep her intake to a minimum. She wanted all her wits about her.

She and Gable had finished their supper and he had led her back upstairs and into the master bedroom at the front of the house. An imposing king-sized bed covered with a padded, frilled quilt dominated the room.

Tessa stood beside the bed and watched Gable take off his jacket.

He turned to her. "Will you undress for me please, Tessa?" he asked, his voice husky. "Slowly, very slowly. I want to watch you. Enjoy you."

I have to seduce him, Tessa thought. I have to be so fantastically sexy that he'll have his climax before he's had a chance to get properly near me. And after that I'll have some more time to think. And maybe, please God, Rex will find me.

She made a little show of doubt and reluctance, then gave a long, resigned sigh. She thought of peeling off her lace-topped stockings and then recalled that men could go quite crazy about stockings and left them on. Pulling down a strap of her dress she slithered sinuously out of it like a snake shedding its skin.

She let it drop in a shiny emerald pool on the floor, then raised herself and faced Gable. His eyes moved lingeringly over her, taking in the cleft of her breasts exaggeratedly pushed up by the cunning wiring of the bra he had selected.

He stood up and came towards her. He turned her round. He ran his hands down her neck, across her shoulder blades and her back, along the curve of her buttocks.

"Imagine Rex doing this," Gable whispered. "Imagine Rex's strong square hands caressing you. Think of his fingers touching and stroking you. Here, and here, and here."

Tessa's mind tracked his words. She released a small involuntary gasp of pleasure.

Gable was in no hurry. Where his fingers had touched, now he brushed her with his lips. Slowly, slowly, his breath warm on her skin. And all the time, talking her through what he was doing. Speaking Rex's name, over and over.

Tessa forced herself not to think of Rex. Just thinking of him

301

was enough to arouse her and make her lose sight of her cool, calculated objective. She must think only of the here and now. The shockingness of it. The dangerously gentle horror of it.

Gable lifted her in his arms and laid her on the bed. He turned her on her stomach and unhooked her bra. His hands massaged the bones of her back, each separate vertebra receiving detailed attention. His hands were moving gradually downwards.

It was dark when Rex drove into Shorton village. There was a local girl singing in the pub there, belting into a microphone, the noise deafening. Everyone was listening, spellbound. No one wanted to talk. He asked the woman at the bar if she knew of any houses surrounded by cornfields. She stared at him. "This is wheat country here. You won't find no cornfields. Not a one."

He got back in his car. The time had moved on to nine o'clock. Maybe already it was too late. And Hickling Green, his last hope, was twelve miles away.

Tessa lay on the bed, naked and dry-mouthed. Gable, clad now in a silk robe, sat on the bed beside her. He felt intoxicated with the pleasure of his power over Tessa and with the anticipation of the sensual delights to come in making love to her. He was confident that he would bring her pleasure. Sex, after all, was a matter of faultless psychology blended with exquisite technique. A matter of manipulation, in its widest and most delicate sense. He looked down at her with a throb of desire, savouring the moment when he would present her with the final stage of his plan. Holding it back from her had been as tantalising as the delay of an orgasm.

"I think we shall have a small glass of wine before we enjoy our lovemaking," he told her, running a finger along her cheek.

"No, not wine, water," Tessa said to him, her mouth parched, her throat raw and dry. She could not believe Gable's stamina. He had been in a state of arousal for what seemed like a lifetime, and yet he was still in control of himself. He had roamed over her body, touching and kissing her. He had stroked the backs of her knees, kissed the soles of her feet, parted each strand of her hair and breathed in the scent of her scalp. And still he was in control.

She sat up, watching him steal silently across the carpet to the small tray of drinks which stood on an oak chest of drawers. She noticed that his bare feet were beautifully narrow and elegant, a blueprint for those of Adam Baddeley. Thinking of Gable's 'son' sent fresh alarm ricocheting through her body as she contemplated Gable's capacity for committing the unspeakable.

She had no idea what the time was. She had left her watch on the sink in the small washroom. It did not matter. Time seemed irrelevant.

She took deep breaths, knowing that now she must try to grasp the initiative. He mixed her iced-water and lemon barley. She drank it down in one long draught, her thirst was so great.

She looked up at him, making her eyes wide with the conflict of longing and reticence. She took his hand and pulled him down on the bed. She knelt over him and undid his robe. His body was white and firm. A fit and beautifully cared-for body. It was not pleasurable to stroke it and place her lips against the silky skin, but neither was it revolting. ·

She saw his eyes momentarily droop in pleasure as her fingers circled the mound of his thighs. She did not look at him, she simply focused on the power she had to bring him to a point where his control would finally leave him.

"How would it be, Tessa," he asked, stilling her hand, "if we were to conceive a child tonight?"

Tessa froze. "I'm on the pill," she breathed.

"Oh no. I've procured information from the database at your doctor's practice. You have had only one prescription made out for you in the past year, and that was medication for food poisoning."

"No," she cried out, "it won't happen."

"Think what a wonderful child we could create together."

Tessa gave a low moan.

"If you were to become pregnant," he continued reflectively, "I could take you abroad until the baby was born. After that I would return you to Rex, I'm sure he'd be waiting for you.

303

Of course, I would keep the child, it would be a wonderful compensation for the baby Belinda could never give me."

Tessa stared at him in utter terror. And then she began to feel a heaviness in her arms. Her legs were growing swollen and leaden. Her eyelids would not hold themselves open, they were weighted with sandbags.

The drink, she thought. He had spiked her drink. The oldest, simplest, most obvious trick in the world.

He lifted her hand from his thigh. He rolled her on to her back and knelt over her. "Just seven-point-five milligrams of a very standard member of the benzodiazepine group," he told her kindly. "You won't lose consciousness, Tessa. Your limbs will be disobedient, but your mind will appreciate everything."

Tessa turned her face away from him, staring blankly at the wall. Now she really was his.

Rex felt the steering wheel slur in his hands. His foot went automatically to the brake. The car lurched, pulling to the left with unstoppable insistence, wayward like a drunken sailor.

His curses were violent as he threw himself from the driver's door, roaring out his frustration to a thick, dark blue sky peppered with stars.

One of the car's front tyres was not only flat, but torn into ribbons, the strips of rubber hanging down, trailing on the ground.

"Hell!" he growled, imagining lads with knives having a great old time wreaking havoc in the Shorton pub car park. Or maybe it was girls. Whoever, whatever, the car wasn't going to get far unless he changed the wheel.

Keep calm. Keep cool. Just do it.

He got out the kit. Wheel-brace, jack, spare tyre – which, thank God, seemed taut and healthy. He squatted down, put the brace on the first nut. Jammed solid. Jesus! The second one the same, and the third and the fourth. He realised they'd all been tightened with a Godzilla grip by that damned machine the mechanics at his garage were so fond of.

He wouldn't have a cat-in-hell's chance of shifting them without a heavy monkey-wrench. He looked around him.

Christ! Was he expecting one to drop from the skies? There was just flatness, darkness, incomprehensibly huge fields stretching away on either side. To the north a thin line of golden light glowed, attracting all of his attention, drawing him.

Leaving the car unlocked, the tools strewed on the ground, he began to run up the narrow road leading to the light. There was a sign a hundred yards along. *Corn-mill Cottage*. He saw it and his brain seemed to explode.

Tessa heard a tremendous pounding. Drums. The sound of drums in her ears. She had been keeping herself conscious by imagining the last movement of Beethoven's ninth symphony. She had studied it at school. It was etched on her heart. She had read somewhere that focusing on a piece of music could work miracles; preserve your sanity, take you through the horror of being trapped in a lift, giving birth. Anything. The theme was running in her head, keeping her brain alive, shutting out Royston Gable who crouched over her, his hands stroking her cheek, his honeyed words dropping like poison into her ears. The music swelled, it grew louder, beating its way through her tired brain. There was the sound of drums, hammering and banging so violently she shook with fright.

And then without warning Gable sprang off the bed. She blinked hard to focus on his face. It was pale and disoriented, agitation shivering there. The first time she had ever seen that expression on his features.

He moved to the door, his head tilted, listening. "It's over, Tessa," he said quietly. "What a shame."

Blinking her eyes to keep them open, she saw that he had already stepped into his trousers, was pulling on a shirt.

She heard him go quietly down the stairs. A door at the back of the house clicked softly shut.

There was a violent shattering of glass at the front of the house. Her mind filled up with fresh terror. She got up from the bed, her limbs like iron girders, her brain a grey mush. But she was on her feet. She was moving. She was thinking. Swaying slightly she grabbed at the green dress and somehow fought her way into it. She moved to the top of the stairs.

Below her she saw an image of Rex, a wonderful mirage

conjured up from the longing that swamped her mind. He looked enormous and dark and fierce and utterly wonderful. He was moving towards her. She fell against him, fighting the swirls of mist behind her eyes. "You came in time," she murmured, "just in time."

Thirty-One

When Tessa woke two hours later, the police had arrived. And the local television crew. An ambulance was also waiting, its blue light revolving.

Tessa found herself curled in Rex's arms, held tightly. Totally safe. "Benny. What about Benny?" she murmured.

"He's fine. A neighbour rang the police to tip them off about a couple who had suddenly gained a nephew who was making a lot of very loud protests. He's back home with Vicky and Doug, reunited with his wormerie."

Tessa smiled. She knew Benny would soon heal. "I love you," she said. "And don't give me a lecture about how stupid I've been."

"Was I really in time?" Rex asked, low and terse.

"Oh yes." She smiled.

"He didn't hurt you? He didn't . . . Are you sure I truly was in time?"

"Yes. He was just about to have his evil way with me . . ." She felt dizzy with happiness. Laughter kept bubbling up. It must be the drug, it had taken away all her normal inhibitions and made her skittish. Or maybe it was simply the relief. And the joy of seeing Rex.

"Don't!" he barked, recoiling from the thought.

"I love you when you're fierce," she giggled. "Just as well really. You're not exactly lamb-like by nature."

"How did you manage to hold him off?" Rex demanded.

"Cunning." She cuddled close against him. "I was absolutely brilliant. And Beethoven was quite good too."

He sighed. "I'm not going to get any sense out of you until tomorrow, I can see."

"Mmm," she laid her head on his chest and sank into a

307

blissful sleep, the throb of his heart beating in her ear. Gable, with his knowledge of developmental psychology, would have been able to tell her that the warm rhythmic pumping was what the unborn child hears, a memory each human carries within them, the last memory of utter peace before being catapulted into a clamouring, dangerous world.

Rex cancelled all his appointments for a week, growling frequently about not being prepared to let Tessa out of his sight, whatever she or anyone else thought to the contrary.

He drove her to her flat and paced the hallway whilst she packed her cases, the bare essentials she would need for a swift removal to his place.

Trudie crept in and whisperingly demanded to be told the whole gruesome story of the abduction.

Tessa shook her head. "It's too soon to talk about it, Trude. Give me time!"

"Oh yes, I'm sorry. But did he . . . you know?" She looked at Tessa with a kind of awe, her eyes wider than they had ever been.

"No," Tessa said quietly. "He didn't. How are you and Oliver getting on?"

Trudie broke into smiles. "Fantastic. I think he loves me to bits, he really is so very darling to me. And, do you know, his mum has been so sweet as well. She can't wait for us to get engaged."

Trudie's innocent joy was catching. Tessa gave her a hug. "Aah, I'm so pleased for you!"

"And isn't Sharon glamorous?" Trudie continued, breathlessly. "I hope I look half as good when I'm her age. We went shopping together at the weekend and she took me to her hairdresser to have my hair restyled. It cost an absolute fortune and she wouldn't let me pay a thing!" She shook her trimmed mane. "Do you like it?"

"It's great," said Tessa, noting the ultra-fashionable Cell Block H fringe and giving a private smile.

Rex carried Tessa's cases through the doorway of his house and set them down on the floor. He enclosed her in his arms.

"You'll just have grin and bear it," he told her grimly. "You're stuck with me now. Night and day."

"A dire sentence!" she murmured, making a very dismal show of putting up a fight.

Lady Collingham telephoned her and decreed that she must have at least two weeks off work to recover from her ordeal. "Lucinda will take over your slots," she told her. "I doubt if she has your edge or your dynamism, Tessa, but she seems to know how to avoid constant conflagrations. I'm sorry if I sound cynical."

Tessa was in a mood to see the humour in this. She found herself able to sit through Lucinda's simpering sychophantic interview with Cherry Ripe without wincing once. She was also entertained to catch an occasional glimpse of Mummy Ripe and the publicity agent from hell hovering on the edge of the set, just within camera range.

After her check-up at the hospital and her interviews with the police, Tessa found herself bombarded with requests for articles for the tabloid press. Nearly every national TV station wanted an interview and two prominent celebrity magazines were falling over themselves to get an exclusive story.

Reputable photographers knocked on the door wanting shots, other *paparazzi* lurked in the bushes in Rex's garden hoping to snatch a picture when she stood near a window or went out with Rex. More than one unlucky hopeful had his camera wrenched from his hands and the film ripped out.

"Blood-suckers," snarled Rex. "Vultures! Damned media hounds. They'd kill their own grandmother to get a juicy story."

Tessa caught his eye. "We're media," she reminded him archly. "Can you honestly say you've never . . ."

"Never!" he cut in. "My grandmothers both died before I was ten."

Royston Gable was news for days after the kidnapping incident. Reporters badgered his professional colleagues and his research assistants. On finding themselves blocked when it came to getting the names of his research subjects they turned their attention to Belinda instead. And even though Belinda kept her mouth tightly shut, they nevertheless painstakingly pieced together some sort of an account of Gable's early life.

Child psychologists assessed the possible effects of his deprived childhood and gave their various interpretations of his personality on radio and TV. They tried to find reasons for Gable, the renowned professor of psychology and genetics, the man who had discovered a gene for intelligence, to have kidnapped a young chat-show interviewer and the nephew of her lover. They tried to imagine what had prompted him into an act of folly that had ruined his career and made him flee the country. He had caused a stir that had sent ripples of unease through the whole of the academic world.

So why had he done it? Was it simply the act of a man crazed with desire for a pretty young TV presenter? Was there some sort of love tangle? Or something much more sinister?

Tessa read each and every report she could lay her hands on, amazed that the dark truth behind Gable's actions was still a closely guarded secret.

When interviewed she always maintained that the kidnapping could be fully explained in the light of Professor Gable's having inexplicably developed an obsession about her. She always denied that he had harmed her, and strongly refuted any suggestion that there had been any flicker of reciprocation of his feelings on her part. He was a man she had interviewed on her show: she respected his research, she admired the sharpness of his mind. That was all she could say.

I've told no lies, she reflected in private. I've simply omitted to tell the more fantastic aspects of the truth.

When Royston Gable had first realised the seriousness of Tessa's determination to discover his most shocking and exciting secret he had made provision for the time when he might become a fugitive. He had emptied his British bank accounts and arranged credentials for an alternative identity.

The day after his abrupt departure from the Cambridgeshire cottage, he had booked himself on a tour called 'The Glories of Northern Africa' which enabled him to leave the country and be herded through customs in splendid anonymity with a big tour company label on his jacket.

The tour took him by rail through France, on through Spain and finally into Northern Africa on the boat crossing from Algeciras to Tangier.

Morocco with its walled cities, its gentle dusty stairways and its various deeply carpeted five star hotels suited him very well as a temporary refuge, where he could relax and plan what to do with the next stage of his life.

He toyed with the idea of writing to Tessa. Of trying to explain himself. It interested him to discover how much he valued her good opinion. She was the daughter he had always longed for, the wife he had not been able to keep, the mother he had always wanted. For him she was the embodiment of intelligent, sexually magnetic and warmly sympathetic femaleness.

His obsessive desire for her had cooled now. It was perhaps something to do with the shock of almost being brought to book and having to slink away from his former life in disgrace. He thanked fate that that had not happened and that he had been able to make the satisfyingly dramatic departure that represented actuality. For now, whatever happened, even if his misdeeds should finally emerge into the light of day, he had some dignity left, the opportunity for a further re-invention of himself, a new life free at last from the dreadful tension of maintaining guard over his darkest secret.

He felt curiously grateful to Tessa for all this. And he had the sense that although she had judged him with fair sternness for the terrible thing he had done, she neither despised nor hated him. Maybe she even understood him a little. He judged Rex Chance to be a man supremely blessed.

A few months later, Tessa and Rex sat together in Vicky's and Doug's garden keeping a watchful eye on Benny whilst his parents went inside to prepare iced drinks and various other lunchtime refreshments.

Benny was contentedly grubbing around the marigolds, a bright green plastic bucket sitting squatly on the earth beside him. Slowly, with silent dogged concentration, he dug around the stems of the flowers with his trowel. Ten minutes ago there had been around a dozen snails clinging together at the bottom of his bucket. Tessa judged that the number would have doubled at the very least by now.

She turned to Rex and saw that the expression on his face as he watched the child was one of great sweetness and tenderness. She reached across and placed a kiss full on his mouth.

"Will we have one like that?" Rex asked softly. "One day?"

"I hope so," Tessa told him.

"I'll wait until you're ready," he said, his eyes dark with love.

She laughed. "Until I'm over the hump of my glittering career? Is that what you mean?"

"Being head-hunted by the BBC isn't to be sneezed at," he pointed out. "A programme of your own. Serious topics, prime slot."

She nodded. "Maybe I need a year or so to get my teeth into all of that. But," she looked across at Benny, understanding what a precious gift he was, "don't let's wait too long."

"I think we'll need to be married first. I had the impression your mother was a traditionalist on that score. A child must have a stable, conventional background and so on."

Tessa smiled. Reflecting on the new happiness of her parents was a source of deep joy. Since Alec had contacted them they had seemed to glow with renewed life. There had been nothing more than telephone conversations so far, but Tessa's mother was sure Alec would soon feel able to be reunited with them in person. "It's like a miracle, Tess love," she kept saying. "You did so well to find him, to bring him back to us."

"I'll marry you any time, Rex," Tessa told him gravely. "The only reason I didn't say that before is because you didn't ask!"

"What. You crazy girl. Of course I've asked. I've been begging for months."

"You just didn't say the actual words."

"Hah! Shall I say them now? Throw myself down in a suppliant position?"

"No. Don't spoil my fantasy of the arrogant, hot-tempered totally impossible lover . . ." She burst out laughing, squirming from his grasp and running across the lawn.

Benny looked up. "Tessa! Look!" He held out his bucket, a shifting, glistening sea of moving shells. "Twenty-nine! Twenty-nine live snails." He gazed at them with loving jubilation, then took up his trowel again.

Rex put his arm around Tessa's shoulders and they walked together under the shade of the trees. The sun shone down through the leaves, dappling the grass with gold coins.

"Will you keep Gable's secret for ever?" Rex asked her suddenly. He had thought long and hard about Tessa's reasons for not exposing the smooth-talking psychologist.

"Most probably. What good would come of making it public?"

"Very little. And you'd run the risk of making some people very unhappy."

"Exactly." She leaned her head against his shoulder. "I've sometimes wondered why you yourself haven't let the information slip out, Rex. After all you're the one who set the Gable hare running."

He gave a small smile, declining to comment.

"I suppose it's only a matter of time before someone speaks out," Tessa mused. "Hilary Charles's mother definitely thought about it. Her decision to keep quiet was simply based on a reluctance to cause distress to her own family and all the other families. But some time, something could happen to make her change her mind."

"Somehow I doubt it," Rex said. "I doubt that Belinda will speak out either." He was silent for a few moments. "And in some strange way I've always considered Gable's secret to be your special property, Tess. That the choice to share it with the world is yours alone."

She glanced up at him. She saw the conflict in his face and pulled him very close to her.

"You know," he said regretfully, "there were moments when I sensed some curious connection between you and Gable. When I felt horribly, painfully left out and jealous."

"There was a connection, that's true," she said reflectively. "A strange kind of fascination. But there was never any feeling of love. Not at all. And there was never any need for you to be jealous, Rex. In fact the whole episode with Gable only served

313

to make me realise how much I need you – and the preciousness of what we have together."

His eyes closed for a few seconds. A nerve flickered at the corner of his mouth. He bent his head down to hers.

Benny twisted around. He saw that two of his favourite people were twined so closely together they looked like one. He turned back to his trowel and bucket, happy with his task, knowing that Rex and Tessa would take very little notice of whatever he decided to do for quite a while.